unprotected

Kristin Lee Johnson

NORTH STAR PRESS OF ST. CLOUD, INC.
St. Cloud, Minnesota

ISBN 978-0-87839-589-7

First Edition: September 2012

Printed in the United States of America

Published by
North Star Press of St. Cloud, Inc.
P.O. Box 451
St. Cloud, Minnesota 56302

www.northstarpress.com

Part One

chapter one

October 2010

Y ou think you're pretty hot shit, don't you? All tripped up on power, like you're queen of the fucking world!"

Amanda flinched, but Leah just sighed. As a brand new child protection social worker, Amanda still wasn't used to being hated. Their client, Marlys, whose children had just been removed two days before in an ugly scene that culminated in Marlys's dropping to her knees and wailing, "My babies!" in her apartment parking lot, clearly despised her social workers.

"It's not like this every day," Leah said under her breath, passing through the door that Amanda held open to the courthouse. "Marlys is a bit dramatic." Marlys was quickly approaching, and Amanda had the sudden fear she was going to body block them to the ground. A size 22 (if she sucked in a lot) and wearing a dress that had to be a tight twelve, Marlys looked like a chocolate sausage stuffed in a leopard-print casing. Amanda managed a simpering smile as she held open the door for Marlys in a gesture of peace.

"Oh, fuck you and the horse you rode in on!" Marlys huffed at Amanda, her face coming within inches of Amanda's. "You think I can't open my own damn door?"

"No . . . I mean yes . . . I'm sure you can open your own damn . . . uh . . . your own door." Amanda cringed, but Leah stifled a giggle.

Leah put her hand on Amanda's arm to allow Marlys to get ahead of them. As Marlys ambled up the stairs, Amanda finally exhaled.

"So, I guess she hasn't calmed down yet." Amanda wiped her sweaty palms on her new skirt, one of the new work outfits she had purchased in an attempt to make her look like she knew what she was doing.

"Hey, at least she hasn't thrown anything at us today." Leah, her more experienced, albeit jaded co-worker, was unphased by Marlys's anger, even when she had informed Marlys that her children were being removed and Marlys hurled her cell phone at them.

"Oh, my god, that was unreal." Amanda said, still shaken and relieved that she had ducked in time.

"Eh," Leah waved her hand dismissively. "I told you it's not usually like this, and besides, she missed!"

* * *

AFTER LOITERING IN THE BASEMENT of the courthouse as long as possible, they finally headed up the three flights of stairs for their hearings. One of the first things Amanda had learned about court was that most of the action happened in the hallway. There were half a dozen attorneys milling around, both men and women, the men in jackets and ties, the women in blazers and slacks. At least double that number of people looked disheveled, but "cleaned up" for court. A man with long hair looked freshly washed and combed and wore clean black jeans and a beer t-shirt: DUI first appearance in court. A younger woman looked meek and frightened accompanied by a well-dressed, assertive woman carrying a clipboard: battered woman with her advocate filing for an order for protection. Marlys's attorneys and the fathers of two of her children with their attorneys stood near the elevator, which was ancient and purposely avoided by people who knew its history of stranding people between floors.

Marlys, also near the elevator, hands on her ample hips, glared at Leah and Amanda as they came up the stairs. Leah breezed right by Marlys, but Amanda made eye contact as Marlys pointedly scratched her nose with her middle finger.

Leah told the bailiffs at the check-in table that they were there for the Baxter and Thomas review hearings. The bailiff directed them to the larger court room usually presided over by Senior Judge Robert Morphew. Unflappable Leah suddenly looked nervous.

"Crap," Leah said as they walked away from the table, the sound of their shoes echoing on the waxed marble floors. "We hardly ever get him any more. This judge is scary."

Amanda tried to walk carefully on the slippery floor in her uncomfortable black heels so she didn't fall. "Why is he so bad?"

"He's a former public defender and very sympathetic to parents. He's really conservative, believes the government needs to stay out of private citizens' lives except in extreme cases. I'd bet my next paycheck he cheats on his wife. He's always flirting with the women attorneys." Leah sat on a bench away from the people waiting for court to review her file. "The Baxter review is going to be rough because Marlys is a screamer, but the Thomas case is going to be just awful."

The Thomases, a well-known family in town, had owned a fifties' style diner since the fifties. The father in the case, Chuck Thomas, had inherited the business from his father. Chuck, his wife, and their five children revolved their lives around the diner. The wife was the hostess, their four sons cooked, bussed tables, or cleaned, and their fifteen-year-old daughter had been a waitress since she was eleven. Outside of that, the boys played hockey and baseball, just like their dad had when he attended high school in town. They were a beloved family in Terrance, some of the biggest fish in the small town pond.

Which is why it was so shocking when the emergency room at the hospital reported that thirteen-year-old Matthew Thomas, the second to youngest child in the family, was treated for a spiral fracture and dislocated shoulder that most likely resulted from his father twisting his arm behind his back with enough force to break bones. The emergency room doctor, immediately recognized the injury as consistent with child abuse and made the mandated report to the police that night while he was still in the ER. He followed up with a report to Terrence County Social Services the next morning. The doctor had no idea whom he was reporting.

When Leah and Amanda's supervisor, Max, read the report during their Monday staff meeting several people gasped. Amanda thought it was because of the severity of the injury. Roberta, the social worker nearest retirement who had lived in Terrence all her life, explained who the family was. Since Amanda had grown up in Apple Falls, just outside Terrence County borders, she did not recognize the name but knew the restaurant. Apple Falls and Terrence had been longtime sports rivals, so she had played softball and soccer in Terrence many times.

The ER doctor told Leah he had made the report because the mother and the son couldn't give any explanation for the injury. He then called in the mother because he suspected Matthew was covering something, and the mother became defensive and resented his implications. She refused to allow Matthew to answer any more questions and wouldn't leave his side after that. The ER doctor wrote a very strongly worded letter that he felt the injury was the result of child abuse based on the nature of the injury and the family's inability to explain what happened. Two days later Matthew told his friend in great detail that his dad actually had broken his arm and made him lie to everyone. The friend's parents called Social Services, and the team agreed they should file a CHIPS (child in need of protection or services) petition to mandate services for this family. With Matthew still refusing to talk, the case was a mess.

Amanda and Leah were sitting on a bench away from the bailiff's desk when they saw Chuck Thomas walk in. He still had the broad shoulders of an athlete, but the belly of a lapsed jock. His thinning dark hair was rearranged as efficiently as possible to cover his scalp. Still handsome, he carried himself with the assumption of being the most important person in the room.

"Charles Thomas," Chuck said quietly, and the bailiff burst out laughing.

"Hey, Chuck!" They heard Chuck laugh and both bailiffs laughed along with him.

"How's the ticker?" Chuck asked. "My wife said she saw you on the course last week!"

They couldn't hear the bailiff's response. Leah looked sick. They had expected him to be well connected with most of the people at the hearing, but seeing it play out was still like a slap in the face.

"It's gonna be fine," Amanda tried to tell her, but Leah was already squaring her shoulders and preparing to walk back to the waiting area. She just reached the bailiffs' desk when Marlys Baxter, wearing that skintight leopard print polyester dress and silver heels, waddled up to the desk. The straps of her silver heels dug into her thick feet, and she had chipping fuchsia polish on her toenails.

"There's the bitch who took my babies," Marlys belted out. The seventy-year-old bailiff waved a finger at Marlys and shushed her. "I'm sorry, sir, but I'm pissed off and sick to death of that woman effing with my family."

Leah approached Marlys, who immediately turned her back. "No, ma'am, I'm not speaking to you. You can talk to my lawyer or talk to the hand," she said waving her hand and snapping her fingers in the air.

"Marlys, I just wanted to see if you had any questions for me," Leah said. Marlys stuck her nose in the air. "I know it's been a concern of yours that I don't communicate enough with you. Since you didn't return my calls, I thought I would try to talk with you here."

"I didn't get none of your calls! If you wanted to talk to me so bad you could have come to my house, or maybe you could just order a pizza and I could come to yours. Hmph!" Marlys flounced away. Leah stood watching her go, obviously fighting the urge to say or do something behind her back.

Chuck Thomas had witnessed the whole scene. He stood near the wall with his hands on his hips as if he was in the courthouse every day. Although the absence of his wife was glaring to Amanda, Chuck looked thoroughly unfazed. Leah was about to approach Chuck, when he suddenly broke away from the group to greet a very tall man in a gray suit and turquoise tie. He had silver hair and the polish of wealth. The man shook hands with Chuck and pointed to a small conference room where they could speak quietly.

Leah turned around and motioned to Amanda to go into another room. She wore a sick smile of defeat and nausea. They went into a conference room big enough for a table, two chairs, and a phone. "That was Skip Huseman," Leah said with her eyes closed.

Amanda knew the name but couldn't place it.

"'No nonsense lawyers who protect your civil rights,'" Leah quoted.

"Shock and Huseman? From the commercials?"

"Where the hell is someone from the county attorney's office?" Leah said. "Barb Cloud said we're getting their new guy on this."

"Why would they assign a new guy to such a big case?" Amanda was supposed to be taking over this case for ongoing child protection case management, but she wasn't sure it was a good idea to put a rookie like her on a high profile case like this.

"CHIPS cases are bottom of the barrel," Leah told her with a snort. "The new attorneys always start with us. As soon as they get good at this, they want to ship out into something else." Leah rifled through her file to find her preliminary caseplan. "Let's find him and at least give him this."

The hallway on the third floor went in a circle around the open rotunda, with a banister where people could overlook to the main floor with a seal of Terrance County on the marble floor. Through the window on the door of the smallest courtroom they could see Skip Huseman talking to a much shorter man who had his back to the door.

"I'll bet he's our attorney," Leah said of the shorter man. "Barb said to look for a short guy with curly hair." Amanda couldn't see him at all, but it wasn't necessary because the door opened, and Skip walked out, quickly followed by their county attorney. Amanda was watching Skip walk away, looking angry, so she didn't immediately turn her attention to the new attorney and was totally unprepared to hear her name.

"Amanda. Oh, my god."

Amanda turned and sucked in her breath.

"Jake."

* * *

IT HAD BEEN OVER FIVE YEARS, and still the sight of him made her stomach lurch and her heart race. She had run away from him the night her mother died, and he told her that he loved her. She wasn't sure which had been more frightening at the moment.

Amanda had barely begun her new job and already her past life was at risk of being exposed. Amanda did the only thing she could think of to do. The thing that she sometimes thought she did best. She ran.

chapter two

A HAZE OF REDDISH DUST hovered over the field, with the beginnings of a June sunset casting an orange glow over the faces of the people in the stands. The University of Minnesota softball complex was huge compared to the run down high school field the team had been playing on. It was a bigger crowd than Amanda Danscher had ever played for, totaling at least 500 appreciative spectators. None of them were there to see her.

Amanda's arm ached only a little, surprising since this was her third game in as many days. Her dark blonde pony tail sticking out of the back of her cap was damp with sweat. Her coach had played her the maximum number of innings possible, saving her to pitch the complete game for the state championship. And with the last pitches of that last inning, Amanda's only thoughts were of the hazy sun, her aching shoulder, and the vague recognition that she may never play this game again.

"Strike three!" The ump motioned the out, and the team went crazy, throwing their gloves in the air and rushing to home plate. Usually softball teams charged their pitcher in celebration, but this team had learned that their pitcher wasn't the jumping up and down kind of girl. Amanda took off her glove and walked toward the dugout, a few teammates clapping her on the back appreciatively. Her coach hugged her briefly, and Amanda patted her back for a moment before pulling away and gathering her equipment.

The trophy presentation took place thrity minutes later as the sun was setting and the lights had just come on over the field. Amanda accepted the MVP award with a handshake and a thin smile. The moment it was over, Amanda gathered up her bag and jacket and made her way to her tiny hatchback. She threw her bag in the back, and waved at her teammates as they made their way to their vehicles. There was going to be a big party at the catcher's home, and while it was mentioned to Amanda, they all knew she wouldn't come.

Amanda had been accepted at the U and would be starting in the fall, so she took an extra look around, wondering which dorm she would be in and where she might attend classes. But it was late and she knew she was expected back soon, so she got in her car and started the drive back to the hospital to see her mother who was finally, officially, dying.

* * *

SCENTS OF RUBBING ALCOHOL, industrial carpet cleaner, and musty fabric combined for that familiar hospital odor. Using the emergency room entrance, she greeted the admissions desk worker by name and made her way past the elevator bay to the general patient wing. Her favorite nurse, Cheryl, was working and greeted Amanda with a hug that Amanda returned.

"You did it! We all knew you would!" Cheryl held Amanda's face in her hands and beamed. Cheryl was a mom of three adult sons, and she doted on Amanda. She playfully yanked on Amanda's pony tail. "MVP! My husband thought you would be. What an honor!"

Ready to change the subject, Amanda removed herself from Cheryl's hug and asked, "How is she?"

"Same stuff, sweetie," Cheryl rubbed the stitching on Amanda's warm up jacket. "We can't get her bowels regulated and can barely keep her hydrated. She's uncomfortable but so proud of her girl."

"Mmm hmm." Her mom enjoyed the attention that she was getting from Amanda's success, but Amanda barely had the energy to be resentful anymore. It was just who her mom was.

Amanda made her way down the gloomy hallway and entered her mother's home away from home for the past two weeks. She expected it would be the last place she ever lived. Ovarian cancer had been cruel and aggressive, and after nearly four years her belly was full of malignancy. The tumors were wreaking havoc on her digestive system, and she was so sick that she required twenty-four-hour nursing care. The old hospital had a hospice wing where April would be moved when, or if, her doctor could get her stabilized.

"Hey, mom," Amanda knew she sounded tired, and she hoped her mom wouldn't realize that she barely had the energy to be there.

April Danscher was lying on her side with the sheet up to her legs. She had always been rail thin thanks to her two-pack-a-day habit, but now she was emaciated. Her knitted cap barely covered the straggly peach fuzz that dotted her scalp. Amanda had hated shaving her mom's head after the chemo had made it fall out in clumps, but one of the many cruelties of April's cancer was that her hair just stopped growing back, meaning that shaving wasn't necessary anymore. Amanda could see that her mom wanted a cigarette because she was holding her fingers to her lips as if she had one in her hand.

"I knew my girl would be MVP. I told all the girls that it would be you." The "girls" were the hospital nurses, and the only friends that Amanda could ever remember her mom having. April and Amanda had spent the last eighteen years of Amanda's life alone and desperately lonely. Amanda had been her mom's only caregiver for the past three and one-half years until ten days ago, when her doctor had to stop chemo because she couldn't tolerate the side effects. It wasn't really working anyway. Then April developed a bowel obstruction, as the tumors in her abdomen were so large that they blocked her colon. After a horrific night when April screamed in pain for hours, Amanda brought her to the ER and she was admitted for the last time.

"Well, it's late, mom, so I'm going to head out. I just wanted to check in."

April nodded understandingly. "Of course, my MVP. You must be worn out." Her mother looked more worn out than three days of softball could ever affect Amanda, but she was grateful for the easy out.

"Good night, mom." April nodded briefly, never one very comfortable with pleasantries, and rolled over to go to sleep.

Amanda slipped back into the hallway and surveyed the rooms in that wing. As usual, most rooms were empty. The single nurse at the nurses' station was charting with her back turned. Amanda edged into the room two doors down from her mom's and went straight into the bathroom to clean up. She lingered in the shower, feeling the grit of the field wash away. Finally she dried off with a towel hanging on a hook and pulled on shorts and a t-shirt. Amanda had slept at the hospital all week, in whatever room was closest. She feared someone would figure out she was the one messing up rooms, but so far she had gotten away with it.

Overwhelming exhaustion kicked in, and Amanda gracefully made her way across the dark room to crawl into the hospital bed. But when she grabbed the sheet, she jumped and yelped as she touched an arm.

"I was hoping you were going to climb on in." The body in the bed belonged to a younger guy with a scratchy voice who sounded like he was ready to laugh.

"Holy shit! I'm so sorry." Amanda backed away, mortified, as the guy chuckled.

"Seriously, there's room." He reached over and turned on a light. He looked to be about twenty with short dark curly hair, dark eyes, and the kind of face that was always smiling. Amanda continued to back away. "You don't have to leave. I never sleep in the hospital. You wanna watch TV?" He picked up the remote and started flipping through channels.

"I'll find another room," she said softly. She looked him over quickly for clues as to possible reasons why he was there. "I didn't mean to bother you."

"Is that woman down the hall your mom?" he asked kindly, sitting up a bit more and adjusting his pillow." I talked to her for a minute when we were both doing laps."

"Um, yeah. She's probably never going home." Her face turned red as she blurted out that bit of personal information.

He nodded with understanding. "Cancer, right?" He motioned to his hair. "Me too. Sucks doesn't it?"

Something about his concern felt genuine, and she felt drawn to talk to him. "Yeah. It's been really rough. She was admitted last weekend for a bowel obstruction, but they can't fix it so they'll be moving her to hospice when she's more stable." More personal disclosure to a perfect stranger.

"Sorry. That's rough." He motioned for her to sit, and to her surprise she did. "I had, or have leukemia. I actually had a stem-cell transplant eight months ago, and I've been doing great. But then I got the stomach flu and everybody flipped out, so I gave in and got admitted for the night for IV fluids. It was easier than dealing with my mom following me around asking me about my bowel movements."

Amanda laughed. "You really do have to talk a lot about your bodily functions when you have cancer." Amanda cringed and wished she wouldn't have used the "C word," but he didn't seem to mind. He was easy and comfortable to talk to, and he was cute despite the pallor of the stomach flu.

"I'm Jake, by the way. Jacob Mann." He held out his hand to shake hers, but the IV tube in his arm pulled tight and he couldn't reach.

Amanda reached out and shook his hand. "I'm Amanda. Happy to meet you."

Jacob and Amanda stayed up talking most of the night. He talked a little about chemo treatments, and they compared doctor stories. Jake had been going to the Mayo Clinic and said he had great doctors with not so great bedside manners. Amanda wondered if her mom's doctors really knew what they were doing, but the nurses had been amazing. Eventually they talked more about music and TV shows they liked, and they found commonalities in the housebound lives they led.

By 3:00 a.m. Jacob started to look groggy, but he seemed to be forcing himself to stay awake. Amanda was flattered but felt guilty, and knew that he was there to rest and recuperate.

"So, I'm going to get going," she said nervously.

"Where? You can't drive home now." His concern was apparent, unfamiliar, and made her heart flutter.

"Just down the hall," she said with a shrug. "Either they don't know or they don't care because I've been staying here all week."

Jake smiled at her a little sadly. "Oh, okay. Goodnight."

How could one word make her feel so good? She headed toward the door and gave a silly little wave. "Goodnight."

* * *

AFTER THEIR FIRST MEETING, Amanda didn't know how she was going to see Jake, she only knew she wanted to see him again. She passed by his room early the following afternoon while her mom was getting help with a bath, but his room was empty. Saturdays were often terribly long at the hospital, especially when Amanda's mom wasn't feeling well. The meds seemed to be kicking in, and she finally looked more comfortable. The doctor said that as soon as they got her IV out she could move to the hospice unit where at least the rooms were bigger and a little more home-like.

The two nurses on duty until shift change at three o' clock were bitchy, so Amanda went to the balcony to sit outside for a few minutes.

She found Jake there, lying on a lounge chair with his shirt off, apparently trying to get a suntan.

"The glare off your white skin is blinding," Amanda said throwing him his t-shirt slung on the railing. "I think you better cover up." Amanda was trying to sound funny and casual, but she was afraid it came out mean.

"Hey, it's my night stalker," Jake said, throwing his shirt on the floor of the balcony. She noticed his IV was out, but the line was still in his left wrist surrounded by tape and velcro. His chest was pale and hairless, and she could see scars from needles and IV's around his collar bone area and on both arms. He noticed her noticing his scars. "You should try to be a little more casual when you're checking someone out. My mom always said it's not nice to stare."

"Oh, man, I'm sorry," Amanda said feeling a flush race up to her cheeks and looked away. "I . . . uh . . . wasn't looking at . . ."

"Don't freak out. I'm used to people looking at me from when I didn't have hair and looked like a zombie. Someday I hope I'll be checked out for my rippling pecs instead of my shiny red scars." Jake put his shirt back on.

Amanda didn't want him to know that she was checking out more than his scars, but it was less embarrassing to let him think she was looking at his lines and radiation tattoos and burns. "I should know by now to look you in the face and make small talk about the weather so you feel like a normal person, and not someone with a disease." She leaned her elbows back on the railing and looked back down at him. "Or at least that's what the cancer brochures tell me to say to you."

"I'll have you know I'm someone who used to have a disease who now has a slight case of diarrhea that requires a team of doctors to make sure I'll pull through," Jake said. He squinted up at Amanda and shielded his eyes from the sun almost directly overhead. "How's the day going?"

"Eh—" Amanda tipped her hand side to side to show him it was a "so so" day.

"I'm going home this afternoon," Jake smiled a weary smile. "If I had a nickel for every time I checked out of the hospital thinking it was my last, I'd have at least a quarter by now."

"Good for you," Amanda said. "But I'm sure it's real because you won't be back."

"I dig your optimism. My mom would have to give you a hug just for saying it." Jake stood next to her at the railing, leaned forward, and ran his fingers through his hair. His hair was dark brown, coarse, and wavy—most likely because it was growing back after chemo. "So what's next for you?"

Amanda knew that he was asking what she was going to do with herself now that her mom had stopped treatment and was officially dying. Amanda didn't have a clue how to answer. She had learned not to plan too far in advance because life revolved around how her mom was feeling from moment to moment. Her focus had gone from college applications, to softball, to graduation, to the state tournament. As her high school career had ended, her adult life abruptly began with the knowledge that she needed to prepare for her mother's death.

"There's actually not much for me to do. My mom wrote her will a long time ago, which was a joke because I'm the only heir, and there's nothing to get. My mom's family had a house fire when she was in high school, and they lost everything, so she's never been big into having 'stuff' because it's just something to lose someday. She knows what she wants for her funeral, she's arranged her own cremation, which is just sick if you ask me, and the doctor said this morning that she's ready to go to hospice as she asked for instead of going home to die. I don't think there's much I have to do until after."

Jake just nodded in reply. Amanda didn't know if talking about death bothered him. He seemed quiet.

"So I guess other than registering for classes during one weekend in July, I'll be here all summer." Amanda's stomach felt hollow at the thought of spending the summer at the hospital. "I suppose I should get a job," she thought out loud.

A woman with short brown hair like Jake's came out to the balcony holding a bunch of helium filled balloons that included a mylar Bozo the clown balloon. She was barely five feet tall so she was nearly covered up by the balloons. She had permanent, deep laugh lines around her eyes and a wide, toothy smile. She was deeply tanned already, and she looked like a bundle of energy. Reaching up to grab Jake's face, she gave him a kiss on each cheek.

"I was looking for you, Jacob," she said, wiping her lipstick off each cheek with a dab of spit on her thumb. "Once you get the nurse to take out that line, you're okay'd to go home." She turned to Amanda. "Is this your friend from last night?"

Amanda's mouth dropped open at the question, and she couldn't believe that he told his mother about her already.

"Mom, this is Amanda"

"Nice to meet you, sweetie," she said, dropping the balloons with their clown paperweight and shaking Amanda's hand with both of hers. "I'm Trix Mann." Then she turned to Jake. "Have you invited her to supper?" Trix still hadn't let go of Amanda's hands.

"I was getting to it, mom . . ."

"Well, hurry up and invite her. I'm making pork tenderloin and it's a big one." She squeezed Amanda's hands before she let them go, grabbed the balloons and started for the door. "I'll get your bag and meet you at the car. See you tonight, Amanda. It was nice meeting you."

Amanda raised her eyebrows and grinned at Jake.

"I guess you heard that you're invited for dinner," Jake said, sheepish and pleased at the same time. "My mom has always made a big welcome home dinner every time I get out of the hospital, which is actually sad that we have to have a coming home from the hospital tradition."

"Your mom doesn't even know me, and neither do you, really, for that matter. Why would you invite me for dinner?" Amanda knew that sounded bitchy, but her skeptical, dark side had kicked in and spoke up before she could stop it.

"If you want to know the truth, my mom tends to fall over all of my friends." He rubbed his palms along the wooden railing. "Her biggest fear when I got sick was that I would lose friends and miss out on things. She has to help me along by inviting people over, and then she set up this amazing room in our basement with a big screen TV, DVD player, pool table, full bar, pinball . . . you name it. She wanted to make sure that people would want to spend time with me even if I couldn't really go places." He suddenly jumped. "Yeow! Sliver. Jeez don't let my mom see that either. She's got a thing with blood. You know . . . leukemia . . ."

Amanda knew what he meant about the blood. "Anyway, your mom seems so great," she said.

"She is. I have to let her do all this stuff even though I'm twenty-years old because it helps her cope." He squinted at his palm and pulled the sliver out quickly, rubbing away the dot of blood that appeared.

Spending an evening with her and Jake sounded wonderful, but Amanda couldn't imagine how she could get out of having dinner with her mom on a Saturday night. "I'd really love to have your mom's dinner, but I can't leave my mom alone here." She sighed.

"I can't imagine that your mom wants you to hang out in a depressing hospital with her when you could have a nice dinner out. She's your mom. You know she'll tell you to go."

Amanda looked down and pushed away the tears that threatened. If you grew up with a real mom who was capable of thinking about someone other than herself, then you would assume that all moms were that way. It was too humiliating to try to explain that her mom would want nothing more than to see her daughter sit in a depressing hospital on a Saturday night to keep her company. Amanda had begun to see that it wasn't out of selfishness as much as a true inability to think about anyone other than herself. Amanda barely held it against her anymore, but the thought of losing a nice evening with Jake and his family brought her mother's attitude suddenly into sharp focus. Guilt, anger, and frustration merged, and she had to clench her jaw hard to keep from crying. Long ago Amanda had stopped allowing herself that kind of emotion, and today with this stranger she was surprised that tears were threatening. Amanda hadn't cried since she was ten years old.

Amanda just shook her head at Jake, unable to speak. She felt that somehow he understood that her silence was about more than her mom being sick, but about a loneliness that started well before the first diagnosis.

"How about this, have dinner with your mom but just tell her you're feeling a little sick so you're not going to eat much. Then you can beg off around 7:30 or 8:00 and we'll wait to eat until then." He smiled at her, satisfied he had solved the problem.

"You can't hold your dinner for me, and I'm not going to lie to her, and I just . . ."

"Quit being a martyr. You need to get away from this place, and she'll have nurses here all night to help her if she needs it. It's not your job to babysit her." He crossed his arms and stared hard at her. "Okay?"

Amanda shook her head and looked down at her shoes. "It's not that I have to babysit her. Other than school, I've just never had anywhere else to go. Our trailer is just a place to take a shower because I can't stand being there. It's just not home. This hospital is the closest . . ." Her throat felt tight again.

"Amanda, calling this place home is so sad I can hardly stand it," Jake said, standing up and wrapping his arms around her in a gesture way more intimate than their eighteen-hour friendship allowed, but he felt so nice she didn't mind. He smelled like hospital soap, but in a good way. She laughed and let herself relax a little.

"I know," she said, with a big shuddery sigh. But she was also smiling.

"You're coming."

* * *

AMANDA STOOD OUTSIDE THE DOOR, trying to figure out what to say. Jake and his mother lived in a split-level house with a tuck-under garage that was probably built in 1972. It looked like it could be any house on any street in any town. There were little wire flags all over the yard indicating the lawn had just been sprayed with fertilizer. Amanda wondered if he played football in this yard and rode his bike on this sidewalk and played basketball in this driveway. It was hard not to resent how normal he was. There was the issue of his cancer, so it wasn't quite fair to call his childhood "normal." It was just that he had all the things Amanda had craved.

Before she could knock, Jake opened the door.

"Was I supposed to sense your presence or was it in your plans to knock eventually?"

Once again Amanda didn't know what to say.

"Don't look all awkward. Just come in and relax." Jake stepped aside and motioned her into the entryway. He took her sweatshirt while she tried to take in the surroundings. Upstairs the dining room and living area were furnished with comfortable but nice furniture. She could smell dinner cooking and hear kitchen sounds coming from upstairs toward the back of the house.

"Hi, sweetie," Trix yelled down. "Show her the basement, Jacob." He rolled his eyes at Amanda.

"I will, Mom. I was planning on it."

"Hi, Mrs. Mann," Amanda said softly.

Trix came out of the kitchen wiping her hands on a dishtowel. "Oh, good lord, sweetie. Call me Trix. I'm so glad you're here! Did you find the place okay?"

The town was not that big, and she had lived there all her life, so of course she knew how to find their house. "I drove right to it," she said. "I used to have soccer games down the street at Miller Park."

"Of course you did, sweetie. Jake told me you're an athlete." She smiled and threw her towel over her shoulder. "Make yourself at home. We'll eat in about twenty minutes."

Jake gave her the grand tour. The basement was fixed up to be an adolescent boy's paradise. A flat-screen TV took up one whole wall, surrounded by gadgets and machines including a DVD player, Nintendo X Box, and Internet service through the TV. There was pool, foos ball, and an actual pinball machine with Elvis on it. In one corner there was a bar with a working soda machine, and Jake pointed out that there was a tap for a keg that they filled only on special occasions. Beer lights, sports posters, and girl calendars covered the walls. Jake said it was a little weird to think of his mom decorating the room with girls in bikinis.

Jake's bedroom was downstairs and also looked like a teenage boy's room. He had a double bed with a plain navy comforter, a desk with a computer, and two dressers covered with ribbons, team photos, and trophies from Punt Pass and Kick competitions and baseball tournaments. Amanda looked at all the photos with him in his baseball and basketball uniforms. She didn't see any pictures that looked like they were from high school.

"That's me in all my seventh-grade glory," Jake said. "My mom and step-dad had just gotten married when I was in middle school, so me and Mike bonded over football. He's the assistant coach in that picture, which he did to try to get close to me I'm sure." Amanda smiled at the rows of boys in huge helmets all with tough looking scowls on their faces.

"Was it weird that he wanted to be such good friends?" Amanda asked.

"Oh, I didn't care. I was glad he was trying to get to know me." Jake shrugged and sat on the edge of the bed. "I never had a dad before, and Mike's a great guy. I couldn't have picked a better guy for my mom to marry. My dad left when I was a baby, and my mom never dated before Mike. I wanted her to have somebody because I could tell she was lonely, so it was a big relief when Mike came around. Being the baby of the family I could tell early on that if anyone was going to stick around with Mom it would be me."

"Were you picturing yourself as an adult sleeping in the basement of your mom's house, parking your car in the driveway, going off to work with a lunchbox . . ." Amanda laughed and realized it was partially true.

"I probably should say it bothered me, but it didn't. Mom and I have always been really close, so it wasn't horrible to think I'd just live my life here. I was a late bloomer, so it seemed like girls never really liked me anyway. It seemed like an easy out to just say that I had to take care of my mom, and that's why I never got married."

"You sure wrote yourself off early!" Amanda was leaning against a dresser because she wasn't going to sit on his bed.

"Even before I got sick, I was shy with girls. After I got sick it pretty much sealed my fate for homecoming and the prom. I missed at least half of my junior and senior years in high school, and people were so freaked around me anyway that it was just easier to avoid the whole thing. After I didn't go to the junior prom, my mom sort of panicked and re-designed the whole basement. She asked me at least once a week if I wanted to invite a girl over to watch a movie, but I always said no. She's practically foaming at the mouth now that you're here."

Amanda blushed and turned around to look at the trophies so he wouldn't see her face. She had no idea how to feel about his invitation— if it was a date, or were they just hanging out as friends, or what. She walked away and asked if dinner was ready.

He jumped up too. "It must be. Come on up." She followed him upstairs where he finished the house tour. The kitchen was big and open, separated from the living area by a large counter-breakfast bar. There were two bedrooms upstairs in addition to the master bedroom, which were designated for Jake's older sisters even though neither of them had lived in the house for years.

Upstairs Amanda noticed the balloons were the centerpiece at the table, which was set for two.

"I have to ask about Bozo the balloon," Amanda said. "Is he another tradition?"

"It's a running joke," Trix said with a smile. "Usually Jacob's sisters are here for his coming home dinner, but both of them are busy this weekend and since he was only in for a couple of days they felt fine about missing it." She brought a beautiful platter with sliced pork tenderloin, surrounded by new potatoes and asparagus. "Jacob has never liked clowns, ever since he saw that awful movie, *Poltergeist*, with that little blonde girl who goes into the TV, and the boy who gets strangled by the clown. Jessie used to watch Bozo in the mornings before school and Jacob hated it. I swear she did it just to bother him. They're only two years apart and they fought like cats. Anyway, the first time Jacob came home from the hospital, Jessie decorated his room with clown pictures and clown dolls. It was kind of her way of saying that he wasn't too sick to pick on."

"I found the nightmares quite comforting," Jake said.

"We always bring out the clowns to remind Jacob that he's just fine." Trix filled water glasses from a large pitcher, brought over a basket of bread, and then motioned them to sit down. Amanda stood waiting to see where she was supposed to sit. Trix finally grabbed Amanda by the shoulder and said, "Why don't you sit here, sweetie."

"Thanks," Amanda murmured. She took her cloth napkin and set it on her lap. Trix hovered over them, serving their tenderloin, vegetables, potatoes, and bread.

"Now I have some things to do, so you two enjoy your dinner," and Trix escaped to her room before either of them could argue.

For the second time that day, Amanda stared at Jake, unable to find words. "She's not going to eat with us?" she finally asked.

Jake shook his head and smiled. "Apparently not. I guess she wants this to be date night."

Amanda let out a snort, then looked away quickly. She felt like an idiot. She kept acting like she didn't want a date with him, when the only real problem was that she was too socially inept to know what to say. They ate quietly.

Trix must have sensed the tension because she came back out and started bustling in the kitchen again. "So Amanda . . . where do you live?"

She tensed at the question. Having no idea how much Jake had told her, she didn't want to admit she lived in a trailer court on the opposite end of town. She also couldn't lie, so she was vague. "Near the mall," she finally said, and quickly added, "This dinner is wonderful."

"I'm glad you like it . . . Maybe I'll have a little something with you." She brought out a plate and served herself full helpings of everything. "When my husband's out of town I usually don't cook. This time he's been gone for so long I think I was happy to have the excuse." She caught herself and was appalled. "Oh' Jacob, I mean I wasn't happy that you were in the hospital. Dear Lord what a thing to say."

"Settle down, Mom. It's fine." Jake helped himself to another serving of pork, which his mother eyed carefully. "Are you still feeling okay, Jacob? You don't want to make yourself sick again."

Jacob seemed to have infinite patience for his mother, as even Amanda was starting to feel a little smothered by all her mothering. "Yes,

Mom. They said it was probably something I ate, so my system should be clear of it by now. I can eat whatever I'm hungry for, and I want more of your delicious pork stuff."

"Tenderloin, Jacob. You help yourself." She watched him until his plate was completely full again, then she turned to Amanda. "Jacob told me you're going to the U this fall. Do you know what you plan to study?"

Amanda chewed slowly to stall for time. This whole experience was a little intimidating, and Amanda didn't want to admit to Trix that she was completely undecided about what to do with her life. College was just the next thing to do because she couldn't imagine trying to hold any job other than Dairy Queen.

"I guess I want to spend a little more time looking into my options," Amanda said.

"Undecided," she said knowingly. "There's nothing wrong with that, sweetheart. Don't you apologize for it." She ate small bites of everything, chewed fast, and swallowed with dainty sips of water. She reminded Amanda of a small, well-run machine the way she moved so efficiently.

"Um, what does your husband do?" Amanda asked, mostly to take the focus off herself.

"He's in sales, bikes and equipment," Trix said. "The company is located in Colorado, so he's there for a good part of February and March to prepare for the big sales season, and then on and off the rest of the year depending on how things go. He's home October and November almost all the time, so it seems to balance out, except that in the middle of winter I start to feel like a widow. I'm in sales too, you know, so we tend to be busy at the same times, which is nice." Trix put another piece of pork on Amanda's plate without asking, and served her more vegetables and bread. "I know you athletes have appetites, so don't be shy about eating a big meal."

Jake smiled at her, and she found herself smiling back. Amanda let out a sigh and tried to relax.

"I rented you two some movies," Trix said, squeezing her knee. "I hope you'll want to stick around for a while. Your mom won't expect you back at the hospital tonight will she?"

Amanda didn't know how much Jake had explained to Trix about her "situation." Amanda put her head down and decided to be direct. "I think she'll be too tired to see me tonight, but she'll still be upset if I don't call or something before she goes to sleep."

"Is there anyone else who helps you?" Trix asked gently.

"I'm not sure what you mean," Amanda said quietly. "Helps us do what?"

It looked like Trix had tears in her eyes. Pity. There was always pity. Amanda looked away.

Trix gave Amanda a watery smile. "I was wondering if anyone helps you take care of your mom, but I can see she's in very competent hands with you looking out for her all by yourself." Trix rubbed Amanda's back and then jumped up with their plates. "I hope you both saved room for pie!"

When they were both stuffed to the point of nausea, they tried to take their dessert plates to the kitchen, but Trix shooed them off. "Go check out those movies, you two."

They both ambled off to the basement. Jake went to use the bathroom, so Amanda went to the TV and noticed that Trix had rented no less than seven movies. She had found something in just about every genre, including a musical, drama, thriller, and three romantic comedies. *Subtle,* Amanda thought. Amanda popped the thriller into the DVD, and then realized that she couldn't figure out how to run the TV with all the remote controls and different boxes. She sat on the corner of the couch and waited for Jake to return.

Several minutes passed, and Trix came down the stairs. "He's been in the bathroom a long time," she announced. She went to the bathroom door. "Jacob, honey, are you sick again?"

Amanda could hear him respond quietly.

"Are you sure sweetie?"

"I'M FINE, BEATRICE. Go away."

Trix turned to Amanda with a weak smile. "Obviously he wants me to back off." She wrapped her arms around her shoulders, hugged herself and shuddered. "It's hell having a sick child, Amanda. You can just never completely convince yourself that everything will be okay. You watch the tiniest things. He was eighteen years old and I was practically wiping his nose for him because he was so exhausted from all the treatments." Amanda knew what she meant. Her mother weighed less than a hundred pounds, but Amanda used to panic whenever her mother complained of being cold because it was one of the first things that happened every time before she went to the hospital.

There was a flush, and Jacob walked out of the bathroom. Amanda and Trix both turned to look at him.

"I had to take a dump, Mom. I managed all by myself, and it looks like I'm going to live one more day." It looked like he was finally irritated with her.

Trix nodded and looked down. She went to the thermostat and spent a moment adjusting it. "It's chilly down here. I just want you to be comfortable." She glanced at Amanda and said, "Enjoy your movies, kids."

Jacob put his head down and sighed with his hands on his hips. "Just a second," he said, following his mother upstairs. Amanda could hear her sniffle, and Jake talking quietly to her. He was back in less than a minute.

"I'm done with my little scene, Amanda. There will be no more 'poor mom' stuff tonight!" Trix shouted down the stairs. "You two want popcorn?"

"Mother!"

"Okay, I'm done. I'm going to bed. Good night, you two."

Amanda settled into the corner of the couch comfortably. It was big and deep, and Amanda told herself not to fall asleep, as she easily could after a big meal and a long day. Jake threw her a blanket and turned the lights down. The TV was huge, and there were speakers all over the room.

"I have to say that with all my mom's overbearing mothering, she knows how to spoil a late-adolescent boy. This home theater system is the best." Jake was pushing buttons on different speakers and boxes to get the sound right. Amanda couldn't tell what the difference was after he monkeyed with it for a while, but he seemed to think it was much better. He grabbed a pillow off the couch and sat on the floor, his back against the couch.

Amanda couldn't remember the last time she felt so comfortable.

* * *

CONTACTS STICKING TO HER EYELIDS.

Ouch.

Amanda sat up in the dark and tried to figure out where she was. She had a pillow from someone's bed under her, and she was covered with two blankets. It was very dark, but she could see two digital clocks blinking 12:00 p.m. and several red lights from electronic equipment.

Jake's house. His basement. She had fallen asleep on the couch. Amanda had no idea what time it was, but it felt and looked like the middle of the night. She got up quietly and looked around. The door to Jake's room was open, and he was asleep in his bed. Suddenly a clock chimed upstairs, and Amanda counted the chimes and found it was 5:00 a.m.

Amanda found the bathroom and a small cup. Luckily, Jake also wore contacts, so she put hers into the cup and added some of his saline. She swished her mouth with water and scrubbed her teeth with some toothpaste on her finger.

Quietly turning the bathroom light back off, she padded back to the couch, sat down and tried to figure out what to do. She had spent the night at Jake's house, on his couch. There was no one at home waiting for her. No real home to go to. Her mother was in the hospital, and the memory of the previous day came back to her, which began in the middle of last night in Jake's hospital room. She had known him for just over twenty-four hours and now she was sleeping on his couch. Even worse, on his mother's couch.

It was all just too weird. These unbelievably friendly and sincere people invited her to their home before they even knew her last name. Even more shocking was that it felt nice. Amanda almost felt her deep chasm of loneliness had been a tiny bit filled by their warmth. She thought she should feel awkward, but somehow it was okay to fall asleep here.

And since it was okay, she decided it would also be fine to go back to sleep for a few more hours. She snuggled back under her warm blankets and drifted back to sleep.

* * *

AMANDA AWOKE TO FIND JAKE sitting in his spot on the floor eating French toast and sausage and watching TV. Before she could even sit up, Trix brought down a plate of breakfast for Amanda. They watched MTV and talked about music.

Amanda dragged herself away at almost noon, and she went straight to her mother's room because she felt so guilty. Her mother was full of questions about where she was, and Amanda decided it was easier just to tell her the truth. Suspicion flickered in April's eyes when Amanda explained where she was.

"What do you mean, you just 'fell asleep'?" April was propped on two pillows wearing her pink "Live to Ride" t-shirt and cut off sweat pants. Her legs were so skinny that her knees looked almost bulbous connecting her bony thighs and calves, and she wore patchwork slippers that had been donated to the hospital by the ladies' auxiliary.

"I don't know what else to say. I had dinner, we watched a movie, and I fell asleep on the couch. His mom had already gone to bed, so I assume Jake finished watching the movie and went to bed later. When I woke up it was after 10:00 a.m. I ate a quick breakfast and came right here." Amanda was sitting in the glider rocker in the corner of the room. Even though it didn't have a chair pad, it was still very comfortable.

"Those are the clothes you were wearing yesterday."

"I just told you I came right here, Mom."

April leaned back and closed her eyes. She couldn't seem to find the words for what bothered her so much about Amanda spending the night at Jake's house, but Amanda knew exactly what the problem was. April wasn't upset because her daughter had spent the night at a guy's house, or that she was wearing the same clothes and the nurses might suspect something. She didn't like that Amanda had somewhere *else* to go.

April finally just shook her head and changed the subject. "I'd like to go out today. Maybe stop at Wal-Mart and get some good socks."

She wanted to tell her mother that she didn't need socks, but there was no point. Going to Wal-Mart would be a long, involved activity that would require bathing, dressing, borrowing a wheelchair, getting in and out of the car . . . It would easily take the rest of the day. Amanda took a deep breath and braced for her mother's response.

"I need to go home for a while, Mom. Why don't you have a nurse help you get dressed, and I'll pick you up around 2:00."

April stared at Amanda. "Have another date?"

"I want to change clothes, Mom. I want a shower. I need to do a few things before I can spend the afternoon at Wal-Mart." Amanda was just trying to be honest, but she knew this would not go over well.

"You know what, Amanda? Just forget it. Forget it. I don't need socks. It's a waste for me to get anything new anyway." April turned away from Amanda and lay back down. "I'm tired anyway. Go take your shower, and I'll see you at dinner if you're not *too* busy."

Amanda heard a familiar scream of frustration in the back of her mind. "I told you I would take you, Mom. Let's just go."

"You can't go now, Amanda. You need your shower and your clean clothes. Forget it." Her mother talked into her blanket. There was no winning this argument, and Amanda sensed that a trip out would be too much for her mom today anyway. She really was withering away before her eyes.

Amanda saw that even sitting up in bed wore her out. She decided to let it go.

"I'll see you in a couple hours, Mom," Amanda said. She leaned forward and put her cheek next to her mom's. April put her hand up and rubbed Amanda's head.

By the time Amanda returned later that afternoon, her mother had forgotten the Wal-Mart argument. They had dinner together and watched *Entertainment Tonight*. April was asleep by 7:00 p.m.

Amanda left the hospital and drove around town. She needed to get a job, both to pass time and save some money for school. Even though her financial aid package included big government grants that paid for nearly everything, she would need money for her book bag, things for her dorm room, college apropriate clothes, and the like. She stopped at Dairy Queen to pick up an application and found Jake and his mom in line for blizzards. She couldn't really call it a coincidence since Jake had mentioned that they often went out for ice cream at night.

Without much resistance, they talked her into getting a blizzard and returning to their place to watch one of the rented movies.

Amanda had her contact lens case in her pocket.

chapter three

A MANDA AND JACOB SETTLED INTO a friendship and a routine. Amanda was hired at the Dairy Queen, so she worked five days out of seven, either the 11:00 to 5:00 shift or 4:00 to close at 10:00 p.m. Jake had decided not to get a job because he was taking two classes at the local college.

At the end of the day, Amanda and Jake always found each other. Usually they watched movies or David Letterman in his basement. Amanda slept every night on his couch. Trix set out sheets for her, which she spread on the couch because she assumed Trix did not want her to drool on the upholstery.

Michael had returned from his long road trip. He was very friendly and didn't act at all surprised that Amanda was spending every night at their home. One Sunday night the four of them even played hearts together. At midnight that night, Michael was the first to get up and say he needed to go to bed. Jake cleared their soda glasses and pretzels off the table. Trix seemed to give Jake a look, and he went in the kitchen and busied himself at the sink.

"Amanda, sweetie," Trix began.

Trix looked serious, and Amanda internally began to panic. She had spent the last two weeks on their couch, and Trix was about to tell her she needed to live in her own depressing home.

"Honey, we love having you here, but the couch is no place for you to sleep every night . . ."

"I know, I know. I'm sorry . . . I . . . I . . . don't know why I've stayed every night," Amanda stammered and felt her throat get very tight.

"Honey, stop right there." Trix grabbed both of Amanda's hands and looked up at her. "I'd just like to get you more comfortable. Would you consider sleeping in Jessie's bedroom? Jessie has probably only slept there a dozen times in her life since we bought this house after she started college. It's big and there's a bathroom and you could be very comfortable." Trix stared at her so openly that Amanda couldn't stand it. Once again tears threatened, but she bit them back.

Trix must have seen her chin quiver. "Oh, honey," Trix said, pulling her to the couch and sitting her down. "I just can't hug you right standing up because you're so tall."

Jake knelt on the floor in front of them. "Just say yes, Amanda," he said. "I think we'll all feel better."

She could only nod and smile. Jake took her hands and pulled her up, leading her to his sister's bedroom. He flipped on a switch, and she looked around the room, which was nicely decorated but felt like a guestroom because it was without anyone's personal items. Amanda smiled when she looked at the bedside stand, upon which Jake must have placed a bozo the clown doll holding a tiny sign that said, "Welcome Amanda."

* * *

AFTER AMANDA GOT HER FIRST FULL paycheck from Dairy Queen, she felt like she needed to buy something for Jake and his family. She had known these people just under a month, but she knew that Trix liked certain antique dishes, Jake collected football cards from the sixties and seventies, and Michael was a huge Twins fan.

One Sunday after Amanda had lunch with her mother and spent a very uncomfortable afternoon trying to give her a pedicure, Amanda told her mom she had to work so she could leave early and shop for the gifts. She walked around the town looking at different stores, trying to decide what to buy that would be casual but appropriate.

She had almost allowed herself to "move in" to Jessie's room. Instead of carting her huge duffel bag back and forth, she unpacked a little and filled two drawers. She kept her toothbrush in the bathroom drawer that had actually become "Amanda's bathroom" to the rest of the family. Amanda caught herself saying "the rest of the family" in her thoughts a few times. It implied that she was part of this family, but her daily trips to the hospital always reminded her that she wasn't.

Amanda had considered at least a hundred gift items, including Twins hats, full sets of football and baseball cards, different dishes that looked like antiques but she just couldn't judge quality, bobble head dolls, joke items, flower baskets, sentimental cards, and even a few religious items since they did have a Last Supper reprint in the kitchen. There was nothing appropriate for her situation, which was hardly surprising but made her struggle no easier.

A saleswoman in a gift store followed Amanda through the aisles trying to be "helpful."

"Are you looking for a gift for a certain occasion?" The saleswoman, Nan, according to her nametag, stood with her hands clasped ready to ferret out the perfect gift.

"Just looking, thanks." Amanda said with her head down.

"It's the time of year for graduation parties . . . we've had so many people buying plaques and inspirational books. So much more personal than cash."

"And there's nothing a graduate likes more than a pile of plaques," Amanda said before she could catch herself. "I'm not shopping for a graduation."

Nan recoiled slightly, but pushed on. "Birthday? Belated Father's Day? Would you like to see some of our albums?"

Amanda could smell her Wind Song perfume, and she wanted to pluck the clip-on earrings dangling on the bottom of her wrinkly earlobes. "I need a gift for the family I'm staying with while my mother is dying in the hospital." It wasn't even the full story, but it was enough for Nan. She was aghast and clearly had no words to comfort anyone in such a horrendous situation, no gifts that were appropriate.

"Perhaps a lovely flower basket from next door . . ." Nan said as she wandered away.

It always came back to pity.

* * *

AMANDA WALKED IN THE DOOR to the Mann house with nothing. Wondering if she would ever get over the feeling that she needed to ring the doorbell, she edged in the front door hoping that she could get into her room before anyone would "catch" her letting herself in. Michael came in from the patio just as Amanda was going up the stairs.

"Hey there, Amanda," Michael said. He had been staining the deck, so his khaki shorts were covered in reddish brown stain, and his hands looked like he had slaughtered an animal. He went to the sink and poured himself a glass of water directly from the tap. "Filthy stinking hot out there. I swear that deck is hotter than an Alabama shithouse."

Amanda just smiled, not knowing what to say.

"And I almost lost my life to a huge family of wasps living under the railing. Luckily I had some foaming insect-killing stuff out with me because there was a thing on the news just last night about how wasps make their nests on decks, among other places. I foamed that bad boy and ran for cover quick." Michael swabbed his high forehead with a paper towel, found an apple in the refrigerator and snapped off a huge bite.

She giggled a little at the thought of him spraying a cloud of foam and running for his life.

"I'm inspired to consume a large slab of cow in honor of my accomplishments." He rifled through the freezer and pulled out several odd shaped blocks of meat wrapped in freezer paper. "We will eat steak," he said, pounding his chest with two blocks of meat. " Wanna help me make dinner?"

Amanda paused, knowing that the kitchen was clearly Trix's territory. "Is that really a good idea?"

Michael laughed. "Are you worried that I'm making dinner or invading Trixie's turf?" Once again, Amanda was at a loss for a catchy reply. He was far too quick and clever, and Amanda loved his humor and felt like a clod at the same time. "Don't worry, kid. She loves it when I make cow."

So Amanda and Michael made dinner together. Michael took a quick shower first while Amanda thawed the steaks and washed the potatoes and salad fixings. Michael made a large production out of making dinner, using many pots and dishes wastefully, seemingly unaware that everything he used would eventually have to be washed.

Trix came in halfway through their meal preparation. She had been gardening and sun tanning by the looks of her. She was wearing a bright red tube top, short denim shorts, and a red sun visor. Trix always looked perfectly coordinated and just right for the occasion. Her toenails matched the red of her tube top, and she was practically a walking Ralph Lauren ad with Ralph sunglasses on top of her visor. Trix had apparently not gotten the news that too much sun was dangerous, for she was deeply tanned with freckles covering her shoulders and face. She stood with her hands on her hips and watched Michael and Amanda bustle in the kitchen together.

"Amanda, you look like you know your way around a kitchen," Trix said, and Amanda knew this was high praise.

"You tear lettuce like a pro, Amanda," Michael added. "Who taught you how to cook?"

Trix gave him a searing look that was impossible for Amanda to miss. Trix bent over backwards to avoid any mention of Amanda's family unless the moment was right, at which time she was never afraid to ask her directly. Trix saved the moment like a pro. "Amanda's like me, Michael. Gals like us operate on pure gut instinct. No teacher required."

Amanda had appointed herself in charge of the salad, so she found the bowls and put together four salads.

"Oh, we only need three, sweetie. Jake isn't coming home for dinner tonight." Trix was a little too nonchalant about it. Amanda nodded and distributed his salad in the remaining three bowls.

"Does he have a late class?" Michael asked.

Amanda saw Trix step on Michael's foot hard. She cleared her throat, stalling for time, and finally said, "he's studying with a friend . . . some friends." Trix continued to jabber about the dinner, but Amanda missed the conversation after that. She moved the lettuce leaf by leaf into the other bowls while she absorbed what Trix had said. Jake was with a girl. Amanda didn't think it would be a big deal if he was truly just studying with a girl, but Trix was acting so weird about it that it had to be more than that. She couldn't figure out what to think or how to feel.

Trix was in maximum overdrive at this point. She was flitting around like a maniac trying to act like nothing was wrong. Michael went out to the deck to check on the steaks, and left Amanda and Trix alone.

"Oh, that salad looks so good, Amanda." Trix fished around in the cupboard until she found some croutons, and then busied herself placing them on the salads.

Amanda nodded.

Trix sighed and put down the croutons. "It's not a date, sweetie."

Amanda mumbled something incomprehensible and looked away, feeling her face turn hot.

"I'm sure he needs the help in this class. He's not the best with school-work, especially in the summer. Working with someone probably helps him stay focused . . ."

"It's okay," Amanda said quietly. "Don't worry about it."

Trix came over and put her hands on Amanda's shoulders and looked up at her face. "I want you both to be happy, sweetheart."

"It's no big deal. Forget it. Really." Amanda didn't meet her eyes while she set salad dressing on the table. Michael brought in the steaks and set them on the table, eyeing them both.

Trix talked loudly through the entire meal while Michael gave Amanda kind looks and smiles. Amanda ate half a steak and excused herself to run to DQ to "check the work schedule." Trix tried to give her a meaningful look, but Amanda got out before Trix could connect with her.

Amanda barely made it out the door before she felt her loneliness rush back on her like a tidal wave. This family was not hers, and she was pretending to have something that she would never, ever have—a place to belong. At that moment, Amanda thought she could jump off the end of the earth and no one would ever know, ask a question, or care.

With nowhere to go and her keys left inside the house, Amanda started to walk and then broke into a jog. She ran, passing house after house filled with families. She ran past mothers walking their babies in strollers, middle-school girls walking in clumps, boys on bikes, elderly couples on lawn chairs inside their mosquito tents. Everyone connected to someone else. No one connected to her.

Amanda ran until she was past the houses and arrived at a park on the edge of town near the dump and the old drive-in theater. Amanda sat against a tree in a marshy, swampy area and stared. Immediately, mosquitoes and gnats swarmed around her. Amanda wondered if even the insects knew she existed. A mosquito landed on her thigh. She watched it penetrate her skin, felt the tiny sting, and watched as it sucked out her blood. It was dusk, and the bugs were heavy, but Amanda did not stop the insects from taking her blood and flying away with it. She discovered the sensation of a mosquito bite was not always the same depending on the part of the body that the bugs bit. On her legs, the sting was not very noticeable, but on her neck it was almost unbearable. With her hands resting on her knees, sweat collected under her palms from the heat and discomfort.

A mosquito landed on the inside edge of her right upper eyelid. She felt as if she should let it sting her as the dozen others had because there was some sort of deep, sick comfort that came from knowing that the insect took away a part of herself. But she couldn't stand the bug on her eyelid, so she came to life with a sudden jolt of force slapping the bug away. It awakened the pain and itch on all the other welts, and suddenly she was scratching herself uncontrollably on her arms, legs, cheeks, and neck. She jumped up and scratched until she had deeper welts and skin under her fingernails. She even dragged her legs across the trunk of the tree leaving trails of scratch marks across her shins.

She ran again, still with nowhere to go, but her mind was clear and afraid. Blood was running down her legs from the scratches she inflicted on herself. She had hurt herself on purpose, and she felt better because of it. She was sicker than she ever thought.

It was dusk, and bats started to swoop out of the giant trees that lined the streets. She slowed down and walked quietly back home, or to the Mann's home, as Amanda really had no home. Thankfully she passed few people. Blood ran down the front of her leg into her shoe. She arrived back at the Mann's home just as Jake was getting out of someone's car. Amanda slowed so he wouldn't see her, but he had gotten out and was leaning through the passenger side window talking to the driver. After a moment he got up and walked inside with his backpack slung over his shoulder. The girl had short, dark, heavily styled hair and sunglasses on her head. She was wearing a short sleeved, off the shoulder sweater, and Amanda could see she was wearing lipstick. At least she hadn't worn off her lipstick. *Study-whore.*

Amanda waited until Jake had been inside for at least five minutes before she went in. Michael and Trix were sitting at the table eating ice cream cones from Dairy Queen, and Jake was helping himself to a blizzard they had saved for him in the freezer.

"Join us, Amanda!" Trix yelled, hopping up. Amanda was going to have to get past all of them in the kitchen to get to her room and her bathroom to clean herself up. Trix would freak if she saw her bloody welts.

"I'm um, not going to . . . um, don't worry about . . . uh, I uh need something downstairs." Amanda ran down the stairs to Jake's bathroom and shut and locked the door. The bathroom smelled like his deodorant and coconutty shampoo. He was pretty high maintenance for a guy.

Amanda looked in the mirror and was shocked. Her face was filthy with sweat and smudges of dirt, and her hair was wild. She had three large mosquito bites on her face including the one by her eye that made her right eye looked half closed. Her neck was blotchy and red. Her arms and legs were dirty and bloody. She had done this to herself, and it scared her to death.

Knowing she had to get in the shower, Amanda turned on the water as quietly as possible. The cold water was a relief for her stinging skin, and it felt good to wash away the muddy sludge all over her body. She stepped out and dried off using a towel that Jake had obviously used before because it smelled strongly like him. The laundry room was connected to the bathroom, and Amanda knew she had a load of laundry in the dryer. She wanted clean clothes, so she wrapped herself in a towel to sneak out and get some clean pajamas.

But she couldn't sneak far with Jake standing in the doorway to the laundry room waiting for her.

"Amanda, are you okay?" He was unflustered seeing her stand there in a towel. Amanda was so shocked she couldn't speak. She stood shaking her head.

"What happened to you, Amanda? You look awful. Did something happen with your mom?"

Amanda was ashamed to admit, even to herself, that thoughts of her dying mother were a thousand miles away.

"I'm fine," she said looking down and trying to edge past him.

"Amanda, come on," he said, grabbing her by her bare shoulders. "What's wrong?'

"Did you get any studying done?" she blurted out, and instantly wanted to suck the words back in her mouth. She was getting more psycho by the second. Jake backed up and sat on the back of the couch in the rec room.

"What do you want me to say Amanda? Are you upset that I was studying with a girl?"

Amanda shook her head. "I just want to get dressed." Jake nodded and backed away. Amanda carefully squatted in front of the dryer, holding her towel tight around her, and found a t-shirt and boxer shorts that she usually wore to bed. She ran back into the bathroom and got dressed. When she came back out, Jake was sitting on the couch watching David Letterman. She started to go upstairs, when Jake asked if she would stay and watch the Top 10 List with him.

Amanda stood for a second, but started walking back to him before she had even made up her mind to watch TV with him. She was going to sit on the floor, but he rubbed the cushion next to him motioning her to sit there. She moved to sit by him without a thought. Jake put a cushion on his lap and gently had her lie down with her head on the pillow on his lap. He rubbed her back and played with her hair until she finally let down her guard enough to drift off to sleep.

chapter four

THINGS SEEMED TO MOVE BACK into their summer routine after that night. Jake took his finals and was done with classes for several weeks so he was around home a lot more. Jake's sisters—minus their significant others—visited for a long, fun weekend during which they played Trivial Pursuit, hearts, and Cranium until after midnight every night. Amanda insisted on sleeping downstairs on the couch while they were there, and no one argued with her.

Amanda worked most days, visiting her mom for an hour or so every day in the mornings. Amanda hadn't spoken with her mom's doctors for at least a month, so it startled her when the nurse on duty one morning pulled her aside and asked her to stay a while longer so the doctor could talk to her when she finished her rounds.

"Why does the doctor want to talk to me?" Amanda was frustrated because Trix had invited her to go to lunch at a restaurant on the lake just outside of town.

"She needs to discuss your mother's condition with you." The nurse was not a day over twenty-two, pretty, and snotty as hell. Amanda had seen her a few times this summer, but it was obvious she was new.

"I need to meet someone in an hour."

"I'm sure you have things that feel like a priority to you, but it's imperative to talk to your mother's doctor today." The nurse glared at her, and it was clear she thought Amanda was a selfish brat, too busy to be bothered with her mother in the hospital.

"Fine." Amanda wanted to tell her off, but she wasn't sure what she could say in her own defense. Amanda used to live at the hospital, but that had changed this summer after she had met Jake and his family. Her reality used to be dictated by her mother's condition minute by minute, but Amanda had reached the point where she couldn't stand to live her life around a sick person, even if that sick person *was* her mother.

Amanda went back into her mother's room and sat in the rocking chair. She looked closely at her mother, and realized for the first time that her mother had changed drastically in the last week. It looked like her body had dried in the sun like a prune. Her skin was gray and looked thin as paper. Her lips were pulled away from her mouth, and her hands looked like they belonged to a one-hundred-year-old woman. Amanda usually came around 9:00 a.m. so she was not troubled that her mom was usually asleep when she got there and slept through most of the visit. But then Amanda realized she hadn't seen her mother fully conscious for days.

The doctor walked in, another young, new face. She was Asian with long black hair in a low ponytail. She wore small, rectangular wire-rimmed glasses, and no make up. She looked businesslike.

"Hi, Amanda. I'm Dr. Sam. I don't think we've met before." Dr. Sam shook Amanda's hand, and Amanda searched her face for signs of judgment on her absence. "Amanda, I want to inform you about your mom's situation. I'm sure you've recognized that she's slipping." She paused, waiting for Amanda to respond, but there was nothing Amanda could say because she hadn't really noticed the difference until today. "Your mom has an advance directive that she changed about two weeks ago. Her former orders stated that she wanted tube feedings and many other measures taken to prolong her life. Recently, she changed her orders to state almost the opposite. She wants no heroic measures other than minimal morphine for pain."

Amanda couldn't absorb what the doctor was trying to tell her. "My mom always wants lots of medicine, especially for pain. She's always bugging the nurses about her pain and asking for something to help her sleep or make her more comfortable."

"She receives morphine every three hours, and otherwise takes nothing. I'm sure you can see that your mother hasn't been able to communicate clearly for at least ten days."

Ten days? Amanda thought. Had she been so wrapped up in herself that she didn't even notice that her mother had been unresponsive for over a week? Apparently, this was what the doctor was trying to tell her.

"I don't understand why you're telling me all this." Amanda stared at her mom, snoring quietly in her same hospital bed, wearing her same Harley Davidson t-shirt.

"I'm telling you this because the nurses feel that you don't realize that it's almost the end." Dr. Sam looked at her intently but with kindness in her eyes and her voice. Amanda just nodded blankly. "She hasn't eaten since Sunday, and even then she was only taking a few sips of broth at every meal. Today on rounds it appeared she had slipped further into a coma-like state. My best guess is that it will only be a few more days." She reached out and patted Amanda's leg. "I'm sorry. Is there anything I can do? Do you have any questions?"

Questions? Definitely she had questions. How had her mother changed her advance directive without talking to her? How had she been unconscious for ten days without Amanda's knowledge? What were the last words she had said to her mother? Have they had a real conversation in days? Amanda didn't know the answer to any of this. What kind of daughter wouldn't have noticed these things? She knew the answer to that.

Dr. Sam was still looking at her closely. "Is there someone I should call for you?"

Amanda knew she didn't deserve any support. She shook her head no and sunk back into her chair.

* * *

THAT DAY PASSED IN A FOG. Feeling that she needed to be punished, Amanda sat by her mother's bedside, watching the nurses come and go. She excused herself a few times when they needed to do the intimate cares that Amanda never wanted to observe. Her mother always preferred to have Amanda help her use the bathroom or bathe, but Amanda hated doing these things for her.

When April came home after her first hospitalization, she refused home health care and relied on Amanda for everything. Amanda was fourteen-years old and had to help her mom get to the bathroom to vomit, or even worse, dump out her buckets of vomit when she was too weak to get to the bathroom. She shaved her mother's head. She managed her pills, and picked up her prescriptions. During one horrible spell, Amanda held cigarettes to her mother's lips so she could get rid of her nicotine fits right after the surgery.

Amanda's life was always about cancer. Her mom asked about Amanda's high school career when it suited her, but Amanda had learned long before that the pleasure that April took in Amanda's life was always related to how it impacted April. She watched Amanda's softball games when it seemed like fun, like on parent's day when Amanda would give her a rose and a hug in front of a crowd. But when Amanda was pitching in the state tournament in previous years, April didn't go because she hated driving in the Cities, or she didn't like to sit with the other parents, or she had something more interesting going on at home. Amanda and April had always lived like sisters or girlfriends. Amanda figured out early, before she had words for the feeling, that she had never really been mothered.

But seeing her mother being cared for by others stirred up a new emotion that she didn't have words for either. It was like the feeling that she had a few weeks before when she had let herself be preyed upon by a swarm of mosquitoes. It was the sense that she didn't even exist at all. It was the knowledge that when everyone else in the world had a family tree, she had a dandelion with two blooms and no roots.

"Mama had a baby and her head popped off."

The childhood rhyme rang in her head as she remembered how she and the other kids in the trailer court used to pick dandelions, sing the rhyme and pop the dandelion flower off with a flick of the thumb.

She was totally, utterly alone.

* * *

BY EARLY EVENING, Amanda was starving so she ate a bag of chips, a granola bar, and two bags of peanut M&Ms from the candy machine in the basement of the hospital, not allowing herself to leave the hospital to get money for anything more substantial. She was drifting off into a bored sleep when Trix and Jake walked in.

"Hi, sweetie." Trix said, squeezing her shoulders. Jake hung back in the entryway, obviously uncomfortable.

"What . . . what are you doing here?" Amanda stood up and stretched, surprised to see anyone other than nurses.

"When you didn't show up for lunch, we figured something had happened with your mom," Trix said. Amanda had completely forgotten about lunch.

"Sorry, I, um . . ." She motioned to her mom and her voice trailed off.
Trix got tears in her eyes and nodded. "I know, sweetie."

Jake had not looked up from the floor since he entered the room.
Amanda wanted him to leave, knowing how hard it was for him to be back
in this hospital watching someone die.

She walked them into the hallway. "The doctor said she's not going
to make it much longer, so I thought I should stay . . ." Her throat tight-
ened. She hadn't said the words out loud yet.

Trix pulled her into a tight hug. A sob came up from the bottom of
Amanda's stomach, and she actually thought she might vomit she sucked
it back so hard. Amanda pulled away stiffly, but Trix wouldn't let go of her
hands. Trix was crying, and she wiped her eyes with her shoulder sleeve
and let out a big sigh.

"Since we're going to be here for a while, let's grab some of those nice
soft chairs from the family visiting room." She squeezed Amanda's hands
tight, and then let go and grabbed Jake. "Help me carry, will you, Jakey?"

Amanda was stunned. "What are you doing?" she asked, following
them down the hall.

Trix opened the door to the family room and popped the door stand
down with her foot. "Let's take both chairs and that big ottoman. They're
all vinyl, but we can grab those nice blankets from the ladies auxiliary."
Jake picked up a chair that was surprisingly light, and carried it into the
hallway and into her mother's room. Trix picked up the ottoman and
headed down the hall.

Amanda went back into the hallway and found Trix digging in a large
cabinet behind the nurses' station. The nurse on duty was gone, but Trix
made herself at home. She came up with a pile of folded quilts and knitted
blankets.

"Aren't these homey?" Trix said as she passed Amanda. Jake was carrying another chair out of the visiting room, and Trix went back into her
mom's room. Amanda followed them slowly, not realizing her mouth was
hanging open.

Trix was tucking blankets into the chairs. Amanda realized then that
she had brought a book bag with crossword puzzles, magazines, snacks, and
bottles of water. "Can you track down some spare pillows, Jakey?"

Jacob left, and Amanda turned to Trix. "I don't get it," Amanda said.
"Who are all these chairs for? It's just me. I don't have any other family."

"Sweetheart, did you really think we were going to let you be here alone?" Trix asked with a watery smile.

Amanda sat on the ottoman with a thump. This family's kindness was never ending, but Amanda felt so unworthy. She shook her head and tried to tell her that she didn't have to stay. Trix sat on the chair next to her and grabbed her hands again. Amanda's tears were dangerously close this time, and she dug her fingernails in her hands to push the feelings away. "But this has to be too hard for you," Amanda finally said in a shuddery voice, April's soft breathing and the beeping of the machines in the background. "You and Jake have spent enough time in the hospital."

"So have you," Jake said from the doorway, a pile of pillows in his arms. "I'm staying. But, mom, you should go." Jake dropped the pillows on the chair and put his hands on his hips.

Amanda nodded at her.

"Okay, kids. We all know we're worried about each other. No more arguing. We're all staying." Trix reached into her bag and pulled out a newspaper, ending the conversation. Amanda and Jake settled into their chairs.

When the next shift of nurses arrived, Amanda was asleep on a soft chair. Trix and Jake had pushed the ottoman under her legs and tried to get her to stretch out so she could sleep more comfortably. Jake turned on the TV without volume and watched music videos. Trix went into the hallway with one of the nurses after midnight to ask what April's situation was.

Amanda awoke at 4:17 a.m. It was still dark outside. Trix was curled in a soft chair with her head resting on two pillows, looking surprisingly comfortable. Amanda saw that Jake was staring blankly at MTV with no sound.

"How can you stand to watch TV without sound?" Amanda asked softly.

Jake jumped a little at her voice, and then turned to smile at her. "Do you really think infomercials are any better with the sound on?"

Amanda stretched, and realized she must look and smell awful. She could taste peanut M&Ms in her teeth. She reached for a bottle of water and swished before she swallowed.

"I don't ever sleep here," Jake said, "so I've always gotten acquainted with the overnight TV schedule on my hospital stays." Jake flipped to Nick at Nite broadcasting and an episode of *The Cosby Show* was on.

"I always did homework," Amanda said, scrunching down under a mismatched quilt with yarn ties that smelled like Rosemilk lotion and antiseptic cleaner. "This is so pathetic, but I actually used to do extra reading, or work ahead in math, or even write papers that weren't assigned because I needed something to keep me occupied."

"Geez, Amanda, let's not play 'Who's the most pathetic?' because you always win this game . . . Couldn't you just have read a magazine?" Jake rubbed his eyes with the heels of his hands and yawned.

"They don't make 'Harley Daughter' magazine, and I just have never been able to relate to anything else. *Seventeen* and all those magazines talked about prom and boyfriends and celebrity crushes, and those things were always light years away from chemotherapy and hospitals." As always, Amanda's attempt at sounding light and funny came out harsh and awful.

Jake reacted.

"Amanda!" Jake said suddenly and loudly, causing Trix to jump in her sleep. "Don't you think you might have had a more normal life if you would have tried to have one? It's like the second any typical life experience presented itself, you said 'piss on that' and went the other way."

"Jacob!" Trix sat up in her chair and glared at him. Amanda didn't understand his anger, but she did understand her own.

"You have no idea what I tried or didn't try to do. You have no idea what anything was like for me, Mr. Perfect Family, so go to hell!" Amanda jumped up and ran out of her mother's room into the neon lights of the hallway. She went into the family lounge and threw herself on the vinyl couch. He could never understand the lonely Thanksgivings they spent at a café, and the Christmases with the fuschia tinsel tree with eight ornaments and three gifts under it. He would never know the feeling of not being able to get too close to friends because eventually she would have to invite them to her house, and she could never let people into that part of her world. Teachers were usually lukewarm, coaches loved her for her ability, and everyone else ignored her. Jake would never know that reading a magazine or a book or watching a sitcom just reinforced how alone she was.

Amanda knew that Trix would come in the room in a few minutes and try to explain to her why Jake was so upset. She didn't want to hear it. With all their kindness and perfection, the Mann family also brought baggage that wore Amanda out. She was even more frustrated because they were in her mother's hospital room, one of the few places she could claim as her own. She wished they would just leave her alone. Connections had their price.

An older nurse named Bonnie passed the family room and saw that Amanda was sprawled on the vinyl sofa. Bonnie had worked a lot with April the first time she had cancer, but had cut back on her hours since her husband was diagnosed with cancer around the first time April went home. Amanda had only seen her a few times since her mom returned to the hospital.

"Hi, Amanda," Bonnie said warmly, sitting next to her on the couch. "I've been wondering about you. I heard you graduated." Bonnie was small and plump with short, graying hair and glasses that she wore on a chain around her neck.

"Yep. I'm off to the U in a couple weeks," Amanda said. She enjoyed talking to nurses like Bonnie because they never felt like they had to try to make her feel better, and they never felt awkward around her. "No idea what I'll major in, but I guess I have a few years to decide."

"Good for you. My daughter is going there too, totally undecided about her life."

"Is this her first year too?" Amanda asked, not remembering that Bonnie had a daughter her age.

"No, she's actually almost twenty-one," Bonnie said. "She's been working the last two years, but suddenly realized her mother is right and she won't get far without a degree. Let me give you her number in case you want to look her up." She pulled a receipt from her pocket and wrote her daughter's address and phone number on the back and gave it to Amanda.

"Thanks," Amanda said, taking the paper but knowing she would never call.

"Who's that in your mom's room," Bonnie asked. "Is that her sister or something?"

Amanda sunk back on the couch. "Long story." She looked away and hoped Bonnie would take the hint that she didn't want to talk about them.

"Do you want them to go? I can ask them to leave if you want."

Now there was a question, Amanda thought. She wanted them to leave in a way, but only so she didn't have to deal with them face to face. It had made a difference to have them sitting with her. She and Trix had played several hands of gin, which made the time pass faster. Jake had barely spoken, but his presence was comforting. Comfort was another new concept in her world.

"No, they can stay," Amanda finally said. "They're just some people I met recently who are trying to help me out. I'm the local charity case, you know."

"Amanda, can I tell you something?" Bonnie leaned forward and put her hand on Amanda's knee. "I know we don't know each other very well, but I've actually seen you here a lot, especially a few years ago when your mom was first diagnosed. I've been through this myself with my husband who passed away last March. I have lots of family—four brothers and a sister, many nieces and nephews, cousins, and my grandma who is still alive. It's really true that in a crisis you learn who your friends are. My brothers didn't have a clue about what to do for me, my sister lives in Florida, and my friends brought food and ran out the door as quick as they could. My sister-in-law, the one who is married to my youngest brother, was the one who came to the funeral home with me to pick out a casket. She stood with me at the funeral, wrote thank you notes with me afterwards, and took me out for coffee every Saturday morning without fail."

"That's nice," Amanda said, beginning to feel awkward. Bonnie was right. They didn't know each other very well, and she didn't know why she was telling her all this now.

"My point is that it isn't easy to support someone through a loss like this, and my family couldn't really handle it. My sister-in-law was the only one who understood what I needed and was truly there for me, and she only married my brother three years ago. I don't think these people would do all this because you're a charity case," Bonnie said.

"I don't know why anyone would do all the things they've done for me," Amanda said suddenly. "You wouldn't believe what these people have done. They just give and give, and I keep waiting to hear what the catch is."

"Maybe they are doing this because they like you, my dear. Maybe they get as much out of being with you as you get out of being with them."

"I can't imagine that," Amanda said.

"Amanda!" Bonnie said, grabbing her shoulders and looking her in the face. "Are you really this cynical, or do you think you're just not worth the effort?"

Amanda sighed and looked at the floor in reply.

"Oh dear," Bonnie said. "I thought so."

* * *

When Bonnie went back to her shift, Amanda saw that the sun was coming up and thought she should return to her mother's room. She found Jake dozing and Trix sitting by the window watching the sunrise.

"Good morning, sweetheart," Trix said quietly. "I was going to chase you down, but I realized you might need some space so I didn't."

"It's okay," Amanda said. "Let's just forget it."

Trix opened her mouth to reply, but realized that she wouldn't be "forgetting it" if she did, so she stopped herself. "Pretty sunrise."

Amanda smiled absently and sat back on her chair, back in her "position."

"Would you like me to run out and get some bagels?" Trix asked.

Amanda groaned. "I'm really not ready to eat yet. I'll wait until after the rounds and see how I feel then."

She figured that Trix somehow knew that she was waiting to see what the doctor thought her mother's condition was before she allowed herself to plan the day. "Pull your chair over by the window so you can see this, Amanda."

Obediently, Amanda sat by Trix to watch the sunrise. She felt like she could almost see the colors becoming more vivid and intense in the sky. But before long, the colors faded into light. The sky became light blue.

A nurse came in and began checking her mother's vitals. Amanda allowed herself to look at her mom's face, something she realized she had done very little. Her eyes were slightly open, though it would be more accurate to say they were not quite closed. Amanda was reminded she didn't know the last conversation she had with her mother—the last time she had seen those eyes open. She would never see them open again. It seemed like she should have said something significant, or that her mother should have said something significant to her. Instead, their parting words had been incidentals.

"Are you the daughter?" the nurse asked coldly. There was a time when everyone in this hospital made a point of knowing who she was. Only three months before, they had hosted her graduation party. Not that much time had passed, but it seemed that they were all strangers.

Amanda got up and stood next to the nurse, reading the chart over her shoulder. Only notes were scribbled, and Amanda couldn't see anything of significance. The nurse pulled the chart away so Amanda couldn't see it.

"Dr. Hamabi will be through in a few minutes," the nurse said curtly over her shoulder as she left the room.

Knowing that she was among strangers caused Amanda's loneliness to swell again, and she had a horrid thought. She just wanted it to be over. She wanted to go eat ice cream and play hearts at the Mann's kitchen table and pretend none of this was her reality. She wanted two parents who had a solid, stable marriage and a middle-class existence to drop her off at college in their minivan and cry when she finally kicked them out of her dorm room. Amanda was having so much trouble staying numb to the pain of too many losses and changes happening all at once. Her chest felt like a boulder was crushing it. She could hear herself almost gasping for air. Her fingernails dug into her palms until she could finally feel blood, her knuckles aching.

A small, balding Middle Eastern man wearing scrubs and a stethoscope around his neck walked in. He smiled kindly at her. "You are family, correct?"

"I'm her daughter," Amanda said, almost whispering.

"Yes. Well," he said, looking at her chart. "You understand she will most likely pass away in few days?"

"Yes, I know."

"There no more patients on this unit," Dr. Hamabi said. "I work on general medicine floor, and I check with you every few hours. The nurse will stay here most of time."

"She's the only person on this whole floor?" Trix asked incredulously.

He shook his head, closed her chart and looked at Amanda. "If her breathing becomes labored, heavy, or if there any big changes on monitors, push your call button."

Amanda could only nod. *When she dies, let us know.*

* * *

AFTER DR. HAMABI LEFT, Trix went to change clothes and pick up some breakfast.

"Let me see your hands," Jake said suddenly. Amanda jumped, not knowing he was awake.

"What? Why?" Amanda said. "When did you wake up anyway?" She sat on her chair next to his.

He sat up and leaned his elbows on his knees.

"I saw you clenching your fists before," Jake said. "Except it looked like you were trying to dig your nails into your hands. I want to see if you cut yourself." He was irritable again.

"Jake, why are you here if you're just going to get pissy and start arguments? Why don't you just go home?" Amanda put her hands under her legs so he couldn't get a look at them.

"You'd love that, wouldn't you? It would add to the melodrama of the lone daughter watching her mother die." He put his head down in his hands and rubbed his hair hard.

"What the hell is wrong with you?!" Amanda yelled at him, her voice shaking with rage and exhaustion. "What are you mad at me for? Go home if you don't want to be here. I never asked you to stay."

"You bet I'm mad at you. I'm sick of you moping around like some victim, just letting shitty things happen to you so people like my mother can rescue you."

Amanda almost fell off her chair in shock. She was furious, but she also needed to cower from his sudden angry attack. She wanted to curl in a corner and disappear like a wounded, orphaned puppy. She couldn't find a word to say. So Jake continued.

"There you go again, sitting there with your chin quivering because I'm yelling at you. Why don't you go scratch yourself up again, or dig some new welts in your hands? Yell at me. Yell at her, your bitch of a mother who did a shitty job being your mom and then goes off and dies on you, leaving you a freaking orphan. Yell at that doctor that cares so much he'll be two floors down, but you can call him when she croaks. Yell at me for being such a bastard. Do something, Amanda! Stand up for yourself or this world is going to swallow you up whole!"

Amanda jumped up and wanted to walk out, but she let herself explode on him instead. "Go to hell, Jacob. I'll be just fine after you and the rest of your family go back to your lives and drop my charity case from your roster. I have a life, and I can take care of myself." She went to Trix's chair by the window and sat down again in a huff. Jake rolled his eyes and shook his head, but Amanda swore he looked like he felt better.

* * *

THEY SPOKE VERY LITTLE THE REST of that day. Trix returned with bags of food, which Jake devoured and Amanda barely touched. Amanda and Trix alternately played rummy and did crosswords together. Jake slept or watched MTV, still with the volume down to nothing. He didn't go home to change, but went into the hallway bathroom at one point to brush his teeth and add some gel to his hair. Amanda called into work and said she wouldn't be coming in until further notice. Michael brought them dinner and stayed into the evening.

April died later that evening uneventfully. Her breathing got faster, then labored, then slower, and finally her chest didn't rise again. Amanda stared blankly at the flat line, and then at her mother. She waited for her mother's chest to rise, as though needing to confirm what the machine was obviously telling her. She was gone. There were five bodies, but four lives in the room. Amanda wondered if her soul was floating out of her, or if a ghostly apparition sat up and walked out, invisible to the mortals in the room. She looked up, as if to look at heaven and try to see if her mother was there yet, but of course all she saw were the water stained tiles of the ceiling.

Michael slipped out of the room, presumably to find a nurse. Jake and Trix were watching her. She was truly alone now that her mother was gone, but she felt no different than she did the moment before she died. She felt no more alone. Trix came over, knelt in front of Amanda and grabbed her hands. Amanda met her tearful eyes and shrugged, almost in apology. No emotion came.

The next hours drifted by in surreal images. The doctor checked her mom's vital signs and confirmed that she had died. There was some discussion about the time it had occurred. A nurse came in and began turning off and unplugging machines. Someone asked Amanda if she would like some time alone with her mother. She shook her head. Amanda could think of nothing to say to her.

"She left instructions about which funeral home to use," the nurse was saying to Trix. A small corner of Amanda's brain registered how strange it was that April left instructions about the funeral home she wanted.

"What other instructions did she leave?" Amanda heard herself ask.

Everyone turned to Amanda, apparently surprised to hear her speak. The nurse looked down at the sheet of spiral notebook paper clipped to her chart. "She wants to wear a Harley Davidson t-shirt when she's cremated. She wants you to keep her ashes and spread them in the ocean or river, or someplace that's close to you wherever you make your home someday. She wants a little ceremony in the chapel outside the hospital. She wants it to be short." The nurse, another stranger, looked up at Amanda. "Do you want a copy of her instructions?" she asked blandly.

Amanda nodded. The nurse went behind the nurses' station and made a copy, considered both pages for a moment, and then gave Amanda the original. *Last Will* it said on the top in all capital letters in her mother's printing. Amanda folded it again and put it in her jeans pocket.

Trix came out of the room carrying a medium-sized box, with her book bag over her shoulder. Michael took the box and carried it, and Amanda realized Jake's arm was around her. They walked silently out of the hospital. She got in the backseat of Michael's car, and Jake took her keys and drove Amanda's car back. They drove home without a word. Michael pulled into the driveway and let everyone out before he pulled the car into the garage.

It was after midnight. Trix tried to offer everyone a snack, but no one was hungry. Everyone just went his or her direction to get ready for bed. Amanda was in her bathroom brushing her teeth with the door open a crack. Trix knocked softly.

"I know you're not ready to talk, sweetheart, but is there anything you need? Anything I can do for you?" Amanda shook her head, but allowed Trix to hug her tightly for several minutes. Even Michael stopped in the hallway, put his arm around her shoulders and gave her a squeeze.

Amanda crawled into bed and stared at the ceiling. She looked at the bozo next to her bed that still held the sign welcoming her to the Mann's home. She had a few more personal things in the room, but otherwise it was bare. She waited for sleep to come, exhausted.

She hadn't lain in bed long when she heard another knock. Jake came in and knelt on the floor by her bed. She turned on her side to look at him.

"I'm sorry, Amanda," he whispered. His eyes were wet. Hearing his apology and seeing his sadness broke something inside of her, and she was unable to keep her grief away any longer. Nearly a decade of tears forced their way out, and she curled into a ball and sobbed. Jake crawled into bed with her and held her while her body quaked. His chest became warm and wet with her tears. He rubbed his cheek against her face, and gradually the sobs dwindled to quiet, endless streams of tears. He held her face with his hands and kissed her eyelids gently, trying to make the tears stop.

Without thinking it through and before he could stop himself, he kissed her again. Her face still wet with tears, he kissed her mouth and cheeks and nose and forehead. She drew her breath in sharply, shocked by his kiss and the intense flood of emotion that came with it. She felt a stabbing in her chest that pulsed down to her toes. She wrapped her arms around him and dug her fingernails into his back. He arched and groaned. He reached down and pulled her t-shirt off with one motion before she could react. Their skin was pressed together, their hearts thudding, their breathing shallow and fast.

Neither knew it for sure about the other, but it was the first time for both of them. He held her hand, his thumb brushing over where she had cut into her skin with her nails.

"Are you okay?" Jake whispered, his breath hot in her ear.

She nodded, willing him not to stop.

They moved together, the intensity so overwhelming for Amanda that she could barely breathe. They were together like this for several minutes, while he kept wiping and kissing her tears away. Finally, his whole body shuddered, and then he was still. Amanda's heart was still racing, but she laid still. He pulled away and rolled onto his back, still breathing hard and fast.

Jake looked over and saw a tear slide down her cheek by her temple. She couldn't look at him. Neither knew what to say. She wondered if he was going to get up and go back to his room.

He took a deep breath and let it out in a sigh, staring at the ceiling.

"God, Amanda," Jake whispered. "Was that okay? Are you okay?" He sounded worried, and possibly regretful.

She nodded.

"I love you, Amanda."

She squeezed her eyes shut. He reached down and held her hand until he fell asleep.

* * *

AMANDA LAY STILL, UNAWARE of the time passing. Jake had rolled over and was facing away from her, his breathing slow and regular. She could hardly absorb what had just happened, what he had just said, what they had just done.

She edged her way out of bed, pulling on a t-shirt and shorts. Some part of her mind wondered if Trix or Michael had heard them. She felt uncomfortable and sore. Her hands were shaking, and her breathing was still ragged. The dull roar in the back of her head had returned, stronger than it had ever been. The urge to hurt herself was almost uncontrollable. Nothing had ever been as terrifying as the feeling she had at this moment. She backed away from the bed and found her two laundry baskets. One was full of folded clothes waiting to be put away. She opened her drawers as quietly as she could and piled the rest of her clothes in the baskets.

The room had never been very dark because of the bright streetlight that shined through the bedroom window. Amanda scanned the floor and decided to grab the most important things to pack in her bags, her eyes barely focusing as the tears fell.

Amanda had sloppily packed two laundry baskets and stuffed some things into her pillow case. She dragged them carefully into the hallway and down the stairs to the entryway. She found her purse with her keys hanging by the door. Carefully she opened the door and set her belongings on the front step.

The house creaked, and Amanda paused. A tiny voice in her head tried to tell her to run back upstairs and crawl into bed with Jake. She imagined the warmth lying next to him under the sheets. Then her stomach lurched, and Amanda choked. It was just too much, and she just couldn't stand to feel everything she was feeling. Tears sprang up again, and she knew she was being a fraud. This was not her life. This was not her world. She would never be allowed to stay.

Amanda pulled the door open quietly, set the lock so the door would still be locked when she left, and pulled the door closed behind her. She dragged her baskets to her car parked in the driveway, loaded them quickly in the hatchback, and closed it carefully. She got in the car and backed out of the driveway before she turned the ignition. She drove away.

When she reached the park a few blocks away where she used to play soccer, Amanda pulled her car over. She held her head in her hands and sobbed.

Part Two

chapter five

October 2010

IN THOSE RIDICULOUS HEELS, every footstep made an echoing clop that announced her departure to the lower floors of the courthouse. She hoped she had escaped before Jake realized she had run away once again.

Finally she found a back door and went outside, blasted by the brisk October air. She decided to walk and attempt to clear her head. She had only been there a month, but she loved her job. Social work was a career she backed into because the sociology classes in college interested her the most. During a seminar, there was a speaker on child protection, about which she was amazingly ignorant. The idea of helping families heal and get back together spoke to her. Families were fascinating to Amanda because she had never really had one of her own. Perhaps seeing other people's families up close would help her figure out how they work, and maybe someday would lead her on a path to having a family of her own.

At least that was the plan in college, before she was actually hired to be a social worker and found herself stupidly staring at Jake outside a courtroom, and her only thought was to run. Run away from memories and emotions so strong they rocketed through her and felt like they could blow her toes off.

Amanda had not allowed herself to think about Jacob much in the past five years since she ran out of his home. During her freshman year in college, Amanda was too drunk or stoned to give him a second thought. With the partiers she had met on her co-ed floor, Amanda had allowed herself to become one of them. They drank in their rooms watching Monday night football, and they went to house parties every Thursday, Friday, and Saturday night without fail. Her friends were wild, fun, and superficial, never asking one another about their families, friends, or childhoods. It was absolutely perfect for Amanda, and it allowed Jake to become a distant memory.

By her junior year, Amanda's stomach was raw from the alcohol, her tolerance to booze was scaring her, and she hadn't accumulated enough prerequisites in any program to declare a major. She settled down and found that psychology and social work classes appealed to her the most. She did enough reading that she gave herself a few diagnoses from her psychology texts. The social work classes taught her what should have happened and who should have intervened to help her and her mom. She had found a purpose, but without the partying to distract her, she was left with an aching, lonely hole in her gut. She had gradually learned to tolerate that hole, but hoped someday to fill.

It took Amanda five years to graduate with all the lost time from her first two years. During Amanda's fourth school year, she met Lucy Ramirez, and they connected and complimented each other. Where Lucy was timid with speeches and speaking her mind, Amanda was fearless, already having conquered many demons scarier than stage fright. Where Lucy was full of love and heart and family, Amanda felt empty and cold except when she was with Lucy, whose heart seemed to beat strong enough for both of them. Lucy was the oldest of five sisters, and a second generation Mexican American. Lucy's entire family embraced Amanda and welcomed her to their home for holidays. It was impossible not to think of Trix when she went to their home and Lucy's mother, Rosie, doted on Amanda, feeding her until she was stuffed. But even then, the thoughts of Jake had been pushed far back, because the pain and regret were too much to bear.

* * *

UNTIL NOW, WHEN JAKE re-emerged in her life as a work colleague, Amanda was hyperventilating so severely she thought she might faint. At least an hour passed with Amanda walking as far away from her office building as she could. She concentrated on her breathing, got into a rhythm with her footsteps and her breaths. Hearing the first fallen leaves swishing under her feet, feeling the crisp air warming a bit in the thin autumn sun, smelling cut grass and fresh asphalt, Amanda's mind finally quieted. She stopped and stretched, and then forced herself to think.

Amanda couldn't let her fear take away the chance to do something meaningful and real. It was true that she accepted this job more for herself than to help anyone else, but helping people was important too. And another truth was emerging: she wanted to see Jake again. Going back was the only option that made any sense.

Slowly Amanda wandered back to work and tried to be nonchalant as she made her way to her cubicle. She tried to walk past her supervisor, Max, who was in his office with Leah, but Max waved her in.

Max was, in a word, fantastic. When Amanda interviewed with him she was immediately at ease because he always smiled and seemed unflappable. He looked vaguely like Barack Obama, without the protruding ears, and was often asked if he was related to the president. Max was in his mid-forties and married for the first time, his office full of pictures of his wife and one-year-old daughter.

Amanda took a deep breath, went in Max's office, and sat down next to Leah.

"Where did you go?" Leah asked pointedly. Tact was not her strong suit, but that was part of what made her a good social worker.

"I was feeling really sick. I'm sorry. How did it go?" Amanda asked quickly to get the subject onto something else.

"I think we're ready to give both of these cases to you," Max said. "You have been shadowing long enough, and I think you're ready to jump in and do some work on your own."

Insecurity crept in. While she was getting very bored following other workers, taking on these two families didn't appeal either. Somehow, she wanted to refuse cases that seemed distasteful, or really anything she could screw up. Was there any such thing as an easy child protection case?

"Is that going to be okay, Amanda?" Max asked her. "You're looking stressed. Was court that bad?" Max leaned forward and looked at her intently.

Amanda suddenly remembered that she was in her boss's office and he needed to have faith in her. She was still on probation as a new hire. If she couldn't handle the job they were under no obligation to keep her.

"No problem," Amanda said, shaking her head a little and smiling. "Where do I begin?"

Leah pulled some papers out of her file. "I got Marlys to sign releases and agree that the kids can't come home until she completes treatment. But the Judge said you have to facilitate visits three times a week while she's in treatment. She's going to stay in outpatient for now, but if she has any further alcohol or drug related incidents she'll have to go inpatient."

Amanda took the file from Max. "The main part of her caseplan is sobriety, but she also needs to do some basic parenting education," he said. "Why don't you meet with her and write up a draft of a caseplan, then bring it to me and we can talk about it?"

"I can probably see her this afternoon," Amanda said.

"No, you have a meeting this afternoon with that new county attorney," Leah said. Already? Amanda's stomach dropped and she looked at the floor to hide the flush on her face. "Skip Huseman pulled all kinds of case law that says his client doesn't have to say one more word to us if he doesn't want to. Our attorney was totally unprepared and had no reply. He managed to get the judge to agree that they could submit briefs on the issue to give him time to figure out an answer." Leah shook her head. "He got really lucky. I can't believe he showed up for court so unprepared."

Amanda managed to ask a casual question. "Did he explain why he's on this case?"

"All he'd say was that Gloria's no longer working in their office so he was given the file this morning, ten minutes before he went upstairs." Leah shook her head knowingly. "You know we'll be getting requests to commit Gloria within the week. She was so doped up these last few months there's no way she can just quit now." Amanda didn't know Gloria or anything about her rumored drug problem. All she knew was that Gloria did many CHIPS cases. If Jacob got her file, he might be taking over the child protection caseload.

"We'd be referring that commitment to another county," Max said. "There's no way any of us should be involved in that . . . small towns . . ."

"Anyway," Leah said. "That attorney wants to get up to speed with you and figure out where to go from here. I'd come too, but I have two appointments this afternoon."

"So I'm going to Jake's office?" Amanda asked.

"That's his name—Jacob," Leah said. "Max, please don't reprimand me for creating a hostile work environment if I say I wanna grab his ass."

Amanda jumped up to put an end to the conversation. "I'll get going on that plan then," Amanda said quickly.

"He said he knows you, Amanda." Leah said with a smile.

"Hmm," was the only reply Amanda could think of as she scurried out of the room. She didn't see Leah raise her eyebrows in question of Amanda's curt response.

* * *

WALKING OVER TO THE COUNTY ATTORNEY'S office, Amanda watched the sidewalk and tried to think of an opening line. During her lunch hour, she had briefly considered trying to get off the cases, but she realized there was no way she could get off both. She had to keep reminding herself that she needed to be more concerned about doing well at her job than figuring out how to deal with Jake.

She entered the same building that contained the courtrooms and took the stairs to the basement. The county attorney's office took up the whole basement level. She had been in the offices once before for a meeting with Gloria. Amanda's meeting with Gloria had lasted five minutes because she had excused herself from the room and never came back. The head county attorney, Barb Cloud, finished their meeting with a brief apology and said Gloria wasn't feeling well. Amanda had spent at least an hour in the office not knowing that Jake was down the hall the entire time.

"Your name?" a woman asked from behind the receptionist's station.

"Amanda. I'm here to see Jacob Mann." Even saying his name out loud made her heart thud.

The woman buzzed Jacob's office. "Amanda is here to see you." Amanda could not hear his reply.

"He just wants you to head back," the woman said, pointing to a row of offices over her shoulder. "He's the third door on this side." There were offices lining both sides of the floor, and about ten desks in the middle, separated by low dividing walls, where several women and one man worked on computers. Amanda breathed deeply and walked to Jacob's office.

"Hey, Jacob." He was sitting at a large metal desk in an office not much bigger than the desk, with one chair in front of the desk, and filing cabinets flanking the chair. Amanda couldn't figure out how Jacob got behind his desk because it was so wide that both sides almost touched the walls. Amanda couldn't contain a smile. "I can't believe they let you have the whole closet!"

"Hello to you too, Amanda." He looked up from the file he was reading and smiled back, in spite of himself. "Welcome to the county."

"I've been here a month, Jacob. I wonder how we haven't crossed paths until now."

Jacob motioned to the chair for her to sit down. "I've been out of state for some training so I could take over the child protection cases. Have a seat."

She smirked. "How?"

He gave her a look, got up from his chair, squeezed around the side of his desk and pushed one of the filing cabinets forward with ease to the front wall of the office. This left at least a foot of space for Amanda to maneuver around and sit in the chair. "I asked for a filing cabinet," he said with disgust. "Somebody with a sense of humor found the biggest ones in the building."

"Nice co-workers," Amanda said as she slid into the chair. He squeezed around her back into his chair. They had run out of small talk, so when he sat back down they found themselves staring at each other.

Jake rubbed his palms along the edge of his desk. "So . . . how've you been?"

She nodded and looked away. "Fine . . . good. Thanks. Anyway, um, are you going to have all the CHIPS cases?"

He shrugged. "Looks that way. Barb said she would back me up, especially in the beginning. The files aren't in the best shape, but one of the paralegals did a lot of covering for Gloria, so I think she'll be able to help me figure out what's going on."

"I don't have a clue about the legal stuff in these cases. I barely know the social work part," Amanda said. "Maybe Barb should take my cases since you and I are both so new."

"Nice try, Amanda," Jake said. "You can't avoid me."

She shook her head in protest and was going to say that wasn't what she meant, but he was right, so she didn't say anything. Thankfully, her heart wasn't thudding anymore.

"Okay, so we're working together, "Amanda said, trying to sound businesslike. "What do I need to know about these cases?" She opened Marlys's file first.

"Well for starters, it would be good if you actually attended the court hearings."

She looked up at his nasty smirk. "Jacob, if we're going to work together, you're going to need to find a way not to take jabs at me," she said more defensively than she intended.

"Amanda, am I supposed to ignore the fact that you ran out of the building this morning? I have to represent you on these cases. I have to know you're going to stick around." He said it with enough force that she knew he was referring to more than that morning.

"I wasn't feeling well this morning," she said quietly.

"You have a history of bolting, Amanda," he said equally quietly. "I need to know if there's anything that I did, or anything I shouldn't do."

Again, this was about more than this morning.

"This is my job," she said finally. "I'm not going to mess it up."

Jake looked like he was going to say something more, thought better of it, and let the subject drop. He nodded.

"So, what's the deal with this Thomas case?" he asked taking a deep breath and opening the file.

"Well I wish Leah was here. She did all the interviews, but the gist of it is that Matthew, the thirteen-year-old son of Charles Thomas, was seen at the emergency room for a dislocated shoulder and compound fracture of his right arm. The ER doctor wrote in his letter that he suspected child abuse, both because of the nature of the injury, and because the kid and the mom couldn't explain what happened consistently. A few days later the kid told a friend in detail that his dad hurt him, but he just shut down during his interview so we don't have a direct statement from him. " Amanda paged through her file until she found the initial report. "It's obvious that the doctor didn't know who he was reporting, and he hadn't made too many child protection reports before." She looked up at Jake. "At least that's what Max said. He couldn't believe the doctor made the conclusions that he did about the injury being 'highly likely' to have resulted from child abuse."

"I saw that, "Jake said. "That doctor is a lawsuit waiting to happen, whether he's right or not."

"That's the really sad part," Amanda said. "Everyone is just freaking out about this because of who the family is, and it makes it really hard to focus on the fact that this kid was beaten up pretty badly."

"Makes it a lot easier to be out-of-towners," Jake said. "I really don't care who he is. But that lawyer is the one who's gonna make it hard on me. I've barely been doing this two years," Jake said. "He's already trying to intimidate the hell out of me, and referred to his experience about eight times in the three minutes he spoke."

"How did he manage to make his experience relevant?"

"In my thirty-four years of trial experience I have never seen such an egregiously overzealous response to an obvious accident." Jake snorted. "Well, in my twenty-two months of trial experience I have never seen an attorney more impressed with his own shit."

"What did the judge think of his shit?"

"Oh, that was even better," Jake said. "Chuck and the judge had to catch up on old times, 'off the record' of course. Then the judge looks at me, and I swear he would have scolded me if he could have, and says, 'how can we dispose of this matter today?'"

"He did NOT!" Amanda said, loud enough for the paralegals in the office to turn around.

Jake waved them off over Amanda's shoulder. "Amanda, you need to find a way not to sound quite so naïve," Jake said scoldingly. "There's very little about this process that makes sense, and nothing happens the way you learned about it in school."

"Knock it off and spare me the lecture," Amanda said, feeling pissy again. "First of all, you don't need to act like you're wise to the world of law and disenchanted before you're thirty. Second, if you're not bothered by what happened in there then you need to find a new job."

"I didn't say I'm not bothered by it. I'm just saying I've seen plenty of it and you will too." He sat back and smiled at her. "I don't fight with any of the other social workers," he said smirking. "It must be you."

Thrown off guard again, she could only smile back.

* * *

THEY SPENT THE NEXT HOUR reviewing the two cases. Jake thought Marlys's situation would settle down and become relatively routine. Her public defender had not put up much of an argument and seemed to know that the kids needed to be placed until she could get sober.

Skip Huseman had demanded discovery on the Thomas case, and he had already filed briefs demanding that the case be dropped citing three different bases in three different statutes. Jake felt that Huseman was trying to drown him in paperwork so he would drop the case and take the easy way out.

"Fortunately, the law is on our side," Jake said, "and I think he knows it. We have a serious injury, a report from a doctor, and the kid's own words, via his friend, that his dad did it. If we charge him criminally we'll have a hell of a time admitting any of this evidence into court, but since it's a CHIPS case, we only have to have a 'preponderance of evidence' that he did it."

"Are you going to charge him criminally?" Amanda asked, finishing her diet coke and twisting off the tab.

"I really don't know," Jake said. "Criminal charges are a lot harder to get, and depending on the situation, sometimes Barb wants us to resolve it in family court instead. I'm thinking I should focus on the CHIPS because that will keep Huseman more off balance, and I'll have a whole lot more latitude to talk about what really happened."

Amanda scrunched her nose. "Those seem like icky reasons."

"Why? Because they have nothing to do with the kid?"

Amanda sighed. "Yeah, I hadn't even thought of that, but that makes it all the worse. I just think the whole thing sounds gamey, and you sound way more interested in beating this lawyer than keeping the kid safe."

"The only way I can keep the kid safe is to beat this lawyer, because this dad isn't admitting a thing and is playing legal games." Jake looked a little hurt. "But don't think that I'm not concerned about this kid. Maybe you need to talk to your people and see if there's something else you want to do about this." Jake closed his file and stood up. "I don't know about the social work part, Amanda. If you want a CHIPS petition, this is how you do it."

Amanda stood, too and gathered up her files shaking her head. "I feel like I'm going to mess this up because I don't know what I'm doing," she admitted.

"Join the club. You just gotta figure it out as you go." He slid around his desk and walked her to the stairs. Amanda was quiet. When they got to the stairs he squeezed her arm quickly. "You'll be fine, Amanda. Just be careful, follow the law as best you can, and don't get sloppy. You can't get in trouble if you are acting in good faith. Remember that."

Even after five years, he still knew exactly what she needed to hear.

chapter six

A MANDA LAY ON HER COUCH with feet up and staring at the TV, not noticing that the news was over and she was actually watching *Wheel of Fortune*. There were so many thoughts swirling through her head that it gave her a headache. Longing for some comfort, Amanda reached for the phone and called Lucy. She almost hung up when a male voice answered the phone.

"I'm sorry, I'm calling for Lucy Ramirez."

"She's right here." Amanda could hear Lucy ask who was calling, and the guy responded in Spanish.

"Hello?"

"Hey, Lucy."

"Oh, Amanda . . ." Lucy started sobbing. Amanda was used to Lucy crying at the drop of a hat, but this time she sounded more upset than normal.

"What happened?" Now she could hear the male voice trying to comfort her.

"Will you come over, Amanda, please? I was just going to call you."

"Of course. I'm on my way." They hung up, and Amanda grabbed her coat and keys and walked out the door. Amanda lived in the upstairs apartment of an old house.

The drive to Apple Falls was almost thirty minutes, just over the Terrence County border. Lucy had found a teaching job immediately after graduation at Amanda's old elementary school. The school had not advertised for a bilingual teacher, but Lucy knew it helped.

Amanda arrived at Lucy's apartment in less than forty-five minutes, parked along the street, and went to Lucy's entrance in the back. Before she could knock, her male friend answered the door.

"Hello, Amanda," he said with a slight Spanish accent. He was broad shouldered and muscular, with large, perfect teeth and friendly smile. He shook Amanda's hand with both of his and almost pulled her inside. Lucy was sitting on the couch crying. There was something in the way that Lucy looked that told Amanda what was going on before Lucy could say a word.

Amanda sat next to Lucy on the couch. "So when are you due?" Lucy looked up at Amanda, shocked, and her friend started to laugh.

"Lucy knew you would figure it out. I told her we shouldn't tell anyone yet, but she said you would know the second you saw her anyway." He sat on the arm of the couch and put his arm around Lucy. "I told you it's going to be okay."

Lucy dried her eyes on her tissue and took a deep breath. "Amanda, this is William. Do you remember me talking about him? We dated in high school for over two years." Lucy looked at her almost begging her to remember.

"Of course, I remember him," Amanda said. "He was all over your photo albums. He wore that awful tux to the prom." William laughed again, and Lucy finally smiled. "I just don't understand why I'm hearing about him now when apparently you two were spending some time together."

Lucy's face darkened again, and she looked down at her tissue that she was tearing into strips. "I don't know, Amanda," she said in a shuddery voice.

"Yes, you do," William said suddenly. "You may as well tell her since we both know it's the truth."

"What do I know?" Lucy said looking up at him angrily.

"We weren't exactly acting like boyfriend and girlfriend, Lucy. We were sneaking around because you didn't want your students to know about me." He was obviously hurt, and Amanda could see this was not a new topic for the two of them. Lucy looked like she wanted to crawl in a hole.

"I just didn't think it was appropriate for the students to see me with a man," Lucy said.

"The only reason you feel that way is because you feel guilty for disappointing your family because you're not a virgin," William said. Lucy jumped at the word and burst into tears again.

"Oh, come on," Amanda said. "Your mom would never hurt you like that."

"You don't understand," William said to Amanda. "It's not going to be pretty with her family, but we'll get through it. Initial reaction will be the worst."

"I don't think you're giving Rosie enough credit," Amanda said. "Seriously, Lucy, she's the kindest person I ever met."

Lucy had shredded her Kleenex into tiny bits that she rolled into a ball. "William's right," she said. "My mother's a very conservative Catholic, and being a virgin is a big deal. She got married as a teenager because she was pregnant with me, and my dad was a jerk. She always made a big deal about being a virgin because of our faith, but it's really just to keep us from making her mistakes. She will be the most upset about the example I'm setting for my sisters. Then there are my students . . ." And her tears started again. Amanda handed her another tissue.

"Your students are first graders," William said. "There's a very easy way to take care of this, honey." He knelt down next to Lucy, and then looked at Amanda and said, "I want to marry her. I've always wanted to marry her. She won't even answer me."

Lucy kissed William on the forehead and then leaned on Amanda's shoulder. "I don't know what's right." She took a deep breath.

"Yes, you do," Amanda said. "You have never gotten over William. I think you knew you'd marry him someday."

"I just hoped," Lucy said, a tiny smile peeking out.

"Can I call that a yes?" William asked, squeezing Lucy's hands.

"I guess you can." And the tears started all over again.

* * *

THEY DECIDED TO HAVE a "milk toast" (William's joke) in honor of the pregnancy and upcoming wedding. Lucy had been at the doctor that day and learned her due date was May 20th. Lucy admitted she hadn't told Amanda about William because they were sneaking and screwing around and felt guilty. Lucy wanted to get married before the baby was born, before she was showing, so they tentatively decided on a New Year's Eve wedding. William talked Lucy into waiting a day or two before she called her family. William said he wanted them to enjoy their "engagement" before the fallout started.

Amanda drove home that night thinking about Lucy's baby. There was no other word for it: Lucy looked maternal already. She looked how all mothers were supposed to look . . . soft, nurturing, motherly. For the first time in a long time, Amanda thought about her own mother. Had

April ever looked or felt maternal? She wondered whom she told first about the pregnancy. April was seventeen when she had Amanda, so she dropped out of high school. Amanda realized she didn't really know who was in her mother's life at that time. Amanda knew that when April was still in high school, her family scattered after a house fire that had destroyed everything they owned. Most likely, April gave birth on her own.

The other topic that Amanda never allowed into her head was her father. April had told Amanda, probably before she was able to talk, that her father was a "bastard" and there was no reason for her to even know his name. Amanda had accepted that as part of her history her whole life without question. When her mother had first been diagnosed with cancer, doctors wanted to know about next of kin. "It's just my Manda and me. It's always been just us. We don't need nobody else."

An image floated up from the recess of Amanda's mind of a Christmas tree. She couldn't have been older than four or five.

An artificial tree, totally white. She was disturbed by the metal branches—they didn't look right. There were balls wrapped in shiny string hanging from the tree, but most of the string was fraying and falling off, revealing the Styrofoam inside. Little Amanda sat behind the tree digging her fingernail into the styrofoam from a blue ball. Through the branches of the white tree she could see her mother, flicking her cigarette into an ashtray and tapping her foot. She was wearing tight jeans and boots. A few gifts were under the tree wrapped in shiny silver paper that must have been aluminum foil. The walls were paneled with cheap wood on the lower half that Amanda was leaning against, and the upper half had wallpaper of canons on a yellowish background. Amanda sensed a smell, but what that smell was slid out of Amanda's mind before she could identify it.

Amanda was surprised at the vividness of the image she likely had forgotten for at least twenty years. The only Christmas tree Amanda and her mom ever owned had been a cheap artificial green one, and she had no memory of ever having a white tree in any of the apartments or trailers they had lived in. The image had also brought with it an emotion Amanda did not have words for, yet it brought tears to her eyes. She sensed that the cold October night with tiny flecks of snow flying through the air had somehow brought out the image. Something about that place was painful.

She arrived at her apartment and went to bed with a lump in her throat.

chapter seven

AMANDA WAS SITTING IN HER cube at work trying to concentrate. Becca, a social worker, whose clients were mentally ill adults and children, was clipping her fingernails. Loudly. Amanda rarely, on any occasion wanted to work with Becca, but her cube was closest to Amanda's so they were nearly office mates. Becca was the only co-worker that Amanda truly did not like. With Becca's marriage clearly on the rocks, Amanda frequently heard her fighting with her husband on the phone, or humphing in response to his snotty emails. The first week Amanda was there, Becca read her a few of her husband's messages: "Working late tonight, you need to pick up kids and actually cook something instead of driving through McDonalds." Amanda tried to be polite but Amanda knew she wanted to keep her distance from Becca.

Soon after, Leah had told her while they were working together on an investigation that she needed to stay away from Becca.

"Seriously, everyone here hates her, and if you associate with her they're going to avoid you too." Leah and Amanda were on their way to a hoarders' house, Amanda's first investigation, and Leah reveled in telling Amanda what she was going to need to do to survive at their office. The first rule was to stay away from Becca. The second was to not be a wuss about hoarder's houses. Leah loved telling war stories about the grossness she had seen in the line of duty.

"There's a smell that's always there in these houses, " Leah was saying. "It's a mix of cigarette smoke, dirty diapers, cats, and general filth. You always sit on a hardback chair, never accept food, never ever use the bathroom, and usually don't wear your coat inside because it will pick up the smell."

Amanda started to slide out of her brand new wool coat. "Can we go home and change if we know we're going to a house like that?"

"Maybe," Leah said. "Definitely change if you had court that day, otherwise it's probably not necessary." Leah had told her that everyone was going to be waiting to hear how she handled her first hoarder house, and they were going to never let her forget it if she was too freaked. Amanda didn't tell Leah that day that the house was no worse than some of the trailers she had played in when she was younger.

The clipping had not relented, and Amanda was convinced Becca must have started on her toes. Amanda decided to leave a little early for her meeting with Marlys's sister, LaToya.

LaToya had lived in a trailer court near the railroad tracks in town. Marlys said she was going to be living with LaToya after treatment since she had lost her apartment, so Amanda needed to check out LaToya's home before the kids could visit their mom there. Marlys did not want her kids placed with her sister, but there was such a strong obligation to place with relatives that she needed to meet with LaToya to discuss relative placement anyway, especially because neither dad was a placement option at this time. They were preparing to get the judge's approval to move the kids if LaToya checked out, but there were issues with LaToya's background so it was going to be iffy.

Terrence was an old railroad town, and the section of town near the tracks was especially seedy. There was an old train changing station with several rows of tracks and two tall abandoned grain elevators scheduled to be demolished soon. Leah said the Terrence police officers said that area was rampant with drug traffic. Max had warned her to lock her car, because the trailer court had several thefts reported in the newspaper in the last several months.

Amanda meandered through the gravel alleys in Shady Court looking for number seventy-seven. As in all trailer parks, there were some trailers that were nicely painted with window boxes and a neat lawn. Most of the trailers, however, had broken windows with duct taped screens, porches with steps that a person could fall through if he wasn't careful, and endless old scooters, trikes, bikes, and wagons with missing wheels or seats.

Amanda found number seventy-seven after over ten minutes of driving in circles, finally going all the way down an alley with trailers numbered in the teens, which abruptly jumped to the seventies. Number seventy-seven stood out because it was encircled by chicken wire at the base of the trailer to the ground, which Amanda knew was an attempt to keep pests from getting through cracks in the foundation and the floor. Amanda tried to put the image of mice or larger pests out of her mind. She parked at number seventy-nine—there was no seventy-eight—because there were two dilapidated cars, one up on blocks, parked in front of seventy-seven.

The steps up to the trailer door were cement blocks. Amanda walked up carefully and knocked on the screen door. There was the sound of ferocious barking, followed by, "Shut up, Gomer! Shut UP, Gomer!"

LaToya peeked around the door. "Sweetie, you're gonna have to get back in your car for a second," LaToya said. "I need to get Gomer to his kennel in back, but he'll lunge for you if he thinks you're gonna go inside."

Amanda nodded silently and gladly went back to her car. LaToya came out, holding Gomer by his frayed collar. Both she and the dog were an interesting sight. LaToya looked like Marlys, with a similar build and sense of style. She wore a gold velour one-piece jumpsuit with a zipper that went from her neck to her crotch. It was at least three sizes too small, so LaToya's belly squished in rolls down the front of the suit. She wore braids of artificial hair that were so full of beads that Amanda thought her hair must have weighed fifteen pounds. LaToya's glasses were enormous, with gold-gilded rims and rhinestones along the bows.

Gomer was an ugly Doberman with some other breed mixed in. La-Toya could barely hold on to his collar when he saw Amanda's car, and he howled uncontrollably trying to get out of her grasp. She kicked him hard with the side of her foot, wrestled him into an orange pet carrier that barely contained his girth. "Don't make me hose you," LaToya yelled. To Amanda's surprise, LaToya actually picked up a garden hose and motioned to turn on the water. Gomer settled a little and looked like he was trying to turn around to lie down.

LaToya turned around, smoothed her jumpsuit over her rolls of belly, and waved to Amanda. "Okay, sweetheart, come on in now."

Amanda felt uneasy getting out of her car, eyeing the carrier, but she obediently followed LaToya. "Watch your step, sugar," LaToya said. She carefully went back up the cement blocks and went inside the trailer.

Amanda had accompanied other social workers on at least half a dozen home visits, but never had seen a home quite like this one. The trailer was typical in that the living room was at the front, with a kitchen in the middle, and a narrow hallway in the back that led to small bedrooms and a bathroom. The kitchen was piled with dishes in both sides of the sink and along the counters. There was a gigantic dog dish and dog bed in the kitchen with water spilled and dog food scattered around the dishes. In the corner was a small table with two old kitchen chairs, and a fuzzy plaid dog bed coated with Gomer's hair.

"Let's go in the living room, sugar," LaToya said, motioning her to the fake leather couch. Amanda couldn't keep back a smile when she walked into the living room. On the wall above the vinyl couch was the largest velveteen blanket-wall hanging she had ever seen, and Aretha Franklin's head and torso were emblazoned on the velvet in shimmery paint. LaToya moved a large electronic keyboard away from the vinyl recliner and flopped into the chair with a plastic-y poof. "Can I get you a coke?" LaToya asked, leaning her bulk forward in preparation to get back out of her chair.

"No, no," Amanda said quickly. "I'm fine. I don't want to take too much of your time."

"That's okay, honey. I want to do anything I can for my sister," La-Toya said nodding. Amanda noted that she wore large, square tipped, gold, press-on nails that clicked softly while she stroked a dog statuette perched on the end table next to her. Amanda couldn't imagine how she could play her keyboard with those dagger-nails.

Amanda dragged her eyes away from the nails back to her notebook. She had written some questions on her pad of paper and was trying to get up the nerve to start asking her personal questions. "Maybe we should start with a little history about you," Amanda said.

"Why, sugar?" LaToya asked, her eyes narrowing. "What difference does my life make?"

"Because the kids are in foster care, and I can't just . . . I mean there's liability and I have to make sure . . . they're just so little and I'm wondering . . ." Amanda was panicking and she knew it. Questioning a total stranger was harder than she thought it would be.

"You have to check me out? Is that what you're saying," LaToya found her cigarettes and lit one expertly. She took a long drag, leaning forward and staring at Amanda. "I ain't got nothin' to hide. Did Marlys tell you about the guns?"

Amanda's heart started beating fast, and her eyes darted to the end table where there was an old cigar box that easily could have contained a handgun. She was alone in a stranger's house and had no way to escape if she would have pulled a gun. This was beyond stupid.

"I used to work for Zigger T," LaToya said with a swagger. "You know, the record producer." LaToya inhaled on her cigarette deeply to allow Amanda time to digest LaToya's importance. "Turns out Zigs was dealing guns. I went down with him cuz I loved Zigger. I done forty-four months in Shakopee." Shakopee was a women's prison. Alone in a trailer with a felon who sold guns.

"Um, okay," Amanda said haltingly, not sure what to do next. "I guess I should write down when you were arrested. We'll have to look into the criminal stuff pretty thoroughly."

"You know Lana James? I love Lana. She's my PO, but we had to be sisters in another life," LaToya ground out her cigarette in a black plastic ashtray, and Amanda could see LaToya's gold lipstick on the butt. "Lana can tell you about how I turned my life around in prison. I got my GED and worked on my singing. I started a gospel choir at Shakopee that's still going strong. Most important, sweetness, is that I discovered our Lord Jesus Christ," LaToya said with a proud smile, and sat back in her chair with her hand on her ample chest.

Amanda relaxed at the news that LaToya had found her lord, assuming that meant she was probably safe.

"Do you have any kids, LaToya?" Amanda asked, looking around and noticing no evidence of children.

LaToya's head dropped to her chest, and the beads clicked and swished. "I guess my sister didn't tell you nothin'." She heaved a large sigh and reached for another cigarette. "I lost my baby, JaMarquis, when he was still a baby," LaToya said, pulling off her glasses and rubbing her eyes with her thumb and forefinger. "I knew I was gonna have to talk about this, but that don't make it no easier," LaToya cried. Tears streamed down her face, and Amanda sat in complete awkward silence. "He was sleeping with me in my waterbed," she wailed. "I just didn't know, sugar. I didn't know babies could die that way! Oh, I'm sorry, sugar." LaToya heaved out of her chair and went to her entertainment center, opened the top cabinet and pulled out picture after picture of her son, JaMarquis. She brought Amanda a framed eleven-by-fourteen picture of a fat, smiling little boy in a blue train conductor suit, complete with hat and red kerchief around his neck.

"He's really sweet," Amanda said. "I love his little outfit."

"His daddy worked for the railroad, so when he met JaMarquis, he brought him that suit." Amanda assumed that meant that JaMarquis's daddy wasn't around much, so LaToya was a single mom.

"Did your family support you?" Amanda asked.

"Oh, that Marlys was so strung out on the crack that she didn't know what happened. We had our babies at the same time and lost them at the same time," LaToya said, kissing each picture before putting them back in the cabinet.

"What do you mean lost them?" Amanda asked, suddenly confused. Marlys had two young children, but she had never heard that Marlys had a baby die.

"Oh, honey you really don't know nothin' do you?" LaToya sat back down and hoisted her plump ankle on her other knee. "When Marlys was still livin' at home with our daddy, she started getting herself in real trouble with the gangbangers. She got initiated in by a whole mess of them who all raped her. She got pregnant." LaToya shook her head and rubbed her hand on her ankle. "Marlys was sixteen, and I was nineteen and pregnant too. I had a real good job working in the WIC office as a secretary. You know what WIC is?"

Amanda nodded. Though she didn't know what it stood for, Amanda knew that WIC was a federal program that provided milk and formula for low-income women.

"Those nurses at the WIC told me to get Marlys to a doctor right now and get her to quit doing drugs. She quit everything and moved in with me right after I had JaMarquis. She had to quit school to help pay rent, but she was doing real good at the Cub store bagging groceries and babysitting. Then the GDs came down here one day pissed at Marly cuz she was supposed to be their dealer, and she wasn't sellin' nothin'. She tried to tell them she was havin' a baby and wanted out. Them dealers beat her so bad she lost her baby. Was a little boy. She was so far along they had to birth the baby dead."

"Oh, my god," Amanda said. "What happened to the guys who did it to her?"

LaToya shook her head at her. "Oh, sweetness, ain't nothin' happened to them. Marly didn't know who got her, and even if she did she wasn't tellin' no one." LaToya stared out the window and lit another cigarette.

Amanda sat incredulous. She had never heard such awful stories. Even with her own childhood as bad as it was, Amanda never really feared for her safety the way Marlys must have. She had been through a lot, but for the first time in her life, Amanda had met someone who had been through so much more.

"Marlys wasn't never the same after that," LaToya continued. "Marly left my house cuz she couldn't stand seeing my baby. She went up to the cities and hooked up with some Asian gang for a while, then went back to the GDs. She didn't come to JaMarquis's funeral. We couldn't even find her. After I lost my baby, I decided to focus on my singing, but you know where that got me. Then Marly started prostituting herself and got pregnant again."

Amanda, who had been chewing on her pen cap, choked. "Are you telling me that Tyler's father is a john?"

"Oh, yes," LaToya said. Amanda found herself liking LaToya, gold jumpsuit and all. She was big hearted, tough and resilient. They talked for over an hour about Marlys's life, almost all of it tragic and sad. A part of her wondered why Marlys never went to anyone to ask for help. The other part of her knew just how stupid that was.

"Well, LaToya, we need to figure out if it makes sense to move the boys here, and if we even can with your, um, background issues. Marlys should be done with treatment in a few weeks. Is it still your plan to have her stay with you?" Amanda tried to get back on track and figure out a visitation schedule for the kids.

LaToya laughed, shaking her head and clucking her tongue. "My sister is coming here. I'll do anything for her. I'd lie down on those tracks right now if you thought it'd help her. But let's be real, sugar. My sister ain't never getting any better."

"She's doing pretty well in treatment," Amanda said, wanting suddenly to defend her.

"I know she is. But, honey, people don't change who they are. My sister ain't never going to quit doing her crack and her johns."

Amanda's mouth dropped open. "You said you'd do anything for her. Why, if you don't think she's ever going to get any better? Why even try? You must have some hope."

"Honey, I got hope I'm gonna see my JaMarquis when the good lord brings me home. I got hope I'll make it on the big stage someday. But there's no hope for my sister. You better try your hardest for her, but I tell you right now: I'll be elected president of the United States before my sister becomes a good citizen."

"But you changed! Why not believe your sister can too?" Amanda couldn't figure this woman out.

"Honey, when you was little, did you play in the neighborhood with all the kids?"

Amanda didn't want to tell her that her neighborhood when she was growing up was much like the one they were in at that moment. "What are you getting at, LaToya?"

"Kids play doctor, right? Or they play house and the two bigger kids go off and be the parents, you know what I'm saying?"

Mikey Quam was the resident doctor in Amanda's neighborhood. "Yeah, I know what you're saying."

"Marly would play hooker. She'd do favors for boys, suck their weenies and stuff, when she was six-years old. It's who she is, baby. There ain't no changin' that."

chapter eight

A MANDA FELT LIKE SHE had learned more in her ninety minute interview with LaToya than she had learned in five years of college. She
found she couldn't do much more than stare at her computer monitor, and
her tropical fish screensaver. A message popped up telling her she had
email. Amanda clicked on the *open now* box.

"When you get back from your visit with Marlys's sister, please bring
me the background check forms and let me know if you want me to send
the rest of the stuff or if you'll be doing it. Zoe."

Crap, Amanda thought.

Zoe was the foster care licensor who gave her a pile of paperwork that
needed to be signed by LaToya. Zoe had reviewed some of it with her, but
she said it was pretty self-explanatory so she should be fine. Amanda had
forgotten about it completely. Once again, she felt like the clueless new
girl.

Max stood outside her cube and knocked on the metal frame.

"Hey, Amanda, did you get my message?" he asked.

She stared blankly at him.

"Guess that's a no," he said, unfazed, sitting down across from her in
her lone chair for visitors. "I want to talk to you about heading up a new
program. I just came from a meeting at the superintendent's office, and she
is asking for a social worker to help with a truancy thing they're doing."

"Truancy," she said stupidly.

"Everyone's favorite thing. But you know how the governor set the
new mandate for school attendance, so the school has to demonstrate that

they are trying to keep kids in school or they could lose funding." Max sat back in his chair, squirming. "Geez, these chairs are terrible."

"Watch out for the crack on the seat," Amanda warned him, pointing at the seat of the chair.

"Yikes, I will. Crappy government furniture. Anyway, they have a new EBD teacher who used to work at Outward Bound, so she wants to do some hiking and rafting with some of the kids as a motivator to stay in school. I thought you'd be great at something like that."

"Thanks," Amanda said, flattered that he thought enough of her to assign her to a new program.

"You bet," Max said, setting a thin manila file on her desk. "These are the notes on the program. Call the EBD teacher, tell her you're the social worker assigned, and she'll take it from there." Max moved to stand up, but suddenly yelped like an injured dog and grabbed his crotch.

The crack must have gotten him. Amanda was mortified. His eyes widened and he was immediately sweating and rocking gingerly on the chair.

"Did you catch your . . . uh . . . skin in the chair?" Amanda asked.

"Important skin," he squeaked. "Oh, god." He lifted his right butt cheek off the chair quickly emitting a final squeak, and then he relaxed, his "important skin" obviously free. He wiped his face with both hands. "Let's keep this horrifying moment between us, Amanda."

"Of course," she said, avoiding eye contact.

"And, I'll get you a new chair."

* * *

AMANDA SHEEPISHLY ADMITTED to Zoe that she had forgotten the paperwork. Zoe was gracious about it, even offering to meet with LaToya to get it signed. Amanda decided she would take care of it on her way home.

When she got into her car after work, something didn't feel right. She was sitting at an angle. Getting back out of the car, she saw she had a flat. Since she was parked behind the building, no one else leaving work would realize her predicament. She glanced at her cell phone but didn't even bother trying it because she knew she hadn't charged it for days and the battery was dead.

First, she tried to get back into the building, but it was locked for the day, and Amanda hadn't been issued a key card yet. Across the street, she could see several attorneys including Jake leaving his building. Her options were to walk downtown, a good twenty blocks, to use a phone to call a garage and spend the rest of the evening dealing with the mess, or ask Jake for a ride and deal with it from home. Since it was almost dark, Jake was the best option.

"Jake," she yelled out weakly, running across the street awkwardly in her high heeled boots. He looked up, waved, and got in his car. "No, you idiot," she said under her breath. "Don't leave!" she yelled. That sounded desperate enough.

He opened his window. "Do you need a ride?"

"I have a flat," she breathed, stopping and panting.

"Hop in," he said, moving two files from his front seat into the back of his VW Jetta. Leather seats. Great stereo. She would have loved a car like this, and thought for the first of a million times that she might be in the wrong profession.

"Thanks, Jake." She slid into the front and clicked her seat belt on.

"Since I have you hostage, you have no choice but to get a drink with me."

She couldn't contain her smile.

* * *

THEY WENT TO LAS MARGARITAS, a tiny bar that was packed with happy hour drinkers. They served fantastic margaritas served in big plastic cups with endless baskets of nachos and real salsa. It was decorated with kitschy jalapeno-shaped Christmas lights and crepe paper limes hanging from the ceiling. Amanda loved the warm atmosphere.

They sat at a table in the front window, and the waitress brought a basket of chips and salsa and two-for-one lime margaritas. Amanda sipped slowly, not knowing what to say.

"So . . ." Jake said, "how do you like the county?"

"Fine . . . good." They had already had this perfunctory conversation, and both of them knew it.

Jake took a deep breath. "Amanda, let's try not to act so weird, okay? Everything that happened was a long time ago. We're going to have to work together, so let's try to be friends."

Amanda took a bigger drink. "It's hard for me not to act weird, Jake. I'm a fish out of water everywhere I go."

He rolled his eyes. "Wah wah, Amanda. Don't start the pity thing." Her jaw dropped. "Pity?!"

He waved his hands in the air in front of her. "That's not what I meant to say, please don't freak out. I just mean that you have always had this thing about being such an outsider in the world, and you're not. You need to quit thinking that way."

Amanda knew Jake was well intentioned, but she couldn't believe his nerve anyway. "Jake, you knew me for three months over five years ago, and we have seen each other three times since then. You don't know me at all." She had never known anyone who was willing to lecture her like a nine-year-old. Not even her mother talked to her the way he did.

"Keeping track, huh?" He smiled at her.

She got up to leave.

"Okay, Amanda, I'm sorry. I'm sorry. Sit down." He handed her a margarita. She glared at him.

"Quit being an ass and we'll get along fine," she finally said.

"A guy can try." He winked.

* * *

THEIR CONVERSATION SETTLED DOWN after that. Jake asked about how she got hired, and she ended up talking about college and how hard she worked in the last two years to graduate. She tried not to act like her first years were wasted with drinking, and tried to look like she had no regrets.

He caught her up on law school in Chicago. Most of the law students he met went to private schools and had a lot of money and a lot of interest in making more money. He lived near downtown Chicago, clerking for the office of public defenders and Cook County Attorney.

"It's drugs and poverty. All we did was prosecute poor people who committed crimes to get drugs, and committed more crimes once they were on drugs.

"Being poor doesn't automatically mean you're going to use drugs," she said, feeling herself reacting again.

"Of course, it doesn't," Jake said. "I'm not talking about not having very much money. I'm talking about the whole lifestyle of inner city poverty. I felt like I was banging my head against a wall."

She tried to squash down her defensiveness. It wasn't always about her.

"So, if you felt so hopeless, why are you still in criminal law? Why don't you go make a lot of money doing something for some big company?"

"Because brand new lawyers don't get hired 'doing something for some big company.' Plus, I didn't go to a private school, and I don't have any connections."

"Now who's feeling sorry for himself?" Amanda said, eyebrows raised.

"The whole law school experience soured me on a lot of things, but not law. Most of the people there came from families of lawyers, and they had firms waiting to offer them clerkships or practices to step into right out of school. During my work in the OPD, I realized I'm more cut out for prosecuting. It's cleaner."

"Well, no kidding," Amanda said, dipping her chips into the salsa. "What's clean about defending criminals?"

"It's really easy to get righteous about it until you do it. These people have a right to a defense, a good defense, too. Just because you're a nineteen-year-old black kid in Chicago doesn't mean you're automatically guilty of whatever they say you did. But I couldn't take it because most of them *were* guilty, but they also had such shitty lives that it's no wonder they were criminals. None of these people had any hope, so they flushed their lives down the toilet in exchange for feeling powerful, or just to feel something until it wore off and they shot up again."

"That's really depressing," she said, now playing with the salt on her glass. Jake held up his hand, waving two fingers at the waitress. She returned instantly with two more margaritas.

"I tried to get everyone into treatment," he said, starting on his second drink with an ironic smile. "Most of the time they got one shot at treatment, and then the funding was refused. A lot of times they just took the jail because it was quicker and easier. The whole thing was a black hole, and I couldn't stand it. It drove Trix nuts because I was so disillusioned. She couldn't stand all the negativity."

Amanda smiled hearing Trix's name.

"She still asks about you, by the way. Asks if I have tried to reach you. I haven't told her that you work here yet."

"I can't believe she still remembers me." She tried to sound casual to disguise the lump rising in her throat.

"Amanda, you were a big deal in our house for a long time, especially after you took off."

Amanda chewed on her glass, biting on the bitter salt. The margaritas were dulling her defenses. Her belly swelled, making her think she was going to vomit. There was no way she could speak, even though Jake was waiting for a response.

She finally swallowed hard. "I thought we were going to let all this stuff go."

"Yeah, well, I lie sometimes." Jake was feeling it too, the tequila and their past.

"Just like a lawyer," she said with a weak smile.

They were quiet for a minute. Then Jake said, "Let's order some food and talk about sports."

* * *

THEY ENDED UP STAYING at the restaurant until after 9:00 p.m. talking about the Minnesota Vikings, Gophers, Timberwolves, Wild, and Twins. Jake had ordered fajitas and used his vegetables to diagram what he thought the Vikings needed to do to bolster their defense. They were having a great time until Amanda suddenly realized that she hadn't done anything about her car.

"We gotta go," she said, jumping up and grabbing the check.

"Hey, that's mine," Jake said, grabbing the bill out of her hands. "I made you come, so it's my bill."

Amanda wanted to argue, but she was too panicked about her car. "It's way too late to get someone to fix it tonight. What am I supposed to do now? I need my car."

They went to the front of the restaurant where Jake paid. "Let's go back and survey the damage," he said. "I'd like to think I could change a tire if I had to."

Jake drove them quickly back to Amanda's car. Amanda started to get out, but Jacob grabbed her arm to stop her. "Wait a minute," he said. "You have two flat tires. Did you notice anything wrong with your car before?"

"I think I would have noticed if I was driving on a rim," Amanda told him. "What are you talking about?"

"We better call the police, Amanda. I think someone slashed your tires."

* * *

After dealing with the police for over an hour, Amanda was exhausted, still a little tipsy, and just wanted to go home. Officer Baer of the Terrence City PD took pictures of her car and confirmed that two tires had been slashed with a small blade. She couldn't muster any feelings other than fatigue.

Jake drove her home without saying a word. She pointed out her apartment, and he parked the car in front of her house. He suddenly turned the car off and looked at Amanda.

"This isn't good," he said.

"I'm not thrilled either, Jacob. It's going to be at least another day before I'll have my car back. It means I'm going to have to rely on people like you to get around." She was hoping he would offer to pick her up for work the next day so she wouldn't have to ask.

"It's not your car I'm worried about, Amanda," he said, looking down at the steering wheel. "What if this wasn't random?"

The idea that someone had intentionally slashed her tires hadn't occurred to Amanda, but when he mentioned it her stomach dropped. "Come on," she said weakly. "That's stupid. No one around here possibly cares about me enough to do anything to my beat-up hatchback. Are you trying to scare me or what?" She regretted admitting she was scared, especially to Jacob. She didn't know if she had any reason to be afraid, but at times like these her aloneness was glaring. During college her purse was stolen in downtown Minneapolis by a guy who ran up behind her, yanked the purse off her shoulder and ran. The incident left Amanda sleepless for weeks, and was actually one of the reasons she began to let herself lean on Lucy for more support.

"I really don't want to scare you, Amanda. But I don't think people go around randomly slashing tires."

"Nobody knows me or my car. You're almost flattering me to say someone knows me well enough to bother slashing my tires." She couldn't let this even be possible. He tilted his head in acknowledgement that she had a point. "Plus, the cop said I might have driven over something."

"He said it was unlikely, Amanda."

"He didn't say it was impossible, Jacob."

They sat in silence for a moment.

"I'm going to go up to my apartment. When I get inside I'll wave to you and let you know I'm in and you can go home. And if you really want to help, you can pick me up tomorrow on your way to work. Goodnight." She opened the door to get out, paused, and forced herself to sit back down. "Thank you for helping me tonight, Jake. It's nice to have a friend in town."

"You're welcome." Jake watched as Amanda climbed the stairs to her upstairs apartment until he saw a light switch come on. In another minute, Amanda waved from the window facing the street before she closed the blind.

In less than five minutes the lights were off and Amanda went to bed, so she didn't see Jake sitting in his car, staring at her apartment for a long time before he finally drove home.

chapter nine

WHAT ON EARTH HAD SHE gotten herself into?
The realization that the assignment to do outdoor education for teenagers was actually a curse did not come all at once. Amanda first began to see what a nightmare the program would be when she met her co-facilitator, Blanche Larson. Blanche could not have been even five feet tall. She was built like a tree trunk—almost a perfect cylinder—with round, hard muscles on her arms and legs, and a round hard torso. Blanche had short, dark hair that was tipped with blonde in the worst home coloring job Amanda had ever seen. She wore polo shirts with the collar turned up so it encased her head, and wind pants that had to be sized for a ten-year-old boy. She had seven gold studs in one ear, nine in the other. Blanche was ageless to Amanda, but from the way she talked about herself she had to be almost forty.

They met over lunch in Blanche's empty classroom. Blanche was the new teacher for kids with emotional and behavioral disorders. The kids were at lunch, followed by various electives, so she wasn't expecting any students back for nearly an hour. Amanda did not bring a lunch with her, but Blanche had to use their meeting time to eat.

"Go ahead and eat, please," Amanda told her.

"Sorry, it's the only free hour I have."

Blanche was orderly in everything she did, and it occurred to Amanda that she must have been in the military at some point. Blanche sat behind her desk in the small classroom while Amanda took the chair next to the desk. From a cooler behind her desk, Blanche took out a large carrot with the greens still attached, something that looked like a rust colored rock that Amanda presumed was a raw sweet potato, a bag of leafy greens tipped in red, and a refillable plastic bottle containing a gray, milky liquid. She set everything in front of her, shook the thermos, and proceeded to chug the gray liquid. Amanda forced herself to turn away because she knew she was staring. She saw charts all over the wall with students' names and symbols next to each name.

"It looks like you have a pretty elaborate system here," Amanda said, getting up to examine the charts more closely. When Blanche didn't answer, she turned to see Blanche eating the raw sweet potato like an apple. Amanda could see her jaws working to chew up the potato, which had to be hard as a rock.

"I'm a vegan," Blanche said in response to Amanda's stare.

"Uh huh," Amanda said. She couldn't remember exactly what it meant, but she was pretty sure it had something to do with the food she was eating.

"I switched when I went into recovery six and a-half years ago," Blanche told her, bits of potato flying out of her mouth as she spoke. "I realized that being clean and sober was about everything I put into my body. Percoset and THC weren't my only drugs of choice."

Amanda just kept nodding because, as usual, she had no idea what to say.

"I lost one-hundred ten pounds when I got clean. I found a whole new person waiting to come out."

So the cylindrical-shaped veggie-eating army brat used to be a spherical, weed-smoking drug addict. "That must have felt great," Amanda said.

"Yes it did." Blanche had polished off the entire sweet potato and tore into her lettuce. She took out several leaves, shook out the water, rolled them exactly like someone would roll a joint, and bit into the end. From a raw potato to plain lettuce leaves. She couldn't imagine what that kind of roughage must do to her digestive tract.

"So what's your story?" Blanche asked, holding the lettuce doobie to her lips like she was going to smoke it, her piercing gaze focused on Amanda.

Amanda shrugged and looked at the floor. "Not much of a story," she said. "I've been at Social Services about a month. Just graduated from the U with a degree in social work." When Blanche looked like she wanted to ask more questions, so Amanda cut her off. "I'm pretty excited about this program. Can you tell me more about it?"

Blanche nodded while she finished chewing her roughage, holding up one finger while she gulped down the last of her gray liquid. "Okay, let's get to it." Blanche systematically put her uneaten carrot and her scraps back in her insulated bag and got out a thick binder labeled EXPERIENTIAL EDUCATION. "I'm all about learning by doing," Blanche said. "These kids need to get their bodies active, efficient, and productive and their minds will follow. I spend most of the week in the classroom with them working on behavior modification. One day a week I want to get out, quit talking and start doing."

"That sounds great," Amanda said. "What kind of stuff would you have them do?"

Blanche rubbed her palms together excitedly. "Oh, man, what won't we do? I can't wait! I want them doing ropes courses, rafting, climbing, tracking, camping, skiing, swimming, hiking, running . . . Anything that gets their blood pumping and their muscles working. Anything intense! I want it to be all-day stuff. I want to get away from the school and get out into the world."

They put together a rough schedule for the next several weeks. Blanche said she would like to start with a group of ten, five social service clients and five kids Blanche chose from her classes. They would start activities in two weeks.

Amanda left the school with a large binder labeled, LEARN BY DOING. There were sketches of kids on high ropes courses, which were essentially telephone poles suspending obstacle courses made of ropes and wires fifty feet in the air. It looked like the kind of thing she might have tried when she was drunk in college.

Amanda approached her car with visions of herself trapped on top of a telephone pole with angry teenagers refusing to let her down. The Honda was fresh out of the service station after having the two tires patched, and she suddenly noticed a dozen deep scratches on the passenger door. She wondered if they were new, or if they could have happened when the mechanic repaired her tires. Then she noticed dents and more scratches around the keyhole on the passenger door, as if someone had tried to pry the lock open.

Amanda looked around the parking lot, trying to figure out if a high schooler had tried to get in her car to steal her cell phone or go joyriding.

There were three girls standing around one of the doorways, and a few scattered students in the area entering and leaving the school. The fall wind was starting to feel bitter, and she thought she felt a few drops of rain. Amanda looked in the car and thought everything seemed normal inside. Not wanting to stand in the cold any longer, she got in her car and drove back to work, trying to ignore the nagging feeling in her gut.

* * *

BACK AT WORK, AMANDA STOPPED at Max's desk to fill him in about the project.

"It has potential, don't you think?" Max asked after hearing her description of what she and Blanche would be doing. Max was between bites of an enormous cheeseburger dripping mayo and ketchup into a pinkish blob on his desk blotter. Quite a contrast from Vegan Girl.

"I hope so," she said, looking away. As someone who ate most of her food condiment free, the mayo-ketchup mixture was revolting.

"Let's talk at staff on Monday about some good referrals." Max tore into his mountainous burger again just as the phone rang, so she used that excuse to bolt.

Amanda spent the rest of the afternoon reading from the Learn by Doing material. The extent of her experiential education before this project was doing the "human knot" exercise at nearly every college "getting to know you" event. She couldn't imagine herself motivating a group of teenagers to build a canoe together, but she was also excited at the prospect of trying.

Shortly before the building closed, Amanda heard several people cooing and laughing outside of Max's office. Max's wife, Christine, had just arrived with their one-year-old daughter, Jade. Max's wife was surprisingly pretty, a contrast to Max's bookishness. Leah said once that Max had found a wife way out of his league, and he should give that gorgeous woman whatever she wants.

Amanda stepped out of her cube in time for Jade to wobble straight into her legs and tumble to the floor. After a second of shock, Jade let out a wail.

"I'm sorry," Amanda said, crouching to pick up the sobbing toddler when suddenly a lump rose in Amanda's throat and her stomach dropped. A picture flashed in her head of a pink-and-blue crocheted blanket and a hard, smooth rocking chair. A console TV, greenish-gray shag carpeting, wood paneling, a smell she couldn't identify . . . The image was homey, safe, and sad, and it swam in front of her eyes as if she were there. The feeling slid away as suddenly as it came.

Still crouching on the ground, Max bent down next to her and held her shoulder. "You okay, Amanda?"

Not wanting to make a scene, Amanda stood up quickly. Christine was holding Jade, who had already recovered and was wiggling to get down again. Amanda mumbled something dumb and backed out of the office before they could ask her what was wrong.

When she was in her car, she sat for a moment before putting the key in the ignition. Closing her eyes, she tried to bring back the image. It stayed away, just beyond where her mind could grab hold. Breathing deeply, she tried to smell what she had smelled before. Eyes closed tightly, she tried to see it again.

As the feeling slipped further away, the immediate surroundings returned. It was dusky outside, and a freezing cold rain began to fall in huge droplets on her windshield. She started the car and blasted the heater.

chapter ten

AMANDA WOKE THE NEXT DAY still in a fog. She lay in bed for nearly an hour before she remembered that it was Thanksgiving.

Amanda was looking forward to the day with Lucy's family. Thanksgiving was always Amanda's favorite holiday with the Ramirezes because there were no church services, no pressure to try to fit into yet another setting where she didn't belong.

Religion was a thread tightly woven into the Ramirez family tapestry, and it served to highlight once again Amanda's barren family heritage. She and her mother never attended church, never prayed, and never acknowledged the spirituality of any holiday. Its glaring absence grew when she attended mass with Lucy's family. They prayed together as comfortably as they laughed together. When the family joined hands during the Our Father at mass, or when they prayed together at the dinner table, Amanda always felt as though her cold hands were the weak link.

The phone rang, and Amanda grabbed the phone she kept by her bed in case someone broke in.

"Good morning, chiquita," Lucy sang.

"You always sound more Latino when you're about to see your family," Amanda told her, settling back down on her pillows.

"I need all the points I can get," Lucy said. "This is the first time I'll be seeing my aunts and uncles since I broke the news."

"Everyone is coming?" Amanda said, sitting up and holding the covers around her, suddenly feeling less excited about the holiday.

"Don't freak out on me, Amanda. I need you today." Lucy sounded small and afraid, and she sniffled like she was going to cry.

"Listen to who is freaking out," Amanda said, unconsciously reaching for a tissue and wanting to pass it to her friend. "You must be a weepy waterfall with those extra baby hormones. It's going to be fine."

"Mama called this morning already," Lucy said. "She's having the whole family, which she loves. But we're all invited to William's house tonight, and she's all nervous about what she's supposed to bring. William told her not to bring anything, and now Mama's insulted and embarrassed. She's all, 'My future son-in-law wants me to look like a dog in front of his parents showing up at his house with nothing.'"

Amanda laughed.

"It's not funny. William's family has money. His father has run his own business for years. His parents are big at St. Thomas's church, and they know a lot of people," Lucy sighed. "It sounds terrible to say, Amanda, but they are very white Latinos."

"Now I know you're freaking out because you never talk like this," Amanda said. "I have no idea what that is supposed to mean, white Latinos?"

"I'm not being critical. I totally understand. It's just that Mama won't. William's father was born in Minnesota. He lived in Minnesota when there weren't a lot of Mexican families here. William's mother is the same, she makes hot dishes! Mama makes tamales." Lucy was crying again. "My whole life we have driven to St. Paul to mass because it's in Spanish. Mama finally joined St. Thomas when it became impossible to get all of us girls out of the house on time to drive an hour. They rarely even speak Spanish at his house."

Amanda was quiet for a minute, running her hand along the smooth edge of her quilt. She could hear Lucy sniffling, blowing her nose, and trying to pull herself together. "All I know is that your mom treats me like a member of your family," Amanda said, "and I know I can't speak Spanish. You're not giving your mom enough credit."

Shuddery sigh. "I know you're right. I guess it's not just that I'm worried about Mama accepting William's family. It's also that . . . I hope she accepts me being part of his family. I'm . . . I'm different around them." Lucy sounded ashamed.

"If you're different anywhere, it's around your family," Amanda said. "You get an accent, you use more Spanish words . . . you call me Chiquita," Amanda laughed a little, but Lucy was in no mood.

"It's not funny! I hope you never have to go through this," Lucy said. "Get married BEFORE you have a baby."

"Yeah, I'd hate to bring shame to my family."

Lucy gasped. "Oh, I'm so sorry! I didn't mean to make you feel . . ."

"Lucy, no no no . . . I was trying to be funny. Don't worry so much. You can't offend me." Amanda knew that no matter what Lucy said, she never meant to be hurtful.

"Before I say anything else stupid, let's just drop it. I'll just need you to keep me in line tonight."

Amanda scoffed. "Yeah, well, I'll have to do it from my apartment. I'm not going to William's house."

"Oh, yes you are," Lucy said. "I have to have my maid of honor there!"

Now it was Amanda's turn to cry. One consequence of her friendship with Lucy was that her tears simply wouldn't stay away anymore.

* * *

AMANDA ARRIVED AT THE RAMIREZ home shortly after 11:00 a.m. They lived in Riverton, a small town just south of the Twin Cities metro area. The town's industry was apples—picking, boxing, selling, processing. Migrant workers provided most of the labor for the orchards and the factories.

Lucy's mother, Rosita, was one of the bakers in the pastry shop connected to the larger of the two orchards. She had moved to Riverton with her brothers when she was still a teenager. They all worked in the factory until Rosie became pregnant with Lucy when she was eighteen. Lucy's father wouldn't marry Rosie, and he moved back to Mexico before Lucy was born. She had never met him. When Lucy was four, her mother married Javier Ramirez, and they had four more daughters. Pictures of Lucy's stepfather were all over the house. He died in an accident at work a few months before Amanda and Lucy met.

Amanda had noticed immediately that their loss of Javier was much different from the loss of her own mother. Amanda almost felt his presence in the house even though they had never met. Rosie kissed his picture all the time, and there were flowers, candles, and palms from church in a little shrine to him. The first time she went to Lucy's house, Lucy "introduced" her to her stepfather. Lucy seemed embarrassed at the display, but matter of fact about his presence in their life.

As she walked up to the front door, Amanda could hear laughing. Lucy's Uncle Joel, Rosie's brother, opened the door for Amanda and gave her a huge bear hug. He was smiling but looked like he had been crying.

"Lucy told us her beautiful news," Uncle Joel said, pulling Amanda inside. "A baby and a wedding . . . beautiful!"

Lucy was sitting on the couch surrounded by her aunts and cousins, laughing and crying at the same time. Everyone had to touch her somehow, rub her arm, touch her hair, hold her hand. Lucy's Aunt Mary was rubbing Lucy's slightly mounded belly. The pale couch was barely big enough for three, but six adults had squeezed together to share Lucy's news. Above them was a famous picture of Jesus rising from the dead. Two shelves that contained candles, statuettes, and palms surrounded it. A rosary hung from one of the shelves.

Amanda was weighed down with crudities, which she carried into the cramped kitchen. Despite the cold outside, the kitchen was well over eighty degrees. The windows had steamed. Stuffing ingredients were still on the table, along with casserole dishes waiting to go into the oven. Rosie was barking at Lucy's fourteen-year-old sister, Marina, who was sulking at the table, the phone in her hand.

"Can't you see how much there is to do?" she asked Marina. Rosie was hurriedly peeling potatoes and cutting them into a large pot of boiling water.

"Hey, Amanda," Marina said sullenly.

Rosie spun around, a potato flying out of her hand. She wiped her hands on her apron and reached out to hug Amanda.

"Hello, chiquita." Rosie squeezed longer than usual, and her voice was softer than Amanda had expected. Rosie had been crying too.

"I brought vegetables," Amanda said.

"You know how I count on you," Rosie said, smiling and holding Amanda's face in her hands. Since the first time Amanda spent a holiday with the Ramirez family, it had been her job to bring vegetables, olives, and relishes for the table. Shortly after they met, Amanda had spent a fall weekend with Lucy at her home, and Rosie had learned Amanda didn't have family. She insisted that Amanda come to their Thanksgiving and assigned her to bring relishes. Amanda realized later how much Rosie looked out for her from the beginning. To help her feel comfortable, she didn't let her show up empty handed, but Rosie also knew that Amanda wouldn't know how to cook. That first Thanksgiving, Amanda arrived with bags of carrots, pickles, olives, beets, celery, and everything else gathered together in a grocery store display labeled *for your relish tray*. Rosie displayed the tray proudly, and made sure everyone ate olives that day.

Amanda found the relish tray and began opening cans and arranging fresh celery and carrots.

"Marina, if you are going to sulk, why don't you just go up to your room until dinner. Amanda can help me." Rosie didn't turn from her boiling water when she spoke.

Marina got up from the table with a flounce. "Gladly," she said, and went up the back stairs to her room. Rosie's shoulders dropped.

"She thinks she needs to invite her boyfriend," Rosie said quietly. "She's fourteen years old and thinks it is appropriate for her boyfriend to spend the holiday away from his family so he can be with ours." She shook her head. "These girls think I am stupid." She was peeling potatoes at lightning speed. "I make traditional dinner for them because they think they need turkey on Thanksgiving. They don't like it when I make tamales." Rosie rubbed her forehead with the back of her hand. "They think I don't know how it is to be a teenager in love. They think I don't remember. But I would never cross my parents by losing my virginity." Except that she had done exactly that when she got pregnant with Lucy as a teenager. Amanda saw beads of sweat on her forehead, and tears on her cheeks. "Now that their sister is having a baby out of marriage, they think the rest of our values don't matter. Last night, I found Cynthia downstairs lying on the floor with her boyfriend under a blanket watching the television. *Never* would I hurt my family like that!" Rosie flinched at the sound of her own voice, and caught herself.

Amanda was frozen, heart pounding. It was Lucy's biggest fear, to disappoint her family. Amanda had told her she had underestimated Rosie, but Lucy had been right. Rosie was heartbroken.

Aunt Mary swooped into the kitchen and began fussing over the sweet potatoes.

"Amanda brought her relishes!" Aunt Mary sang.

Rosie turned and smiled, their conversation forgotten for the moment. "You know how I count on my Amanda."

* * *

AMANDA HELPED WITH THAT MEAL more than she ever had before. Lucy was usually at her mother's side during holidays, but she was so swept up with family that she never made it to the kitchen. Amanda forced herself to figure out what needed to be done, trying to be as helpful as possible. Rosie didn't bring up the topic of Lucy's baby again.

There were twenty-four all together for dinner. Amanda put herself in charge of the kids' table in the living room, filling the little ones' plates and making sure they all had milk to drink. She never actually sat down to eat, but was quite content to busy herself with the little cousins. When Uncle Joel lead them to pray from the dining room, Amanda joined hands with the two youngest cousins in the living room.

Dinner was uneventful, other than Anna dropping her jello on the floor. As the kids cleaned their plates, they started chanting "*Sopapillas! Sopapillas!*" They were Rosie's traditional dessert, and Amanda loved them as much as everyone else.

"No no, little ones," Rosie said, getting up from the table and beginning to clear dishes away. "Remember we are having pie with Lucy's fiance's family! Her special pumpkin pie!" Rosie's tone was of forced cheer. Amanda looked over at Lucy and saw a sick smile stuck to her face. Lucy seemed to realize that this was a difficult day for Rosie too. Lucy's aunts Marina, Clarice, and Mary shuffled around the table collecting dishes while the men retired to the living room. Lucy stood up from the table and grabbed Amanda's hands, pulling her to the hallway leading to the stairs.

"What am I going to do, Amanda? She's so angry with me!"

"Marina was being difficult, that's all," Amanda told her friend.

Lucy looked over at her Aunt Marina, who winked at her. "They are all so excited about the baby. My Uncle Joel said he has always liked William, and asked if he needed a job at the orchard. Everyone has been wonderful, but Mama's hardly spoken to me."

"It's probably hard to see her oldest daughter growing up! Your mother is pretty young to be a grandmother," Amanda said.

Lucy smiled. "If I have a girl, I hope Mama will teach her how to make her special blankets." Then she dropped Amanda's hands and looked down. "I hope she will *want* to teach my baby."

"Hey, there, I think she could teach your sons too." Amanda held Lucy's bony shoulders. "It's going to be fine." Amanda tried to find more words of reassurance, but she wasn't as sure as she once was that all would be fine between Rosie and Lucy.

* * *

THEY MADE A CARAVAN to William's parents' home. Amanda drove Lucy and her sisters Cynthia and Marina. Cynthia, a senior in high school, had just received her ACT scores and was disappointed that she didn't score as well as she had hoped.

"I'm going to be stuck at a state school," Cynthia told Amanda.

"Watch it," Lucy said. "We both went to the U and loved it."

"The U is a good school," Cynthia said resignedly, raking her long hair with her nails. "But I wanted to go to LA or Texas, some place that would give me a scholarship because Mama can't afford the tuition, and I'll never be able to come up with the money on my own."

"At least you're getting out of here!" Marina snapped. "I have four more years of Mama ragging on my ass."

Lucy whipped around in her seat. "Marina! Don't you dare talk like that about your mother!"

"Shut up, you little tart," Marina shouted back. "Ever since you got knocked up, Mama has taken it all out on me."

Amanda saw Lucy recoil back in her seat.

"She's taking it out on you because you're a mouthy little brat," Cynthia told her. "And you better watch it, or I'll tell her exactly how you've been spending your noon hours."

"Shut *up*!"

In the rearview mirror, Amanda could see that Marina was about to slap Cynthia.

"Marina, put your hand down!" Amanda ordered. "Nobody's smacking anyone in my car. You'd probably get me fired. I'm a freaking social worker, remember?" Lucy was crying again. Marina crossed her arms, swore under her breath and looked out the window. "Now, we're almost there. You all need to stop this, get along, and eat the damn pie with smiles on your faces."

Lucy found a tissue and blew her nose quietly. Cynthia leaned forward, hugged Lucy over the back of her seat and kissed her shoulder. Marina continued to stare out the window.

* * *

THEY ENTERED THE RICH AREA of Riverton, if there was one. It was a new development, and it looked like the house had been built within the last ten years. Every home was the same earthy shade of taupe. The trees in the neighborhood were small enough that someone could reach around their trunkd with both hands. The homes they passed either had driveways full of cars of their Thanksgiving guests, or they looked deserted.

William's parents, Desi and Elena Roberts, lived in the largest house at the end of a cul-de-sac. They parked on the street and walked slowly up to the house. The garage had three stalls, all of which were open to reveal two newer looking sedans and a row of well-equipped bikes. Amanda was suddenly hit with intense déjà vu, which was ridiculous because she had never been anywhere in Riverton except Lucy's house.

William greeted them at the door and gave Lucy a kiss on the cheek. He was smiling and relaxed, and he put his arm around Lucy, sensing her anxiety. Amanda followed Lucy and William inside the chic, modern entryway to the sunken living room/dining room where most of the guests were gathered.

For the second time in a month, Amanda nearly fainted from shock. From across the room, there was a squeal, and before William had a chance to introduce his bride to be, Trix Mann shouted, "Amanda!"

* * *

THE ENTIRE ROOM, WHICH HAD been bustling with happy energy, quieted as Trix squeezed through bodies to the entryway. Trix devoured Amanda with a hug. Amanda was speechless and awkwardly hugged the much shorter woman back.

William was smooth and unfazed. "While those two get reacquainted, let me introduce my fiancé, Lucy Ramirez." While William's family moved forward to greet Lucy, Trix moved Amanda to the stairs on the other side of the entryway and pulled her to sit down.

Trix held both of Amanda's hands in hers and shook her head in disbelief.

"I can't believe it's you, Amanda! It's so wonderful to see you! I guess you must be here with William's fiancé . . ." Amanda nodded, still unable to speak. "We've known the Roberts for years . . . Desi is one of the first salesmen who worked for Michael. Now I daresay that Desi is more successful than Michael. He got the market in the Cities, and sales just took off." Trix was positively beaming. "Oh, honey, Jacob is going to be so excited to see you. Just a minute, let me go grab him . . ." Before Amanda could protest or explain anything, Trix had hopped up to locate Jacob.

Amanda cupped her hand over her gaping mouth, trying to get her brain to catch up with what had just happened. Her best friend's fiancé's father worked for Jacob's father. The chances seemed astronomical, although the logical part of her brain, the only part that could function at this point, recognized that the two towns were relatively small and close to each other.

Trix weaved her way back to the stairs holding Jacob's hand. She stopped in front of Amanda, threw his hand down, and said with disgust, "You work together?!"

Amanda could only nod.

"Mom," Jacob said, as gently as he could, though Amanda could see he was exasperated, "we just reconnected a couple of weeks ago. It's not like I was hiding anything from you. It's just that I thought you might get a little weird about it. Obviously I was wrong." Jacob put his hands on his hips, his familiar gesture of frustration.

Michael walked up and stood behind Trix.

"Hey, Amanda," Michael said, leaning forward and squeezing her shoulder. "It's great to see you again."

"They work together, Michael," Trix said. Amanda couldn't tell if her irritation was genuine or for show. "Jacob was hiding her from us."

"Mom . . ."

At that point, the doorbell rang again. A man Amanda assumed was Desi came around the corner and greeted Rosie and two of her sisters, followed by several of the little cousins. Desi was exactly like his son—warm and gracious. He gently kissed Rosie on the cheek, and did the same to both of Rosie's sisters. William was suddenly by his side and escorted Lucy's aunts, while Rosie entered the living room on Desi's arm. Amanda watched Rosie look up at the vaulted ceiling and the wall of windows overlooking the river valley.

"Which one is Lucy's mother?" Trix asked.

"The one with Desi," Amanda said. Michael, Trix, and Jacob all turned to look at Amanda, who finally pulled herself up from the stairs.

It was the first time she had spoken, and they all finally remembered why they were there.

"So, Amanda," Jacob said, asking the question for all of them. "How did you end up here?"

Amanda, always the outsider, was relieved and proud to have a role. "I'm going to be Lucy's maid of honor."

Trix's eyes twinkled, and she hooked her arm around Michael and gave him a squeeze.

"Of course you are, sweetie," Trix said. "Because Jacob is the best man."

* * *

AFTER A TENSE THANKSGIVING MEAL with the family, Lucy finally relaxed at William's house, looking happy and at home. Trix talked Amanda's ear off until Amanda finally broke away and headed for the bathrooms. Lucy found Amanda and slid her arm through Amanda's, pulling her into the bathroom and locking the door.

"Oh, my God, Amanda, what was that?" Lucy's eyes were wide. "You know Jake?"

"I did know him five years ago. I can't believe you know him." Amanda paused. "Have you been spending time with him?" Jealousy flickered as Amanda wondered when Lucy and Jake could have spent time together, and why Lucy wouldn't have invited her too. In college, Amanda and Lucy had been inseparable, and any social outing that involved one of them always included the other.

"Will talks about him a lot, and we've hung out a few times since graduation. But, Amanda, how do you know him? You've never talked about him."

"Actually, I have. He's 'the guy.'" Amanda whispered even though the door was locked, and they were at the end of a long hallway. "The guy I met in the hospital when my mom was really sick."

Lucy looked at her blankly.

"The guy whose family I lived with all summer? Trix was the mom. Jake was the guy." Lucy still just stared. "I can't believe you don't remember this story. He was kind of a big deal."

"Of course I remember," Lucy said, awestruck. "You mean Jake is the one?! The one you lived with? Your *first*?" Lucy whispered the last sentence and completed her transformation to adolescence. "This is like destiny."

chapter eleven

Their staff meeting that Monday morning after Thanksgiving was relatively uneventful until Maddie, the front desk receptionist, poked her head in the door. "One of Patty's clients is here and said she's scheduled for a drug test." Patty worked with many of the drug addicts and alcoholics. She had just had surgery so she was out for at least a month. The rest of the social workers were dividing her duties until she returned.

"Gotta be Amanda's turn," Roberta said. "Especially if it's Roxy."

Maddie was young, energetic, and unfailingly kind, so she simply nodded and grinned.

"Oh, it's definitely your turn, rookie." Leah raised her eyebrows and grinned. "Have fun."

Amanda worked hard to keep her face neutral. "You mean a urine test?"

"Oh, yes," Zoe said. "I'll take you back to get a test kit." They walked past the front lobby where a very tall, angry woman leaned against the doorway. Zoe patted her arm. "Excuse me, are you Roxy?"

The woman had a few rotting nubs where teeth used to be, and her face was full of healing sores and scars. She had dull blonde hair and amateur tattoos down both arms. "Where's Patty?" she asked in a voice full of gravel and smoke.

"She's on a medical leave, so this is Amanda, and she will be doing your test." Amanda tried to look authoritative in a non-threatening way.

"New girl. Whatever." Roxy started to follow them, but Zoe said that they would get the test and come back to the front to head to the bathroom.

"Patty is working with Roxy on a voluntary child protection case. Roxy was arrested for driving while high on meth, and her kids were in the car. She completed treatment and her kids are back home with her. Patty actually really likes Roxy, but she's pretty gruff."

"Super. Just the person I want to follow into a bathroom stall."

Zoe pulled out a cardboard box and opened the test kit. "You need to fill out this form with her, put these two identifying stickers on the cup, and then give the cup to Roxy. After she fills it, you put the cap on tightly, put a sticker across the top, and seal it in this plastic bag. Put the form and the bag in the box, and add the box to outgoing mail." Amanda nodded, still working hard not to groan out loud. "And, Amanda, you have to really watch to make sure she hasn't brought in urine."

"Brought in urine? How could she . . ."

"Women can, um, insert a balloon or a plastic vial." Zoe raised her eyebrows with a grin.

"Oh, my gosh, seriously?"

"Yep. One time Patty was doing a test, and there was a loud plunk and a splash. Patty thought she had pooped or something. But when the woman tried to flush the vial, the toilet plugged and overflowed."

Back in the lobby, Amanda asked Roxy to follow her back to the restroom, which in their ancient building was actually a row of private bathrooms that were dark, damp, and smelled like a locker room.

"Could I get your information?"

"Want me to just fill it out? Just give it here." Roxy started to grab the form, but Amanda held tight to it, thinking that she shouldn't hand it over in case there was some sort of protocol that didn't allow clients to fill out their own paperwork.

"That's okay," Amanda said with a pathetic, nervous laugh that made her cringe. "I've got it."

"Okay, new girl." Roxy repeated her information and signed and initialed the form. Amanda added the stickers and handed her the cup. "You comin' in?" Roxy asked with the door half open and her pants unzipped.

Amanda hustled in the door and pulled it closed behind them. Roxy pulled her pants down without any hint of shyness, and sat down. The stall was barely big enough for two people, so Amanda had to press her back against the wall to avoid bumping Roxy's knees. Roxy reached through her legs and held the cup under her, and then just sat silently.

Trying to avoid eye contact, Amanda also didn't want to miss it if Roxy attempted to alter the test by dipping the cup in the toilet water. She kept her head down but watched Roxy's crotch out of the corner of her eye. Roxy stared straight ahead. Still no urine.

A full minute passed in awkward silence as Roxy shifted on the toilet. Finally, Roxy held the cup out to Amanda and said, "I can't go."

Keeping her arms at her sides, Amanda said, "Let's give it another minute." Amanda did not want to go back into her staff meeting urineless. She turned on the water in the sink. "Maybe the sound of water will help."

"You think I'm three years old? Jeez!" She stuck the cup back between her legs, strained, and farted loudly. "You wanna get that in a cup too?" Roxy was getting angry.

"Um, no." Like that required an answer.

Finally there was a slow trickle, and Roxy handed her the warm, wet cup with less than an inch of urine. Roxy pulled up her pants and walked out of the bathroom. Amanda looked in the mirror at her own bright-red cheeks and wide embarrassed eyes. She attempted to package the urine in the way Zoe had explained, and then headed back into the staff meeting, greeted by applause.

"Now you're really a social worker," Zoe announced with a grin. "Fully initiated!"

"Did she fart? Patty says she always farts."

At that, Amanda finally had to laugh.

"What a bunch of juveniles," Max said with that presidential grin. "Anyway, Amanda, I've got another new case I'd like you to take." He pulled out a green file and turned to the last section with the casenotes. "Jill just finished this assessment. Do you remember the report about the mom who spanked her three-year-old with a belt and left big red welts on his back?"

"Yep. The one with the infected nose ring?" With so many cases, they often boiled down families to one quick descriptor that stood out.

"That's her. You up for another new one?"

"Sure." The mother, Hailey Bell, was twenty-four and had been charged with gross misdemeanor malicious punishment for striking her three-year-old son, Charlie, with a belt numerous times. His preschool teacher discovered the welts when she put her hand on his back and he winced. He wouldn't say what happened, but allowed them to lift his shirt to reveal at least ten raised, red welts, some of which were scabbed and bloody. The teacher called social services and the police, and Hailey was arrested, booked, and spent the night in jail before she was released on bail the next day.

"She cried through the whole interview," Jill said. "She was pretty testy with me, but I think she'll be pretty good to work with. Charlie is at Hailey's mom's house, and Hailey is more than willing to leave him there to avoid foster care. She's coming in at 1:00 today to sign some forms, so Amanda, you can meet her then."

That afternoon Amanda walked to the other side of the building to Jill's office. Jill was in her forties and had three hockey-playing teenage boys, so she was always running out the door at the end of the day to drive one of them somewhere. She was also recently divorced, and Leah was reasonably sure that she was in a relationship with a woman, but Jill wasn't talking.

"Come on in," she said, snapping her phone closed. "Stevie has a game in Woodbury tonight but forgot his helmet. I told him he needs to track down his dad to bring it up to him because I am working, as my lovely children often forget. It's hard to get the proper tone of disgust to come across in a text, but a mom can try."

Amanda couldn't help scanning her desk for photos of a forty-something woman or girlfriend, but all she had were the requisite hockey pictures. Maddie buzzed Jill to tell her that Hailey was out front.

"I'm going to introduce you," Jill said, "and then I need to leave. You can use my office if you want." Amanda nodded, suddenly nervous because she wasn't prepared to meet with her client by herself.

Amanda also wasn't prepared for a client like Hailey. She was Amanda's age and very pretty, with a red hair cut short in a pixie haircut, freckles covering her cheeks and small upturned nose—still puffy but minus the infectious nose ring, and full pink lips. Her beauty was clouded by the shame that almost oozed from her pores.

"Hailey, this is Amanda."

Hailey shook Amanda's hand limply and sat in the chair across from her desk, hanging her head. Jill briefed Hailey on the process of ongoing case management, had her sign a few forms, and then left for her son's game.

Amanda asked Hailey a few questions and started to fill out some additional forms. Hailey wouldn't look up and answered her questions in a near whisper. After several minutes, Amanda put down her pen.

"Hailey, I just want to get a few things straight. I don't think you're a horrible person. I know you love your son. And we are going to get this figured out."

Hailey looked up at Amanda. "I'm just so sorry."

"I know you are."

"Tell me what to do, and I'll do it. I'll do anything to make it up to him and bring him back home."

Hailey had done terrible things to her son. Amanda had seen the photos of those bloody welts and could only imagine how her son screamed and cried when she beat him. But Hailey wasn't a monster. The surprises in this job just never seemed to end.

* * *

THAT AFTERNOON, THE EXPERIENTIAL education began. *I'm going to ask for a raise,* Amanda told herself, as she worked her way backwards out of a makeshift igloo. In one day she went from collecting urine to interviewing a devastated mom to making snow forts with teenagers and calling it education. Amanda was shimmying backwards on her belly, trying to stay low so she didn't cause any more snow to collapse. A bunch of snow slid up inside her jacket onto her bare skin, and she yelped.

"Were you talking in there?" one of the boys asked her. His face was pierced in at least five places, including a ring in his nasal septum, and Amanda constantly had to fight the urge to grab the ring and yank.

"I was wondering why I went back in, leaving my back exposed to the five of you," Amanda said, plopping down in the snow outside the igloo and tossing a handful of snow in the boys pierced face.

"I don't think you're supposed to say stuff like that," a boy with orange and black hair told her.

"Do you find my negativity offensive, Chad?" There was that sarcasm again. In the two weeks since she and Madge had started their experiential education program, Madge had talked to her several times about her sarcasm, which came across as negativity to troubled kids. Madge reminded her that it was their job to model a positive attitude. She was sure that Madge was questioning why she got stuck with someone like Amanda for this project. Amanda was wondering that herself.

In all fairness to herself, Amanda had to remind Madge that she had been very open to trying many of the projects Madge suggested for their first unit. But when they received fifteen inches of snow in the first week of December, they changed course because Madge insisted on winter survival as their first unit.

"I *hate* doing things in the snow," Amanda had told her. "I'll do just about anything but this, especially for our first group."

"Oh, Amanda, but think of the enthusiasm we can harness if we get out and play in the first snow of the season." Madge's eyes always lit up when she talked about experiential education.

"Oh, Madge, but think of how cold we'll be."

Madge won, partially because Amanda didn't have any better ideas. They spent a week reviewing curriculums, and decided on a group igloo-building project. They would each lead a group that had to build an igloo that would hold all the group members. They were given a few tools, but otherwise had to come up with the design on their own.

Her group consisted of five students at risk for failure or expulsion due to truancy and behavior problems. They were all freshmen, fourteen or fifteen years old. Among the five of them, Amanda was aware of seventeen body piercings, although she was only able to visually confirm thirteen.

During her high school years, Amanda had very little contact with peers of this sort. If she hung out with anyone, it was usually her teammates. Since she could only base her expectations on stereotypes, she assumed the kids in her group would be dumb, angry dope heads. There was some truth to this. The three boys were serious dopers, and all of the kids in the group were intensely angry about any number of life issues that had brought them to this point. But the surprise was that none of them were dumb. Even Chad, the boy with the Halloween hair who had achieved straight F's for the past three years, was much savvier than she had expected. He was the one who recognized the challenge of building a snow structure that could hold the five of them without collapsing on top of them. He didn't have any ideas about how to prevent the collapse, but he correctly predicted that it would.

Actually there were lots of surprises about these five adolescents. The two girls in her group, Brittany and Katelyn, had been on and off friends for years. Neither of them wanted to do anything in the snow, so they stood on the sidelines for the first week absolutely refusing to touch the snow or any of their snow tools. But when Chad had announced that none of

Amanda's suggestions were going to work, Brittany came to her rescue and had some ideas. Brittany wanted to build a mound of snow, pack it down, and burrow tunnels through the middle. Unfortunately, this was the system they were using when the entire thing collapsed on top of Katelyn and Chad. Amanda went back in for their hand shovels, the realization dawning that she was assigned to this group because she was the new girl and couldn't say no.

Matty, the boy with the nose ring, looked expectantly at Amanda. "Now what are we supposed to do, teacher? We still don't got no f-ing igloo."

Amanda had stood up and pulled her shirt and jacket away from her body, trying to shake the snow out of her clothes. Some snow slid down her pants and she yelped again. Tyler, a short, thin blonde boy who was usually pretty quiet, muttered something under his breath to Chad.

"Oh, you're sick, man," Chad bellowed, shoving Tyler against the snow bank.

"What?" Katelyn asked, grabbing on to his arm. Katelyn had a thing for Chad and wasn't at all upset when the two of them got stuck in the snow together.

Chad eyed Amanda and said something quietly to Katelyn. She turned to Tyler. "Keep dreaming, pervert," she said. "She would never stoop so low."

Amanda looked at Tyler, who met her stare in an intense way that gave Amanda the creeps. Funny, none of her social work classes addressed what to do if one of your clients makes suggestive remarks and gives you the willies.

* * *

FOR THE SECOND DAY IN A ROW, Amanda's group ended their session without an igloo or anything remotely resembling one. Madge's group, however, had built a respectable snow structure that fit three people. Madge was disappointed that they weren't able to meet their goal of fitting all six of them, so she had them start working on a second igloo.

As they were walking back inside with the full group, Madge asked, "How is Amanda's crew coming along?"

"This is impossible," Brittany whined. "We tried to build something and Katelyn and Chad almost got killed when it collapsed. "I say we forget the whole thing and do a music appreciation group instead."

"Oh, come on," Madge said. "You're not ready to give up already, are you?" She put her arm around Brittany and launched into a long-winded pep talk.

"She's a freakin Nazi," Chad said, falling into step next to Amanda. "She's a cheerleader Nazi, rah rah, you can do it blah blah. She makes me wanna puke." Chad added with a grin, "and I think she's a lesbo."

Amanda was utterly sick of Madge, but couldn't let a comment like that slide. "Knock it off, Chad."

They went in the back door of the high school and trudged back to Madge's classroom as the bell rang for the end of the day. The students dropped the snow equipment in a large storage closet in the entryway of Madge's classroom. They shoved their way into the room, grabbed their backpacks, and took off. Amanda plopped into a chair by Madge's desk, wanting to catch her breath before she packed her belongings.

Brittany hung back. "Hey, Amanda? Do you have a minute?" she asked, standing next to her chair.

"Sure," Amanda said, trying to sit up. "Have a seat." Brittany slid into a chair in front of Madge's desk. Madge was still sorting equipment in the storage closet.

"You do, like, child protection, right?"

"That's one of the things I do," Amanda said. "Why? Is there something you need to tell me?"

"Yeah, but it's not about me. I don't even know if there's anything anyone can do." Brittany crossed her arms tightly in front of her skinny chest. She was wearing an arm full of bracelets, a skin tight t-shirt, and tight low rise jeans. Amanda could see her belly button ring through her t-shirt and mentally checked one more piercing off the list that she had visually confirmed.

"You can tell me the problem, and I'll tell you some options. We might not be able to do anything, but sometimes there's another option that you may not have thought of."

Brittany let out a deep sigh. "Like I said, I just don't know if anything is happening at all. It's just that I was at my cousin's house last weekend, and my cousin is like a total prep. She's really good and doesn't get in trouble or anything. Her friend was sleeping over, and her friend was just kind of freaking out. Her friend had snuck out of her house, and I guess she does that all the time. She stays at my cousin Jess's house, and my aunt and uncle don't even know."

"So your cousin isn't completely perfect if she lets her friend sneak over all the time," Amanda felt compelled to point out.

"No, it's the totally right thing to do," Brittany said. "Jess told me the next morning that her friend will do anything to get out of her house. Jess doesn't even know what all has happened to her because her friend won't say, but she thinks it's pretty bad."

"Why does she think that?"

"Cuz Jess's friend has this perfect skin, and she's totally gorgeous. Jess is kind of zitty so she's all jealous. So Jess was asking if she takes zit pills or something to make her skin better, and her friend just got all weird and freaked out. So Jess just kept bugging her and said she wouldn't tell anyone, but Jess really wanted to try some."

"Jess wanted to use someone else's prescription? Why didn't she just ask her parents?"

"Because they're all weird about money. They'll never give her money for movies or anything, so Jess has finally got a job just so she can have decent make-up."

Amanda shifted in her chair and motioned to get Brittany to move along. "Anyway, what's the weird part? I think we're getting off the subject."

"Well, you asked why Jess wanted her pills, and it's totally not her fault that her parents are controlling freaks about money!" Brittany tossed her long, jet-black hair from side to side. "Okay, so here's the thing. Jess said that her friend is on birth control!"

Amanda tried not to roll her eyes, especially because Brittany was so worked up.

"Brittany, birth control is prescribed all the time for acne. That doesn't mean anything."

Now it was Brittany's turn to be disgusted. "No, that's not even the thing," Brittany said. "Jess tried to get her to share some of them. A few pills here and there. See if it would work. But her friend just freaked and said she HAD to be on the pills."

"Maybe she was afraid that if she didn't take them regularly, she wouldn't get the same effects and her zits might come back."

"No, it's not like that. Jess said her friend was afraid she would get pregnant. But she doesn't have a boyfriend!" Brittany sat back in her chair and crossed her arms, looking appalled.

Amanda raised her eyebrows at Brittany. Amanda leaned forward and whispered, "Sometimes, I've heard that kids 'do it' even if they aren't, like, boyfriend and girlfriend."

"No! This girl isn't like that. She doesn't have a boyfriend, she doesn't go out with boys, she doesn't do anything social. She stays *home!* Get it?!?"

"Yes, Brittany, I get what you're saying. But you don't have any reason to believe that something awful is going on."

"Yes, I do," Brittany said. "Jess is really upset, and I told her you would help. I think you need to talk to her."

"I can talk to Jess if you want," Amanda said, sympathetically. "I can't talk to her friend. I have no right to do that. It would make it into a whole investigation, and there are all kinds of procedures that go with that. Believe me," Amanda was thinking about the Thomas case about which she had a pre-trial late that afternoon. "People are usually not happy about their children being interviewed by a social worker."

Brittany looked defeated. "I'll try to get Jess to talk to you. She'll tell you. Something nasty is going on with her friend."

chapter twelve

A MANDA BARELY MADE IT to the courthouse in time for their 4:00 conference with Skip Huseman. Jacob said Huseman had requested discovery, which was lawyertalk for records and paperwork. Amanda and Max had reviewed the Social Services file and submitted the records that Max thought were part of the subpoena. Jacob reviewed the records and submitted them, and now Huseman was taking the unusual step of wanting a face-to-face meeting with Jacob to go over the records. He said Huseman thought the Social Services records were incomplete, so he wanted to meet to discuss his concerns. Jacob asked Amanda to be there to answer questions.

Amanda walked into the county attorney's office just as Jake was walking out.

"Hey, Amanda, nice of you to show up." Jake looked flustered.

"I told you I had something at the high school until 3:30. What's the big deal?" She had to walk quickly to keep up with him.

"The big deal is that I wanted some time to prep with you before this meeting," Jake said, suddenly turning toward her. Amanda jumped back, startled.

"Why do we need to prep? I'm not testifying, right? This is just an informal meeting." Her heart starting beating very fast, reacting to Jake's nervousness about the meeting.

He looked away for a minute and then back at her. "I don't exactly know what his plan is, but meetings like this are tactics."

Amanda glared at him. "What do you mean?"

"He doesn't have questions. He might be trying to intimidate you. He might be trying to waste my time. He might be trying something else. But this meeting is not about questions about your records."

"Well, obviously he's doing a good job if he's trying to intimidate you. Geez you're a mess, Jake. Is the case that weak, or are you just that flappable?" Amanda was mad that he was so nervous, mostly because it shook her confidence too. She needed him to tell her they were going to be fine.

"The case isn't weak, Amanda, but it's sure as hell messy. We've got a classic child abuse injury with an implausible explanation, and the statements of a thirteen-year-old who said the kid told him his dad beat him up. That's it. We both know Chuck Thomas beat up his son, but I don't know if I can prove it!"

They were interrupted by the sound of expensive shoes clicking on the marble floor. They were still outside of the county attorney's office near the elevators, and around the corner came Skip Huseman with two paralegals in tow. Jake looked like he'd been punched in the stomach.

Skip puffed himself to his full height as he leaned forward to shake Jake's hand.

"Hello again, Mr. Mann," Skip said, pumping Jake's hand. He turned cordially to Amanda. "I don't believe we met. Are you Ms. Danscher?"

Amanda tried to answer, but let out a cough. She cleared her throat and tried again. "Yes, I'm Amanda Danscher."

"Well, it's good to meet you, Ms. Danscher. This is Ken Brooks and Ashley Daniels, two of my favorite clerks. We actually came down together for a late lunch. This is my hometown, you know."

The tactic suddenly became clear to Amanda. The good ol' boys network was alive and well. She glanced over at Jake, who seemed to be squaring his shoulders to match Skip.

"Then I'm sure you'll enjoy coming down to your old territory for this case." Skip turned to look at Amanda, and she forced herself to meet his stare. He looked at her a little longer than necessary, and she saw something nasty cross his face for a second. Then his smile was back.

"Are we meeting in your office, Mr. Mann?" Skip asked.

Amanda could tell just by the smug look on his face that he knew there was no way they would all fit in Jacob's office.

"I thought we'd use the law library," Jake said. "Pardon me for a moment while I get the rest of my files. Amanda, will you lead the way?"

Amanda turned to glare at Jake, as he had to know that she had no clue where the law library was.

He understood her glare. "Luckily it's on this floor so you all won't have to risk using the elevator again."

"Oh, yes," Skip said heartily. "I've used it a few times in my day."

They followed Skip down the hall to the modest law library. Amanda studied his well-pressed suit and wondered if he had been in court that day or if he always dressed to the nines. The lawyers who worked for the county dressed down every chance they got, but Skip actually looked at home in his suit. It reminded Amanda of women on TV who look like they could run a marathon in high-heeled shoes.

Jacob joined them after a minute, carrying two large files and his briefcase. She wondered if he had downed a cup of coffee, as he looked alert and much more in control.

"Sorry about that," Jake said, sitting on one side of the table with Amanda. Just like in a movie, Skip and his paralegals took the other side of the table. Before they could get started, Janice, a paralegal from the county attorney's office, came in with a tray of coffee and cups.

Before Janice could offer anyone a drink, Skip asked, "Decaf?"

"Oh, no, I'm sorry, it's regular," Janice looked embarrassed and apologetic. "I can sure run back and grab you a cup if you like."

"No no, that's fine. I don't think we'll be long here." Skip turned to look at Jake, who held up his hands to say he didn't know. Janice looked at Jake, who shrugged her off and thanked her.

"Well, Mr. Huseman, I didn't call this meeting," Jake said, leaning back in his chair, trying to look comfortable. "I'm assuming there must be a serious agenda for you and two of your associates to take the afternoon to come down here."

Point for Jake, Amanda thought, making Huseman look like he didn't have anything better to do but drive down to Terrance with two staff for the afternoon. Amanda was glad Jacob got some kind of jab in, because all the points thus far had to go to Huseman.

Skip tilted his head and shrugged. "Actually we won quite a large settlement this week on a pharmaceutical trial," Skip said. "Ashley and Ken were instrumental in the settlement, so I decided to get them out of the office and take them out for lunch for a little perk, other than their fat bonuses of course." Ashley and Ken smiled on cue, but otherwise looked like Skip's personal robots, wearing almost matching conservative blazers and writing on legal pads in identical leather binders. Skip had wrestled that point away too.

"So did you go to Thomas's diner?" Amanda asked. The smiles disappeared. Skip's eyes flashed to Amanda, and then he focused his full attention on Jacob.

"I think that would be a little distracting for Chuck," Skip said, his voice quiet and full of concern. "Truth be told, Jacob, he's pretty unsettled by this whole mess."

"I imagine he would be," Jake said blankly.

"You know, I grew up with Chuck and his brothers," Skip said, resting his arms on the table, hands crossed in front of him, head down in thoughtful consideration. "I graduated Class of '81. Chuck was Class of '83. I played some ball, but nothing like how Chuck played. And on the ice . . . whew . . . some people thought Chuck could have gone pro."

Amanda and Jake were unresponsive, and Amanda thought they probably had the same look on their faces. They let the good ol' boy reminisce about the good old days, and they bit their tongues.

"Funny thing, though. I never played hockey, but one thing you know about hockey players is that they can be some rough fellas. Some of those guys . . . you know they're playing hockey just because they get to slam other guys into the wall." Skip chuckled. "You know how that is. Did you ever play?"

Jacob cleared his throat to stall for time. "Hockey? No, I never played hockey. I was in the minority in this state."

"Oh," Skip said knowingly. "Wrestler."

"Basketball," Jake said. Amanda thought back to his bedroom with the seventh grade basketball team photo on his dresser. Jake spent his varsity years getting chemotherapy.

Skip laughed out loud. "You are in the minority in these parts," he said. "I guess you were a point guard, huh? Small and fast?"

Now that bastard was making jokes about Jacob's height. Amanda wanted to reach across the table and slap his face. She could feel herself getting red, and she shifted in her chair. Skip took the hint.

"That's neither here nor there," Skip said, sitting back in his chair again. "My point about the hockey is that Chuck wasn't one of those rough guys. He just wasn't, Jake. None of the Thomas boys were like that." Skip shook his head like a great travesty had just occurred. He was silent, waiting for Jake to respond.

Amanda looked over at Jake, who was silent also. Jake stared straight at Skip without a word, without a trace of emotion on his face. He was resisting Skip's bait, not allowing himself to be drawn into a debate of the merits of his case, not allowing himself to be intimidated by the good old boy network. Skip was actually trying to intimidate Jake into dropping his case on the sole point of, "He's not one of those people." Jake's was silent, which left Skip out flapping in the wind.

Skip cleared his throat, visibly becoming annoyed with how the conversation was going, or not going. "You must be pretty comfortable with your case, pretty solid on your facts, accusing a man like Chuck Thomas of child abuse." Skip had heard their conversation earlier, and he was using it as ammunition. The wind had changed in their meeting, and it was now coming from the cold north.

"What did you need today, Skip?" Jacob asked, emphasizing his name, not afraid to use it.

Skip tapped Ashley the robot clerk on the shoulder, and she produced a thin manila file. "Here's what we want, and a schedule of when we want it. We want your witness list first because we will be deposing all your witnesses. We want transcripts and copies of all audio and videotapes. We will also be submitting briefs requesting dismissal of the case on several different merits.

"This is a CHIPS petition . . ."

"Oh, I am well aware that you are unable to bring forward a criminal complaint. I am well aware that you are manipulating the law that protects children from real abusers in order to abuse my client instead. I am aware that your social workers," *Here comes the attack on me*, Amanda thought, "completed a shoddy, unprofessional, incomplete investigation that is dragging a man revered by his community through the mud." Skip leaned forward and narrowed his eyes, "I haven't lived in this town for twenty years, but it's still my home. You are in dangerous territory, Jake," he spat the name like a swear word. "I advise you to think very carefully about whether or not you wish to proceed."

Whoa. He issued his warning like a Mafioso just before they whacked the guy and dumped him in the river with cement blocks chained to his feet. Amanda watched Jake. His face was unreadable. The paralegal robots sat still, staring at their identical notebooks.

Finally Jake stood up, hands by his side, making no move to shake Huseman's hand.

"We'll be reviewing your discovery request, and we'll be making our own," Jake said, standing very straight. Skip stood up, and rose to his full height at least a foot taller than Jake.

He put his hands on his hips and shook his head in disgust.

"We'll have one more conference before trial," Skip said. "I'll give you one last chance to make this right." He walked out of the room before Jake could answer, leaving the para-robots to gather his briefcase and trail behind him.

Amanda and Jake watched him leave. Amanda started to speak, but Jake held up his hand, signaling her to be quiet until they were sure he was gone. Jake went to the door and closed it quietly.

He turned to Amanda and let out low whistle. "Something is going on here that has nothing to do with this case."

"Why do you think it has nothing to do with the case?" Amanda said, pushing out the chair next to her and putting her feet up. Amanda hugged her knees to her chest, unconsciously trying to protect herself.

"That guy was scared," Jake said, leaning back against the door and crossing his arms. "I don't get that."

"You think he was scared?" Amanda said.

"His reaction is something beyond business. He warned me not to pursue this CHIPS case. This *little* CHIPS case in a *small* town against a *small-time* restaurant owner. Unless that's how he operates in all his cases, which I doubt, I think this lawyer has a stake in this somehow."

"Jake, that doesn't make any sense. He's not named in the case. It was an incident between this guy and his son. I'll bet Skip Huseman hasn't even set foot in this town for ten years."

"I know it doesn't make any sense. But this guy's reaction doesn't make sense either. Usually when attorneys meet, it's a pretty cordial thing, especially at first. Remember, in law school I clerked for a criminal defense attorney in the public defenders office. Even on the big cases, most of the lawyers know each other, so they kind of cut each other some slack. They know the other guy is just doing his job, so it's pretty friendly. Later on in a case, it can get pretty ugly, but that's usually when the stakes are high for either side." Jake sat on the edge of the table next to Amanda. "In the two years of clerking for that attorney, I probably sat in on a hundred attorney conferences. I'll bet ninety of those conferences were business as usual with a fair amount of time spent discussing golf or football. The other ones, even when they were a little heated, never were like this. Sometimes they would get gamey to try to get the other guy to tip his hand. Sometimes people got a little pissy. A few got nasty because somebody pulled a tactic or some kind of last minute trick to throw the other guys off. But never have I seen anything like this. Never."

Amanda tried to imagine what Skip Huseman could have invested in a CHIPS case like this. "Maybe it just offends him, that a couple of pip-squeaks like us could go after somebody revered by his community," Amanda said. "Maybe it offends his sense of how the world is supposed to work."

"Maybe," Jake said. But he didn't look like he believed it.

* * *

ON A DAY THAT BEGAN with a cup of urine and ended with a snaky attor-ney, Amanda was more than ready to go home. She trudged up the steps to her apartment and paused at the landing when she saw a set of boot prints in the snow just outside her door. Landlord? She had never had a male visitor, and she had not seen her landlord since she moved into the apartment.

Deciding to ignore the footprints, she inserted her key into the lock in the doorknob, but the knob rattled in her hand as the door pushed open. The lock was broken, and there was no way she could ignore that. Amanda found her landlord's number in her phone and dialed it, but there was no answer. Her aloneness hit her again like a slap. She hesitated and finally called her only friend in town.

Jake was standing on the landing within ten minutes.

"It doesn't exactly looked forced, but I'm no expert." Bolstered by Jake's presence, Amanda found the nerve to go inside. They walked through the apartment and didn't find anything out of order. "I think we should call your landlord and have him get you a deadbolt. I can't believe you don't have one already. Until then, I guess it's you and me." Jake put his hands on his hips and grinned.

"You and me . . . doing what?"

"Amanda, there's no way you're staying here if you can't lock your door. Pack up. Let's go to my place."

"Hey there, Mr. Bossypants. Do you really think you're my only option?" Amanda was annoyed at the flush creeping up her neck.

"I'm sorry, Amanda. Do you have a secret boyfriend I'm not aware of?" His voice was dripping with saccharin, and he raised his eyebrows and crossed his arms.

"Maybe I do. Maybe I have a couple." Inwardly she cringed, knowing how lame that sounded.

"Well, aren't you just a player. I promise I won't try to compete with any of your various boyfriends. Now come on. I've got a comfortable couch and a new carton of peanut butter fudge ice cream. Let's go."

Amanda grabbed an overnight bag and packed toiletries and work clothes for tomorrow. Avoiding the boxer shorts she usually slept in, Amanda found some flannel pajama pants. Jake drove them across town to his apartment.

Amanda got out of the car, relieved that she didn't have to stay at her apartment alone, and still a little unsure if this was Jacob making a move on her. He used his key to open the first door, and punched in a security code to get in the second door. His apartment was on the main level, number 109. He opened the door and said, "Welcome to my humble abode."

His apartment looked like a thousand apartments just like it, with plain drywall, light pine trim, and cheap looking light fixtures. It was nice enough to charge good rent, but utterly lacked character, so that no one would want to stay long. In his living room, he had a black leather sofa, but nothing else to sit on. There was a huge entertainment center with a widescreen TV, DVD player, and stereo surround sound system. No art on the walls. No dining room table. The kitchen was separated from the living room by a half bar, and there was nothing on the kitchen counters but a very nice coffee maker.

"Dang, you are boring," Amanda said.

"Tell me about it," Jake said, turning on a lamp by the couch.

"Obviously you don't entertain much, judging by all the seating room," Amanda said. Jake went into the kitchen and turned on the coffee maker.

"Right again," he said. "I can offer you peanut butter sandwiches and the ice cream. Otherwise, I have no food, and nothing to drink other than beer and milk."

"I'm not much of a coffee drinker," Amanda said. "I feel like I should start, though, just to feel like a grown up."

"Eh . . . it's just another addiction. Probably better to avoid it if you can." He made two sandwiches and grabbed the ice cream and two spoons and sat on the floor in front of the TV.

Amanda slid onto the floor next to him, took the other spoon and helped herself to some ice cream. Jake had grown quiet, and they allowed themselves to get engrossed in reruns.

At 9:00 p.m. Jake got up, found some extra blankets and a pillow and brought them out to the living room.

"You're welcome to use my bed," he said, unfolding a blanket. "I can sleep out here."

"This is fine," Amanda said awkwardly, hopping up to grab the blanket out of his hand. "Don't worry about it."

"Okay, then," Jake said. "I'm gonna go to bed if that's okay with you. I'm used to an early schedule I guess. Here's the remote when you're done watching TV." He walked down the hall to his bedroom, stepped back for a moment and said, "Goodnight."

Amanda was not expecting Jake to make any moves, but she was a little surprised that he went to bed so abruptly. She headed back into the bathroom, which was uncomfortably close to his bedroom. He had left his bedroom door open a crack, so she tried to look away as she passed his door. The bathroom was also very clean and non-descript. She knew from past history that he wore contacts too, so she searched for his saline and found several large prescription bottles. Seeing all the medicine reminded Amanda that she had almost forgotten about his cancer. She hadn't asked about his health once since they had rekindled their friendship, or whatever it was that they had. As quietly as possible, she turned the bottles to read what the medicines were, but the first three were nothing that she recognized. The fourth was one that she did recognize: Zoloft. Amanda was pretty sure it was an antidepressant, but she planned to look it up tomorrow to be sure. She wondered if Jake was sick again, if his cancer had returned. He didn't look sick, but he didn't look sick the first time she met him either.

Amanda went back to the couch and tried again to fall asleep. She realized her heart was thudding in her chest. She pictured him lying in his bed, and wondered if he was asleep. She wondered if he was sick again. She wondered how he felt about her. It took a long time for her to fall asleep.

chapter thirteen

DECEMBER PASSED QUICKLY and before Amanda knew it, the last day of work before the Christmas holiday had arrived. Becca, Zoe, Leah, Amanda, and Max were the only social workers working that day, so Zoe brought a tray full of Christmas cookies into their staff meeting.

"Are you excited for the twins' first Christmas?" Leah was asking Zoe as Amanda sat in her typical spot at the end of the table in their meeting room. Zoe, after nearly three years of fertility treatment, had given birth to twins the previous February and was just coming back to work from maternity leave when Amanda started her job.

"Yesterday I made a ton of cookies and tried to get them to help," Zoe said, holding her hands over her coffee cup to warm them. "Surprisingly, nine month olds can't do much with a mixer or a rolling pin, so Sam ended up dealing with them most of the day." Zoe was dark-complected with dark hair and eyes, and always made Amanda feel at ease. She was warm and funny and reminded Amanda of Lucy.

"What did you get them for Christmas?" Max asked. "Did you go ridiculously overboard like we did?"

"Not too bad," Zoe said. "They have everything except toys, and there's not much they'll play with yet. I'm dying to get Olivia a dollhouse, but she wouldn't know what to do with it yet. Sam would love to get Dylan a basketball hoop, but that seems premature too. We ended up buying a plastic play gym for the basement playroom."

Amanda enjoyed hearing them talk about their kids, though it always brought a pang of sadness too. She couldn't ever imagine her mother talking with such excitement about what she bought Amanda for Christmas. The holidays were always pathetic and sad without extended family to visit or money to buy gifts. Sometimes April tried to do something rebellious like grilling hotdogs on Christmas day just to say, "F you," to the rest of the world celebrating the birth of their lord. Other times, Amanda and April went to a café and ordered the Christmas special. The worst was when Amanda was ten and had been relieved because they were going to church services on Christmas just like everyone else. That false expectation made it all the worse when she realized they were at church for the free Christmas meal. That year had been particularly hard for them financially, and April couldn't afford to buy presents or food for a nice meal. Santa Claus came to the dinner and embarrassed Amanda by presenting her with a bag full of candy canes and peanuts and a gift that turned out to be a Strawberry Shortcake lotion and perfume set. There was a tag on the gift that read "school-age girl."

"What are you doing for Christmas?" Max asked Amanda, bringing her out of her trip down holiday memory lane hell.

"What?" Amanda asked to stall for time. She had known eventually her co-workers would ask about her family, and she hadn't completely made up her mind how she was going to answer them. "I'm doing the traditional Christmas thing," she said vaguely. "Turkey, presents, church . . ." That was the truth, because she would be doing all of that with Lucy's family. Amanda looked down at her notebook and calendar, shuffling them around and trying to signal to him that she wanted to start the meeting.

Max took the hint. "I don't have much for staff this week," he told them. He had a thick file with a few papers clipped to the top, which meant that a new report had come in on a previously closed case. "It's just a call from a school social worker that the Swazis are completely broke, and they didn't sign up for the Christmas project or Toys for Tots, so their kids won't have anything for Christmas.

"Oh, no," Leah said. "Max, we must have something for them, don't we? I know Jackie would want us to scrounge something up."

Amanda knew that the reference to Jackie, another child protection social worker, meant that the Swazis must have been one of her old cases.

"I can call my church this morning," Zoe said. "I'm sure they'll find a hundred bucks in the social-needs fund for them."

"Make sure they get a gift certificate for Wal-Mart," Leah said. "Don't give them the cash. I think the dad is drinking again."

"Another success," Becca said, speaking up for the first time that morning. She was in a particularly bad mood that day, so Amanda suspected she was not looking forward to the holidays with her crabby husband.

"The main thing we have is that a meth lab got busted over the weekend," Max said, and told them about the trailer that had been raided on a search warrant. They'd found several grams of methamphetamine. Also confiscated were various meth-making supplies such as boxes of cold medicine tablets, batteries, coffee filters, and gun cleaner. When she had first learned how meth labs worked, with people making their own drugs using a complicated, multi-step process, Amanda was shocked that any of their clients could pull it off. The substances used to make meth were highly toxic, so the people exposed to the process, even if they never ingested the drug, could be poisoned by it.

"The mom had four kids, ages nine, five, four, and ten months," Max said, and they all groaned.

"And I have to say is meth protocol is horrible," Zoe said. "Mary Clark called me this morning and said the kids were all basket cases by the time they got to her house." The Clarks were the foster parents on call for December." She was pissed. She said they all had Band-aids on their arms from blood draws, and all of them had full physicals at eleven o' clock at night in the ER." The group groaned collectively again.

"That's the meth protocol," Leah said. "Those kids have been exposed to so much toxic crap that they need to find out right away if they have any health issues that need immediate treatment."

"Yeah, well, it sounds like the whole crew was a little overzealous, with this being their first meth bust since the protocol was put into place. The nine-year-old told Mary that the police came in hazmat suits and gas masks. The little kids were completely out of their minds. Then they get dragged to the ER and get very complete physicals with blood draws and hair samples taken. They did sexual abuse exams on all of them too. On top of all that, Mary is just hostile about getting four kids right before Christmas."

"I'll bet they're not too thrilled either," Amanda blurted out, furious that a foster parent would be mad that these miserable kids were placed at her house. "Why does she do crisis care if she doesn't want kids placed with her?"

"She does want kids placed with her," Zoe said. "She wants pleasant, clean, grateful children who are free to be adopted and have no behavior problems."

"Oh, *those* kids," Leah said sarcastically. "Tell her we save the good ones for ourselves."

"Okay, I'm crabby because she was so nasty to me this morning," Zoe said. "Mary is usually pretty good, and her husband is fantastic with the kids."

"I'll share my Prozac with her if she'll promise to cheer up," Leah said.

"Anyway, " Max said. "Let's get back to this before Leah starts writing prescriptions. We need someone to write the CHIPS petition, and someone to check in with the kids. I'd like you to take this case, Amanda, since it looks like it will be labor intensive and your caseload is still small."

"Okay," Amanda said, wondering when she was going to get some easy, fun cases.

"I need to deliver a bunch of Christmas gifts today," Zoe said. "Amanda, if you want to come along, we can stop at the Clarks' house and you can see the kids."

"How about a Christmas visit?" Leah asked.

"The police report says that both parents are in jail," Max said. "Amanda, you can ask the nine-year-old where they usually spend holidays. I'll also call the jail and ask the mom if she has any family in the area. Maybe they've got some wonderful grandparents who can pick them up and give them a great Christmas."

"Yeah right," Leah said.

"I doubt it," Zoe added.

"Tough crowd," Max said.

* * *

AFTER THE STAFF MEETING, Amanda and Zoe loaded Zoe's minivan with garbage bags full of Christmas gifts.

"We have four stops," Zoe said. "Most of the clients and foster parents picked their stuff up last Friday. We still have a bunch of watches that were donated by the Lions Club, so I wrapped those and we'll bring them to the Clarks for the meth kids. One of Jackie's teen moms doesn't drive, so I said I'd drop her stuff off. Then we need to go to Harlan's and Freitag's."

"Do the kids get anything good?" Amanda asked, remembering her perfume set.

"I don't know. What do you mean by 'good'?" Zoe asked.

"When I was a kid, it was My Little Pony," Amanda said. "Does anybody donate the big gifts that all the kids want?"

"That's an interesting question," Zoe said. "I guess I never really noticed. Sam and I usually donate a few things. This year we gave a bunch of board games."

"Just curious . . ." Amanda said, drifting back into her thoughts of her own sad Christmases. She wondered if her mom even knew what the cool gifts were. Amanda stared out the window at the houses in the different neighborhoods. The further they got from the downtown area and the old railroad station, the nicer the houses appeared to be. Zoe pulled into the driveway of a newer looking two-story house belonging to Kathy and Joe Freitag, foster parents for an eight-year-old girl whose mother was developmentally delayed. Zoe grabbed two of the smaller bags to bring inside.

Zoe knocked on the door and was greeted by the foster child, Jasmine, holding a new beagle puppy that was wrangling to get outside. Jasmine was a beautiful blonde with fair skin and hearing aides in both ears.

"Did Kathy and Joe get a new puppy?" Zoe asked as they stepped inside.

Jasmine beamed. "Her name is Bubbles. They let me name her." Zoe led the way into the kitchen where Kathy was trying to fit a huge turkey in the refrigerator to defrost. She gave it a final shove, closed the refrigerator door, and turned around patting her hair down. Kathy was no older than thirty with blonde hair and light skin that almost matched Jasmine's.

"Jasmine, sweetie, will you take Bubbles downstairs and play chase with her so Zoe and I can talk for a minute?"

Jasmine coaxed Bubbles to follow her into the basement while they all watched her go.

Kathy suddenly turned to Zoe with tears and anger in her eyes. "Why do we have to let her do an overnight visit on Christmas? She doesn't want to go. Her mom has ended the last two visits after an hour. How is this woman going to take care of her all night?" Amanda was shocked at how quickly Kathy went from beaming to seething.

Zoe tried to be sympathetic. "Jackie said mom's attorney pushed for an overnight for the holidays. Isn't the grandma supposed to be there too?"

"She's almost ninety," Kathy said, wiping her eyes with a tissue. "How much longer do we have to do this?" ·

"It's been almost six months, and obviously the mom isn't making progress," Zoe said. "Jackie is hoping that mom will decide to terminate her rights voluntarily without going through a trial."

"I just don't understand," Kathy said. "Her mother doesn't even want her! But she gets to spend Christmas with Jasmine when she hasn't wanted to spend more than an hour with her all month. What's going to happen in the morning when Jazzy needs to put on her hearing aides? Her mom isn't going to know how to do it, so Jazzy will go back to spending all day in silence because her hearing aides are too hard for her own *mother* to understand." She spat the word "mother."

"Do your best to hang in there," Zoe said. "Jackie is pretty confident that this will settle quickly." Zoe pointed to the bags on the table. "Here are a few things donated to us for foster kids. Coloring books, a little dollhouse, and a watch."

"She really doesn't need anything else," Kathy said, smiling for the first time since they arrived. "We got her a Barbie townhouse, a bike, rollerblades, a new backpack, three new outfits, a new winter coat and snow pants set . . . And I know my family bought her a bunch of things too."

"You could send these things along with mom on the visit," Zoe said, and Kathy's face darkened again.

"That's probably true," Kathy said darkly. "I'll bet that woman didn't get her anything."

Zoe sighed. "We'll say goodbye to Jasmine before we go." Zoe and Amanda went to the stairs just as Jasmine was coming back up.

"Bubbles peed on the floor!" Jasmine burst out, running into the kitchen.

"That's okay, sweetie. We'll clean it up." Kathy grabbed a bunch of paper towels and followed Jasmine back downstairs. Zoe and Amanda let themselves out.

"You know, sometimes I think it really doesn't matter what I say in foster parent training about how the system works," Zoe said as they walked to the car. "When foster parents get scared and attached, it all goes out the window."

They both climbed into their seats in the van, and Zoe backed out of the driveway to head for their next destination.

"Guess she doesn't care for Jasmine's mom," Amanda said.

"Jasmine's mom tries, but she just doesn't understand parenting. She's too low functioning to get it. Jackie's pretty confident that we'll get the guardianship, but there'll probably be liberal visitation. That's going to drive Kathy crazy. Kathy and Joe don't have any kids, and Jasmine was their first placement. They completely feel like Jasmine is their daughter, and they just get hostile at the idea of sharing her with people who won't treasure her the way they do."

"It seems like it should be so easy," Amanda said. "Kathy can take care of Jasmine, and her own mother can't. Seems like there shouldn't be anything left to decide."

Zoe rolled her eyes. "It's never that easy," she said.

As they drove through town, it was apparent that it was nearly Christmas Eve. Kids were out of school and playing in their yards, and several people were unloading bags of food or presents from their cars. Some homes looked abuzz with lots of company, and other homes were obviously empty, their owners traveling for the holiday. Over the past three years that she had spent holidays with Lucy's family, she had learned to almost enjoy the holidays in a way she never did while she was growing up. Now that she had somewhere to go, she allowed herself to acknowledge December 25 as something other than an extra day off from school and work.

Zoe turned into a run-down apartment complex and pulled into a parking spot labeled for visitors. "That teen mom lives here," Zoe said. "Do you want to come in?"

"Sure," Amanda said. She was done shadowing other social workers as part of her training, but she still appreciated the chance to watch other people work since they all had different styles.

They trudged across the parking lot into one of the apartment buildings. Zoe opened the door, and Amanda immediately noticed the smell. It was a combination of dirty diapers, cigarette smoke, and garbage. Zoe led the way to apartment 112 and knocked on the door. A red-haired girl named Jenn, who looked well over twenty, answered the door. She was wearing a tank top and pajama bottoms and holding her baby in one arm. She wore a cell phone head set, which made her look like Brittney Spears in concert.

"I work with Jackie," Zoe told her. "Jackie asked me to drop off some Christmas gifts for the baby."

"Cool. Just a second. Ash, my social worker is here." Jenn motioned them to come inside. The apartment was sparsely furnished with a couch that had no legs so it rested on the floor. Two plastic crates were set in front of it to serve as a coffee table. There was a beanbag chair, and a curved floor rocking chair that Amanda remembered lots of kids had in their dorm rooms. An old console TV blared "Teen Mom" on MTV. There were several empty Mountain Dew cans on the crates. On the floor were about fifteen balled up dirty diapers, as well as dirty paper plates with grease marks and globs of ketchup. There were clothes all over the couch and floor, possibly clean, possibly dirty. Two ashtrays on the TV were full of cigarette butts spilling ashes on to the TV screen. Only a small patch of the floor was visible with clothes and garbage covering most of the rest of it.

"You can set the presents in the corner," Jenn said. There was no Christmas tree, but she had set up a lava lamp and draped tinsel all around it like it was a tree. There were two other gifts by the lava lamp wrapped in Sesame Street paper. "I can't believe he would do that to you. He's such a fucker." Jenn was still talking to her friend on the phone, but since she wasn't actually holding a phone, it seemed to Amanda like she was either talking to them or herself.

"Can you tell your friend you'll call her back?" Zoe asked.

"She's fine. She'll wait," Jenn said.

"Please hang up for a minute," Zoe said.

Jenn glared at Zoe for a second. "The social worker wants me to hang up. I'll call you back. Bye." She tapped something on a box attached to her pajama bottoms.

"Happy Holidays, Jenn. Jackie tells us that things are going pretty well for you, but I'm worried about how your house looks today. You need to clean up in here," Zoe said. "You can't just leave diapers on the floor after you change the baby. You need to throw away all the garbage on the floor, pick up the dirty clothes, and get rid of the pop cans that are everywhere."

During the entire time that Amanda and Zoe were at the house, Jenn held her baby with one arm facing away from her. The baby was very fat, and amazingly did not fuss as he was bounced all over the apartment with his mother.

Jenn glared at Zoe. "You know, it's not exactly easy to clean when you have a baby to take care of." Suddenly Jenn turned the baby around and held him close to her face, cooing at him for the first time since they arrived. His face burst into a smile, and he cooed back and drooled.

"I know it isn't," Zoe said. "I have two of my own at home. But that doesn't change the need for you to throw away your garbage."

"Are you done?" Jenn asked.

"That depends on whether or not you are going to clean up after we leave," Zoe said.

"I have to get ready for Christmas," Jenn said. "I need to bring, like, two salads to my aunt's house." Even this girl had somewhere to go on Christmas.

"Will it help you remember to get it done if I come back in a couple days to check on your progress?" Zoe asked pleasantly.

Jenn glared. "I'll clean up, all right? Jesus!"

"That's all I wanted to hear," Zoe said. "Happy Holidays!"

They let themselves out again and trudged through the parking lot.

"Do you think she'll end up keeping her kid?" Amanda asked as they climbed back into the van again. "It looks like she isn't too focused on her baby."

"You know, I think this is the girl who Jackie said does really well with her baby," Zoe said. "If she doesn't keep her baby, it will be because she does something stupid like hooking up with a sex offender or drug dealer. If she manages to stay away from all the bad influences, she might do okay. Her baby looked good."

"How could you tell?" Amanda asked as they drove away again.

"I don't know. I guess you can't tell in a five-minute visit," Zoe said. "The good things were that he looked smiley, she made eye contact with him and he cooed back. That's big. It looks like she holds him a lot—big too."

"She probably had to hold him with all the junk all over the floor," Amanda said.

Zoe tilted her head to concede that point.

As they continued their trek through town, Amanda thought about Jenn. Her own mother had been about Jenn's age when she'd had her. The lava lamp tree stuck in Amanda's head for some reason, and a vivid memory played in her head:

Wood paneling . . . if she picked at the white covering on the Christmas tree, the fake snow came off revealing bare metal wires. She didn't like the way the metal looked, but she couldn't stop picking. She was hiding, trying to be very quiet, so she could stay. She wanted to stay in this house with the white tree.

"Are you coming in?" Zoe asked, interrupting her memory. They had pulled into a trailer court, but it wasn't the same one where she had visited Marlys's sister. There was one very wide, paved road, and twenty-five to thirty neatly kept mobile homes on either side of the main road. They pulled up next to a mobile home with a painted sign that said, *Beware: Grandchildren Spoiled Here.*

Amanda wordlessly climbed out of the van and helped Zoe carry in several large bags of toys and clothes.

"Hello, sweetie!" A small, round woman with snow-white hair and a permanent smile opened the mobile home door.

"Merry Christmas, Gracie!" Zoe yelled out.

"You wait right there, sweetheart, and Lars will come help with all those packages." Gracie moved aside to allow Lars to pass through the doorway, because he never would have fit with her standing there. Lars was well over six feet tall with long arms and huge hands. His face was worn with deep laugh lines around his blue eyes. He looked like he could have picked up Gracie and palmed her like a basketball.

"Thank you, sir," Zoe said, and Lars nodded. He held out his arms as they piled on gifts and bags. He nodded for them to walk ahead of him inside the mobile home.

When she walked inside, she felt like she had entered Mrs. Claus's home away from home. On every surface was either a porcelain house or a Santa Claus figurine. There were ropes of Christmas lights and tree garland encircling the doublewide living room. The couch was draped in an intricate red-and-green quilt embroidered with Santas. The enormous tree was proudly displayed in the front of the living room, and was filled with ornaments.

"Lars, honey, please set the gifts under the tree. You girls, come sit and share a cookie before you go." Gracie hooked her arm through Zoe's and led her to the dining room table.

"Gracie, this is Amanda. She's our new worker. Amanda this is Gracie and Lars Harlan. They have been foster parents for twenty-eight years." Zoe beamed as she introduced them.

Gracie smiled modestly. "We've had 112 foster children in our home. Legally adopted six of them. Another three took our name after they turned eighteen. Loved each and every one of them." She scurried to the tiny kitchen and brought back a platter of beautifully decorated Christmas cookies. There were intricately frosted Santa Clauses, trees, angels, and stockings.

"These are too pretty to eat," Amanda said, afraid to touch the masterpieces.

"Oh, no, sweetie. If you don't eat them they'll just go to waste. Now do you want cold milk, hot chocolate, or coffee with your cookies? Ooh, and I also have spiced cider." Lars had finished unloading the gifts under the tree. He sat in the recliner nearest the tree and drank his coffee from a Santa coffee cup. As he rocked in his chair and watched his wife, he had an amused smile on his lips.

They both requested cider, and as Gracie went off to the kitchen to prepare their mugs, Amanda watched her with an emotion that closest resembled longing. This home was like nothing she had ever experienced. She imagined children being delivered to this home, pulled away from their parents due to drug use, abuse, or abandonment. She pictured Gracie cooing at toddlers and putting her arm around teenagers. She wondered if kids ever wanted to leave Gracie and Lars, or if they begged to stay forever.

Amanda knew that she would compare herself to the children she worked with when she started this job, because there were clearly times while growing up when she could have been removed from her mother. When Amanda was in first grade, they lived in a frigid garage with a space heater for heat, and they had to pee outside. And there were countless times that Amanda slept on a stranger's floor while her mother got high and then disappeared into a bedroom with another faceless, scary thug. The irony was that even though she was employed to provide this safety net for other children, she had always believed in her own life that with her mother was better than being anywhere else. Yet now that she had met Gracie and Lars, she wondered what difference a foster home like this might have made in her own life.

Two little boys, ages four and seven, padded down the hallway and stood behind Gracie, pulling her pant leg.

"Is our mama here, Gramma?" the older one asked.

"No, precious, it's Zoe and her friend," Gracie said, wiping her hands on her apron and turning around. "Remember, honey, your mama isn't coming today." Gracie held the boy's face in her hands. "Oliver, I feel very lucky because I get to have you and Stevie at my house for Christmas this year." Oliver grabbed onto Gracie's wrists while she was still holding on to his head and tried to lift his feet off the ground so that she was holding him suspended in the air. Gracie let her arms drop, and Oliver fell to the ground laughing.

"Gramma, you dropped me!" Oliver yelled. Little Stevie was jumping up and down next to Oliver, wanting his turn to fall on his back.

Zoe stood up. "Will you jump with me, Oliver?"

"Yea!" He grabbed Zoe's hands and began jumping wildly up and down. Stevie jumped up and down next to her until she gave him a turn, too.

Gracie maneuvered around the boys with two steaming cups of cider. She set them down next to Amanda, and then sat herself in the chair on the other side of Amanda.

"I love to meet the new workers," Gracie said, patting Amanda's knee. "So, are you enjoying being a social worker?"

Amanda smiled at Gracie and wanted to answer, but suddenly felt a lump rising in her throat.

Gracie leaned in, watching Amanda's face closely. Amanda willed her chin not to quiver, but she was still unable to speak. Gracie reached down and held Amanda's hands in her own soft, wrinkled hands.

"You look like you'll be a wonderful social worker," Gracie said quietly, looking Amanda intently in the eye and squeezing her hands.

The boys finally tired of jumping and ran over to Lars, climbing on his lap. "Can we play marbles, Grampa?" Lars stood up and reached for a Chinese checkers board and a bag of marbles that was resting on top of Gracie's curio cabinet. He set them on the floor next to the boys, and Oliver immediately grabbed the velvet bag and dumped the marbles out on the floor. The boys scrambled to retrieve the marbles that were rolling under the furniture.

Zoe sat down next to Amanda. "You have your hands full with these two," Zoe said, a trace of worry in her voice. "Has Jackie told you how long they're staying?"

Gracie shook her head and whispered, "I think their mother is gone. She hasn't visited the kids since Thanksgiving, and Jackie said their mom didn't show up for court last week. Their dad passed away. Suicide," she whispered. They all watched the boys sadly. "We'd adopt them if we could, but I'm sixty-six and Lars is seventy. It's just not fair to them."

They sat for a minute, finishing their cookies, and then Zoe reluctantly stood up. "I suppose we should go . . ."

"Wait a minute girls," Gracie said, popping up with surprising quickness. She went to the freezer and took out two little packages. "Here are some cookies for you two to take home." Lars came over and stood by the door as they left, having not spoken a word the entire time they were there, but still making them feel like he was glad they were there.

As they were walking to the car, Zoe said, "I love visiting them. I could stay all day." Amanda got back in the van and buckled her seat belt, staring out the window to hide the tears running down her cheeks.

* * *

THE CLARKS LIVED IN A BIG, beautiful house in a new development on the edge of town. It was beige, like every other house on the block, with a three-car garage that was open and showed off a BMW, a huge SUV, and a substantial boat. They parked on the edge of the driveway, and Amanda marveled at an elaborate playhouse in the backyard that had rope ladders connecting it to two large trees, each of which had a small tree house built in it.

"This house must be heaven for all the kids who come here. How do you ever get them to go home?" Amanda asked.

Zoe looked at her. "With a few exceptions, kids always want to go home, no matter how great the foster parents are."

They stood at the double door entrance and rang the bell. Mary Clark opened the door and stepped back, wordlessly inviting them in. The house was even more impressive on the inside, with vaulted ceilings and an open floor plan. The large, modern kitchen was on their left, and to the right was the living room with tall windows along the back wall overlooking their wooded backyard. The house looked like it had been professionally decorated for Christmas in ice blue and white, and their huge Christmas tree matched with blue tulle and icicle ornaments dangling from every branch. It was like a model home, gorgeous and impersonal. Amanda followed Zoe's lead and immediately slipped off her shoes.

"Mary, this is Amanda. She's a new worker with our office. She'll be taking the new case." Mary was tall and willowy, with expertly highlighted blonde hair and icy blue eyes. She looked like she could have won beauty pageants, except for the frown. Mary nodded at Amanda for a brief second without offering her hand, and then looked back at Zoe.

"We weren't supposed to be on crisis care in December." Mary glared at Zoe. "I'm hosting a party tonight. Kids aren't invited."

"Mary, you agreed to this after the Jacobsens quit."

"No, Larry agreed to this. I wanted this month off."

"I'm sorry if there was a misunderstanding. Maybe you can hire a babysitter tonight to watch the kids during the party." Zoe was trying to keep her voice down in case the kids were close by.

"Actually I'd like them to go to respite care until the twenty-sixth." Mary said.

Amanda's jaw dropped.

"Mary . . ." Zoe said, looking angry but choosing her words carefully. "I think it would be really rough to have them go somewhere else for Christmas. They've been through so much already."

"They barely know us. Why would they care if they spend Christmas here or someone else's house?" Mary's expression was unreadable. Something else was going on here.

"Mary, may I ask what this is about. You seem very angry about this placement, but it really seemed that you were okay with getting placements when we met last week. We talked about the party, and last week you said it would be fine if you got some kids."

Just then they heard a door open in the basement, and kids voices. Mary suddenly turned and walked back to the kitchen, ignoring the kids who had just come back inside. Amanda looked at Zoe questioningly, and Zoe looked back and shook her head. Mary busied herself in the kitchen as her husband, Larry, walked upstairs holding a rosy-cheeked baby in his arms.

"We got the tree," Larry said, his eyes shining. He noticed Zoe and Amanda still standing in the entryway. "Oh, hey, Zoe, Merry Christmas."

"Merry Christmas, Larry," Zoe said quietly. "And this must be Anthony." The baby put his head down on Larry's shoulder and wouldn't look at Zoe and Amanda.

"He won't let me put him down," Larry said. "Last night I tried to go to the bathroom without him, and he sat outside the bathroom door and screamed. I finally gave up and let him come in with me. He slept in our bed last night. There was no way he was going to sleep anywhere else." The cupboard doors in the kitchen slammed shut. The situation with Mary suddenly became clear.

"Larry this is Amanda. She's our new worker, and she's going to be the worker for these guys." Larry smiled at her, and switched the baby over to his other side so he could shake Amanda's hand.

"Nice to meet you," Larry said. He looked like he could have been Mary's brother, with dark-blonde hair and a smile that made him look like a news anchor. "You're gonna love these kids. We just cut down a tree in the backyard, and they just had a blast. They've never had a real Christmas tree before, so I said we had to get one. Then I realized that we don't have a tree stand for a real tree, so I need to run down to Target and get one. Do you have extra car seats or should I pick those up too?" The cupboard doors slammed again.

Larry turned around and looked at his wife. He walked over to where she was standing in the kitchen, put his arm around her waist and gave her a squeeze. Amanda could see him whisper in her ear. She put her head down in response. Anthony reached out and grabbed her hair, and Mary immediately recoiled. Larry grabbed Anthony's hand and pretended to gobble it up.

"Let's go and check on your brothers and sister," Larry said, flying Anthony through the air, making the fat little boy guffaw. "They've probably found a way to set that tree up by now. Come on down and meet the kids, ladies."

Amanda looked at Zoe, and Zoe motioned her to follow Larry. Zoe looked like she wasn't sure if she should try to talk to Mary or go downstairs. Mary was pulling things out of the refrigerator, ignoring everyone else in the house. Zoe followed Amanda down the stairs.

They could hear the kids before they could see them.

"Blaze and Justice! That's enough!" The nine-year-old daughter, eldest of the four, was standing in the corner of the room holding the enormous tree up against the wall. She was dark complected like Anthony with round brown eyes, a high forehead, and long mousy-brown hair. The boys looked like they had peeled off their wet shoes and socks and were running around the basement. The room was large and decorated in traditional Minnesota north woods style with knotty pine wall boards and Terry Redlin prints on every wall. There was a beautiful gas fireplace on one wall surrounded by a large denim sectional sofa. The boys raced across the sectional, bouncing on each cushion, until the cushions fell off the couch.

"Hey, let's make a fort!" the older boy yelled.

"Dudes! Slow down a sec," Larry shouted. "Come here and meet Zoe and Amanda."

"No, we're making a fort!" The five-year-old didn't look up, but the four-year-old obediently stood up and came over to Larry.

"Thanks, dude," Larry said, rubbing the boy's dark shaggy hair. "Ladies, this is Justice. He has been my worker man today." Justice stared up at them with the same brown eyes as his sister. His gap-toothed smile revealed he was missing both of his front teeth, and Amanda could see that several of his teeth were capped silver. He was still a gorgeous little boy.

"Blaze, buddy, stand up and come say hello to the ladies. Now." Larry didn't sound angry, just serious. Blaze flew up from under the cushions and raced over to stand by Larry. "And this is Blaze." Blaze waved at Amanda and Zoe, and he seemed to have so much energy he was quivering. He had the family brown eyes, but his lids seemed to droop, making him look sleepy. His skin was dark and the bridge of his nose was flattened. Actually, his whole face seemed to be flat.

"Hi, boys," Zoe said. "You look like you're having lots of fun with Larry."

Blaze jumped up and down and nodded his head wildly. Justice batted his eyes that showed his joy.

"Okay, guys, go play." They bolted away again, climbed on the back of the couch, and dove onto the cushions on the floor. Larry was unfazed by their energy or by the havoc they had wreaked on the furniture.

"Wow," Zoe said. "That is a lot of energy."

Larry nodded happily. "You can't imagine. They're just great though. We had such a great time cutting down the . . . tree!" Larry suddenly veered around to the corner where the boys' older sister had been standing, silently holding the tree propped against the wall. "Oh, crap, Angel, I'm sorry." Angel rolled her eyes and shrugged. Larry gently allowed the tree to rest on the floor, still awkwardly holding Anthony, who refused to be put down.

"We're sorry, too, Angel," Zoe said. "We've been standing here babbling while you were holding that prickly thing against the wall."

Angel went to a recliner closest to the fireplace and sat down. She was indifferent to them, aloof.

Larry looked nervous for the first time as he knelt next to Angel's chair. "I'm really sorry we didn't notice you right away." Angel shrugged again and wouldn't look at Larry. "You were a big help getting the tree." He looked up at Amanda and Zoe. "Angel is going to be a great mother some day. She had those boys under control out there. She could teach me a few things." Angel turned her body away from Larry and stared out the patio doors. Larry squeezed her knee, got up and stood next to Zoe. "Can we talk for a few minutes?" he said under his breath.

"Sure," Zoe said. "Amanda, how about if you get to know the kids a little bit?"

Zoe and Larry went back upstairs, Anthony still on Larry's hip, beginning to look like he was attached. Amanda stared at the kids, no clue what to do next. The boys were on the floor building their fort. Blaze was jumping from the cushionless couch to their pile of cushions and blankets. Justice patiently set the cushions back up every time Blaze knocked them down. Angel continued to stare out the window, but when Amanda sat on the floor by the fireplace, Angel turned slightly toward her.

"Hi, guys, I'm Amanda." She wasn't sure if they knew or cared who she was. "I'm going to be working with you for a while."

"Doing what?" Angel asked, not moving.

"I, um, I'll be helping your mom, with her, uh . . ."

"When are we going home?" Angel interrupted angrily.

"Yeah yeah yeah!" Blaze bounced on the cushions and then draped himself over Amanda's back and wrapped his arms around her neck. "I wanna go home now!" Amanda almost tipped over.

"Whoa, careful, Blaze." He ignored her and kept bouncing.

"Home home home." Amanda felt herself getting frustrated as Blaze kept knocking her in the head with his head. She unwrapped him from her neck and tried to push him back to the couch where Justice was still setting up cushions. Angel stared at the fireplace, angry and braced for the response.

"We're not going, are we? We're never gonna see our mom again." Angel spat the words, trying not to cry.

"Oh, no, Angel, you'll see her. It's just going to take some time to get things figured out."

Angel's chin started to quiver slightly. "How long?" she said.

"I don't know," Amanda stammered. "Cases usually last six months but . . ." At that point, Angel started to cry. She fought valiantly to hold her tears back, but the situation was too much for her nine-year-old mind to handle. She covered her face with a hand and turned her chair toward the patio door.

Suddenly she heard a wail. Amanda turned to find Justice burying his face in the cushion, sobbing.

"Whatsamatter, Dustish," Blaze asked from his perch on the arm of the couch. "Angel, Dustish is sad." Justice jumped up and ran to Angel, burying his head in her lap and sobbing. Angel was still crying silently, but she held Justice's head and rubbed his back.

Amanda gulped back her own sobs. She didn't know who was supposed to tell the kids what was going on, but somehow she had just told them. Knowing that she had screwed up, she wanted to fix it for them, but many of the problems seemed unfixable.

"Don't you like it here?" Amanda asked. "I think Larry is really great. Didn't you have fun cutting down the tree?"

"I wuv dis house," Blaze said. "I want dis a be my house."

Amanda relaxed slightly.

Angel turned to Amanda with a vicious stare. "This isn't our house. We don't live here. *She* doesn't even want us here." Her voice broke again as she said the last sentence, but this time Angel stared straight at Amanda as tears rolled down her face. Amanda wondered if the hurt was more about being away from home or feeling rejected by Mary.

"I don't think that's true . . ."Amanda attempted.

"You KNOW it's true. She's trying to get rid of us for CHRISTMAS! I HEARD her say it. She HATES us." Angel put her head down and sobbed. This made Justice cry harder. Blaze froze when he heard Angel yell. He jumped off the couch, ran to Angel and started to cry, burying his head in her lap next to Justice's tiny wailing head.

Seeing the three of them clutch each other and sob pushed Amanda over the edge. The stress of the day, and seeing these families struggle through a holiday that everyone else seemed to treasure, was all too familiar. She tried to wipe the tears from her cheeks before the kids noticed. "I'm so sorry guys," was all she could muster.

At that point, Zoe and Larry pounded back down the stairs. "Is everybody okay down here," Larry asked, "we heard . . ." Zoe and Larry both stopped when they saw the kids huddled together and stared at Amanda.

"What happened?" Larry asked.

Zoe looked at Amanda questioningly.

Amanda stood up quickly shaking her head. "I was just trying to talk to them, but they wanted to know . . ." She stopped, afraid she would cry again. Zoe nodded knowingly.

"Had you talked to them about how long they would be staying?" Zoe asked Larry under her breath.

"No," Larry said. "We didn't know what was going on."

"Now they know," Zoe said. Larry crouched next to them, putting his hand on Blaze's back.

"Hey, guys, don't you like it here?" Larry asked. "We've been having fun, right?"

Zoe shook her head. "I'm sure it's just really hard because they miss their mom."

At that, Justice started to wail all over again. Larry snapped his head back and looked pointedly at Zoe.

Angel sat up and looked at Larry. "Where are we going to be for Christmas?"

Larry looked nervous.

"Angel," Zoe began, rescuing Larry. "Do you have any relatives that you usually spend Christmas with?"

Angel was wise beyond her years. The look on her face showed that she knew exactly what that question meant. She squared her jaw. "No. We don't have any grandmas or cousins or anything. Nobody in my mom's family talks to her."

"Okay. I got it," Zoe said with a sigh. She looked at Larry again. "Guys, I think we have to get some things figured out . . ."

"You'll be here," Larry interrupted. "We're all going to have Christmas here."

Zoe turned to Larry, her face showing that this was a change from what they had decided upstairs. Larry looked determined. Amanda wanted to hug him.

"Is Santa gonna come?" Blaze asked, hopping up, grabbing Larry's hands, and trying to flip himself over.

"That depends," Larry said. "Have you been naughty or nice?" Larry tickled Blaze's tummy and he dropped to the floor in hysterics.

As Angel watched Larry play with Blaze, her face softened a bit.

chapter fourteen

AMANDA LAID OUT HER GIFTS one last time before packing them into bags to bring to Rosie's house. She felt good about everything she had purchased, and was proud to be able to give something nice to all the girls. She checked the clock. It was 11:15. She gathered her relishes and a new relish tray she bought at the Rochester Super Target, an extra special treat that was worth the drive. Then she carefully packed the gifts in a large shopping bag and carried them out to the car in two trips. The second time, Amanda locked the door, almost dropping the relish tray down the slippery stairs.

Amanda pulled away to Bruce Springsteen's version of "Santa Claus is Comin' to Town" on her car radio. This was her third year spending Christmas with Rosie's family, so she was starting to feel like she knew the routine, starting to feel like she had a place at the table, and if she wasn't there they would miss her.

This was also the first year she didn't feel much of the leftover pain from all the years of sad and pathetic holidays. Seeing Angel sob about spending the holiday away from her mother was gut wrenchingly familiar, but somehow Amanda was able to separate herself from Angel and keep her own past in the past. Visiting with Gracie and Lars had actually been harder, she supposed because Gracie was so maternal. Amanda had learned that she was drawn to the rare souls who were natural mothers. Gracie was one of those moms who could get away with pinching just about anyone's cheeks. But even though there was a part of her that ached because she never had someone like Gracie in her life, that feeling didn't sit like a cloud over her today. It was still in the past.

The drive passed quickly, and Amanda arrived at Rosie's before noon. She was whistling as she pulled into the driveway, but slowed down as there were several unfamiliar cars. Usually Christmas Eve was spent with the immediate family, and they didn't see the rest of the family until midnight mass. Amanda parked in the street, gathered her packages, and went to the door. Hesitating for a second, she remembered what Rosie had always told her to do and let herself in.

From the second she walked in the door, Amanda could feel the tension. A young Hispanic male, no older than sixteen, sat on one side of the sofa, staring uncomfortably at his hands. He looked up when Amanda arrived, but neither of them knew what to say because they didn't know each other, and no one was in the room to introduce them.

Then Amanda could hear the yelling.

Lucy's two youngest sisters, Susanna and Anna, ran through the living room carrying armfuls of Barbies. They brushed past Amanda without saying a word and headed for the semi-finished basement that served as their toy room. The girls were apparently oblivious to the fight occurring in the kitchen, the voices just muffled enough that Amanda couldn't tell what they were saying. She could hear Rosie's shaky voice.

Amanda looked at the boy on the couch again and decided she would rather barge in on the fighting than hang out alone with him. She smiled at him briefly, set her gifts by the tree in the corner on the other side of the couch, and slowly entered the kitchen.

Rosie was standing at the sink wrestling with a ham. Cynthia was standing next to her, tears streaming down her face, arms crossed in front of her in defiance.

"There is no way I'm sending him away, Mama. No way!" Cynthia said.

"The way you talk to me! How dare you speak to your mother like this!?" Rosie shook her head, and Amanda could see Rosie was crying too.

Amanda realized her initial thought was wrong, and hanging out with mystery boy in the living room would have been better than this. She set her things on the kitchen table as unobtrusively as possible.

"How dare you try to put someone out on the street!"

Amanda had never seen Cynthia so angry. Cynthia had grown up in the past year, going from a gawky sixteen-year-old to a stunning seventeen-year-old. She had her family's good looks and a gorgeous figure complete with a booty that would make J-Lo envious. Her entry into the dating world scared the daylights out of Lucy, especially because she was friendly and funny along with being beautiful. Lucy had told Amanda that Cynthia was dating a lot, but so far it was very innocent. Seeing Cynthia, who was usually the family comedienne, like this was completely out of character for her.

"Christmas is for going to mass and celebrating the birth of Jesus. It is a time for family!" Rosie yanked the last of the wrapper off of the ham and stared at it angrily.

Amanda carefully set her bag on the table and quietly started to back out of the kitchen.

"Family, huh? Well then why is Amanda here?"

Amanda felt like she had been punched in the stomach.

"Amanda is family," Rosie said. Tears sprang up in Amanda's eyes at Rosie's words.

"She is not. If she was family then you wouldn't be so nice to her. You'd be a bitch to her like you are to the rest of us." Cynthia's eyes got wide as she realized she had gone too far. Way too far. Rosie's head snapped up as if she had been slapped. She wiped her hands on the kitchen towel, turned and walked out of the kitchen through the door that led to her bedroom. She went into her room and closed the door. Cynthia stood frozen, like she was afraid to move.

Amanda stood by the door with her mouth hanging open, horrified at what she had just seen and heard. Cynthia made eye contact with Amanda for a minute, looking ashamed, and then stormed past her out of the room.

The girls never swore around Rosie. To Amanda's knowledge, none of them swore at all. They had always been respectful to Rosie, never displaying this kind of scene. She assumed the fight was about the boy in the living room who obviously was Cynthia's boyfriend. This must have been a continuation of the fight Amanda had witnessed at Thanksgiving, when Rosie was fighting with Marina and still furious with Cynthia for being under the covers in the basement with her boyfriend watching TV.

But the fight on Thanksgiving had blown over enough that they still had dinner, and the day was bearable. Amanda couldn't imagine Rosie getting over this one enough to even come out of her room.

Amanda could feel the roar beginning in the back of her head that usually came when she was overwhelmed. Not wanting to go there today, she needed to distract herself somehow. The ham was still in the sink, but they usually didn't eat traditional Christmas dinner until Christmas day. Amanda picked up the ham, set it in the roasting pan next to the sink, and put it in the refrigerator. On Christmas Eve, Rosie usually made homemade tortillas and other traditional Mexican food. Amanda had no clue how to make any of Rosie's specialties, but Lucy did.

Her gut was starting to ache. Where was Lucy anyway? Lucy's car hadn't been in the driveway when she arrived.

With nothing else to do, Amanda put together her relish tray and set it in the refrigerator. The clock on the stove said it was 12:37. Usually the family hovered in the kitchen together most of the afternoon making home-made tortillas and fillings, and *sopapillas*. Rosie was usually in her glory on Christmas Eve because she got to teach her girls about their heritage and pass on a Mexican family tradition.

Amanda returned to the living room to find Cynthia defiantly draped across her boyfriend, who was still frozen watching TV. She could hear the little girls downstairs. Not knowing what to say to Cynthia and desperate to find a distraction, Amanda went downstairs to check on Susanna and Anna.

The unfinished basement had been converted into Barbieland. They had two Barbie cars and a jeep, a huge townhouse, and at least fifty Barbies. Since all the girls in the family were obsessed with the blonde and beautiful Barbie at one time or another, they had managed to accumulate everything Mattel had ever made.

Anna looked up at Amanda shyly, but Susanna ran over to Amanda and grabbed her hand. "Hi, Manda."

"Hey, girls. Merry Christmas."

"It's not gonna be," Susanna said solemnly. Anna sat in the corner by the townhouse, trying to arrange the Barbies in the beds for an apparent sleepover.

"Why do you say that? Are you worried that Santa won't come?"

Susanna rolled her eyes at Amanda. "I'm a little old for that, Amanda," she said, precociously. "Anna doesn't even believe that old story anymore."

Amanda found that very sad. "Wow, you girls are getting old," Amanda said. "So if you're not worried about Santa, why won't this be a good Christmas?"

Susanna was trying to get a pair of very tight spandex pants onto the Barbie she was holding. They slid up over Barbie's incredibly long legs, but were stuck at her curvaceous hips. Amanda had never noticed exactly how out of proportion Barbie was. Amanda held out her hands, and Susanna gave her the Barbie so she could try to dress her.

"Mama is so mad at everyone. I don't even know if we're gonna open presents. Lucy got in a fight and left, and now Cynthia was yelling at her. Mama hates all men. That's the problem, you know."

Lucy got into a fight and left. Amanda wanted to ask what she meant by "left," but the girls were more worried about their mom. Amanda pulled and tugged at the spandex pants with no luck. She finally grabbed on with her teeth and moved them a centimeter. "I don't think your mama hates men."

"Yes, she does. She hates them. Lucy and Cynthia were talking about it. Lucy said that her dad was really mean to Mama. Lucy has a different dad, you know," Amanda glanced at Anna, who was unfazed and apparently knew this bit of family history already. "Then Mama got married to our dad, but he died. Now she doesn't want anyone to have boyfriends or get married or anything because she said men are no good."

"My gym teacher is a man," Anna said, putting a Barbie in the jeep next to Ken, who was driving. "He's good. He lets us play trench and soccer and jump rope."

"I'm sure everything will smooth over," Amanda said, not at all convinced or convincing the girls. "Families fight sometimes."

"Our family fights all the time," Anna said.

"Lucy said she's gonna run away and get married," Susanna said, "cuz of Mama."

"Their wedding is all planned. She won't run away," Amanda said, but the words "run away" made her stomach drop.

"I don't even think Mama will go to the wedding," Susanna said. "She's supposed to be making dresses for all of us, and she's hardly started. They're never going to get them done in time."

Susanna, who wasn't playing with anything any more, looked miserable. Amanda couldn't believe Rosie would refuse to go to the wedding. In the years she had known this family, Amanda had been present for a few arguments. One year Marina wanted to wear a very short skirt and tank top to midnight mass. Both Lucy and Cynthia told her she looked terrible.

When Rosie saw her, she gasped, and Marina flounced back to her room to change without another word being spoken. Another year Susanna and Anna were fighting and Susanna pulled Anna's hair hard. Lucy broke up that fight before Rosie found out.

"Susanna, did you say that Lucy left?" Amanda asked.

Susanna was brushing spandex Barbie's long blonde hair. "Yep. She says she's not gonna be here for Christmas."

"But . . . of course she is . . ."

"No she isn't! Lucy and Mama got in a fight about William. Lucy said, 'I've had it,' and ran out the door. She said, 'Merry Christmas, Mama. I won't be back.'" Susanna had tears in her eyes. "That means she won't be here for Christmas."

Amanda swallowed hard. The last time she and Lucy had spoken, Lucy reminded her to be there by noon. She didn't say anything about being with William's family for Christmas, although Amanda realized that Lucy would probably go to his family's house at some point over Christmas. But this was different. Susanna said that Lucy left and wouldn't be back.

Amanda's stomach dropped as she wondered where that left her.

* * *

AMANDA DRESSED A FEW MORE Barbies with the girls until boredom and worry got the best of her. She returned up the stairs. The situation in the living room with Cynthia and her boyfriend hadn't changed, except they were now lying down together on the couch under a blanket. Her hair looked messy, like they actually had the nerve to make out with Rosie one room away.

Back in the kitchen, Marina was sitting at the table eating Doritos. Of all Lucy's sisters, Amanda was the least comfortable with Marina. It seemed that Marina caused the most conflict, though it was never anything like this.

Amanda sat at the table across from Marina. "So . . . Merry Christmas, huh?"

Marina glared at Amanda, but she also seemed anxious to talk. "Bet you wish your mom was still alive so you didn't have to deal with this."

Amanda was shocked that Marina made reference to her mother. She never knew how much Lucy had told her family about Amanda's situation.

"Actually, my Christmases were never much when my mom was alive. We'd probably be eating at a soup kitchen or something like that."

Marina's eyes widened. "Really? Was your mom crazy?"

Hard question, though Amanda had definitely considered it before. "Not crazy, exactly, just messed up."

Marina nodded. "Mama's messed up too. Our whole family is messed up."

"You guys have never seemed messed up to me. I think your family is wonderful."

Marina snorted.

"Seriously, Marina, you don't know how lucky you are. A lot of people would give anything to have a house and a family that loves them." Amanda was one of those people.

"Yeah, well, I don't know about any of that. Mama's losing it. Lucy and Cynthia don't see it because they're too busy screwing their boyfriends, but I see it. She can't remember stuff. She cries when nothing has happened. She sleeps all the time." Marina looked worried, and much older than her fourteen years. Amanda always had the impression that she wanted to be as distant as possible from the family, but today she looked like she just wanted her family to be okay.

"She sounds depressed," Amanda said. "People sleep a lot and can get really groggy and out of it when they are depressed."

"You're probably right," Marina said.

"She could get on medication, and that could help a lot."

"Yeah, right. There is no way she would take medication. If she's sad, she thinks that's what God wants for her. She would think she deserves to be sad. She probably thinks Lucy getting pregnant is her fault because she is a bad mom, so she's coming down on the rest of us twice as hard." Marina started to cry.

"Do you really think she's that upset about Lucy being pregnant? You think that's the cause of all of this?"

"Mama said to Lucy today that William is just like Lucy's father. Mama *hates* Lucy father, and Lucy knows it. That's why Lucy got mad and left."

"You don't think she's coming back?"

"She said she's not. I was standing there when she left. She told me 'sorry.'"

The roar in the back of Amanda's head just got louder.

* * *

AMANDA AND MARINA SAT at the table a while longer, until the little girls came upstairs wondering what was happening. They all felt the tension and no one knew what to do about it. Finally, Amanda and Marina decided to start cooking in hopes that they could draw Rosie out of her room that way.

After an hour of attempting to make shredded beef and refried beans (with Amanda trying to find recipes and Marina trying to remember spices and oven temperatures), it became apparent that Rosie was not going to come out of her room on her own. Marina knocked softly on her bedroom door. When there was no reply, Marina opened her door a crack, stared for a moment, and then closed it again.

"She's sleeping," Marina said tearfully. "She didn't move when I opened the door or whispered her name. I don't know what to do."

Amanda didn't either. Amanda didn't feel like she could approach Rosie and talk to her because she was afraid Rosie would see her actions as disrespectful. But she was afraid that eating their special meal without Rosie would be disrespectful too.

"I think we should wake her in time for her to get ready for church," Amanda finally said. "We know she won't miss that. Then hopefully she'll perk up, and we can eat after church."

So the Ramirez girls and Amanda, minus Lucy, awkwardly sat around the house until it was time to get ready for the Christmas Eve mass at 4:30. At 3:30, Marina brought the little girls to their rooms to get dressed. Amanda cleaned up the kitchen. Cynthia, who defiantly hadn't left her perch on the couch, wandered out to the kitchen.

"So what's going on? Is everybody still going to church?" Cynthia asked, not acknowledging any role she might have in the family conflict.

At that moment, Amanda wanted to slap Cynthia. The letdown from preparing for Christmas and having it fall apart was unbearable. Amanda was much angrier with Lucy for abandoning the family, and especially for abandoning her, although she knew it was selfish to be more concerned about herself when the family was in such crisis.

"Of course everyone's still going to church," Amanda said brusquely.

Cynthia put her hands on her hips. "All right, Amanda. You don't have to get pushy too. It's bad enough that I get it from my own family."

Another jab at her outsider status. All of this was so out of character for Cynthia, and part of her wanted to ask her if she was okay. A bigger part of her still wanted to slap her. Cynthia flounced out of the room.

By 4:00 the kitchen was presentable, with the pans covered and put into the refrigerator hopefully for dinner after church. With nothing else to do, Amanda found her purse and went to the hallway mirror to check her hair and put on lipstick. Cynthia and her boyfriend were putting on their coats.

"We'll meet you there," Cynthia said to Marina, who was doing Susanna's hair in the bathroom. Cynthia and her boyfriend went out the door before anyone could answer. Susanna looked up at Marina silently, watching for her reaction.

Suddenly they heard Rosie's bedroom door open. She emerged from the kitchen wearing her church clothes. Her face looked gray and tired, and her eyes seemed to be half open. She didn't look at anyone as she silently took her coat from the hall closet.

Anna ran to her Mama and hugged her. Rosie held her for a moment with her eyes closed. The group shuffled out the door to Rosie's van in the garage, still not acknowledging that Cynthia and Lucy were not there.

* * *

WHEN AMANDA LOOKED BACK on that Christmas Eve, she realized that the reason it hurt so much was that she thought her years of pathetic holidays were over. After spending December 23 going to clients' and foster parents' homes, each with a different sad Christmas story, she believed she was finally on the other side of the fence. Amanda thought she was officially part of the world that didn't ache from Thanksgiving through the New Year. She thought that she had finally become normal, at least in that regard.

Which was why Lucy's abandonment and the Ramirez's terrible family feud hurt so much worse than any Christmas spent at a soup kitchen. The ugly truth was that Amanda thought she was better than that.

Even though the day improved slightly after church, the gnawing in her gut never went away. Church seemed to calm Rosie, so that when they went back to the house they ate a subdued dinner with store-bought tortillas. Cynthia brought her boyfriend back to the house, and Rosie was civil enough to pass him the sour cream at dinner. The little girls were excited about their gifts, and Rosie gave Amanda a warm smile when she opened her certificate for a massage. But when all the gifts were opened and there were piles of wrapping paper and boxes everywhere, there was still a small group of unopened gifts under the tree.

Somehow Amanda expected Lucy to return that night. She never believed that Lucy would truly stay away from her family, and Amanda, on Christmas.

Everyone went to bed early that Christmas Eve. Amanda slept in Lucy's bed, just as she usually did when she spent holidays with the Ramirezes. She lay in bed awake for a long time, stinging emotions swirling in her head. She was barely aware that her fists were clenched, fingernails digging into her palms

chapter fifteen

THE WEEK AFTER CHRISTMAS PASSED quickly at work, and before Amanda knew it, New Year's Eve, the day of Lucy and William's wedding, had arrived. Amanda had managed to avoid Lucy all week by turning off the ringer on her phone and unplugging her answering machine so she could legitimately say she did not know Lucy had called. Not knowing whether or not Lucy had tried to call was difficult too, but the need to avoid her was stronger than her curiosity.

Amanda had also avoided Jake all week at work, so she had not spoken with anyone about the final wedding plans. She didn't know whether Rosie finished the dresses, or what kind of flowers Lucy had chosen, or what time to be at the church to get ready.

Instead of dealing with her personal life, Amanda focused on her job and the people who were officially crazier than she was. Amanda learned that Angel, Blaze, Justice, and Anthony actually had a very nice Christmas at the foster home, despite the bitchy Mary. Amanda spent over two hours with Angel one afternoon, chatting with her about volleyball, school, and about her family. Angel was rather tightlipped about her mother, but she had no problem talking about the other people they had come into contact with in their travels. Angel, age nine, told of the man who was HIV positive who took so many medicines that he could swallow handfuls of pills at once. She talked about the house they lived in that had an actual hole in the bathroom floor that her mother covered with heavy cardboard so they could use the toilet. Then there was the trailer they lived in that had no heat or running water, so they peed in a five-gallon bucket and showered at swimming lessons, which they attended on a scholarship. Angel told Amanda that her father was in prison, and she had never met him, although her mother showed her his mug shot on the Department of Corrections website on the public library computer. Blaze's dad was the one Angel remembered the best and feared the most.

Amanda also finished the reunification plan with Hailey, and Hailey and Charlie started having regular visits at Hailey's mom's house. Hailey had actually decided to move out of her own apartment at the end of the month and move back home with her mom so she could be with Charlie every day. Hailey seemed intent on changing her life, and she was working hard.

Amanda spent New Year's Eve morning catching up on casenotes about Hailey, and writing the long, sordid social history for Angel's family. The detachment with which Angel described her life was disturbingly familiar to Amanda, though Amanda also knew that she wasn't nearly as detached as she used to be. Amanda credited Lucy for helping her break down her defenses and participate in her own life. Unfortunately, Amanda had realized over the past several weeks that she couldn't seem to get her defenses back up when she wanted them back.

The office closed at noon, so Amanda reluctantly went home to prepare for the wedding she didn't want to face.

When she parked on the street by her apartment, Amanda could see the wardrobe bag that must have contained her dress hanging on the screen door. She climbed the steps carefully, noticing only one set of footprints in the snow that had fallen that morning. Whoever delivered the dress came alone. Amanda wondered if it was Lucy, or if someone was helping her handle the last minute arrangements.

Amanda grabbed the dress and brought it inside, finding a note attached to the hanger.

"Amanda, where have you been, sweetie? I've been trying to call you all week. I hope nothing is wrong. Here is your dress. William's aunt finished them last night, so I hope it fits. See you at the church at 3:00. William's cousin will go there to do your hair if you want yours done. Love, Lucy."

No mention of Christmas.

Amanda threw the dress on the table with her purse and keys. The hurt that she had felt all week turned to anger at Lucy's lack of acknowledgement. Family used to be the most important thing to Lucy, but now it seemed that she was so self-absorbed that she didn't care about any of them.

Amanda decided that if Lucy could skip Christmas, it was her turn to skip the next big event. Even if that big event happened to be Lucy's wedding.

Amanda turned off the lights and went to bed.

* * *

SHE WASN'T SURE WHEN SHE realized she was awake. There was some kind of noise, but it could have been part of her creepy dream. Amanda had been dreaming she was getting married to Cynthia's adolescent boyfriend. They had been holding hands in the front of Lucy's church, and Amanda looked back and saw that no one was on her side of the church except for Lucy and William. The only people on the "groom's" side of the church were homeless people there for the free meal.

Amanda rolled over to find Jake leaning over her bed. She screamed and clutched the covers to her chest for some meager protection.

"Hey, I'm sorry. I'm sorry. You have got to start locking that door," Jake said, looking worried and annoyed.

"What the hell are you doing in here? Jeez, Jake, you scared me to death." Amanda sat up, embarrassed and angry, trying to pat down her hair and rub her cheeks to wake up.

"I'm here to pick you up, sleepy. You're going to be late." He went back to the kitchen and brought her dress into her bedroom. Already in his tuxedo, Amanda realized for the first time in a long time how good looking he really was. "I can't believe you're not dressed yet. You women take forever getting ready. Are you dressing at the church?"

Amanda was looking at her blanket and gritting her teeth, feeling embarrassed and exposed. "I didn't ask you to pick me up."

He lifted his hands and stared at her. "What's the problem, Amanda?"

She swallowed hard. "I'm not going." She sounded like a six-year-old.

"What?" he said skeptically. "Get up. Come on, you're gonna make me late too."

Amanda stuck her chin out defiantly. When she said it out loud, skipping Lucy's wedding sounded horrible. It would be a friendship-ending act. Amanda didn't want to end the friendship, but it was hard to think past her hurt to know what she did want to do.

Slowly, Amanda dragged herself out of bed and went to the bathroom to change.

* * *

THEY DROVE TO THE WEDDING in silence. Amanda was surprised that Jake didn't ask why she was sleeping when she should have been getting ready. She frowned at her black shoes, frustrated that she didn't have time to shop for something better.

They arrived at the church a few minutes after 3:00. As they climbed the stone steps and went inside, Amanda thought that she had attended St. Joseph's enough times with Lucy's family that it felt like her home church, if she had one. It was the largest church in town, easily seating 500 people. The aisle that Lucy would walk down stretched past at least thirty pews.

"I think the women are downstairs," Jake said, and he left in search of William and the men.

She took the stairs slowly, suddenly very nervous. Not only had she never been a bridesmaid, Amanda had actually never been in a wedding. She didn't know how to act or what to say.

When Amanda reached the bottom of the stairs, she could hear laughing and talking in the room ahead of her, which was the bridal dressing area next to the bathrooms. She pulled in a deep breath and walked in.

Cynthia walked by her first, smiling and flushed, on her way to the restroom. The room was very hot with at least fifteen women squeezed in trying to see themselves in the mirror. Marina was gathering her hair to make a high ponytail, bobby pins sticking out of her mouth.

"Hey, Amanda," she said, also surprisingly upbeat.

Amanda recognized most of the women from William's house. Through the tangle of bodies she could see Lucy sitting in the corner, her short legs stretched out under her dress. Right after she and William got engaged, Lucy found her perfect wedding dress, which she had modeled for Amanda and her sisters on Thanksgiving. Lucy had chosen a straight, simple white dress that actually had some spandex to move with her growing breasts and belly. It was straight and slightly gathered on the bodice with spaghetti straps, and the fabric dipped a little to show off her newly acquired cleavage. As Lucy was getting her hair done, Amanda admired the dress's elegant simplicity all over again.

"Oh, Amanda, you can't wear your hair like that," Cynthia said as she breezed back into the room. Cynthia wore her hair in a low ponytail with a rhinestone clip. Amanda hadn't done a thing to hers except brush it quickly after she yanked her dress on. "Let's give you big Barbie hair." Cynthia grabbed one of several curling irons and a big vent brush.

"No way," Amanda said. "If you want big hair, do your own that way."

"Come on," Cynthia said. "I've never gotten to play with blonde hair before."

"Oh, shut up," Amanda said, but she smiled and let Cynthia have her way. Amanda's hair was "Minnesota blonde," which was the same washed out dark-blonde color that many Scandinavian girls in Minnesota had. Cynthia pulled it back into a tight ponytail that she curled into smooth curls that sat at the base of her neck.

"Oooh, Amanda, look at you," Marina said as she made her way over to them. "Your hair is beautiful, but please let me give you some make-up."

As the girls put on her face, Amanda watched the other women in the mirror. Everyone in the room was bubbling and happy, including Cynthia and Marina. William's mother was there painting Lucy's nails, and his cousin was still working on her hair. A few other women who looked like William's relatives were working on each other's hair, and another who must have been William's seamstress aunt was fussing with Lucy's dress. Lucy still had not seen or acknowledged Amanda's presence. She wanted to ask what was going on, but she was afraid to stir up tension.

"Where's Amanda?" Amanda heard Lucy ask. "Please tell me she's here somewhere."

Amanda couldn't find her voice to answer.

"We're over here," Cynthia yelled. Lucy turned around and saw Amanda in front of the mirror.

"Hey, sweetie. I've missed you this week." Lucy freed her arm and reached out to grab Amanda's hand. Amanda smiled weakly at her friend, who had always been pretty, but today was luminous. Amanda wanted to let go of her anger, but she couldn't seem to push it away. Lucy watched Amanda's face, looking like she wanted to say something, but then just smiled faintly and looked away.

Rosie came up behind Amanda, placing her warm hand on Amanda's back, and handed her a bouquet of flowers. Rosie was wearing a dress similar to the bridesmaid dresses, but more matronly. She moved among the women, quietly handing out the bouquets to her daughters, and pinning flowers on the rest of the women. Rosie and William's seamstress aunt shared a few words and hugged. Somehow they had resolved the issue of the dresses, and there appeared to be no hard feelings. Finally, Rosie carried the bridal bouquet to Lucy, who was getting the finishing touches on her hair and veil. Lucy stood in front of her mother, and Rosie took Lucy's hands.

"My chiquita," she said softly. Rosie held out her arms, and Lucy melted into her mother. This time Lucy wasn't the only one who cried away her mascara.

* * *

THE CEREMONY WAS A BLUR for Amanda until the vows. The priest was kind enough to tell them that the maid of honor and best man should join the couple as they said their vows. William and Lucy stood across from each other, holding hands, and Jake and Amanda came up and stood a step up from them on either side of the priest.

Lucy never stopped smiling or crying. William looked serious at first as he said his vows, as if he wanted Lucy to know how much he meant his promises. His voice cracked with emotion. When it was Lucy's turn, she never took her eyes off him. As they exchanged rings, they never let go of each others' hands.

Lucy and William went to their kneelers, and Jake and Amanda sat down. There was a blessing, and then Lucy and William were pronounced husband and wife. They kissed and hugged and kissed again, and then went back down the aisle holding hands as husband and wife. Amanda stood watching them until Cynthia nudged her in the back, reminding her to take Jake's arm and go back down the aisle. As they made it to the back of the church, they found Lucy and William holding each other. Jake patted William on the back, and they finally let go of each other. William and Jake hugged, and then Lucy practically lunged at Amanda and hugged her.

"Thank you for being here for me, " Lucy whispered.

Amanda hugged back, feeling awful because she almost wasn't there for her best friend. "Congratulations," she managed. "I know you're both going to be so happy."

William's mother arrived and whisked Lucy and William back into the church to excuse people from their pews.

Jake edged back over to Amanda and pulled her aside.

"Here, you're a mess," he said. He took out a handkerchief and wiped the tears off her cheeks that Amanda didn't even realize were there. "You're not used to make up or weddings," he said quietly. "You girls always cry at weddings."

"I've never been to one before," Amanda said, softened by Jake's gentle gesture.

"Yeah, well, I've been to a lot of them, " he said, pushing the handkerchief into her hand. "The vows always get me too."

* * *

AMANDA RODE TO THE RESTAURANT for the reception with Jake and a couple of ushers, two of William's innumerable cousins. When they arrived they headed for the bar instead of the reception hall. Jake bought them a round of drinks, and she noticed he had a Coke. Amanda ordered a glass of the house wine. They were quickly joined by several of William's friends and family, who all ordered pitchers of beer and bottles of wine.

When they finally moved to the reception area, many members of the wedding party had a festive buzz starting. Amanda wanted to provide a good example for the bridal party, who were all quite underage, but Jake seemed to make sure her glass was always full. She sat down at the head table next to Jake and found she was feeling more than a little tipsy herself.

"You look like you're having a better time," Jake said as he settled in next to her and dug into the mixed nuts.

"Better than you, apparently," Amanda said. "You're the only one not drinking tonight."

"Doesn't mix with my medications," he said as Cynthia sat down next to him. Amanda stared at him, unsure how to react and wanting to ask what he meant. She knew from snooping that he was on several medications including an antidepressant, and she was still afraid the medications meant that his cancer was back. Neither one of them had said a word about cancer, his or her mom's, since they had renewed their friendship.

William's uncle grabbed a microphone at the entrance of the hall and announced that Mr. and Mrs. William Roberts were entering the room. William and Lucy ran in the room together, holding hands and still laughing.

Lucy and William worked the room together, hugging friends and family at every table.

Amanda still stared at Jake, trying to summon the courage to ask about his medications, but he was wrapped into a conversation with Cynthia and William's cousin.

The wedding dinner was a new experience for Amanda. People clinking silverware on their glasses to get the couple to kiss, telling stories and making toasts at the microphone, coming up to the head table to congratulate the new couple and meet the bridal party.

As their delicious and very Minnesotan walleye and steak dinner was being cleared away, the waitress brought another bottle of wine. Jake refilled her glass but still didn't take any for himself. Trix and Michael came to the head table to say hello to Jake and Amanda.

"You look gorgeous, sweetie," Trix said, grabbing her hands.

Amanda smiled in reply.

They all watched as Lucy and William fed each other cake, another tradition Amanda had only seen on TV. William gently tried to edge his piece in Lucy's mouth, but then Lucy smudged some frosting on his nose.

"That Lucy is an absolute doll," Trix said. "Did you two meet up at the U?"

Amanda forgot that Trix knew her before she went to college. The summer she spent with them was so distant, yet still such a strong memory for her. "We met during my third year of college and were roommates the next two years."

"Jakey and William practically grew up together," Trix said. "When Michael and I were still just dating and Jakey was in grade school, we would go to Michael's house for New Year's Eve and the Fourth of July, and William's family was always there. It was harder to stay connected when Jake got sick, so we missed out on William dating Lucy in high school. I remember hearing about her around prom time from William's mom. She just adores Lucy."

And Rosie can't stand William and compares him to Lucy's deadbeat dad, Amanda thought. Or at least that was how she used to feel. The sudden reconciliation between Lucy and Rosie was a mystery.

It was also surprising to hear Trix talk about Jacob's cancer. Amanda searched Trix's face for signs of worry about Jacob's current health. Trix didn't seem preoccupied or stressed, and she wasn't fussing over Jacob.

Susanna and Anna were going from table to table handing out dessert plates with cake. Anna brought Amanda a piece of cake and giggled. "Is he your boyfriend?" Amanda blushed like a grade schooler. Jake put his arm around the back of her chair. Trix beamed.

* * *

THE DANCE STARTED SHORTLY after dinner. The DJ started them off with a song for the bride and groom: "What a Wonderful World" by Louis Armstrong. Lucy wrapped her arms around William and closed her eyes.

The DJ announced that the bridal party should join the couple for the second song.

Amanda's eyes grew wide. "That's us again," Jake said. Somehow Amanda forgot that there would be dancing at the wedding too. Jake took her hand and led her to the dance floor. He wrapped one arm around her back and held her other hand. The scent of his cologne brought back the memory of their night together so strongly that it took her breath away. She put her head down, embarrassed and afraid he could read her mind. She had conflicting urges to wrap her arms around him and push him away and run at the same time.

"So you've really never been to a wedding?" he asked.

"You know I haven't," Amanda said, still unable to make eye contact.

"So you don't know about the tradition where the best man and maid of honor sleep together on the wedding night." Jake was straight faced.

Amanda stopped dancing and stared at him.

Jake laughed out loud. "I'm kidding!"

Amanda turned bright red, afraid that she had given her thoughts away.

"It's fun to leave you speechless," he said. "When I razz you, you either bite my head off or your mouth drops open and you don't say a word. I haven't figured out how to predict which response I'll get."

"That doesn't seem to stop you, does it?" Amanda said, still trying to regain her composure, still smelling his cologne, still feeling his arms around her. The wine had lowered her defenses and made it harder for her to think.

"It's way too much fun to harass you. I couldn't leave you alone if I tried."

She couldn't help but smile at that.

* * *

THE DANCE PASSED QUICKLY for Amanda. She danced several more times with Jacob, once with William, and she had a hilarious spin with Michael around the dance floor when he tried to teach her to polka.

It was after 11:00 p.m. when the DJ announced the last dance. Jake found Amanda sitting with Cynthia and Marina, who were both exhausted, crabby and rubbing their feet from the uncomfortable dress shoes. He took her hand and led her out for the last dance.

They were both quiet for several moments. "I'm staying at my parent's house tonight," Jake finally said quietly. "You're welcome to stay there too."

"Oh, I should probably just go back home," Amanda said. "I didn't plan on staying here."

"You didn't plan on coming at all, you mean," Jake said.

He caught her off guard. "No. I wasn't going to come," she admitted with shame.

"Do you know how much that would have ruined this day for Lucy?"

"I'm here, Jake, okay? I don't need a lecture." Amanda started to pull away from him.

"I'm just saying that it would have been awful. For both of you." He pulled her back so she couldn't leave. "What could Lucy have done that was so bad that you'd stand her up at her own wedding?"

Amanda sighed. Nothing was that bad, and she knew it. Amanda was very glad that Jake picked her up and made her go to the wedding. But somehow she wanted to explain herself to him.

"I was just upset because Lucy skipped Christmas. By the time I got to her mom's house on Christmas Eve, Lucy had gotten into a fight with Rosie and left. She never came back and never called. She didn't spend Christmas with any of them . . ." It still hurt.

To Amanda's surprise, Jake didn't chew her out. Instead he nodded understandingly. "So you spent Christmas with Lucy's family, but no Lucy."

She nodded. Jake pulled her a little closer. "For future reference, you are always welcome with me and my family on any holiday, or any regular day for that matter."

Validation, she realized at that moment, was all she needed to let it go, and his offer seemed to bring her feet back to the ground with the rest of the world. Amanda put both arms around Jake and hugged him, inhaling his familiar, soothing cologne and wanting the moment never to end.

chapter sixteen

AMANDA WOKE UP STARING at Bozo the Clown. She was confused until she remembered where she was. Jake had brought her back to the Mann's house after the wedding. Trix served them ice cream at the dining room table before anyone could argue. Then without even asking, Trix brought Amanda a t-shirt and shorts to sleep in. Amanda took them and went to bed, saying goodnight to Jake as he headed downstairs to his old bedroom. Amanda had watched him go, wondering if this is what he meant when he offered that she could spend the night at his parents' house.

She rolled out of bed and found Trix in the kitchen making French toast.

"Morning, sweetie." Trix had already showered and was dressed for the day. Amanda realized her hair was still frozen into her stiff style from the night before. She started pulling at the bobby pins. "Have a seat. I don't think Jake is up yet. That boy is approaching thirty, but he can still sleep like a growing teenager."

Pulling on her sticky hair added to Amanda's already pounding headache.

"Do you think I could have some Tylenol?"

Trix smiled and passed her the bottle that was already on the counter. Amanda sat at the bar stool on the other side of the counter.

"So how do you like your job," Trix asked, opening a package of sausage.

"I think I like it, " Amanda said. "There's so much to learn, but I think I'm getting the hang of it."

"Were you as surprised as Jacob when you two were assigned to that case together?"

"Yeah," she admitted. "Really surprised."

"I'll bet he's a good lawyer," Trix said. "He's always been so smart and so good with people."

Amanda nodded. "I think he's very good. I haven't seen him in action much yet, but he seems to have good instincts."

"I've always had good instincts," Jake said, as he made his way upstairs and plunked himself down next to Amanda. His curly hair was sticking up all over his head, and he rubbed his eyes like he had a headache even though he had no alcohol that Amanda ever saw.

The smell of the sausage browning made Amanda realize she was famished in the hung-over way of her college days.

"How did you like the big-bucks lawyer in that case, Amanda?" Trix asked, scrambling eggs in a pan. "Jake told us he was a worm."

Amanda looked quizzically at Jake, surprised he had told them about their meeting with Skip Huseman. Jake didn't seem to notice her look.

"I don't know. I thought he was working very hard." Amanda thought a minute. "I guess it was like a power play. There was nothing genuine about him, even though he leaned across the table and tried to talk to us like he had known us forever."

Jake smiled. "Like I said—he was a worm."

"Who is . . . Skip Huseman?" Michael said, coming in the kitchen in running clothes. Amanda remembered that he always ran in the morning.

"He's the one," Jacob said, and turned to Amanda. "Michael graduated with Skip."

"I didn't know you were from Terrance," Amanda said.

"I don't exactly claim it," Michael said, maneuvering around Trix to get some coffee, and he helped himself to Tylenol. "I grew up in California, but when my dad died, my mom moved us to Terrance to be closer to her family. I was in tenth grade when we moved there." Michael stuck out his tongue and made a face.

"So you didn't like it there?" Amanda said.

"No, I did not," Michael said. "I'm sure there are many fine people who live there, but it also has more than it's share of total scum. Skip is a classic Terrance guy. He always thinks he's the biggest fish in any pond."

Michael was usually so laid back and easy going that it was unusual to hear him sound almost hostile.

"Amanda, you must see some of what Michael is talking about," Trix said.

Amanda shrugged, not really sure what he was talking about. "The only thing I have noticed about Terrance is that there are 'Terrance people' and then there's everybody else. People who grew up in Terrance have lived there all their lives and want it to be their own little society."

"I think that happens in any small town," Trix said, "at least to some degree. I grew up in Nebraska, and any time I go back for class reunions there are the people who stayed and raised their families there, so they update us on the town gossip." She pulled a coffee cake out of the oven, and Amanda wondered exactly how early Trix must have gotten up that morning. "There's something different going on in Terrance."

"Different how?" Amanda asked.

Jake and Trix both looked at Michael to explain. Michael sighed. "I don't exactly know how to explain it. When I moved there, I never really got to know anyone except a couple of other kids who had recently moved there too. No one would let me in. The guys stuck in the same crowds they had been in since kindergarten, and they dated only certain girls. There was a group of about twenty jocks who moved their way through this group of girls. Each one dated a different one, then it was almost like they would yell switch and suddenly everyone had a new girlfriend."

Amanda shrugged. "I think my high school was kind of like that. There were certain girls who wanted to date the entire football team, so they made their way through them."

"No, this was very different." Michael looked serious. "It was like they were a bunch of Quakers. The girls didn't socialize with the guys. At hockey games or parties, the girls were in one group and the guys were in another, but at the end of the night everyone would pair off and disappear. And the girls wouldn't talk to anyone other than their boyfriend. It was like they couldn't."

Amanda looked at Jake, who was frowning and nodding. "People in my office talk about it."

"Talk about what," Amanda said, still trying to understand. Amanda wasn't alive at this time, so it was hard for her to know how guys and girls interacted in those days. Maybe this was surprising to him because he came from California where everyone was more relaxed. "What do your coworkers say?"

"A couple of the attorneys who have been around forever talk about it. With the true 'Terrance people,' the men are in charge of their wives. The boys are in charge of their girlfriends from an early age. And Terrance seems to have an unusually large number of girls who mysteriously move away for about nine months."

Amanda thought back to her own high school. She was vaguely aware of rumors about a certain girl moving away, having a baby while she stayed with relatives, and then returning to school the following year with no baby. But there were two others in Amanda's class who had their babies and came back to school, and it wasn't a big deal. "So there are a lot of girls who get pregnant," she said.

"A lot of pregnancies, no babies," Trix said.

Amanda sat back, thinking about one of her social work classes that had a panel of speakers come in to talk about teen pregnancy. Two girls kept their babies, and two girls placed them for adoption. All of the girls had worked with a pregnancy counselor in a private agency who had helped them think through their options and make the decision that was right for them. All of the girls talked about why they made their decision. Amanda had written a paper about the options available to teenagers who were sexually active and got pregnant, and she found that Minnesota had more services than most states. What Michael was describing didn't fit with what she had learned in her class. The girls on the panel were all empowered to make their choices. The girls in Terrance didn't sound like they were empowered at all.

chapter seventeen

WITH THE NEW YEAR ON ITS WAY, school resumed and Amanda returned to the igloo.

The class of truant kids was surprisingly upbeat, considering they had to be back in school full time. Chad and Katelyn both had new piercings. Katelyn had added several studs to the top of her left ear, and Chad had put a large expander in his ear that would stretch the hole wide open. Amanda couldn't stand to look at his bright red ear lobe, stretched so far it looked like it would tear apart.

They were in back of the school again, and Madge had spent her Christmas holiday researching igloo building. She was full of ideas for her group, though she insisted on giving them hints and not doing their work for them.

"Hey, teacher," Chad said, jumping up and down trying to fight the cold. "Can't we just flunk igloo class and go inside?"

Amanda was on the ground again, this time with Matty, who shocked her by volunteering to dig a hole in the snow. Amanda ignored him, growing more frustrated by the minute. Brittany stood shivering in a short leather jacket, no hat, mittens, or boots. She put her hands on the back of Chad's neck.

"Hey, like I'm not effing cold enough," he yelled.

Brittany laughed and whined. "Give me your hat, Chad. I'm gonna freeze to death."

He groaned but gave her his plain black stocking cap. She put her hands in it and held in to her face. Katelyn, who was standing on the other side of the igloo, jealous, moved over to the other side of Chad.

"What are you gonna give me?" Katelyn asked Chad.

Tyler mumbled something, and Katelyn turned around and punched Tyler in the stomach. The ensuing fight happened before Amanda could get herself off the ground. Tyler grabbed Katelyn's arm and twisted it behind her back until she screamed. Chad grabbed Tyler, pulled him away from Katelyn, and threw him on the ground.

"You fucking puss, beatin' up a girl?" Chad yelled in his face. Tyler, who was lying face down in the snow, pulled himself up and charged at Chad and knocked him to the ground. Chad was twice Tyler's size, and immediately had Tyler on his back. Chad hit Tyler in the face several times before Amanda almost jumped on Chad's back.

"Get off of him!" she yelled, holding his right arm with both of her arms. Tyler's nose was bleeding, but he lay in the snow staring venomously up at Chad without saying a word. Still holding his arm, she made Chad stand up.

"Brittany, go get Madge. Matty, run inside and tell the secretary in the office that we need the school cop and the nurse." Amanda tried to give Tyler her scarf for his nose, but he wouldn't take it. He stood up and started walking toward the school.

"Hey," Katelyn yelled at Amanda. "You gonna let him get away with attacking me just because he's got a little bloody nose?"

"He's not getting away with anything," Amanda said, watching him walk away with his hands by his side, blood running down his face. "Right now that kid needs some space."

* * *

DEALING WITH THE AFTERMATH of the fight took the rest of Amanda's day. The school liaison officer called two more officers to the school. Chad was arrested and taken to a secure detention facility for adolescent males. Tyler left the building and was located by another officer, who tried to bring him back to the school. Tyler refused to get out of the squad car, so he was eventually taken to the secure detention center also. They all had to give verbal and written statements to the police officer.

When the police were done, Amanda had to try to explain herself to Madge, the school principal, and Max. The four of them met in a conference room outside of Madge's room.

"I honestly don't know how it got started so fast. The whole thing lasted less than sixty seconds. The kids were standing there talking one minute, and the next minute they were on the ground."

"The girls say Tyler said something to instigate the whole thing," Madge said. "Supposedly Tyler said something crude about Katelyn, she punched him, and then he really went after her.

The principal, a fiftyish man who was used to being the most important person in the room, questioned whether or not two women should be in charge of ten emotionally disturbed students that far away from the building with no back-up nearby. Madge was deeply offended by this. They got into an argument, and Amanda and Max could both see that the principal was not exactly a fan of Madge's program.

The meeting finally ended with the principal telling them to stick to more traditional teaching methods until further notice. Madge was indignant but quiet, and Amanda wasn't sure if she was angry with the principal or with her. Amanda walked with Max to the parking lot.

"I feel like I really screwed this up," Amanda said as they passed a group of students who Amanda could hear were talking about the fight.

"No," Max said with a deep sigh. "One of the commissioners wanted a social worker in the schools as a concession to the cops so they could have more guys on the streets. This was a tough assignment for anyone. This isn't your fault."

Amanda still felt horrible that she couldn't handle a bunch of fifteen-year-olds any better than this.

Max got in his truck and went back to the office, and Amanda headed back to the classroom to collect her files. As Amanda walked by a large group of lockers, Brittany ran up to her and grabbed her arm.

"Amanda, I have to talk to you right now." Amanda knew that Brittany was in the program for kids with behavior problems because of her history of depression and suicide attempts, and because of her ability to disrupt by creating drama where none existed.

Amanda sighed. "I really can't right now, Brittany. I haven't even had lunch yet."

Brittany was still holding on to her arm. "It's really serious, Amanda. Really serious. My cousin Jess said her friend told her what's happening to her and it's really bad." Amanda barely remembered the conversation she and Brittany had before Christmas about Brittany's cousin's friend.

"Are you saying she wants to make a report about something?" Amanda asked. "Because if she does we need to do this in a more formal way . . ."

"Amanda." Brittany looked worried and a little excited at the same time, and Amanda knew she was enjoying the drama as much as she was concerned about this girl's welfare. "This is not a girl who's going to sit down and do an interview with the cops. Please just come talk to her."

Her lunch didn't seem to be a good enough reason to put Brittany off, so she reluctantly followed her to the girls' locker room.

"I'll tell you right now," Amanda said as they were walking into the locker room. "We are not doing this interview in the bathroom."

Amanda's irritation melted away as she entered the locker room and found three girls sitting on a bench between two rows of lockers, and another girl slumped in a corner, red faced and shaking. One of the girls stood and motioned to Amanda to talk in a private corner.

"You're a social worker, right?" the girl asked, wiping her eyes with a soggy Kleenex.

"Yes. Are you Jess?"

The girl nodded, and Amanda could see the slight family resemblance between her and Brittany. Jess was prettier and looked less rough around the edges than Brittany.

"I'm so scared. She's just freaking out. She won't talk anymore. We've been sitting here for an hour and can't get her to move." Jess played with the ends of her long blonde hair, absent-mindedly stroking her face with her hair as if it was a make-up brush.

"What started all of this?" Amanda asked, looking at the girl in the corner more closely. She was curled into a ball and stared at nothing. Even though she was clearly traumatized by something, she was still beautiful with long dark hair and a perfect complexion.

"She has a bruise on her cheek by her ear. She was covering it with her hair, but I finally saw it before lunch," Jess said. "I tried to ask her about it, and she snapped at me. I told her it looked like someone punched her, and she said, 'I wish.' I didn't get what she meant by that at all, so I told her I didn't get it. Then she just started breathing funny and said she didn't think she could stand it any more. She came right in the locker room, and I followed her here." Jess's eyes filled with tears. "Then she just lost it. She started screaming and wouldn't stop. I got so scared I just tried to grab her and make her be quiet. She was crazy. She said she couldn't deal with anyone else touching her. Finally she just slumped in the corner and she's been there ever since."

Amanda looked over at the girl, who had put her head down on her knees and was gently rocking.

"What's her name?" Amanda asked Jess.

"Rachel Thomas." The name didn't register to Amanda at all at that point. She crouched next to Rachel.

"Hi, Rachel. My name is Amanda." Rachel didn't move. "Your friends are really worried about you." Rachel still didn't register anything, and Amanda wasn't sure what to say. She had never really dealt with a kid in the moment of a crisis before. "Is there anything you want to tell me?"

Rachel shifted her body slightly. It felt like she did want to tell.

"I want to help, Rachel. I want to see if we can stop whatever is happening to you so you can feel safer." Rachel shook her head at that, seemingly saying that feeling safer was impossible. "Can you talk about who's hurting you?"

Rachel took a big deep breath and let it out in a shudder. "I want some water," she finally said. Brittany ran to the sink and brought back a Dixie cup of water. The girls leaned in, waiting for Rachel's big disclosure. Rachel drank the water and sighed again.

Amanda looked up at the girls waiting expectantly. "We can talk somewhere more private if that would help," Amanda said.

Rachel tilted her head. "Who are you?"

"I'm sorry," Amanda said quickly. "I should have told you right away. My name is Amanda and I work at Terrance County Social Services.

Rachel suddenly sucked in and clapped her hand to her mouth in horror. "Oh, my god."

Amanda couldn't believe her reaction. No one ever knew who she was, but this girl recoiled as if she said her name was Lucifer.

Rachel pulled herself off the floor and started to walk toward the door. "Hey, wait!" Amanda said. "I need to know that you're okay."

Rachel wheeled around and pointed at Jess with fire in her eyes. "Are you completely stupid!?" Jess shrank back as if she had been slapped.

"Rachel, I'm sorry. Brit thought Amanda could help you. I didn't know what to do."

"Stay out of my business. Stay out of it!" Rachel whipped back around and ran for the door.

"You can't just keep letting yourself get raped!" Brittany yelled the words, not realizing the effect they would obviously have. Jess turned toward Brittany in horror. Rachel, her hand on the locker room door, froze. She turned around and gave Brittany an icy stare.

"You don't know what you're talking about." Her words were short and detached. "Stay. Out. Of. My. Business." She turned and walked out of the locker room.

*　*　*

AMANDA STAYED WITH THE GIRLS for a few minutes to help them calm down. Jess wrapped her arms around herself and cried, and Brittany, who didn't know Rachel but was caught up in the drama, sobbed like it had all happened to her.

"You need to do something, Amanda. You need to help her."

Amanda was so exhausted from the day's events that it was difficult for her to process what she needed to do next. She realized Rachel hadn't made a single disclosure or anything close to a disclosure, so there was nothing she could do. Everyone in the room knew that something was happening, but they were powerless because Rachel didn't want any help.

"You girls have to realize that sometimes it takes a long time for people to deal with what's happening to them. She needs support, not pressure." The girls finally settled down, and Amanda was able to collect her belongings and go to her car.

She shuffled through the pile of junk on the passenger seat until she found a granola bar from earlier in the week, still wrapped. She tore into it and ate it in three bites, washing it down with a warm diet Coke from the morning. She started her car and sat back with an exhausted sigh, waiting for it to warm up. Rachel's face stuck in her mind. Suddenly, the realization nearly knocked the wind out of her. The resemblance, the name . . .

Rachel Thomas was Chuck Thomas's daughter.

*　*　*

WHEN SHE GOT BACK TO WORK, her message light was blinking at her. Amanda spent the ride back to work playing back the conversation with Rachel, trying to remember if Rachel had said anything that constituted a child protection report. Hoping something was reportable. Hoping there was an obvious answer, and realizing there probably wasn't.

Amanda walked across the hall into Max's office. "Have a minute?"

Max was looking at something on his computer. "Sure. Have you recovered from your day?"

Max was referring to the fight, which had become the furthest thing from her mind.

"Actually, something else happened as I was leaving school." Amanda replayed the conversation with Rachel. When she said Rachel's name, she waited to see if he recognized the name. His blank look showed her he didn't.

"I suppose that's the risk of having a social worker in the school," Max said, leaning back in his chair, and hoisting his foot up on the edge of his desk. Max was wearing hiking boots and socks with reindeer on them. He noticed Amanda noticing. "The socks were a gift."

She smiled obligingly at the socks. "Rachel Thomas is Chuck Thomas's daughter. I just looked it up. Somebody is hurting her, and it looked like she was ready to tell. Then she recognized my name, freaked out and left."

Max sighed deeply. "I'm sure you're right, Amanda. The thing is, we don't know who or what may have hurt her, and we certainly don't have a shred of evidence to prove it."

"I knew that, I guess. I just feel like I need to do something. I can't just have this knowledge and do nothing."

"What knowledge do you have, exactly?"

Amanda replayed the conversation in her mind again. Rachel said she couldn't handle anyone else touching her. For all Amanda knew, she could have an abusive boyfriend, or something could have happened on a date. It was a pretty big leap to assume someone in the family was hurting her. But even if it wasn't someone in her family, something was happening to Rachel, and Amanda knew it but couldn't help.

"I know it's hard, Amanda." Max said, seeing her frustration. "Sometimes we have these very frustrating situations when our hands are completely tied. It seems like we should be able to help, but we can't."

Amanda nodded.

"Why don't you head home," he said. "You've dealt with enough for one day."

"I need to stop by and see Hailey Bell. I'll go home from there. My brain is completely fried."

* * *

HAILEY HAD JUST MOVED IN with her mother, and it had been a rocky start. Hailey's mother, Nancy, doted on her grandchild and subtlety undermined her daughter every chance she got.

Today Nancy met Amanda at the door and stepped outside with her, pulling the door almost closed behind her. "She was real short with him last night again. She was giving him a bath, and I could hear him splashing, and she just yelled, 'Stop!' Real loud."

"So what has she done well lately?" Amanda had staffed this case last week, and her coworkers suggested asking Nancy that question to see if she had anything positive to say. Overall, Hailey had been doing very well with Charlie, and it was becoming clear that Nancy was more of a hindrance than a help to Hailey. When they were working on her social history, Hailey described the string of abusive men that Nancy brought into their lives. While she had only been hit a few times herself, she had watched her mother get dragged across the carpet by her hair, and that wasn't the worst beating she ever took. Hailey had dropped out of school and moved in with her older boyfriend when she was seventeen, a mistake that started her down the path of her own abusive boyfriends.

"What has she done well?" Nancy repeated. Sadly, the question stopped Nancy in her tracks. Hailey had passed GED testing with flying colors, enrolled in technical college, and was almost done with her anger management class. It wasn't a difficult question.

"I just need to meet with Hailey for a few minutes." She stepped around Nancy and went inside, where Hailey stood just on the other side of the door. The ache in Hailey's eyes revealed she had overheard the conversation.

"Hey, Amanda," she said sadly. Charlie was hiding behind his mom, and when Amanda entered he plowed into her, hitting her kneecap with his skull so hard that it brought tears to her eyes. Hailey either missed the blow or ignored it. Charlie ran through the living room and down the stairs to the space that he and his mother shared.

"How's it going, Hailey?" Amanda tried to keep her voice steady despite the pain. Charlie had crashed into the knee she had injured sliding into third base during her junior year, and it felt swollen already. Nancy finally came back inside and went straight to her bedroom, where she probably could hear their conversation best. "I just need to get a release signed for the evaluation we set up for Charlie." She handed Hailey the forms and showed her where to sign.

"God I hope he can get on some meds. He's so wild I'm afraid he's going to hurt someone."

Amanda's throbbing knee proved Hailey's point. Amanda and Hailey had completed a screening questionnaire about Charlie that had indicated some areas of concern regarding his behavior and overall development, so Amanda was setting up a more in-depth evaluation.

"It should give us some good answers," Amanda said as she took the papers back from Hailey. "That's all I need for today." She headed for the door, but the look on Hailey's face made her pause. "Are you okay?"

Blinking back tears, Hailey ran her hands through her enviable red hair. "Sometimes, I just wish I had a normal mom. The kind who can think of someone besides herself." Her words came out in a shaky whisper. "I mean, I'm glad she let me move back home, and I know she adores Charlie. But she didn't take good care of me. She was too busy making it all about her all the time. And, every once in a while, I just wish I would've had the kind of mom who stuffs you full of cookies and can't stop bragging about you. You know what I mean?"

Yep, Amanda thought. *I know exactly what you mean.*

* * *

AT THE END OF ANOTHER EXHAUSTING DAY, Amanda left Hailey and drove across Terrance to the bad side of town where LaToya lived so she could drop off one last form. The streets were narrow and the homes very close together in these neighborhoods. The railroad tracks ran parallel to the street Amanda was driving on, and were surprisingly close to the backyards of the homes. She stopped at a stop sign and looked over at a pink home with three butterflies mounted on the siding by the garage. For the third time in as many months, Amanda felt a surge of déjà vu so strong it took her breath away. She stared at the pink home, noting the mint-green shutters by the front window, with shutters missing on the left side. A gray army blanket blocked the front window. Several pumpkin garbage bags, faded and falling apart, were piled by the garage door. An image of ceramic gnomes with crumbling faces and faded bodies popped into her head. Plastic lattice leaning against siding . . . a tractor tire sandbox . . . matchbox cars and faded pink buckets.

Amanda finally drove through the intersection, but she couldn't allow herself to pass by that pink house. She turned around and parked on the street, across from the pink house. When she got out of her car. She could only stare. The winter sun was setting behind the house in vivid pink and orange brush strokes. Amanda asked herself what she was doing, why she was approaching the house, and what she would do when she got there. She had no answers but kept walking.

The snow was only a few inches deep, and it had melted and frozen enough times to create a thick crust with a few blades of grass sticking through here and there. The driveway had never been shoveled, but there were ruts where cars had driven a few times. Amanda walked slowly in the yard by the driveway vaguely aware that she was approaching the backyard. She peeked around the hedge in the back of the house, her heart pounding for reasons she couldn't explain.

Partially due to hunger, partially to shock, Amanda nearly fainted with what she saw. Crouching in a row against the back of the house where a flower garden would be in the spring, there they were, gnomes.

* * *

AMANDA COULDN'T PROCESS WHAT she saw and felt. Stumbling back to her car, she drove back to her apartment, barely remembering how she got there. She went straight to her bedroom and curled up on her bed. Though she felt vaguely afraid of the mystery emerging from her subconscious, she was mostly overwhelmed by emotion. Utterly exhausted, she fell asleep.

* * *

AMANDA WOKE UP AFTER MIDNIGHT long enough to take out her contacts, brush her teeth, change into pajamas and get back into bed. She felt calmer as she fumbled around her bedroom in the dark. She turned on the TV in her bedroom that barely showed two channels, but she needed the reassurance that nighttime TV could provide. As she was falling asleep, the realization came to her slowly but surely, as if the fog that had covered this part of her life had dissipated, revealing the truth that, at some level, she had always known.

That house belonged to her grandmother.

chapter eighteen

SOMEHOW, HAVING FAMILY IN TERRANCE should have been more earth shattering than it was. For the next several days, Amanda went about her daily routine as if nothing was different. She still got up every morning and went to her job at Terrance County Social Services, and at the end of the day she still went home and spent almost every evening alone.

What was different was the knowledge that she was no longer alone on the planet, and in fact never had been. She had family.

The question was what to do with the knowledge. She basked in it for a day, feeling reassured that there was at least one more person who was connected to her. Sitting at her desk, she had stretched her mind for more memories of that house, and a few rolled in. Amanda remembered sitting in that yard by the gnomes watching ants crawl through the flower garden and up and down the gnomes. She remembered sitting on the tire sandbox, and she sensed there were other kids there, but she couldn't pull up any of their faces. And she remembered playing with matchbox cars there. Her mother's running joke that she was going to be a stockcar driver because she loved matchbox cars probably began when she played with the cars in her grandmother's sandbox.

Grandmother.

The problem was that her grandmother didn't acknowledge her. And then she became obsessed with the question of why.

Amanda tried to remember if her mother had ever talked about her own mother. She couldn't recall any conversations, but the subject of family was always taboo with April, and suddenly this made much more sense.

She suddenly remembered her grandmother had called once. Amanda was about eight years old, and they were living in an apartment complex that Amanda loved because it was full of kids. As a teenager she drove by and realized that the complex was low-income housing, and understood better why many of the kids she knew there as a child were struggling as teenagers.

She and her mother were in the living room watching a rerun of *Happy Days*, eating a TV dinner of salisbury steak and French fries when the phone rang. Amanda answered it, and a woman was crying on the other end. Amanda didn't speak, but her bewildered look must have prompted her mother to grab the phone away from her. She listened for a moment, and then told the woman to stop calling and "give it up." Amanda asked her mother who called, and her mother suddenly blurted out, "It was your grandmother, but she's nothing but a troublemaker so just forget about her." Amanda did as she was told.

After three days, Amanda got up the nerve to pick up the phone book to try to look up her number, when another startling revelation came to her—she didn't even know her grandmother's name. She looked up Danscher but only found herself, of course. When Amanda had driven by every day on her way home, though it wasn't accurate to say it was on her way home because Amanda lived in the opposite direction, there were never any signs of life at the home, yet it still appeared to be lived in. The fleeting thought came that her grandmother might not even live there anymore, but that would close a door that Amanda simply wasn't willing to close yet.

Zoe walked by lifting her coffee cup, signaling that it was break time. Amanda sighed and went to the break room to chat with her coworkers for a few minutes.

Lois and Sharon, the two workers responsible for maintaining the computer tracking system, were in the breakroom lamenting the new system to Becca. They were in the process of switching to a nationwide computer database that held information about every person who had been found "guilty" of child abuse nationwide. The system piggybacked their statewide computer system that held the same information, in addition to being the computer system that they used for all documentation on every case. Lois and Sharon were both in their sixties, and defied the stereotype of the young, tech savvy computer programmer.

"The system now contains the name of every victim, perpetrator, and social worker involved in every state," Lois was telling Becca. "It's a huge amount of information, and I completely object to the names of victims being included."

Amanda tuned out at that point, realizing that she might be able to find her grandmother in this new system. She found herself hoping, strangely, that her grandmother had been found "guilty" of child abuse so that her name would be in this system. She slid out of her chair at the break room table, and headed for her office.

"Did we bore you already?" Lois asked, taking knitting needles out of a bag.

"No, I, uh, just have something I need to do." Amanda knew she looked guilty as hell. They had been clearly instructed that they were never to use this system for anything other than work. She sat back at her desk and logged into the system.

The screen that allowed social workers to locate clients required as little as a last name and location, but could take more information to reduce the search. She typed in Danscher and Terrance, and paused before hitting the enter key. She considered how much trouble she could be in for using the system this way. She could claim that this was part of a case she was working on if she ever got caught. She couldn't imagine that someone was monitoring the system that closely anyway. Glancing up, she saw that Max's door was closed, and it looked like he was on his phone. She sucked in her breath and pushed enter.

The word, "searching" blinked on the screen for about ten seconds.

What came next shouldn't have caught her by complete surprise. Living the life that she had lived, she should have been prepared. But she wasn't. What she saw felt like a punch in the stomach, and in an instant made her question everything she had believed about herself.

April Danscher.........perpetrator
Amanda Danscher...........victim

chapter nineteen

IN ONE OF AMANDA'S SOCIOLOGY classes—Diversity and Social Work Practice, the professor had lectured on the use of language in social work, and how it could affect their future clients. They had discussed using the terms African American and Caucasian, versus black and white. They discussed terms like chemically dependent, alcoholic, welfare, abuse, and addict. But the word that garnered the most heated debate was one of the more straightforward words in their practice—victim: one who suffers at the hands of another. Some of the people in the class wanted to use the term survivor. Others thought that was ridiculous and overdramatic, especially when dealing with child abuse. Clearly a child could be considered a victim at the hands of the person who was expected to keep him safe. Yet, the term incensed some members of the class who said the term implied weakness. The professor said the term also implies vulnerability, which is very hard for many people to acknowledge in themselves.

Yet there it was, written plainly on the screen in front of her. Victim, at the hands of her mother, Amanda's only known relative until a few days ago. There were no other Danschers. Her grandmother remained anonymous.

Amanda only wished that this information could have remained locked away as well. Anyone in her office could do the same thing and find out that Amanda was once a client of this office. Perhaps they already knew. Max might run all names through the computer before interviews.

Amanda sat frozen at her computer until she realized someone could walk in and see her computer screen. She closed the window, and absently shuffled papers around on her desk. The phone rang, and she jumped.

"Hey, loser." It was Jacob, and he was teasing her about the teams she picked to go to the Superbowl in his pool. She coughed and tried to speak, but couldn't.

"My gosh, a sore loser at that. It was only twenty bucks to get into the pool. Maybe next year." Amanda still couldn't think of anything to say. "Are you there, Amanda?"

"Mmhmm."

She was going to cry, so she hung up the phone and got out of her office, and out of her building before anyone saw her. Unfortunately, her car was in front of the building and there was a lot more traffic in that direction. She walked, just trying to get away.

They're going to find out about me. The words marched through her head like a playground taunt. Flashes of scenes that never actually occurred played themselves out in her head—Leah interviewing her mother. Zoe driving her to foster care, dropping her off with icy, angry Mary Clark. Would her mother have tried to get her back?

Her steps slowed. What had been reported? Who reported it?

It was the same street she had walked a few months before the day she saw Jacob in court for the first time. In her Minnesota winter uniform, a heavy sweater, wool slacks, and dressy boots, she was relatively warm, even without her coat. She had walked several blocks before she started to wonder if anyone would notice she was gone. She couldn't remember if she had any appointments scheduled. At that point, she could barely remember what day it was.

From the first day on the job, Amanda had realized there was a line drawn between "us" and "them." She supposed it was how they all tolerated all the painful things they encountered. Her coworkers were devoted advocates for the kids they worked with, and oftentimes the parents too. But consciously or unconsciously, right or wrong, there was a line between workers and clients.

Was she more upset because she was a victim, or was it the fear of having her life exposed? In Terrance, she was always being asked whom she was related to, when she graduated, or how she fit into the town that its residents fiercely claimed as their home. Would anyone still think she was competent if they knew who she really was?

As she walked, she listened to her boots squeak on the hardened snow. The air was cold, but not frigid. The tears running down her cheeks made her face colder. She was oblivious to her surroundings until a car pulled up next to her, moving with her slowly on the deserted residential street. She started to feel nervous, like she was being followed, until she looked over and saw it was Jacob. He parked and motioned for her to come over. She looked at him, not moving, so he got out.

"Hey." He was carrying her coat. "When you hung up on me, I thought I better come over and apologize. Max said he saw you leave out the back door without your coat . . ." He put her coat around her shoulders, holding the lapels together in front to keep the coat on. "What happened?"

Amanda shook her head, too ashamed to tell him anything. She looked down, trying to hide her tears.

Jake put his arms around her and held her tightly. Amanda held her breath, trying not to cry anymore. "Max told me you had a rough day yesterday. He said to tell you to just go home for the day if you needed to."

Victim. Pathetic, pitiful victim. Too weak and pathetic to work. She shook her head, both at the thoughts running through her head, and the suggestion that she just go home. She couldn't admit to Max that she was weak. She tried to stuff down the sadness and shame, but her feelings wouldn't squash down the way they used to. They were on the surface more and more lately, and she had no idea how to handle them. Every emotion she had seemed to knock the life right out of her.

Jacob pulled back and tried to look at Amanda, but she avoided his eyes. He could still see her jaw clenched, holding back tears.

"Whatever it is, Amanda, it's okay." He stroked her hair. "Let's go to my place, and I'll make you some lunch. We can sit around and watch MTV all afternoon." He was going to take the afternoon off to be with her, but all Amanda really wanted to do was go home and go to bed.

"Just take me home," Amanda whispered. "I just need to get some sleep."

"No. You can sleep at my place. You're not going to be alone."

He always knew just what to say.

* * *

JACOB WARMED UP SOME of Trix's homemade wild rice soup, and they ate on the couch sitting under blankets. They watched MTV, and then switched over to the game show network to watch a *Price Is Right* marathon. The soup, the blanket, and the company made Amanda start to relax. Jake always had an amazing way of being with her and tolerating her being emotional.

At some point, Amanda dozed off on Jake's couch. When she woke up, it was nearly dark out. Jake was sitting on the floor by the couch, working on his laptop, but stopped when he saw Amanda sit up.

"Feel better?"

Amanda nodded, embarrassed.

"What happened, Amanda? You looked so sad."

Amanda let out a heavy sigh. She was so tired of feeling this way. So tired of feeling pathetic and alone. She was becoming her own worst enemy because she was letting her history get the better of her every time it became an issue. She hated people feeling sorry for her, but the person who felt the sorriest for Amanda was always Amanda.

"I'm okay, Jacob. I was upset, but I'm over it. I'm ready to move on."

Part Three

chapter twenty

MARLYS ACTUALLY WORE A BOA to her discharge meeting. "I know I got a long way to go," she said, enunciating her words clearly and proudly, "but I'm here today and I'm sober today, and that's alls I can do is take care of to-day."

Marlys' primary counselor, Mavis, nodded. Mavis was in her early sixties, and she had been a counselor for over twenty years after becoming sober herself. Amanda knew this because Mavis talked about her own sobriety almost every time they talked about Marlys. "That's right, Marlys. So tell your social worker what you're going to do to stay clean and sober tomorrow and the next day . . ."

Marlys turned to Amanda, sitting at the table in the conference room at the outpatient treatment center where they were having their meeting. The only other person in the room was Glady, the court appointed guardian ad litem who was assigned to the case to look out for the best interests of the kids. Glady was in her fifties and African American, and she had a calm and competent demeanor that gave her instant credibility with clients and providers.

"I'm already going to the NA or the AA almost every day. I still needa job, but I know there's a meeting somewhere every day, and I need my meetings. I also needs to stay on my medication so I don't get so depressed about my past and all the things I've did."

"The medication is a biggie," Mavis said. "Shame is a big trigger for you, and you started handling that shame much better when you started your meds."

"Amen," Marlys said. "I'm ready to be a new person, a new sober person for my kids."

Amanda nodded and took this as her cue to speak up. Meetings like this intimidated Amanda because people like Mavis were so experienced, and she knew Mavis could immediately tell if she said something stupid.

"About your kids . . . I think we'll be ready to increase your visits now that you're done with primary treatment." Amanda opened her file and pulled out the caseplan for Marlys. "We said at the last meeting that your visits would increase to all day, and we'll start working toward unsupervised visits in the next few weeks . . ."

"Weeks! I ain't waiting weeks! I'll have my apartment next month, and then I want them home." Marlys sat up straight in her chair and leaned forward with her eyes bulging. Glady sat back slightly in her chair.

Amanda cleared her throat and felt herself turning red. "I know you do, Marlys, but we need to make sure that, uh, that you aren't going to, uh, I mean that your treatment has really worked . . ."

"You see!" Marlys yelled, banging her hand on the table. "Nobody thinks I'm gonna do right. Everybody's expecting me to fail. Why should I even try?"

Mavis sat back and crossed her arms. "You're being a victim, Marlys. You don't need your social worker's permission to get sober. This has to be about you taking care of yourself."

"I done all this for my babies, but she's the one who decides what happens to my babies. I can't get my boys back until *she* say so."

Amanda cleared her throat again. "The law says that I have to try to get your children back to you . . ."

"The law says! See! You don't think I'm doing nothing. You're just doing what the law says. Did the law say that my babies' daddy don't hafta pay me no child support? No. The law says he s'posed to, but he don't pay nothing. When you start getting the law to make him pay, then you can use your laws on me."

"Don't argue, Marlys," Mavis said, "It gets you nowhere. Your drug addiction got you into this place. Not his failure to pay child support. You're blaming again."

Amanda closed her file, and cleared her throat, trying to sound more authoritative and confident. "Marlys, I really do want to get your boys back home. This is a great step that you made, getting through treatment like this. We just have to make sure it's really going to work this time, because you have relapsed before, and we don't want to let that happen again. I'm not saying that to make you mad. I'm just trying to talk about it so we can make sure it doesn't happen again."

Glady spoke up at that point. "We all know that kids do best with their mamas, as long as their mamas are healthy. We want to help you be healthy so you can be the best mama."

Glady's words soothed Marlys enough to help her settle down and talk about the next steps.

They ended the meeting with the agreement to meet in a week, during which time Amanda would set up a more intensive visitation schedule and parenting education for Marlys during her visits. Marlys hugged Amanda before she left, tearily thanking her for "being a bitch when I needed a bitch."

It was the end of the day, so Amanda decided to go straight home instead of bringing her file back to the office. The treatment program was in a strip mall next to Target, and Amanda felt the store calling her. She decided to go to Target and look for some winter clothes on clearance.

She wandered around the women's clothing section looking at sweaters and wishing that she had a reason to buy a swimsuit that was already on display for winter vacationers. Several people in her office were going to Mexico or Florida on a cruise or just to a resort. Amanda didn't have the funds or the vacation time to do anything other than take an afternoon off and sit in the hot tub at the Y. Her mood had improved in the past month after she had joined the Y and started running almost every day. It was a good distraction from the stress of her job, and the feeling that her head and all these crazy memories were messing with her. She still drove by the house with the gnomes, but she didn't have the energy to do anything more about it.

Amanda found a blazer and slacks on the clearance rack that she picked up and thought about trying on. She carried them with her as she continued to wander, when her phone vibrated in her purse.

Dinner tonight? The message was from Jacob. He had been wrapped up in a trial he was working on, so they had not seen much of each other since the day he picked Amanda up on the street.

Somewhere cheap, she replied, thinking of her credit card bill that she was still paying down from Christmas and Lucy's wedding. She wandered to the shoe section and tried to find shoes to match the makeshift suit she was considering. Some spikey boots were on sale, but she wasn't sure if they were right for court. Her phone buzzed again.

You've always been a cheap date, but we're not going to DQ tonight. I'll pick you up at 6:30.

K, she replied, and dropped the phone in her purse. Looking down at her suit, she knew that if she was going out for dinner she didn't have extra money for clothes anyway. But she couldn't leave Target without something, so she grabbed a cinnamon scented candle and headed to the front of the store. There were at least a dozen men in line, holding cards or flowers or another small gift. Then she noticed the paper hearts hanging from the ceiling and remembered that it was Valentine's Day.

* * *

BACK AT HER APARTMENT, Amanda stared at her closet with no idea of what to wear.

He called her a date. A cheap date, but a date nonetheless. And since it was Valentine's Day, restaurants would be full of couples. Knowing this, Jake asked her to go to a restaurant with him, on Valentine's Day. Did that make this a date? Amanda had been enjoying their friendship, but she had never noticed him making any moves toward anything other than friendship. The night her mother died flashed in her head, and her face flushed with the memory of being in bed with Jake. Sharp and bittersweet, and she rarely let herself go back to that night, but for a moment it was all there: sounds of summer outside the open window, a whiff of Trix's lavender fabric softener on the sheets, Jake's sweaty grip on her bare shoulders. And then there was the shame. Many people probably used sex to comfort themselves after a loss, but she still felt guilty. She was also just simply afraid. Jake told her he loved her, but she didn't believe him. And then she ran away.

Amanda pulled in a deep breath and tried to calm down. She had been out for dinner many times with Jake, although it was usually a casual happy hour that extended far enough into the evening that they both were starving and ordered food. This felt different. He'd called it a date.

Just because he called it a date didn't mean that she had to consider it as anything other than another night out with her friend. Amanda went on three dates with a guy in college who clearly had a thing for her, but

Amanda was so uncomfortable with his obvious interest that she never allowed him to even hold her hand. After three dates and not a speck of interest in him returned, he gave up. Amanda didn't want Jake to give up on their friendship, but she wanted him to clearly know that this was a night out as friends.

Amanda turned away from her closet deciding not to make the effort to change clothes, not just for a night out with a friend.

* * *

JAKE ARRIVED A FEW MINUTES before 7:00 and came up to her apartment just as Amanda was pulling on her coat. He knocked and then opened the door, which Amanda had not locked.

"As you see, I can clearly let myself in, as can any intruder who wants to harass you when you don't lock your door." He stood with his hands on his hips in the entryway and glared at her seriously.

"Hello to you too." She folded her arms and waited for the argument. Jake dropped his hands by his side and shook his head.

"Just want you to be safe," he said, almost to himself. He seemed to be willing to drop the nagging for now. "Ready to go?" Amanda followed Jake to his car, which Jake had left running so it was warm.

"You look nice," Jake said a touch formally. Amanda looked down at her sweater and pants that looked a little wrinkled and tired after she wore them all day. She couldn't remember Jake ever commenting on her appearance before.

"Just my work clothes," Amanda said a little too brightly. Jake took a road away from downtown, so Amanda asked where they were going.

"Out to the lake," he said. "There's nowhere fun to eat in Terrance." She nodded and looked out the window. Yep, this was a date.

* * *

THEY WENT TO THE BOATER'S INN, a restaurant on Lake Pepin just over the border in Wisconsin. It was a new place that had just received excellent reviews in the *Star Tribune*. It was crowded and there was a wait for a table, so they went to the bar. Amanda ordered a glass of wine, and Jake a diet coke. He led her to a tall table near the window that overlooked the now dark lake. She couldn't help staring at his drink. Once again, he was abstaining, and it had happened enough times in a row that it was clearly not a coincidence. She pictured the pill bottles in his medicine cabinet he didn't know she had seen.

"Great view, huh?" Jake said, motioning at the darkness.

Amanda nodded, trying to decide if she was going to mention his tee-totaling.

"Being here reminds me that I didn't get on a boat once last summer," Jake said. "We should go waterskiing next summer. Michael has a great boat when he's home to use it."

She nodded again. "How's your diet coke?" she asked pointedly.

"Refreshing," he said. "You ever skied before?"

Amanda wanted to say something sarcastic to remind him that her life had been far too dysfunctional for such pastimes, but she was trying to get rid of the "poor me" attitude, so she just shook her head. They looked out the window in silence for a moment.

"How have you been feeling lately?" The question was blunt, and her tone was clear that she meant more than his general health. He looked straight at her with his eyebrows raised slightly, and his jaw clenched just enough for her to notice. His cancer had become a touchy subject, only because they hadn't spoken of it since they had become reacquainted.

"I'm good," he said. "How are have you been feeling?" Her shoulders dropped, and she looked down. Obviously the subject was not open for dis-cussion. He said he was feeling fine, and that should have been enough. But it wasn't. His reaction meant something was going on.

"My sisters are great waterskiers," he went on, filling the awkward si-lence. "Both of them wanted to be part of the Tommy Bartlett Water Show at the Dells." The Dells— actually the Wisconsin Dells—and Amanda had participated in this Midwestern tradition. The Dells was actually a tiny town and an area in the middle of Wisconsin that had become a family vacation haven because of its many waterparks, minigolf courses, and waterski shows.

The conversation stayed away from Jake's health and lack of drinking, and they both relaxed. Amanda didn't order another glass of wine because she felt strange about drinking when he was pointedly not drinking. After nearly an hour they were seated in the dining room, which was soothing beige and white and decorated with sailing paraphernalia. It felt like a breath of summer in the depth of winter.

Amanda had pasta and Jake had a steak, and they both had a nice time. Despite it being declared a date and the earlier awkward discussion, they finally relaxed and chatted easily about the upcoming Twins season, politics, and William and Lucy. William had been updating Jake on Lucy's progress almost obsessively. Lucy had been emailing less, but Amanda was working hard not to take it personally. She knew Lucy was uncomfortable, stressed and scared, so Amanda had been calling more. Lucy sounded wearily pleased every time Amanda called, so she knew it was her time to be selfless with her friend.

"Will sounds just nervous," Jake said. "It's like he's tiptoeing around Lucy for fear that walking too loud will put her into labor."

"Nine months is way too long to be pregnant," Amanda said as though she had some sort of first-hand knowledge. "I hope she goes the second the baby's healthy enough to be delivered."

"Do you think you'll ever have kids?" Jake mumbled, looking at his plate. She thought she misheard him at first, but his discomfort showed that she heard him right. The question surprised her, and it was actually something she had given very little thought in her life. She must have taken too long to answer, because Jacob looked up at her nervously.

"I honestly don't know," Amanda finally said. He nodded and looked like he was ready to say something more when someone approached their table.

"Well hello to both of you," a tall man in a dark suit said without an ounce of genuineness.

Amanda looked up and groaned inside: Skip Huseman. How could they have been so unlucky? He was wearing a red tie and matching pocket scarf, and he stood over them like a watchdog ready to pounce.

"Skip." Jacob made a point of using his first name again. "Enjoying the evening?"

"My wife and I are celebrating nearly thirty years together. She's a local girl too, so we always like to come home for Valentine's Day." Amanda and Jake nodded, not wanting to say anything that would extend the conversation and encourage him to stay. Skip caught the eye of someone across the room and nodded and smiled.

"Say, Jacob, I've been meaning to ask, how is your health?" He said it like a statement, not a question. Jacob flinched slightly, but then turned his head and tried to look unfazed, although he was clearly affected by the question.

"Quite well." Jacob's eyes darted to Amanda questioningly, bordering on accusingly.

Skip was nodding. "Cancer can be so devastating. Glad to hear that you beat it."

Jacob looked down, his jaw muscles working. Then he looked up at Skip. "Enjoy your evening."

Skip smiled condescendingly. "Oh, we will. Same to the two of you." Skip made his way back across the room, slapping backs and shaking hands as he went. Jacob was staring into space. She opened her mouth to say something.

"Don't," he said, the mood of the night spoiled. He raised his hand to motion to the waitress at the next table. "Check please."

chapter twenty-one

L UCY WAS ENORMOUS. "Forty pounds. I've gained forty pounds, and I've almost twelve weeks to go." Lucy, stretched out on her couch with her feet resting on several pillows, didn't have shoes that would fit her swollen feet, and her ankles disappeared as her calves ended at her shoes.

"You look great, you really do," Amanda said, sitting on the old Lazy Boy recliner next to the couch. William was up north ice fishing for the weekend, and Amanda had agreed to spend the night with Lucy so she wouldn't be alone. Amanda had been looking forward to the weekend with just the two of them, the way they used to spend many weekends in college when they were too poor to go out. Amanda had rented or borrowed several movies, and Lucy wanted to start a scrapbook for the baby, so they were looking through pictures of Lucy and William to start the book.

"I'm a whale," Lucy said. "Everything hurts. I'm bloated. I can't sleep. I'm so crabby I can't stand to be alone with myself. I don't know how you're going to stand spending twenty-four hours with me." Lucy tried to sit up with an audible grunt, but just flopped back and closed her eyes.

"What can I do for you? Would anything make it better?" Amanda couldn't help smiling because Lucy had always been so good natured, but she was so grouchy it was endearing.

"Nothing, unless you can convince little bambino that he needs to be born *right now*." She pointed and gestured hopelessly at her heaving belly.

"Hmmm. Not much help there." Amanda shuffled through the large stack of movies to find something funny and distracting. "Let's watch something that will get your mind off your misery."

"Impossible. But I know what you can do for me." Lucy's eyes lit up. "Tell me about Valentine's Day." Big grin.

Amanda's smile drooped. "What are you talking about? What's to tell?"

Lucy raised her eyebrows. "I happen to know that Jake was trying to be casual about Valentine's Day, but he kept asking William about it, and finally he let it slip that he was going to have dinner with you."

"What did you do?" Amanda asked, hoping to change the subject.

"Don't change the subject. We had a very nice night at home and William cooked, but we're talking about you. He's so weird about you, Amanda. It's like he's terrified of offending you, so he overthinks everything."

Amanda pulled a pillow on her lap and shrugged. "I don't know. I mean, we're friends, and I want him to stay my friend. I don't want anything to mess it up because I can use all the friends I can get. Every once in a while it gets weird and intense, and it seems like he wants something more. But then it just blows over, kind of like he just thought better of it. I don't know what to think."

Lucy raised her eyebrows. "I know that I want you two to get married, buy the house next door, and we'll all be best friends forever. But you've never said what you want."

Amanda buried her face in the pillow. "I told you I don't know. Sometimes I think I do, but when he called our night out a date, I got nervous and acted casual." Amanda pulled in a deep breath and looked up at the ceiling. "I guess it's just that there are times when it seems like he's thinking of me as more than a friend. We went out to this nice place for dinner on Valentine's Day. It was a date by anyone's definition. But while we were out, he was totally platonic. It was like I didn't know what I wanted, and he didn't know what he wanted. He didn't say anything other than our typical chatting, and at the end of the night he took me back to my apartment. But, maybe that's not a good example because Skip Huseman was at the restaurant, and he asked about Jake's cancer."

Lucy sat back, her eyes wide. "Oh, not good. William can barely go there."

"I know. Jake and I haven't talked about it once since we started working together. And that's kind of surprising because when we met it was more matter of fact. He seems way touchier about it now." It made his mystery medication more confusing and worrisome.

"William's dad said it was all pretty scary for a while when Jake was first diagnosed. He talked about Trix being a wreck, and Michael was home a lot trying to support her. That's actually when Desi's business took off because Michael had to be home for Jake. Jake was in the hospital for weeks at a time, and they didn't know if the treatments were working. William didn't see Jake much because he couldn't have visitors, and Will was a self-centered teenager, so he didn't do much for Jake. I just think it was an awful time for all of them, so you can see why he wants to forget about it and put it behind him."

Amanda was quiet. She didn't realize it was life or death for Jacob. When she met him he looked and seemed fine. She thought of how desperately Trix wanted her to stay and be Jacob's friend. Amanda had been so focused on herself that she didn't realize that Jacob might have needed her as much as she needed him.

* * *

THE DAY PASSED QUICKLY and comfortably. William called twice to check in, and spoke with Amanda to make sure that Lucy was really as okay as she said. Amanda promised she was.

Amanda slept on the couch, despite Lucy's insistence that she could sleep in their bed. While she had shared a bed with Lucy many times, sharing her marital bed with her was a line Amanda was not going to cross.

Lucy went to bed apologetically at ten, saying there was no way she would be able to stay up any later. Amanda fell asleep quickly and had the most vivid dream she had ever had.

She could see pictures in pretty gold frames. Shelves full of pictures. Gray shag carpet. There were good smells . . . Grandma was sitting in her recliner, wearing jeans and a blue-and-gold sweatshirt. She asked Manda to sit on her lap and look at a book full of pictures. "Daddy was the best player on the team." Daddy . . .

* * *

"AMANDA . . ." IT WAS A WHISPER. Lucy. She sounded afraid. Amanda awoke with a start, hopped up and ran down the hall. In the bedroom she found Lucy sitting up in the dark.

"What's the matter? Are you okay?"

Lucy was holding her belly. "I don't know. I feel like I'm having contractions, but they're probably just Braxton Hicks." Lucy glanced at the clock. "It's just that they're pretty hard contractions, and I didn't think Braxton Hicks contractions were supposed to wake me up."

Amanda went in and sat on the bed next to Lucy. "I don't know what to tell you. Should we see if they continue, or do you want to just go to the ER right now?"

Lucy slumped back and got tears in her eyes. "Maybe we can call the OB unit and tell them what's happening?"

"That sounds good," Amanda said. She found the phone and the number in Lucy's birthing book on her dresser next to her already packed hospital bag.

Lucy called and explained that she had been having hard contractions for over an hour. She was sitting up in bed with her hair standing up and her eyes wide and teary, and Amanda's heart sank for Lucy looking so terrified. Lucy said okay a few times and hung up.

"They said to give it about thirty minutes and see what they do. If the contractions are still intense after thirty minutes they want me to come in." Tears began to roll down her cheeks, and she covered her mouth with her hand while she put her other hand on her belly. "I'm so scared, Amanda. This is way too soon. I'm only twenty-seven weeks. This just can't happen."

Amanda crawled into bed next to Lucy and put her arms around her. "It's going to be okay. You don't know that this is any big deal right now. For all we know, everybody has contractions like this right now." Amanda squeezed her shoulders and pulled back to look at her. "But I think you should try to relax. Freaking out isn't going to help and might make the contractions worse."

Lucy sniffed and nodded. "Okay. Talk to me about something else." She sat back on her pillows and smoothed the sheets over her lap.

Amanda thought about the dream she was having before she woke up.

"Well, if you really want to be distracted, I guess I could tell you about these dreams I've been having." Amanda told her about the dreams and pictures that came to her at different times, the house with the gnomes, and her conclusion that she was remembering her grandmother's house.

"Amanda, that's incredible. Just incredible! Do you think this woman is still alive? Do you realize that you may still have family alive?" Lucy rolled onto her left side and hugged the body pillow she had started sleeping with.

Amanda flinched at Lucy's reference to family, the reminder that she was alone in the world, but Lucy was scared and Amanda was trying not to be so reactive these days, so she let it go.

"I realize. But I have to say that I don't think anyone is living in that house right now. It just doesn't look inhabited." Amanda leaned back on the headboard and tried to ignore that she was lying on William's pillow.

"There are ways you can find that out," Lucy said excitedly. "You could check at the county recorder and see who owns the home and who pays the taxes there."

"I suppose I could . . ." Amanda couldn't explain the hesitance. "I may do that. I don't want to explain who I am or why I'm asking."

Lucy nodded. "And once you ask, then you have the answer and you have to figure out what to do next."

"Exactly," Amanda said. "I don't know if I want to do anything next. I mean . . ." Amanda paused and saw that Lucy's face was contorted in pain. "Another one?"

Lucy nodded and her chin quivered. "They're getting worse."

* * *

THEY WENT TO THE EMERGENCY room entrance, and an OB nurse was waiting with a wheelchair at the receiving desk so they went straight to the unit. There was already an OB doctor on the unit who wanted to check her immediately. Amanda gave Lucy a hug and said she would call William and be in the waiting area as soon as she could. They had called him from the house, so William had already left the cabin he was staying at with his uncles and was waiting for an update. Unfortunately the cabin was on the Canadian border, the only place where there was still solid ice left, so it was going to take close to eight hours for him to get back. Amanda promised to call him every hour with updates and to make sure he was staying awake on the long, dark drive.

Amanda went up to the OB unit and asked at the desk about Lucy. The doctor was in with her, so she said Amanda could wait in their family room. Amanda made her way down the hall and stood at the nursery window to look at the babies. There were only two little boys in the nursery, even though there were at least ten rooms occupied with new moms, so she assumed that the rest were in with their mothers.

Amanda thought back to Jacob's question on Valentine's Day asking if she would ever have kids. For the first time in her life, she thought seriously about whether she would ever be a mother. She didn't think of herself as "mother material," but that was mostly because she was never mothered herself. But looking at the babies wrapped like little papooses, she had the urge to stroke their little cheeks and count their toes. She thought of Jacob and flushed, even though no one was there, no one could read her thoughts. But then, unbelievably, she looked up and there he was and she flushed again.

"Hi," she said, barely able to meet his eyes. They hadn't had much chance to speak since Valentine's Day, and there was a new awkwardness.

"Hey." He smoothed his shirt and seemed uneasy too. "William called me and asked me to be here with you and Lucy. How's she doing?"

"I don't know. The doctor is in with her now."

He nodded and they both looked at the floor. After a moment a young looking male doctor came out and spoke with the nurse at the station, and she nodded and picked up a phone. The doctor approached them.

"Are you Amanda?" She nodded. "I'm Dr. Banks. Lucy asked me to come and talk to you about what's happening. Let's head down to the family room."

Amanda looked at Jacob with big eyes. They both knew that having a talk in the family room was never a good sign. They went in and he motioned for them to sit, but Amanda shook her head so they all stood.

"Lucy has pre-eclampsia and she is in preterm labor. Her chart also says that they have been watching her for placenta previa. I gave her some medication to stop the labor, but I'm sending her by ambulance to the University Hospital where she can get some additional testing. It might just be for a few days until they can get a better handle on what's going on, or they may need to keep her there until she delivers, which they obviously will try to postpone as long as possible." Dr. Banks spoke quickly, but he used plain language and he was sensitive and likable. One of the better doctors Amanda had ever dealt with.

"How's the baby doing?" Jacob asked. Amanda was impressed that he had the wherewithal to think of a question, because Amanda's brain was frozen.

"Pretty well, " Dr. Banks said. "Lucy's hooked up to a monitor, and the baby's heartbeat is steady and strong. If she was staying here I would do an ultrasound to get a better look at the baby and see where that placenta is, but I'm sure they'll do that at the U." Dr. Banks clapped his hands together. "I don't want to rush you, but I have two other moms in heavy labor and it's just me here tonight. Do you have other questions?" They both shook their heads, and he shook Amanda's hand. They watched him rush down the hall into another room, where they could hear some faint moaning.

Amanda turned to Jacob, trying to swallow the lump in her throat.

"She's going to be okay. The doctor was concerned, not alarmed. You and I both have enough experience reading doctors to know that this is a bump in the road, not an emergency. I'm going to go call William." He pulled her into a quick hug and kissed the side of her head, before he headed down the hall to make a phone call. Despite everything that was happening with Lucy, she couldn't help but wonder about his hug.

* * *

THE HOSPITAL AT THE UNIVERSITY was huge, and the map they got from the nurse didn't help much. After an hour of driving around the campus looking for parking lot F, they found where they were supposed to be. Amanda talked to William twice, who talked very fast and sounded near tears. Amanda tried to be reassuring even though they didn't have much information yet.

They wandered around the hospital hallways before finally finding the OB unit. They found Lucy's room, but the nurse at the desk said that she was sleeping and said it would be better if they left.

"Lucy wanted us here, and we're not leaving. Amanda is going to sleep in her room until her husband gets here, so it would be great if you could bring her a blanket and a pillow so she can sleep comfortably on the chair."

The nurse pursed her lips at Jacob, but he stared back until she shrugged and said, "Be extremely quiet. There are a lot of women on this unit who need their sleep."

Amanda crept into Lucy's room. Lucy was lying on her side, but woke up as soon as Amanda entered the room Lucy's tears started again. Amanda sat on the chair next to her and reached over to hold her hand.

"You're okay. This is just going to be a bump in the road." Lucy nodded and closed her eyes. It was nearly 3:00 a.m. Lucy tried to go back to sleep, which was difficult with the fetal monitor connected to her belly and an IV in her arm.

Amanda was dozing when William arrived. He came in and put his hand on Lucy's shoulder and kissed her head. Lucy opened her eyes and her quiet tears started again. William crouched on the floor in front of her. He held her hand and stroked her hair. Amanda was on the opposite side of the bed by the window and felt like an intruder as she watched the two of them together. Neither of them spoke, but William put his hand on her belly and closed his eyes. Amanda could hear him saying a prayer to "Mary, Mother of God."

Amanda slid out of her chair and left the room without either William or Lucy noticing. She stood in the hallway not knowing where to go next. Jacob was sleeping on the couch in the waiting area at the end of the hall. She went to the waiting area and sat in a vinyl chair opposite him and watched him sleep. She thought about what Lucy had said about Jacob being "weird" about her, and realized she had to agree. But she knew she was weird about him too. They hadn't dated anyone else during the time they had known each other, and Amanda knew that she didn't want to. But the idea of "dating" Jacob didn't appeal either, at least not now. He was just hers. That was all she knew for now. She watched him sleep and knew that she didn't want to share him with anyone.

chapter twenty-two

A MANDA DROVE TO THE CLARK foster home with apprehension, dreading what she had to tell them. It was March 1st and nearly fifty degrees. March was officially coming in like a lamb, but Zoe had said that morning that there was no reason to think that it couldn't go out like a lamb too.

Mary was outside sweeping the front step as Amanda pulled into the driveway. Justice was on the steps next to her playing with matchbox cars, wearing an expensive looking winter coat and matching hat, but no mittens. In the past two and a half months, Mary had formed a close bond with Justice, and had conjured some warmth for the other three kids. Anthony still couldn't leave Larry's side, and Angel was distant from both parents but stayed close to Blaze. They brought all four kids and a nanny with them for a two-week vacation in Mexico, so Mary was tanned, which looked out of place with her turtleneck and ski vest.

"Hey there, Justice," Amanda said. "Cool cars. Looks like you made a race track." She turned to Mary. "How are you, Mary?" she asked formally. She still was intimidated by her chill, but forced herself to try to be a grown up and a professional and talk to her anyway instead of shrinking away.

"Fine, thanks." Mary put down her broom and walked inside, and Amanda followed despite the lack of invitation.

Justice trailed in after them and obediently stood on the rug by the door, waiting for her to strip off his jacket and boots. She threw them outside on the front step, too dirty for her house, but Amanda noted that she allowed him to walk to the kitchen with his muddy pant legs dragging across the wood floors.

A woman was sitting at the table with Blaze doing puzzles. Blaze popped up and ran to hug Amanda around her legs. She patted his back, and he ran back to the table, knocking off puzzle pieces as he sat. The woman reached down and picked up the pieces silently. Amanda knew that the woman was his skills worker, which was someone paid by the state to work with Blaze several hours a day on his social skills and daily care.

"We doing puzzles," Blaze shouted.

"Inside voice, Blaze," the woman said,

"We doing puzzles," Blaze said, slightly quieter.

"Very nice, Blaze," Amanda said, using a soft voice in attempt to encourage him to quiet down.

Mary said, "Jane, could you bring the boys downstairs for a while?" Jane silently started picking up puzzles pieces, but Blaze screeched, threw his body across the table and pushed the entire puzzle onto the floor, along with the centerpiece of fresh spring flowers in a white vase. Jane gasped as water from the vase spilled on the floor, and she looked almost fearfully up at Mary. Mary closed her eyes, took two towels out of a kitchen drawer and crouched on the floor to clean up the mess.

"Blaze, look what happened," Jane said. "You need to come back . . ."

"I've got it," Mary said tersely.

"Dr. Simons said we're supposed to . . ." but Jane trailed off. Obviously Mary knew what Dr. Simons said, but her look told Jane to take the boys downstairs.

Amanda stood awkwardly with her files in her arms, wondering if she should help clean up as Blaze sprinted and Justice strolled downstairs, with Jane following behind.

Mary set her vase right side up and pushed on the towel to soak up the water in the carpet. She picked up the wet puzzle pieces and set them on the towel, and brought the whole mess to the kitchen sink.

Amanda stood in the doorway to the kitchen and asked if she could help.

"No, I'll just leave it for now. Blaze makes fifteen messes a day, so I usually end up cleaning after they all go to bed." Mary wiped her hands on a dishtowel. "Can I get you anything to drink? Coffee?" she asked, motioning to the fresh pot.

"I'm fine, thank you," Amanda said. She followed Mary and sat at the kitchen table.

"How are things going now that Blaze has more help?" Amanda asked. Mary had been ready to give up on the kids in January, but Amanda went to her staff and asked for ideas to preserve the placement. She was able to set up regular respite care twice a month and qualified Blaze for PCA services.

"It's definitely better, " Mary said. She looked like she was going to say more, but stopped. "Any word on Anthony's dad?" Mary looked down as she said it, and Amanda thought she sounded hopeful.

"His home study was approved," Amanda said quietly. "His dad is ready any time."

Mary nodded and sighed hard. "So that's that? He just goes to his dad now?"

"We have court tomorrow, and I requested in my court report that the judge approve Anthony moving in the next week. His dad will be in court tomorrow, and he's able to stay for the week. Max suggested that we have his dad spend a couple of afternoons here this week and get Anthony really comfortable with him before he takes him back to Michigan with him.

Mary nodded again. "This is going to be awful for Larry."

"I'm sure it is," Amanda said. "I really feel like we ask foster parents to do the impossible. We want you to keep these kids, treat them like your own, but be willing to let them go and not have any control about who, where, or when they go." Amanda had discussed this situation for a long time at their staff meeting last week. Amanda was worried about separating the kids, but their mother was looking at a five-year jail term for violating her probation and selling meth again. Even without the jail term, she had told her attorney that she was done with her kids. They had no choice but to look to relatives for the kids to be with, starting with their four dads. Paternity had never been established for Blaze, but the other three had dads who received notice of the CHIPS hearings. Only Anthony's dad responded, and he actually came to the initial hearing and spent time with Anthony. He had recently completed a successful stint through drug court, and he wanted his son. Amanda completed extensive paperwork to request a home study where he lived in Detroit, and he was cooperative with the process and the home study was approved. Amanda tried to keep Larry and Mary aware of the entire process, but there was so much for her to do that she often forgot to talk to Larry and Mary about the details until they asked. Larry finally started emailing Amanda at work every few days asking about progress on placements. It had become clear that Larry wanted to adopt the kids, but Mary's position was harder to figure out.

Mary folded her hands in front of her face. "I suppose it's terrible for me to say I'm a little relieved." She didn't make eye contact as she spoke. Amanda was surprised that she was sharing her feelings at all, because Mary was usually all business with Amanda. "It's been difficult to go from no kids to four. But even with Blaze's behavior, I feel like we could do this with the other three."

Amanda took a deep breath. "Actually, I'm not sure it's going to be three."

Mary's head snapped up. "Who?" she asked, without any pretense. Amanda knew exactly whom she was asking about.

"It's Justice," Amanda said, cringing, knowing his was the name she was hoping not to hear.

Mary put her head in her hands. "But he's had the paperwork for months and hasn't done anything. It's going to take you months to check him out, and by that time the six months will be over. He doesn't deserve a son he never even asked about."

Mary assumed it was Justice's father, a man who was recently released from prison and had not responded to any of the court notices. "It's not him," Amanda said quietly. "He has a cousin. It's his dad's cousin who took care of Justice after he was born for several months while Angel and Blaze were still with their mom. She just found out about the petition. She lives in Chicago now and is doing pretty well apparently . . ."

"No." Mary spoke so quietly Amanda could barely hear her.

She paused for a moment. "I'm sorry, I couldn't hear you very well . . ."

"You heard me. I said no." Mary stood up, grabbed the kitchen sponge and started cleaning the counters aggressively.

Amanda stared at Mary's back and tried to figure out what to say. Was Mary saying no because she thought it was up to her, that she could stop this somehow? "She's a nurse now, working at a hospital in Chicago. She has a son of her own who used to help take care of him . . ." Amanda hoped that explaining the situation somehow might help Mary feel okay about losing Justice.

"This is not going to happen." Mary spun around angrily and looked at Amanda with tears and hatred in her eyes. "I will not let you take him just to send him off with some woman, a third cousin for Christ's sake, who hasn't seen him for three years. He's happy here. He's going to preschool and can write his name." She gulped back a sob. "He calls me mom." Mary pushed the tears off her cheeks with the palm of her hand. "You're not taking him."

Amanda stared back and had no words. She really didn't know if Mary had any right to fight Justice's eventual placement with his cousin. She didn't know what her position was supposed to be. Mary hadn't said a thing about fighting for Anthony, even though she had said that Larry would be devastated. "I can check with Zoe to see what your options are . . ."

"We will be hiring an attorney. Today. You can wait to hear from him." Mary walked out of the kitchen and down the stairs toward the boys, seemingly to keep Amanda from taking Justice right now.

"Mary, you know that we have to follow the law. You are licensed by my office to provide care for the boys. You're getting paid to . . ."

Mary wheeled around furiously. "You brought these children into my home. You asked me to keep them, to care for them. To be their mother."

"Foster mother," Amanda couldn't help saying.

"You want us to care for them like they are our children, and then let them go when you say so, to some fourth cousin twice removed from bumfuck Egypt who hasn't seen him for three years. I can tell you this isn't happening. You are not taking him." On cue, Justice came running up the stairs and wrapped his arms around her legs. Mary picked him up and held him close, his head on her shoulder. Amanda felt like a kidnapper.

"I'm sorry," Amanda said quietly. "I'll talk to my supervisor and get back to you." Amanda hurried out the front door before Mary could say more.

* * *

DRIVING BACK TO HER OFFICE, Amanda dialed Jacob's direct phone number at his desk.

"Terrance County Attorney, Jacob Mann." Amanda smiled at his formal greeting.

"I am so freaking tired of feeling like an incompetent baby snatcher." Amanda said by way of hello.

"If you work at it, you might become a good baby snatcher." Jacob said, and she could hear the smile in his voice.

"I doubt it. Remember the meth lab kids? Another relative came forward, this time for the four-year-old boy. You know we have to look at any and all relatives who come forward. I told them this from the beginning."

"Told who? The kids?" Jacob asked.

"Not the kid. He's four years old. I'm talking about the foster parents. Try to keep up," It sounded like he was typing and not really listening.

"Okay, Snappy. Jeez. What did the foster parents say?"

"She said no, you're not taking him. Like she can even say that." Amanda groaned. "She can't say that, can she? I don't even really know. That's the other thing I'm so tired of. I feel like I say ten times every day: 'I'll check and get back to you' or 'Let me ask my supervisor.' For once I would like to know the answer to a situation without having to ask someone."

"In other words, it's just another day working for the county," Jake said. "I expect not to suck at this sometime before I earn my ten-year plaque."

"Well, if you suck too, don't you think you should get someone else in your office to take my cases? Because I don't think incompetence should work with incompetence."

"Okay, first of all, I never said I was incompetent. And, second, you need to stop trying to get rid of me. I'm not going away, even if you get mean about it." He paused significantly. "So are you asking me what to do about these foster parents who won't surrender this kid?"

"I guess that's what I'm asking. But I'm probably not asking yet. I was just trying to tell her that a relative has come forward. I'm not even sure this will pan out, but she needs to be aware."

"Sure she does," Jacob said. "This has to be horrible for her, to get attached to these kids and then have to let them go."

"It's more like 'attached to one kid,'" Amanda said. "She's pretty willing to let the baby go, but the one with the cousin who wants him is her favorite."

"Well, no fair playing favorites," Jacob said. "She lost my sympathy."

"I know. And she's not a very sympathetic character to begin with, but I still feel bad."

"Yeah, well that's why you get the big bucks, Amanda."

"You're no help on this at all. New topic—have you heard from William today?" Amanda was back at her office and pulled into a parking place right next to the building, and then sat in the car to finish her conversation.

"Yep, he emailed this morning from his laptop. They are going to send her home tomorrow, but she's going to be on bed rest until the baby comes. He also said something is wrong with the placenta that means she needs a C section. Not terribly wrong, but not great either."

"It's called placenta previa," Amanda said. "It means that the placenta is blocking the cervix."

"Uh huh. And that is all I want to know about that."

"You're such a guy. I'll see you tomorrow in court."

* * *

MAX WAS ALREADY GONE when Amanda got back, so she found Zoe making coffee in the break room and told her about the meeting with Mary.

"Oh, yuck," Zoe said. "This is going to get ugly."

"That's what I thought. What are we supposed to do?" Amanda asked.

"Take one step at a time. The cousin isn't ready yet. Put everything in writing. And then get ready for a battle."

"Well, that's just great. I've been here for eight months, so I clearly feel ready for a big ugly trial," Amanda said.

"You're doing a great job, Amanda. Really great. I've seen how you talk to people, and I appreciate how direct, but still kind, you are. I think there's a good chance you can talk them through this."

Amanda smiled at the praise. Zoe was one of Amanda's favorite people in the office. She was the easiest person to talk to, and she felt like a person Amanda would want as a friend. "Thanks. I hope so."

"Where did you learn to be such a diplomat? Are you a middle child?" Zoe asked. It was a benign question for anyone who wasn't a former client.

"Only child, " Amanda said. "How about you?" Always deflect personal questions.

"Middle. So so middle. I had to sit in the middle of the backseat of our station wagon for every family vacation because my brothers would pummel each other if they sat together. I never complained, even though their hairy legs rubbed against me for three days when we went to the Grand Canyon. It just seemed easier to stay quiet. That's a middle child for you." Zoe leaned against the wall holding her coffee cup in both hands.

"Funny," Amanda said, edging toward the door. Amanda had daydreamed about having a big brother when she walked into her high school on the first day, thinking that an older brother who played football would protect her from unnamed girls who were sure to commit terrible hazing acts. In reality, on the first day of high school she had been invisible.

"No siblings, huh?" Zoe said. "What was that like?" Zoe smiled kindly, assuming that there was no option other than two doting parents. That one question had revealed Zoe's pleasant, middle class, intact family upbringing as clearly as a family movie. Amanda had never refined a good answer to family questions. In college she often responded with bitter sarcasm or just ignored the question altogether. But now she was making a concerted effort to lose the chip on her shoulder.

"It was just my mom and me," Amanda said hesitatingly.

Zoe nodded kindly. "Working with families the way we do really makes you think about how you grew up, doesn't it?" Amanda smiled in agreement. "It makes me realize that my mom making me come home at midnight on prom night wasn't such a tragedy."

Amanda was still hoping to make her way out, but Leah walked in, so Amanda was stuck in the room. "What wasn't a tragedy?" Leah asked as she moved toward the coffee maker, cup in hand, but stopped when she saw there was fresh coffee coming.

"Having a twelve o'clock curfew on prom night," Zoe said. "My parents were a little overprotective."

"Holy crap, I guess so," Leah said. "I was doing indecent things to my boyfriend, soon to be husband, soon after to be ex-husband, in his pickup while you were getting a good night kiss on your front doorstep."

"My husband was my prom date too and we were doing more than kissing, but I was still home on time," Zoe said, pulling the pitcher off the coffee maker and pouring herself and Leah a cup. "So what time did normal teenagers have to be home after the prom?"

Leah snorted. "Don't ask me. Both of my parents were drunk for most of my adolescence, so I came home when I felt like it." Someone else with a crazy life? Amanda relaxed a little, and she admired how Leah was able to talk about it with just the right balance of sarcasm and resolution.

"You're mom is doing great now, though, right?" Zoe asked.

"Sober for seven years," Leah said. "We go to the same meetings now."

"Okay, well now I really need to know," Zoe said. "How about you, Amanda? What was your prom night curfew?"

Amanda spent prom night in the emergency room with her mom, who had spiked a fever after her last round of chemo. Since she had no intention of going to her prom, the fever didn't spoil anything but a night watching Harry Potter movies. "2:00 a.m.," Amanda blurted.

"Well, there you go. That sounds more normal," Zoe said.

"What year did you graduate again?" Leah asked.

"It was five years ago, " Amanda said trying to make her way back to the door casually.

"Did you graduate with Steve Tubman?" Leah asked. "He's my ex's stepbrother, and is the cutest kid. You should date him, now that I think about it. I know he's single, and If I wasn't so angry at my ex every minute of the day I would call him to get Steve's number."

New dangerous territory. Amanda didn't want to talk about her dating life any more than she wanted to talk about her home life. "I graduated from Apple Falls, not Terrance. Anyway, I should get some casenotes . . ." she said heading out the door.

"You don't need to set up Amanda with anyone," Zoe said with a smile. "I think that new county attorney is smitten."

That got her attention. Amanda turned around and was so flustered that she knew she was blushing.

"Look at you!" Leah said. "You're smitten too!"

Amanda tried to will the blood to leave her cheeks, but could not come up with any sort of response, as usual. This was not good. Leah would never let this go.

"Call me a cougar to use a horrible cliché, but he's yummy." Leah said.

Zoe grinned. "He is super cute, but Leah you would destroy his gentle spirit, and anyway, Amanda's got dibs."

"I don't have dibs," Amanda, said, suddenly regaining the power of speech. "He's just a friend." Old friend. True friend. Yummy friend . . . An image of her hands sliding over Jake's naked back popped into her mind, and she looked away to keep them from somehow gazing into her dirty mind. "I'm going to work now." Amanda walked away, realizing that she was completely busted.

"You love him . . ." Amanda heard Leah sing-song as she went back to her cube. Of course she loved him, in some sort of capacity she was unable to define, but there was no way she wanted anyone to know that, least of all Jacob.

chapter twenty-three

A PRETRIAL HEARING IS JUST a formal way to get the parties together one more time before the CHIPS trial, and to settle any discovery or other trial issues. Shouldn't be a big deal," Jacob said as he packed up his files to head up to the courtroom. He was wearing a suit, not just a jacket and tie, and he looked nervous, though he was trying to act like he wasn't.

"What do you need from me?" Amanda asked.

"I think you just need to sit by me when we talk to him and make sure that I'm saying everything correctly. You know your file way better than I do, so you'll understand the social work stuff." Jake held the door open for her, and she walked through.

They headed up to the courtroom on the third floor where they would be having the hearing. Chuck Thomas was already there, chatting with the bailiff about turkey hunting. Skip Huseman was not there yet. Jake and Amanda strolled the hallways, Amanda looking out the window and Jake reviewing his file occasionally.

Skip Huseman arrived forty-five minutes late and barely glanced at Jacob. He breezed by the bailiff and Chuck Thomas, saying, "We're ready to go in."

The bailiff, a long-time sheriff's deputy with dozens of grandkids that he bragged about to anyone who would listen, stood up and followed Huseman. "Ready for the judge, already? Aren't you going to meet with Mann and the gal first?" Jake and Amanda had moved toward the bailiff's desk assuming that Skip would accompany them to a meeting room to hammer out issues about evidence and witnesses.

"I said we're ready now." Skip said. Edgy. His chill made Amanda very nervous. They followed the bailiff and Skip into the court room silently. Amanda and Jake sat at the table on the left, Skip and Chuck, minus any of Skip's associates, sat on the right.

"All rise," the bailiff said, and Amanda stood up, once again feeling like she was in a TV courtroom. A judge walked out that Amanda did not recognize. Jake looked down with what Amanda realized was a suppressed grin. "The Honorable Judge Matthew Bach presiding. Court will come to order. You may be seated."

"Good morning," Judge Bach said and nodded to both tables.

"Good morning, Judge," Skip said, his voice thick with schmooze. "And welcome to my hometown, as coincidence would have it." Ballsy, Amanda thought. He may as well pee in the corner for as much as he was trying to claim his territory.

"This is the case in the matter of the welfare of the child of Charles and Vivian Thomas, court file JV-78778." Amanda was pleased that the judge was not going to acknowledge any claim staking. "Please note your appearances for the record."

"Jacob Mann, two N's, Terrence County Attorney's office."

"Amanda Danscher, Terrence County Social Services." The judge's head popped up and looked at her a beat too long. Judge Bach appeared to be in his early to mid forties, with graying blonde hair and a soothing voice like a radio announcer. This judge was familiar looking, and Amanda got lost in her thoughts trying to place him.

"I expect to call both social workers," Jacob was saying, which brought Amanda back to the present. Judge Bach looked at her again, or maybe he was looking at Jacob. She had completely lost track of what was happening.

"We'll set the final hearing for May 4th," the judge said. "We'll get an order from today in just a moment." A petite clerk popped up from the desk next to the judge and moved to the room behind the courtroom to make copies of the order she had just printed.

Jacob looked at Amanda with his eyebrows raised and a small smile. He looked pleased, but Amanda hadn't a clue why.

The bailiff stood and moved toward the judge. "Permission to approach, Judge?"

Judge Bach stood and leaned across to shake the bailiff's hand. "Good to see you, Ed."

Ed, the bailiff, shook Judge Bach's hand with both of his. "Sorry to hear about your mom, Matt."

They were talking loud enough that it was impossible not to hear, but it still felt like they were eavesdropping.

"Thanks, Ed. We were praying for her to go in the end, but it was still really tough."

"I know Ellie said that she was relieved for you," Ed said. "She said you barely left her side, and that's too much when you're the only one."

The judge looked down in response, and Amanda glanced sideways to see that Jacob was listening too. The clerk returned and brought them copies of the court order from the hearing. Chuck Thomas took the order and leaned toward Skip to say something. He gave a one word answer, snapped his briefcase closed, and walked out of the room. Chuck Thomas followed looking angry.

"That went well," Jacob said, as they gathered their papers slowly enough so they did not have to talk to Skip and Chuck in the hallway. "Judge Bach is a good judge, and even though he's from here, he's not from here. He actually lives about twenty miles out of town, but he's based in St. Paul. Could you see how frustrated Huseman was that we had a different judge?" Amanda could only nod because she hadn't paid attention to anything. "This judge is a good guy," Jake said. *Trustworthy*, Amanda thought. Safe.

"I'm glad you feel good about him, " Amanda said.

He stopped to look at Amanda. "You didn't pay attention to this hearing at all. You were a million miles away."

She paused a moment too long. "No, I wasn't."

"Are you worried about testifying?" His eyes were wide and serious.

She met his eyes and felt her stomach drop a bit. "It'll be okay. I can handle it."

"Oh, I know you can handle it. You're a natural witness because you're smart and articulate, and very likable. I just don't want you to worry about it." They stopped by the elevator, and he shifted his books to his other arm to push the button for the basement.

"I'm fine." Amanda said, warmed by his compliments. "And thank you."

* * *

DRIVING HOME THAT NIGHT, Amanda's thoughts wandered back to Judge Bach. She remembered how Max had talked in their last staff meeting about how sometimes foster care just makes things worse for kids, because it shows them what they could have had. Amanda had always known that her life was not normal, but she had never spent much time thinking about what could have been. Would she be the same person if she had happy, healthy, normal parents? What if she had a blonde brother who was a senior when she was a sophomore and they blasted their music as they drove to school together? Who would she have been if she weren't alone?

She turned off Main Street and drove toward the railroad tracks. Amanda had not visited the house for several weeks because she just didn't know what to do about it. A part of her thought she was delusional for thinking that the house belonged to her grandmother based on only the vaguest sketches of memories. Another part had no doubts. She pulled over onto the hardened crust of ice, sand and snow that lined many streets in the winter. Had her mother walked out that front door, never to return? Did she regret the estrangement? She imagined her mother carrying her inside when she was brand new, showing her off. What did her grandmother say? Was she proud? Her mother was eighteen when she had her. Does that mean her grandmother was angry with her? At some point, they got along well enough for Amanda to play at her house. Why did that end?

Amanda suddenly ached for answers. If there was someone else in her life, where was she now? Amanda thought about going to the door and meeting the person who lived inside. Would it be that easy to meet her grandmother, if her delusion was actually real?

Amanda got out of the car and walked across the street and up the driveway and looked at the butterflies attached to the siding by the garage. Shades of a lighter tan peeked through the current pinky brown siding. The front door was hollow looking wood and worn to splinters. Had she been on these steps before?

With a gulp, Amanda forced herself to knock. The sound was empty and cold—no footsteps or voices. There was a small square window in the door that appeared to be covered with newspaper. Blinds covered a larger window by the front door, and Amanda peaked through an opening in the blinds. The carpet in the living room was flat, dark green, and very old. There was no furniture on the carpet. The house was empty.

Empty. If Amanda's grandmother had lived there, she wasn't there anymore. Back to being alone.

The idea of going home to an empty apartment was miserable. Amanda took out her phone and dialed. Her friend answered on the first ring.

"Hey, Lucy. Can I bring you some dinner?"

* * *

DURING HER FIRST TWO YEARS of college, Amanda spent a lot of her time with the guys on her dorm floor. She found them easier to talk to, because they didn't want to talk about anything of substance most of the time. They watched football and college basketball and played Nintendo. As the token female, she fell into the role of preparing the food, but Amanda enjoyed it. She did not grow up with a lot of homemade meals, so she prepared the foods that were familiar: frozen pizza, French fries, and spaghetti with sauce from a jar. Her most requested meal was just a giant sub made from a large loaf of French bread and deli meat, but the guys loved it. Since Lucy was still on bed rest and forced to lie on her left side most of the day, Amanda stopped at the grocery store and bought ingredients for her famous sub since it would be easy to eat lying down.

The sun was setting as she drove to their home, and she noted with a Minnesotan's relief that the sun was setting later and later. She pulled into Will and Lucy's driveway when the sky glowed orange and the stars were coming out.

Amanda knocked and walked in the door.

"I'm so happy you are here!" Lucy yelled from her perch on the couch. "Please come and distract me. If I watch any more daytime TV my IQ will drop below the room temperature."

She went into the living room and found Lucy lying on the couch on her left side, black hair standing up crazily on her left side. Normally petite and almost frail looking, Lucy's face was round and puffy. She was wearing a scoop neck nightshirt and flannel pajama pants, and her pregnancy breasts were spilling over the neck of her nightie. Amanda smiled at the sight of her, and felt a surge of gratitude that she had such a sweet and loyal friend.

"How's Oprah?" Amanda asked on her way to the kitchen.

"You know, I have to tell you that she's kind of bitchy sometimes. And patronizing." Lucy was trying to sit up a little higher so she could see

Amanda over the back of the couch as she prepared dinner. "I don't think she would be any fun to hang out with."

"So tell her you're busy next time she calls." Amanda said.

"I'm too desperate for company," Lucy said. "I'd even hang out with Dr. Phil if he called, and think how awful that would be."

"Yeah, I wouldn't be going to that dinner party," Amanda said. She pulled out the ingredients and started assembling her sandwich.

Lucy dragged herself to a sitting position. "How's work? How's your life? Tell me something interesting."

Amanda pondered how to answer that question. Her instinct was to be vague and superficial, but she decided to just tell the truth. "I went to that house. The familiar house that I thought might belong to my grand-mother, or someone like that."

"Okay that's interesting," Lucy said with wide eyes. "So you went up to the door or what?"

Amanda put the top bread on her sandwich and pushed it down lightly. "Yeah, I went up to the door. I knocked but there was no answer. I could see past the newspaper taped in the front window, and there was no furniture in the room or anything." She let out a sigh.

Lucy made a sad face and looked like she could cry. "Are you sure? Maybe there's something else you could do to find out who lives there."

Amanda nodded. "I suppose that's possible." She cut the sandwiches and served their dinner on plates, bringing them to the coffee table. She sat on the couch next to Lucy's feet, laid back and covered her eyes with both hands. "I don't know anymore. This is a delusion anyway. Thank you for humoring me, but I need to rejoin the real world."

"I'm sorry, Amanda." Lucy shifted and sat up next to Amanda on the couch. "So how are you doing? Were you really hoping that you would find someone in your family?"

Amanda looked down to hide her own tears. "I don't know. A lot of times my life is okay and I don't think about how awful it was for me grow-ing up. But it always comes back to this horrible aching feeling that I am so completely alone."

"Oh Amanda . . ."

"I know, Lucy. I know you're my family, and I'm so grateful for that." Amanda smiled a little as she realized that she really did trust that Lucy was her family. "It just would have been nice to have someone who shares my biology. The kind of family that can be considered next of kin. You know what I mean."

"Sometimes biological family is highly over-rated," Lucy said with a smile as she bit into her sandwich.

"I won't tell your baby that in fifteen years when she comes to her Auntie Amanda and says that she can't stand her family and wants to be emancipated."

"Thanks for that." Lucy said, one hand on her belly, the other on her food. "Great sandwich, as always."

"That's home cooking for you." Amanda said.

"Anything new at work?" Lucy asked. "I really do want to hear about the world outside of these doors."

"Bed rest is not your friend, is it?" Lucy just stared at her and waited. "Jake and I were in court today on our big ugly case."

Amanda went on to tell her about Judge Bach and how the attorney tried to suck up to him but it didn't work.

"Impressive," Lucy said, "although it really shouldn't be. Judges are supposed to be impartial, right?"

"Of course, but that seems so much harder in this town," Amanda said, realizing it was true. "Everybody knows everybody. It matters who you were when you were sixteen. That's what pisses me off. When I was sixteen I was nobody. I was less than nobody." Amanda heard how she sounded and tried to find something to say that didn't sound so bitter and sad. "Anyway, I really liked that judge. He seemed really fair and thoughtful." Amanda's cheeks got warm as she thought about him again. Lucy noticed and raised her eyebrows.

"Looks like you liked him. *Do you* like *him or just like him?*" Lucy leaned forward as far as her belly would allow.

"Oh, gosh, Lucy. I just thought he was a good judge." Amanda got up and started clearing their dinner.

"Clearly." Lucy said. "Remember that you are betrothed to Jacob, and the two of you have to get married and buy the house next door to ours so our kids can grow up together."

Amanda's stomach dropped and she smiled involuntarily. "You need to get a grip on reality."

Lucy sat back looking exhausted and full, even though she ate about a quarter of her sandwich. "I understand reality just fine, and the retired couple next door is talking about getting a townhouse. I'm just saying . . ."

* * *

Amanda dreamed about Judge Bach that night. She was pitching softballs at him, and he was a goalie in a hockey net making glove saves. He was on the ice, and she was on a softball field. He wasn't wearing a goalie mask, so she could see his face clearly as he gave her pointers on her pitching. Jacob was on the sidelines with Trix, Michael, Lucy and William cheering her on. Jacob brought her a hockey stick and told her she needed to start playing hockey, but Amanda argued and told him that she needed to stay on the pitcher's mound. Judge Bach approached the mound and told her to keep throwing softballs because he could handle anything she threw at him. Jacob threw up his hands and left the field. Amanda threw another ball at Judge Bach and hit him in the face. Amanda could see blood dripping on the ice and watched the paramedics load him on a stretcher when she woke up, still feeling guilty that she injured a judge. Then she was embarrassed that she dreamed about a judge, and grateful that no one knew how good it felt to see his face, even if it was in a dream.

chapter twenty-four

IN THE DAYS THAT FOLLOWED her dream, Amanda's caseload became so busy that she had little time to do anything but work. One one particularly hectic afternoon, Amanda was standing in the doorway of LaToya's trailer watching Marlys' boys play with JeMarquis's trains. LaToya stood by Amanda, facing the wall, so the boys couldn't see her tears.

"I knew this would happen. I told you it would happen. It still don't make it any easier."

"I know." Amanda said. Marlys had left her halfway house three days ago, and she wasn't responding to anyone's calls. Amanda went to LaToya's house to inform her that Marlys had just been arrested for felony drug possession and distribution. With her prior record, Jacob expected that she would serve a minimum of three years in prison.

LaToya blew her nose and heaved a deep sigh. She wiped her eyes again with her hands and Amanda noticed that she wasn't wearing artificial nails any more. She was wearing a Chicago White Sox baseball jersey and jeans. The boys were building towers with painted blocks and then knocking them over wildly.

"What's does this mean," she asked bluntly, "for them." She motioned to the boys who had sent dozens of blocks flying across the room. They scrambled after them fighting about who could get to the biggest blocks first.

Amanda exhaled. "Well, that's what I wanted to talk to you about. You've had the boys here a lot, and you do a great job with them. You helped Marlys with every part of parenting them, from attending school concerts to driving them to swimming lessons. She would have probably gotten them back after the next court review at the end of the month, mostly because of your support."

LaToya dropped her eyes modestly.

"Both the boys' dads have said that they're unable to take the kids full time. I think they would want to keep doing their visits. But they have also both told me that they want the boys to stay together."

LaToya nodded and blew her nose. "They would both be so sad if they weren't together anymore."

"I know. That's why I would like to recommend that permanent custody be transferred to you."

LaToya looked up at Amanda with apprehension approaching anger. "Don't fool with me, sweetheart."

"I'm not," Amanda said. "Our hope was that your sister would get her kids back, and our "plan B" was that they could go to their dads. Neither of those plans worked out, and we all kind of assumed that your criminal conviction would rule you out for the kids long term. It still would for foster care, but we could do a direct transfer of custody. As long as the judge agreed it was appropriate and safe, despite your criminal conviction, then we could do the custody transfer. I really think the judge will go for it."

LaToya was speechless. She devoured Amanda in a hug and heaved big sobs of joy and relief. Amanda wasn't sure if it was appropriate, but she happily hugged back.

* * *

FROM LATOYA'S HOUSE, Amanda drove to Buckhorn Elementary to meet with Angel. Social workers need to meet with children in foster care monthly, and Amanda found that the easiest way to see her was to go to school.

Angel slid into the chair across from Amanda, folded her arms and put her head down with an angry sigh.

"Hey there, Angel. Not in the mood to see me today?" After Angel's initial distrust, they were getting along pretty well.

"I hate Mary." But she didn't sound angry or hateful.

"Did something else happen or is it just the typical stuff?" Angel always had a list of Mary's offenses ranging from wicked crabbiness in the mornings to obviously favoring Justice and ignoring the rest of them. Perceptive Angel was definitely keeping score, and Angel believed that Mary was only tolerating her and Blaze so she could keep Justice. It was clear that Larry adored them all, but Angel barely talked about him.

"She's a bitch." Again, no venom behind the cursing, which Amanda ignored even though she vaguely felt that it was her responsibility to correct it. "She and Larry fight a lot. Why'd you put us somewhere with parents who don't like each other?"

"It looks to me that they do like each other." For all her chilliness, Larry did seem to love his wife. "Sometimes adults are pretty private with that stuff, though. And even if they're fighting that doesn't mean they don't still love each other."

"Larry loves everybody. He's a freak like that." Angel suddenly sat up and fixed her headband to get her hair out of her eyes. "They want to get you fired." Said for impact, Angel seemed to be reveling in this juicy announcement.

Involuntarily, her eyes widened, but she sucked back her gasp. "Hmm," she managed to say casually.

"They think you don't know what you're doing because you're going to hand us out to anyone who asks, just to save money." Angel seemed to be trying to read Amanda's face to see if it was true.

Ouch. Had they actually said this to Angel, or at the very least in front of her? Money had actually been a very small part of the discussion the many times they had staffed this family. Max and the other workers had focused on the many mandates and guidelines that dictated child placement, and the conundrum of keeping fathers involved while keeping siblings together. The situation was messy, and every option came with significant downsides, but they had eventually agreed that they were going to have to separate the siblings, at least to some degree, because Anthony had the opportunity to live with a biological parent. Anthony would have been with his dad already, but Mary and Larry filed a motion in court to ask the judge not to separate the siblings, so they had a new hearing scheduled in two weeks. "Angel, I just want you to know . . ."

"Yeah, I know. You already told me that you have to get kids with their parents and all that. But that girl, Heidi, told me that she's going to tell the judge that she wants us all to stay together." Angel looked smug and satisfied to have so much adult information, and to have an adult on her side. Heidi was the Guardian ad litem assigned to these kids, and she and Amanda had spoken frequently. If Heidi had taken this position, she hadn't shared it with Amanda.

"Heidi told you that?"

"I heard all of them talking. Mary said a bunch of times that she didn't think Justice could handle moving again, and then she went on and on about Blaze and his helpers and how good he's doing. Mary said that you guys are just trying to save money instead of doing what's best for us. And Larry was crying and stuff, but he kinda cries a lot. They don't like you at all, and they said you're too young and new to know what you're doing."

Even a nine-year-old could tell that she was in over her head.

Amanda let out a heavy sigh. "Angel, I'm going to be really honest with you right now. You and your brothers are very important, and we all want to do what's right for you. The problem is that it's hard to know what the right answer is. We know that kids need to be together, and we also know that kids really need to be with their parents. Both answers are right, and both answers have problems. Now, I told you that we would have to send Anthony with his dad because he is a biological parent."

"I know. But if you let him leave we'll never see him. He lived with us a while, remember? He was a jerk, and he *hated* Blaze. Larry loves Anthony the best, and he'll freak out if Anthony leaves. And if Larry freaks, then he might not want any of us, or he might not take care good care of Blaze, and Blaze has never ever done this good in his whole life. Nobody likes Blaze but me and Larry, and even Mary kinda likes him too." Angel was as animated as Amanda had ever seen her. "You can't let Anthony go. It's bad for Anthony, bad for Larry, and bad for all of us. Please listen to me. Please!"

Amanda's gut had spoken to her a few times in her life. It told her not to get in the car with drunk Harrison Peters when she was thirteen and he was seventeen, it told her that she should be a social worker, and it told her that he should have dinner with Jake that first day she met him at the hospital. Today her gut spoke to her again, and she decided to listen.

"Okay Angel, I hear you." She looked into this child's hazel eyes and could almost feel the weight of these four lives on her shoulders. "I can't promise what the judge will decide, but after reviewing all the information, I've changed my mind. I will write in my report next week that I want the four of you to stay together."

Amanda sent Angel back to class and headed for her car. There were such similarities between Angel and herself. Angel had that hardened exterior that kept her safe from the pain in her life. She was incredibly tough, and Amanda admired her immensely. This girl was a survivor.

The image of her own name on the computer system, followed by the word victim, popped in her head. Angel wasn't a victim, and this life she was living wasn't her fault. In fact, it made her the scrappy little girl that she was. For the first time, Amanda understood why people thought she was so strong, and she may have even agreed.

* * *

THE FIRST DAY OF SPRING is March 20th, but in Minnesota that could mean anything from seventy degrees and sunny to a blizzard or anything in between. March had remained almost balmy, which had caused the snow to melt early and quickly, leaving peoples' yards full of mud and puddles. Amanda avoided the grass and walked on the sidewalks, wearing shoes instead of clunky boots and feeling hopeful.

Madge had decided they should do a course on the identification of Minnesota flora and fauna, which meant long nature walks in the area's parks and trails. As Amanda parked at the high school and changed into tennis shoes, she wondered about the kids in her group. After the fight, Chad and Tyler were suspended and both went to a correctional facility. She assumed they had both been released by now, but she didn't know for sure. The principal had almost axed the program altogether, but the superintendent had actually intervened because he wanted to keep the collaboration with Social Services. Amanda felt pressure to make this program successful so she had been reading about experiential education programs with adolescents. The main thing she had learned was that a relationship with these kids was key, but she had no idea how to make that happen.

As Amanda made her way through the hallways to Madge's classroom, Brittany stopped her. "OMG, Amanda you have to come with me right now." Brittany's eyes were wide.

"OMG, Brittany we both have to get to class." Amanda said, and then remembered that she was supposed to be working on their relationship. "What's going on?" She looked at Brittany and saw she truly looked scared.

"I don't know, but something's wrong with Jess."

Amanda felt torn with the scrutiny on the program and the need to connect with these kids. "Brittany, we have to go to class, and so does Jess, but I'll talk to both of you after school. That's only a couple hours from now."

"Thanks for nothing!" Brittany flounced away and disappeared among the sea of students passing in the halls.

Madge looked different when Amanda arrived in her classroom. Her usually slicked back hair was dry and stood out in all directions. She was sitting at her desk staring at the computer and barely looked up when Amanda came in. The students in Amanda's group and in Madge's group were sitting on desks talking to each other, indifferent to both Amanda and Madge. The bell rang, but no one moved, including Madge.

"So, I've been reading about spring wildflowers, and I think I might recognize a brown-eyed susan if I see it."

Madge didn't take her eyes off the screen. "Study hall today," she muttered.

"Study hall? Here? We've never done that . . ."

Madge just waved a hand at her and didn't respond. Amanda looked at the students around the room. None of them looked like they had any intention of taking out a book. Katelyn was sitting in the back of the room listening to her iPod. Amanda crouched next to her desk and asked how things were going for her.

Katelyn shrugged. "Okay. I'm failing geometry again." She was drawing a face with big black tears.

"So, whatever happened with Chad?" Amanda asked. Tyler was in the classroom, sitting by himself staring at the clock.

"He got sent." Katelyn said. "Ninety days minimum."

Amanda assumed that Chad must have had a prior record that caused him to be in more trouble than Tyler. She tried to ask Katelyn why she was drawing tears, but Katelyn didn't feel like talking. She was able to convince Katelyn to work on her homework, so Amanda spent the rest of the hour "building a relationship" with Katelyn by struggling through geometry with her.

At the end of the hour, Amanda went to the office to try to find Jess. The two office support staff workers were chatting with a student helper.

"I love watching softball," one of the secretaries was saying. "My daughters all played, so I spent ten years in the bleachers. I miss it now that they've all graduated."

The student nodded. "My parents love it too. It's all we've done for the past five years every summer. All our vacations revolved around the season."

"I heard you're playing Apple Falls today," the secretary said, still not noticing Amanda. "They used to be so tough." Amanda felt her heart quicken at the sound of Apple Falls softball. She hadn't thought about her best sport for a long time.

"I know. My sister played when they had that all state pitcher that no one could hit."

"I remember her. Apple Falls won state that year, mainly because of that pitcher."

Amanda had been that pitcher. Her cheeks grew red, and she almost got tears in her eyes. She wanted to introduce herself and talk softball with these women who knew her only as a great pitcher. But she needed to find Brittany, so she interrupted to do her work.

"Excuse me, I need to find a student, Jessica . . ." Amanda realized she didn't know her last name and couldn't remember Brittany's last name.

The older of the two secretaries, the one whose daughter played softball, smiled kindly. "I'm sure you know we'll need more than that."

Amanda felt stupid. "Yeah, I know. She's a tenth grader, I think. Her cousin, Brittany, is in Madge's EBD class."

"Brittany Coleman," the student said.

"That's her," Amanda said.

"Her cousin is Jess Peters," the student went on. "Her dad was my doctor when I was little."

"I'm sorry," the secretary said. "I just need to know who you are because I can't just give out . . ."

"Of course," Amanda said. "I'm from Terrance County Social Services. I work with Madge. I'm helping in her classroom. We do experiential classroom learning."

The secretary nodded absently. "Neat." She pulled up a schedule on her calendar. "Jess has been marked absent all day."

"Okay," Amanda said, trying to figure out what to do next. Brittany loved drama, and Amanda wasn't sure if she was creating drama by chasing her around. Even though she wasn't due back until the next week, Amanda decided to come back tomorrow and try to see Brittany then.

She walked back outside and headed to her car. The softball fields were on the other side of the parking lot, and Amanda watched as the

Apple Falls bus pulled up next to the field and the players started exiting the bus. Amanda remembered the feeling of anticipation before a game. She usually sat alone on the way to the game, but was always distracted and indifferent to being by herself. On the way home, she sometimes sat with the JV coach, who was also the pitching coach, and they discussed her game. As the girls headed toward the field, she also saw several people getting out of their cars and unloading picnic chairs and coolers. Parents. She wondered if there was someone on the bus like her, all alone, who never had someone cheering just for her. Amanda wanted to go to the game, and cheer for just that girl. Then reality set in, and Amanda realized that she wouldn't know who was alone, and most likely there wasn't anyone as alone as she was. Amanda got in her car and drove home. Alone.

* * *

THE EVENING PASSED SLOWLY, with Amanda trying to find something to watch on TV. She realized that she needed a hobby, a class, something to fill the rest of her time. Five years of college had filled her evenings with constant studying, papers to write, tests to study for. Now her evenings were hers, and she didn't know how to spend them. The Twins had played a spring training game during the day, and Amanda smiled as the sports announcer on the news was wearing short sleeves as he reported from Fort Myers, Florida. Then the weather forecast came on, with news of a major change coming in the next twenty-four hours. The temperature was supposed to drop at least forty degrees, with rain changing to snow overnight. With the winds picking up there would be near blizzard conditions. The weather forecaster's eyes seemed to sparkle with the excitement. *Stupid Minnesota*, Amanda thought. Can't put away the boots quite yet.

Amanda has fallen asleep on the couch, so the sound of knocking startled her awake. Jimmy Fallon was on TV. Amanda's contacts felt fused to her eyelids, and she could barely open her eyes. More knocking.

Amanda went to the door and found Jess and Brittany standing on the deck. Brittany's eyes were wide, and she had her arm intertwined with Jess's. Jess's teeth were chattering, her dark-blonde hair was unkempt, and she had mascara smudged under her eyes.

"Jess got raped," Brittany said. Jess flinched at the word.

Amanda stepped back and let them inside.

chapter twenty-five

J ESS STEPPED INSIDE AND STOOD, FROZEN. Brittany looked at Jess's face, and then at Amanda. "She's been like this all day. She was in the back of her car until noon. I found her there after fourth hour and tried to get her to come out. I brought her some food, but she wouldn't touch it. That's when I tried to get you, but you wouldn't come." Jess's teeth were still chattering.

Amanda's worst days were in the hospital with her mom, mostly when she was younger before she got so numb. Her favorite nurse brought her a quilt made by the hospital auxiliary, and somehow that quilt made those days a little better. It was heavy flannel, and she had imagined that her grandmother made it for her. Amanda still had that quilt. She went to the foot of her bed and pulled the quilt off and brought it to Jess, wrapping it around her shoulders, and then led Jess to her old couch and helped her sit down. She sat stiffly on the edge of the cushion. Amanda found an envelope of hot chocolate and made her a mug. Amanda brought it to Jess and tried to put it in her hands, which were ice cold.

Brittany sat on the couch next to Jess, and put a hand on her back. "She's so freaked out," Brittany said, speaking as if Jess weren't there, which appeared to be accurate anyway. "She won't talk."

"If she won't talk, how do you know that she was . . . how do you know what happened to her?" Amanda asked.

Brittany looked like she was struggling for words, for once not just talking a hundred miles an hour. "Cuz, she came to my house this afternoon. My mom is on second shift so no one was home. All she wanted to do was take a shower. I kind of saw her in there. I mean I wasn't staring or anything, but she was so weird that I didn't want to leave her alone. She was, like, scrubbing herself, um, down there. And the way she's acting too . . ."

Tears were running down Jess's face.

Amanda reached out and touched her frigid hand. "Jess, can you talk to me?" Amanda put the warm mug in Jess's hand and tried to get her to take a drink. Jess put her hands around the mug and took a sip. Before she was going to be able to talk, she was going to need to know she was safe.

"Let's just let her sit for a while and warm up," Amanda said and went to the kitchen. Brittany followed her.

"Oh, my god, I am so scared," Brittany said, her voice cracking. Here was the drama Amanda expected.

"I know, Brittany, "Amanda said. "Where was she last night?"

"I don't know," Brittany said. "There was a bonfire at Schmitty's farm. I know that Jess parties sometimes, so she was probably drinking. But that doesn't mean people can just have sex with her if they want to."

"Of course it doesn't, "Amanda said. "I'm just trying to figure out who she was with." They could hear a cell phone beep from the living room, indicating that someone was receiving a text message.

"That's the other thing," Brittany said. "She's been getting texts all day. She won't respond. I thought it might be her mom so I called her mom and said Jess was going to sleep over and help me study for a test. I'll bet if you get her phone you'll know who she was with."

Amanda found a can of soup, poured it in a bowl and heated it in the microwave, working slowly to give Jess a few moments to relax. She brought the bowl into the living room. Jess was lying down with her eyes closed, the blanket wrapped around her like a hooded cape.

"Jess, I know you might not want to, but I think you should try to eat. Brittany and I are here, and you're safe, and I just want to help you feel comfortable." Jess looked at Amanda with wide, woeful eyes, the trauma and horror showing behind her glassy stare, and she gave Amanda the first of her many surprises of the night.

"Okay," Jess said, and took the bowl in her hands.

* * *

IT WAS NEARLY 2:00 A.M. WHEN Jess actually found her voice. The words came out under her breath, too horrific to speak out loud. She was at the bonfire, got in the car with a group of guys, and lost her friends at the party. They had been drinking sloe gin, and she was foggy. The jocks were talking to her, and she felt important. The car was black, and they rode to someone's house. Someone's basement. More drinking. And then the fog set in, and she must have passed out. She awoke feeling worse than hung over. Naked, on the floor between the bed and the wall. And then she started sobbing with gasping, shuddering heaves. Amanda was thinking like an investigator, wanting to know who, where, when.

Looking at Jess's face she could see that those details were not important right now. As Jess talked, her face began to relax, while Amanda felt her shoulders get heavier. Amanda told Jess to close her eyes and try to get some sleep. Jess rubbed her hands over her face, pulled her cell phone and her keys out of her pocket, and lay down. She was snoring quietly within seconds.

Brittany had been sitting on the floor with Amanda, crying along with Jess as she told her story. As soon as Jess was asleep Brittany grabbed her phone and started scrolling through her messages.

"Weird," Brittany said, rolling off the floor and going to the kitchen. "She has twelve missed calls from Rachel Thomas." She touched the screen a few more times. "She has a bunch of texts from her too, just saying to call her. They must have been together at the bonfire last night."

"Why don't you text her back, tell her we need to know who she was with last night." Amanda followed her to the kitchen. She was exhausted, her eyes watering with fatigue.

Brittany's eyes were bright. "Got it," she said. Amanda poured herself a glass of water, and put her head down, too tired to drink.

"Whoa, she texted back already," Brittany said to the buzz of the phone. "'Who is this? Where is Jess?' I wonder how she could tell it wasn't Jess. I tried to make it seem like I was Jess."

Amanda rolled her eyes. "Brittany, why don't you give me the phone?" The phone rang with an actual call.

Brittany saw it was Rachel calling again. "Hey, Rachel, it's Brit . . . what? Yeah, she's okay, I mean, I guess she's pretty messed up actually . . . well, we're at Amanda's house. The social worker from my group. You remember her . . . Rachel?" Brittany looked up at Amanda. "She hung up."

"Well it's almost three in the morning," Amanda said. "We can try to check in with her tomorrow. Speaking of that, do your parents know where you are?' Amanda asked.

"I told her we were sleeping over at Jess's place so we could study."

"Same thing you told Jess' mom. What if they talk to each other?"

"They never talk," Brittany said. "No one in our family can stand my mom."

Too tired to respond, Amanda just nodded. "I think you should sleep in the living room with Jess. Tomorrow we'll be talking to both of your parents, but I think at this point it would create more problems than it would solve." Amanda didn't have any more blankets, but she found a sleeping bag she bought for camping in college, and unrolled it for Brittany. She went back in her bedroom and gave Brittany her pillows since they were the only ones in her apartment, and she headed to her room to go to bed.

* * *

AMANDA HAD LAIN IN HER BED less than a minute when she heard a car door slam outside. The wind was picking up with the impending storm, and she noticed that a soft rain had started to fall. She thought about Lucy, still stuck on bed rest for another three weeks at least, and wondered if she even noticed what was happening outside her apartment. She had expected to fall asleep immediately, but sleep wouldn't come.

And then there were footsteps on her stairs coming up to her apartment, and she heard the door open. Brittany must have let someone inside. Amanda jumped out of bed, pulled a sweatshirt on and went out to find another teenage girl in her apartment, looking frantic and angry.

"Brittany, what's going on?" Amanda asked, recognizing the girl but unable to place her. She had long dark hair that was messy and wild, and her wide eyes looked frantic.

"Don't you remember? This is Rachel." Rachel went straight to the living room.

Rachel Thomas. Of course. Amanda was instantly uneasy about having this girl in her living room, and wondered if this would somehow mess up her case that was heading to trial very soon. She could hear whispering so she went in the living room to find Rachel trying to wake up Jess.

"Rachel," Amanda said, louder than she meant to, but she was feeling protective. "Jess needs to sleep."

"Stay out of it!" Rachel snapped, and turned back to Jess. "Come on Jessie, wake up. Let's go to Sydney's."

Amanda didn't know who Sydney was, but she knew that she was not going to allow Jess to leave with Rachel in the middle of the night. "I'm serious, Rachel. She's not leaving."

"You need to stay the *fuck* out of my family's business, for your own good as well as everyone else's."

Amanda's heart started to beat faster. "What do you mean, your family's business? How is Jess part of your family's business?"

Rachel's head snapped around to look at Amanda, her face showing a sudden fear.

"Did this happen to Jess at your house?" There are four boys in the Thomas family . . .

Rachel shook Jess's shoulders again, and this time Jess's eyes fluttered. "Come on, Jess. Let's go to Syd's." Jess opened her eyes and looked at Rachel, and then looked around, not appearing to know where she was. "There, you're awake. Let's go." Rachel started to pull on Jess's arm, but Jess wouldn't move.

Brittany lunged forward. "You're not taking her," Brittany said, and she sat on the end of the sofa and put her hands on Jess's legs protectively. Her eyes narrowed as she leaned toward Rachel. "It was your brothers, wasn't it? Both of them, I bet. They're such jerks I wouldn't put it past either one."

"You need to listen to me," Rachel said, her voice dropping. Amanda saw that her hand on Jess's shoulder was shaking. "Stay out of it." She looked down at Jess. "I'm serious now. Let's go."

Jess sat up slowly, groggy. She looked at Rachel, her eyes narrowing. "They do it to you, too. Don't they?"

Rachel pulled her hand away and stood up. "Fuck this."

Rachel ran for the door and grabbed the doorknob, but Amanda put her hand across the door. "Rachel." Amanda looked her in the eyes. "This can end today."

Rachel's eyes welled with tears. She looked back at Jess, who looked at her pleadingly. Slowly, Rachel's hand slid from the knob and dropped by her side. She lifted her head as tears ran down her cheeks, and she breathed one word, "Finally."

chapter twenty-six

THE FOUR OF THEM SAT in the living room, Jess still on the couch, and Brittany, Amanda, and Rachel cross-legged on the floor. Rachel wrapped herself in the sleeping bag, shivering as she talked.

There were many girls. Rachel had been eight-years old when she realized that her older brother, now in college, was bringing girls back to the house. There was usually drinking involved, coming from the ever-present supply of liquor in the basement. She didn't know until she was older that most parents didn't allow their sons to have girls "sleep over." Sometimes they left in the middle of the night. Sometimes in the morning. When she was young, she thought her brother must be a bad boyfriend because the girls always looked glassy eyed and scared when they were leaving.

"But I can't believe one of those girls was my friend," Rachel said. "I can't believe they would do that to her." The tears flowed again.

"Rach, it's not your fault," Jess said, looking stronger than she had since the night started. "How can you blame yourself for what your brothers did?"

"You think you get it, but you really don't," Rachel said.

"Help us get it, "Amanda said. "What about you?"

Rachel shook her head.

"Who hurt you?" Amanda asked again.

"Everyone," she blurted. "Everyone does what they want, but now it's my fault too. Can't you see that? It's my fault that they do it to me. It's my fault that they do it to her, and all those other girls. All of it is my fault." Amanda knew that girls who were sexually abused blamed themselves, but it was still shocking to see it actually happen in front of her.

"None of this is your fault," Amanda said. "You're a kid, and you haven't done anything to deserve any of this."

Rachel glared at Amanda, and she seemed to be making a decision about whether to continue. She rubbed her face with her hands. "If they're doing it to her, they can't do it to me," she snapped. "I hide. I barricade my door. I stay over with friends. I do whatever I can to keep them away from me, but if they don't have me, they just get it from someone else. It's just what men do, and I need to accept that."

Those were someone else's words. And Rachel said men.

"Rachel," Amanda started slowly, afraid of shutting her down again. "What do you mean by that last part, 'It's just what men do'."

"It is," Rachel said, shaking her head. "It's how they are."

"Who said that to you?"

She scoffed. "I just know that. I've lived it."

"But, your brother's aren't really men yet . . ."

She rolled her eyes. "You think it's just my brothers?"

Amanda's heart started beating faster. "Are you saying . . ."

"How do you think my brothers learned it? Chuck showed them. Chuck made them."

Brittany sucked in her breath. "Holy shit."

Rachel seemed to be irritated by Brittany's response. "Uh, yeah. Holy shit about covers it. You have no idea." Her eyes got wider as the words just spilled out. "They kept having boys until finally they got their girl. That's what he always tells people. They wanted a girl. They wanted me for a toy. I was five years old and they were doing it to me. All of them. And it probably happened before that too. I went to a sleepover birthday party when I was in second grade, and I kept wondering when her dad or her brother was going to come in and start on us. Because that's what men do." Tears ran down her face, seemingly unnoticed, as she kept talking so fast she seemed to be afraid to stop. "When I was little I used to tuck myself into my bed so tight just hoping that would stop them. At least slow them down. He started giving my brothers alcohol when they were twelve. It got so much worse when they were drinking. My oldest brother is drunk all the time. He's going to kill himself someday just by alcohol poisoning. He started bringing other girls home to his bedroom, and it was like Chuck was proud of him. They call it the mancave, like they're being funny. He would get the girls drunk with booze that Chuck supplied. He was practically their bartender. I told myself that if they got girlfriends, it would be better, so I was always relieved when the girls came over. But that's when Chuck would go after me even worse. I didn't even know what to wish for anymore."

The other girls stared in shock and horror. Jess was quietly sobbing.

"But I never wished this for you," Rachel said to Jess, looking angry and ashamed. "I'm so sorry they got you."

Jess shook her head, the fear and shock turning to anger. "Stop apologizing," she said wiping her face with the sleeve of her sweatshirt. "I'm sorry they have been getting you your effing whole life."

Amanda was trying to think like a social worker, but she was almost shaking herself. Rachel and Jess both seemed to be getting stronger as they told their stories, and she could see relief in both of their faces. For Amanda, the opposite was happening. She was becoming overwhelmed, knowing that she was the only adult in the room. It was her job to help them, and to finally make this stop.

Rachel and Jess were leaning against each other, both silently crying. Brittany held Jess's hand, crying too. Amanda went to the kitchen, found her workbag, and pulled out her digital recorder usually used for dictating case notes. She grabbed her pen and notebook and went back to the living room.

Rachel saw the notebook and immediately began shaking her head back and forth. "No. I can't. No." She looked at Amanda in fury. "You know him. You already saw what he did to my little brother. You saw it. That was my fault too, you know. I tried to refuse, and he went after him. Even if you get me out of there, don't you see what's going to happen to him?"

Amanda's jaw dropped. The broken arm was retaliation for Rachel, and was obviously a very effective way to keep her quiet. "Rachel," she began, thinking fast and choosing her words carefully. "If you start talking about this, then everyone in your family can be kept safe."

"Chuck owns this town. No one will believe me over him," Rachel said.

"But it's not just you, Rachel," Amanda said, gesturing to Jess. "It's Jess too. And from the sound of it, there are lots more girls. You can make this end tonight."

Rachel curled into a ball and hid her face in her hands. A full minute passed. Then Rachel took a deep breath in and exhaled shakily. Finally she spoke. "Okay."

* * *

AMANDA DID HER BEST to interview her the way she had seen Leah interview kids. Surprisingly, Rachel nodded when Amanda took out her digital tape recorder, and she allowed Amanda to record their interview. Amanda was just grateful that she had her work bag at home. She asked basic, non-leading questions and let Rachel do much of the talking. Amanda focused on the interview, but the trauma of Rachel's life was almost unbearable to hear about. Amanda tried to think of the details she would need, things like when and where, how many times, was there penetration every time . . . ? Cold, direct questions that have to ignore the pain behind the answers to get to the facts. It had started early in Rachel's life, in her bedroom and in the "mancave." Chuck would touch her, and make her touch him. He brought the brothers in too. He would make the brothers watch what he did, and then make them repeat it. Rachel talked about how she would "go away" when it was happening, and she would lose all feelings and sometimes even all awareness. At some point Rachel had "gone away" during their interview. Her words were flat and emotionless, and her eyes had slid to a far away place.

After nearly an hour, Rachel said she had had enough. "I can't talk anymore," she said, rubbing her eyes. It was after 5:00 a.m.

"Okay, Rachel," Amanda said, knowing she had not heard everything, but hoping for now it was enough. "You did great. Thank you." Rachel lay back down on the floor next to Jess. Brittany had fallen asleep on the couch, and Amanda guessed she would be sorry that she missed the interview. "Why don't you girls try to sleep for a few hours, and I'll let you know what comes next." They both nodded and curled up on the floor under the sleeping bag. Amanda went to her room and pulled the comforter off her bed, realizing that she never did sleep that night, and she brought it to the girls, who were already asleep.

Amanda walked back into her kitchen with overwhelming fatigue and a desperate desire to close her eyes for a few minutes, but she knew she could not. She needed to put this together into some type of report and bring it in to work immediately. She knew that the county attorney, probably Jake, would need the details in order to proceed with the case.

Amanda shivered at the thought of what might come next. Sadness for Rachel combined with a tiny thrill of being able to make something as horrible as this finally come to an end. This was why she wanted to do this job.

Amanda pulled out her laptop and started writing.

chapter twenty-seven

AT 7:00 A.M AMANDA FINISHED her report, making extra sure that she saved the documents carefully. She closed her laptop, pushed away from the kitchen table where she was writing and went into the bathroom to take a shower. Looking out the bathroom window she could see that the rain had changed to heavy, wet snow. Most of the season's snow had melted, but this storm had already covered the ground with four inches of new snowfall.

Even with the shower on, Amanda could hear the wind wailing outside. She dressed quickly and warmly. She had already emailed the report to herself, but she decided to bring her laptop with her in case email was slow or down. She needed to tell Max about all of it first, and then she assumed she would bring it to Jake for a CHIPS petition and criminal charges. She pictured Jake's face as she told him the news, again feeling a rush of excitement and pride that she was going to help bring this horrible abuse to an end.

The girls were all still asleep in the living room when Amanda left for work. She arrived at her desk early, and was surprised to see so many of the offices empty.

"Dark over here," Jeanne said as she walked by Amanda's office. "Everyone left last night for that judge's conference." Amanda remembered that she and Jeanne were scheduled to be the only ones in the office most of the day.

"That's right," Amanda said absently. She was trying to decide if she should talk to Jeanne about Rachel and Jess. Jeanne had worked there forever, but she rarely handled child protection cases, and she wasn't sure what kind of advice she would get. She decided against it for now.

"Have a nice day," Jeanne said.

Amanda wondered what kind of day she would have as she called Jacob.

"Hey," he answered on the first ring.

"Hey, Jake. You're not gonna believe what I'm about to tell you."

"Well, tell me quick," he said distractedly. "I'm one of the only attorneys here and there was a drug bust this morning."

"It's about Chuck Thomas."

"You have my attention."

Amanda took a breath. "He's been having sex with his fifteen-year-old daughter for years."

Silence. Then he said, "Holy effing shit."

Amanda told him that Brittany went to her first, and then Jess, and then Rachel came to try to get her to stop talking. But then Rachel started talking, and she told about the years of abuse.

"You interviewed her? Are you trained to do that?" Jake asked.

"I have attended training about interviewing," Amanda said quickly. "She was ready to talk, and I thought I better let her talk when she was ready. She had been quiet for so long. I know sometimes Leah has to do more than one interview if there's a lot and the kid needs a break. I know someone may have to talk to her again, but it just seemed like the right thing to do. I have a report ready to go . . ."

"A cop is going to need to do the complaint. You guys usually work with Kemper, right?""

Amanda thought that Investigator Pete Kemper did most of the child abuse investigations, but she had never met him. "Yeah, I think that's who Leah usually works with. Everybody in my office is at that judge's child abuse conference, so I can't ask her."

"Tell me about it. My office is cleared out too. Send me the write up, and I'll get Kemper to review it and sign the complaint. He's working on the drug bust, but he owes me big so he can help us out."

"Okay, good," Amanda said, relieved that someone else would take responsibility for the criminal part. "I'll get my CHIPS letter ready. I'm sure we'll need to pull all the kids."

"Even after he gets arrested? Where's the danger after Chuck's gone?"

"The brothers were in on it too. Rachel's terrified of all of them, and her mom knew at least part of what was going on."

"We're going to have to do complaints on all of them?"

"I . . . I guess so," Amanda said. She hadn't thought about all those boys getting arrested too.

"Send me the report and we'll go from there."

"Sounds good." Amanda hung up and emailed her report to Jacob.

"So what are you working on today?" Jeanne was back in her doorway.

"I'm working on an investigation," Amanda said. For some reason she didn't want to tell her any more than that. "Do you have Max's cell number, or maybe Leah's?"

"You can try, but cell phones aren't getting through very well because of the storm. There was a huge accident on 35W and it's completely shut down. This whole part of the state is a mess, and it's supposed to get worse as the day goes on." Jeanne was like so many Minnesotans and got a little rush from a big storm.

Amanda took the phone numbers, and Jeanne looked a little disappointed that Amanda didn't want to talk longer. Amanda tried to call both Leah and Max but couldn't get through to either. The phones just beeped like they were busy. Amanda went back through her report and tried to review it critically, the way Max or one of her senior coworkers would. Had she covered her bases? Was she thorough in the interview? She thought about the girls and realized they would be awake by now. She tried to call her house but no one answered, and she didn't have any of their cell phone numbers.

Amanda got to work writing her CHIPS letter, detailing the history with Chuck Thomas, beginning with the alleged assault of his youngest son, and culminating with the lifelong sexual abuse of his daughter. It took some time to find all the information she needed to include in the letter. She tried calling Max and Leah one more time, couldn't get through to either, and decided to head over to Jake's office.

The walk across the street was brutal, with a frigid wind and heavy snow swirling around her. There were few cars on the road as school was canceled, and some businesses were even closing because of the storm.

There were more police officers than attorneys in the county attorney's office. She said hello to the receptionist, Bonnie, and went to Jake's tiny office.

Jacob looked up with wide eyes. "Good God! I'm speechless." He pointed at his computer where her letter was pulled up on the screen. "I mean, I knew this guy was a complete bastard. But, this . . ."

"I know. I still can't even believe it." Amanda squeezed into the chair across from him.

"I forwarded it to Kemper, and he's on his way here to sign the complaint. I think we can pick him up today."

"So you really are going to arrest him right away?"

"We'll see what Kemper says, but I think there's clearly enough for an arrest here."

Amanda's heart was thudding, and her overwhelming fatigue made it hard to think. On cue, Kemper stuck his head in Jake's doorway. "Nice office, Mann," he said with a smile. Pete Kemper was about forty-five, dark haired and balding, with a rich voice that reminded Amanda that he was a high school sports radio announcer on the weekends.

"Did you read it?" Jake asked.

"Can't fucking believe it," Kemper said. "The second oldest kid has been at my house. Friends with my Kelsey. She and I will be talking tonight."

"Enough to arrest, wouldn't you say?" Jake asked.

"Enough to string him up by his testicles. It would warm my heart to call him out from behind that filthy lunch counter and arrest him during the lunch rush and drag him by his hair to my squad." Kemper's face working as he was wondering if anything could have happened with his daughter.

"Julie's got the complaint. I'll let you know when the judge signs it." Kemper turned around and left to sign the complaint.

"Thanks for introducing me," Amanda said.

"You know I suck at that," Jake said with a grin.

"God, I'm tired."

* * *

AMANDA STAYED IN JAKE'S OFFICE editing the petition on his laptop while Jake was reviewing the complaints for the drug bust.

After forty-five minutes, Jake got a call from Kemper. He nodded a few times and gave Amanda the thumbs up. "Can't wait to see that mug shot."

Amanda gave a weary smile. Jake beamed. Her pride and her fatigue made it easy for her to ignore the nagging feeling she had in her gut. The feeling that should have told her that this situation was about to go terribly wrong.

chapter twenty-eight

IT WAS NEARLY 1:00 WHEN they started talking about food and Amanda remembered she hadn't eaten anything all day. The staff left in the County Attorney's office was getting ready to order food so they didn't all have to leave and fight the storm. Jake said that Amanda would probably like a Caesar salad and a diet coke. He raised his eyebrows at her in question that the order was correct. She nodded and smiled that he knew what she wanted, and felt confident enough to order for her.

She and Jake had spent another half-hour editing and waiting for Chuck Thomas's mug shot to go online when Jake's expression turned serious.

"Barb wants us in her office right now." Jake was reading an email from Barb Cloud, who was the lead county attorney, an elected official who supervised the entire office. Something in Jake's face made her afraid to ask why.

They walked down the hall to Barb's large office, where she was on the phone. She motioned for them to sit down in the cushioned chairs in front of her. Barb's office was incredibly neat, which fit with her well-coiffed appearance. She was a politician, but she was also a brilliant lawyer and expected to win a judgeship as soon as one became open. She pushed the speaker button on her phone and set down the receiver.

Amanda's heart thumped hard as she recognized Skip Huseman's voice. "The lawsuit is coming. Your only hope at this point is to minimize the horrific damage and possibly save your job by getting him released immediately and issue a statement accepting full responsibility for this egregious and outrageous atrocity that has been committed to my client."

"We stand by our investigation. This is a solid arrest, Skip."

"How can you stand by your investigation when your alleged 'victims' are in my office stating that your social worker coerced them into making a statement at her home and would not allow them to leave."

They recanted. Oh god.

Barb and Jake turned to look at Amanda. Amanda tried to process all the implications of the girls recanting their statements, and internally she started to panic. Jake rolled his eyes and began to scoff, but his face dropped when he saw Amanda's stricken look.

Barb's eyes narrowed as she studied Amanda's face and she allowed a momentary pause before responding. "We have statements, Skip." But her voice was not as sure sounding as it was a moment ago. "Look, Skip, I've got bedlam here with the storm and a major drug bust, so we're done for now. He'll appear in front of a judge at eleven o' clock Monday morning, and we'll take it from there." Barb pushed the disconnect button abruptly and pointed her pen at Amanda. "What the bloody hell is he talking about?"

Tears stung her eyes and the familiar, dangerous roar resumed in the back of her head. "I didn't coerce anyone," she said desperately. "They came to me."

"Came to you?" Jake asked, his voice rising. "What does that mean, 'came to you'?"

Anger and panic clouded his face. She gulped and tried to steady her voice. "Brittany wanted to talk to me in school, but I had to get to class."

"Are you a teacher?" Barb frowned looking confused.

"She helps in a classroom for troubled kids." Jake said quickly, motioning her to continue.

Amanda nodded. "I tried to find her after school but couldn't. So I went home. I had fallen asleep on the couch and heard a knock on my door. It was Brittany and Jess. Brittany is a student in my room, and Jess is her cousin." She tried to describe the way Jess looked, the haunted, vacant trauma, and she thought she saw Barb's face soften. When she described Rachel's arrival, Jake leaned forward.

"How does Rachel Thomas know where you live?" His anger was still brewing, but she could feel his concern too.

Amanda paused. "I don't know. Brittany said she knew I lived by the middle school, and she recognized my car in front. Maybe Brittany told

Rachel?" But Amanda knew that wasn't right because they were all shocked when Rachel arrived. But regardless of how they found her house, she did not want them to doubt what had happened. "I know he did this. Rachel did not make this up."

"It doesn't matter what you know," Jake said, his words clipped, his face darkening. "It matters what we can prove. If those girls recant their statements, we can't prove anything, and then we have just arrested a prominent community leader for freaking first-degree criminal sexual conduct with no evidence."

"What's worse, this investigation is contaminated no matter what the girls say now." Barb craned her face up at the ceiling shaking her head. "You just don't do this. You don't conduct interviews at your home. I can't believe Kemper signed this complaint. He got screwed on a technicality a few years ago, so he's always by the book."

Jake turned to Amanda, the realization slowly coming to him. "We didn't put it in the complaint." He looked down as he said it, and Amanda could see the shame in his eyes. Fear washed over Amanda as she considered the implications for Jake and for herself.

Barb looked from Jake to Amanda, her expression hard. "You conducted interviews in your home, and then you withheld it like you had done something wrong. Which, now, you have."

Amanda squeezed her eyes shut, her priority now to fix this for Jake. The girls recanted, and she wouldn't be able to change that, but she could at least clean up this investigation. "I have taped statements," she blurted. "Rachel spilled the whole thing. I'm sure she's terrified. Kids recant. All the time." Amanda recalled her training on sexual abuse and how the majority of sexual abuse victims recant all or part of their statements when they realize what they have said.

"This investigation is so tarnished that there's no way we can get these charges to stick," Barb said angrily. "You need to get those statements just to cover our asses."

Amanda followed Jake out of Barb's office.

"Jake . . ."

He whipped around at her, his eyes wide. He rubbed his face with his hands. "Good god, Amanda, how could you do this?"

"I don't know, Jake. I did the best I could . . . They came to me . . ." Her words got stuck in her throat. "I didn't mean . . ."

"Just go get those statements." He didn't meet her eyes and pounded back into his office.

Amanda felt her insides slide as she made her way to the door, Julie holding her salad out to her and then pulling it back when she saw Amanda's face. Outside the snow was falling almost horizontally as sharp, icy flakes pelted her face. The few cars on the road were skidding and fishtailing, and a plow groaned faintly in the distance. Sobs finally escaped as she fought her way to her car. Inside she turned on the heat and waited for the windshield wipers to clear the snow. She flashed back to the night she left Jake's parents' home when she ran to her car in the middle of the night. The urge to run away was back, as strong as ever.

Amanda pushed the thought away and tried to think. Once she got the recordings she would make Jake listen to the girls himself. They couldn't lose sight of what the girls said, because it justified what she did. She squirmed as she wondered why she didn't just tell them the interview was at her house. It looked guilty, unprofessional and embarrassing. The only fix at this point was those recordings. Ignoring the tremor in her hands, she finally pulled out of her parking spot and headed for home.

* * *

WITH THE WIND, THE PELTING SNOW, and the ice on the roads, Amanda barely drove ten miles per hour on the city streets. She jumped when a police car with lights and sirens flashing passed her, seemingly appearing out of nowhere. She had advanced another block when a second police car passed, followed by a fire truck. She turned onto her street. Squinting, Amanda could see that they all seemed to stop about three blocks ahead, very near her home.

Her gut knew first, and everything seemed to move in slow motion. Thick black smoke cut through the blowing snow to create the appearance of a gray tornado. Another fire truck, an ambulance. Sirens and howling wind. Black soot and burning embers floating past her car.

Amanda had to stop almost a block away, as the emergency vehicles took up the road. It was impossible and surreal. Her home was on fire. Images of her broken lock, her slashed tires, and footprints on her outside landing flashed through her head, and the truth hit her like a truck. They had been following her, they had been at her home before, and they had started this fire now. She imagined Rachel's brothers, and perhaps Chuck

Thomas himself, finding the girls at Amanda's apartment and making them leave. Taking them to Skip's office, telling them what to say. She was in a whole different kind of trouble than she had known.

Fears about the case faded as an even more frightening truth emerged: everything she owned was in that apartment. The few traces of her past—photos, softball trophies, her baby blanket—all gone. Her home and everything from her past was destroyed, and soon her career and everything she had built for herself, including her friendship with Jake, would follow.

The roar in her head and the fierce pounding in her ears were paralyzing. Her phone vibrated in her purse, but the sound was foreign and confusing. The vibrating continued. Through the relentless snow, Amanda watched a part of her roof collapse over where her living room used to be. The vibrating persisted, so finally she picked up her phone and saw that she had four missed calls and had a text message from William.

Lucy in early labor. Both baby and Lucy in trouble. Get to Children's Hosp. ASAP! She's asking for you.

Clarity returned as Amanda drove away from her home and the disastrous mess she had created, and toward the only part of her life she had left.

chapter twenty-nine

S T. PAUL CHILDREN'S HOSPITAL was bright and welcoming, with large colorful paintings and mobiles in the entryway. The cheeriness of the décor was a sharp contrast to the faces of the people inside. Amanda had overheard someone saying that a bus full of high school basketball players had been part of a multicar pileup on the interstate, and there had been fatalities. Local news crews were setting up. A command center had been established at the hospital for family members awaiting news, and so near-hysterical parents surrounded Amanda.

Amanda felt like her soul had been lifted out of her body, and the empty shell that remained was moving through the hospital like a zombie. Somehow she found the OB unit and the family waiting area that had been taken over by Lucy and Will's family. William was perched on the edge of a couch with his head in his hands. He was wearing hospital scrubs, and her stomach lurched when she saw blood on his boots. Cynthia, Marina, and Rosie were seated in a row on another couch, Rosie clutching a rosary in one hand and Kleenexes in the other. William's dad was on the phone, and his mother was rubbing Will's back.

Will got up and immediately wrapped Amanda in a huge hug. Tears popped into her eyes, and she willed him not to speak so she didn't have to know. He pulled back and looked at her, but the words would not come. He shook his head and opened his mouth to tell her, but instead just crumpled into a sob. She held him again, and crisis Amanda re-emerged from a place long gone. Crisis Amanda had sat alone in surgical waiting areas at age fourteen, had held her mother's head while she vomited, and had collected her mother's ashes from the funeral home alone. Crisis Amanda didn't feel things.

Patting Will's back, Amanda whispered, "I know, I know." She did not tell him that it would be okay, because she knew it might not be.

"I'm sorry," Will said, pulling back and trying to compose himself. "I might lose them both." He clasped his hands over his head and tried to breathe. "It just went so fast. She woke up and said it hurt, and the next thing I knew she was bleeding. I don't know how there could be so much blood." An image of Lucy, wide eyed, bleeding and terrified popped into her head, and she swayed for a moment before recomposing herself.

Will sat back down and his mother put her arms around him again. Amanda turned toward Rosie and saw both her daughters leaning into her, Marina with her head on Rosie's shoulder. An image of her own mother popped into her head, and she wondered when, if ever, her mother comforted her instead of the other way around.

* * *

THE ROOM WAS COLD, STERILE. Amanda wanted to go to the nurses station for some knitted blankets, but this was not her hospital, and she was not at home here the way she was at her mother's hospital for so many years.

Amanda sat on a chair near William, and his mother whispered to Amanda what they knew so far. Lucy was in surgery because of massive hemorrhaging due to suspected placental abruption. Lucy was barely conscious by the time they got to Children's by ambulance, the weather slowing them down and resulting in more blood loss. The baby was in distress, and even though he was at thirty-one weeks gestation they assumed they were going to have to deliver him. Survival rates at thirty-one weeks are around fifty percent depending on other circumstances, and in this situation the placental abruption did not improve his chances. And yes, Will's mother said tearfully, the baby is a boy.

Amanda absorbed this information without reaction, her emotions simply absent. There was nothing to do but wait.

* * *

DARKNESS CAME AS THE STORM raged on. Amanda left the waiting area to get coffee and hot chocolate for everyone, paying with the money she should use for her rent, her stomach lurching for a moment when she remembered that rent was no longer an issue for her. In the cafeteria she overheard that the only fatality from the bus accident was the driver, but six teenage boys had life-threatening injuries. She approached the cash register behind a familiar-looking news reporter talking to her cameraman.

She carried two trays of coffee and hot chocolate back to the waiting area, but found that everyone already had Caribou Coffee and sandwiches, courtesy of William's uncle, who had just arrived. She felt ridiculous holding the trays and didn't know what to do. Rosie, who had been clutching her rosary with her eyes closed, looked up and smiled weakly at Amanda. Grimacing she got up from her plastic sofa and crossed the room to take one of Amanda's hot chocolates. She kissed Amanda's cheek and whispered, "*Gracias, chica.*" Crisis Amanda wasn't as stoic as she used to be. With great effort, Amanda squashed down her tears.

* * *

LUCY AND JUDGE BACH ARE drinking hot chocolate sitting in front of a fireplace. Jacob and William are playing chess, the baby in Will's arms. Trix is serving cake. Amanda is afraid to approach them until Trix spots her and tells her to sit down. But Amanda doesn't belong so she doesn't move. Zoe appears next to her and whispers, "Your mom did the best she could." Amanda whispers back, "I don't fit here. I'm a victim, a client, one of the people we work with. I'm alone." Zoe shakes her head. "You're surrounded by people who love you. You're only alone in your head."

Amanda awakened suddenly, her neck sore from sleeping awkwardly in a chair. Will was gone, but everyone else looked different—smiling and relaxed. Cynthia ran over and hugged Amanda. "Lucy's okay!"

Amanda glanced over at Rosie, who was politely smiling and nodding at Will's mother sitting next to her. "What about the baby?"

"Javier William is a fighter." Rosie beamed. They named the baby after Rosie's late husband.

"Will is with him now. He's in an incubator and has a machine that breathes for him," Will's mom said, patting Rosie's leg. "But the doctor said his weight is good and his lungs are quite strong for thirty-one weeks."

"Wow. That's so great." She rubbed her face and tried to wake up. "How long have I been asleep?"

"Like four hours," Marina said. "We all whispered when the doctor was in here."

"Wonderful."

"Nobody else can see the baby tonight, and Lucy is still asleep, so we're getting ready to go." Cynthia was pulling her coat and mittens on. "Mom got us a hotel room across the street."

"Hotel room," Amanda said worriedly. That would be easier, but she wasn't sure if she had enough room on her credit card to pay for a hotel. Again, without any rent to pay, she had plenty of money right now. She wondered which hotel they were in, and if she would even be able to get a room for herself. She looked around the room and knew from experience that she would be allowed to sleep here too.

"*Vamonos, chica.*" Rosie stood in front of Amanda and held her hand out to her. "It's time for bed."

"I call sharing a bed with Amanda," Marina said with a grin while Cynthia made a face.

"Come on! Mama farts in her sleep," Cynthia groaned.

Rosie swatted at Cynthia. "You will sleep in the car if you don't watch out." But she smiled as she held onto Amanda's hand and led them to the elevator. Overwhelmed with humility and gratitude, the thought occurred to her that it might be time to accept that she really did have a place in this family.

chapter thirty

A MANDA AWOKE BEFORE THE OTHERS, Marina inches from her face and
snoring loudly. All things considered, she was comfortable. Worried
about Lucy and the baby, but in a contented state of denial. It was Saturday, so she could avoid dealing with the disaster that was her life for at
least one more day. She had turned her cell phone off and appreciated how
she had no choice but to live in the moment.

It was after nine o' clock before the rest of them started to move.
Amanda knew from experience that everyone in Lucy's family was edgy in
the morning. The girls took turns in the bathroom while Amanda peeked
outside and saw that the storm had finally lifted. The sky was gloriously
blue. A truck fitted with a plow was scraping the already dirty and melting
snow into huge mounds at the end of the hotel parking lot.

Since none of them had packed any clothes, they could only brush
their teeth with courtesy toothbrushes from the front desk. They checked
out of the hotel by ten and returned to the hospital.

As Rosie and the girls went to visit with Lucy, Amanda drifted away
and wandered through the hospital. She wanted to give the family a chance
to see Lucy and the baby, and she knew she had nowhere else she wanted
to be.

Amanda allowed herself to think about her mess of a life. She knew
she had to go to work on Monday, and she decided to offer to resign. If
they allowed her to quit instead of firing her, she was considering returning
to school for a Masters Degree in Social Work. Hopefully she could learn
enough not to make such a colossal mistake again. Since she didn't have a

home, she could move anywhere, but ideally she would go back to the U. She even thought about going back to Apple Falls to live close to Lucy and William and help with the baby.

Amanda made her way to the cafeteria for a bagel and diet coke. Her plan felt adequate for now. Focusing on helping Lucy took some of the sting out all the loss. With aching sadness, Amanda realized for the first time that she really loved her job. In the past year, Amanda had learned how to be proud of herself, and how fulfilling it was to give something back instead of always feeling like she was taking from other people. Despite what she had done, Amanda still believed that she could be a good social worker. She truly felt that her history made her more empathetic, more understanding, and more respectful to the families she worked with. Her pride allowed her to believe that she had something unique to offer, and she couldn't let this one mistake take everything away. She owed herself more than that.

* * *

THE DAY PASSED SLOWLY. She found a lounge area outside of the oncology unit that had a TV showing a Twins preseason game. None of the big players were in, but it was still a pretty good way to pass time. She eavesdropped on two dads making sports small talk. They both acknowledged that they were "out of the baseball loop." One dad's little girl had just received a bone marrow transplant, and the other's son was newly diagnosed, so they also talked a little about doctors and treatments and nurses on the floor. They both had the familiar look of hospital families—unshaven, rumpled clothes from sleeping in chairs, and tears barely below the surface that could come out with any or no provocation.

By late afternoon, Amanda figured that most people of Lucy's family would have left, so she went back to the maternity wing. She found Will coming out of Lucy's room and gently closing the door.

"Hey, Amanda, where have you been?" He looked utterly exhausted.

"I just wanted to give everyone some time with Lucy and the baby. How're they doing?"

"Javier is okay. I don't think I really understood what it means to be in the NICU. He's full of tubes, he has tape over his eyes . . ." Will's voice caught on the word tape, but he collected himself and seemed to want to avoid falling apart again. "They kept talking about how many grams he is, so I finally asked how much he weighs in pounds . . . Two pounds, one ounce." Will shook his head slowly. "He's just got so far to go."

"Yeah, he does." Amanda reached out and rubbed his arm. "But he has you and Lucy for parents. I know that a day in the hospital can feel like a month, but before you know it you will be bringing him home. And someday you'll tell this great big kid about how tiny he was when he was born, and he won't even believe it."

Will smiled shakily at the image of his baby being a kid, and then he heaved a big sigh. "I'm so tired I can't even think straight," he said, rubbing his eyes with the backs of his hands.

"Why don't you go home, Will? I can stay here with Lucy tonight, and you could go home and sleep in your own bed."

"No, I can't leave them."

"Javier is going to be here for a while," she said as gently as she could. "I can't stay here every night, but I can stay tonight. Go home and get some real sleep. Lucy and Javier are going to need you to be strong for them, but you can't do that if you're exhausted."

Will looked at Lucy's door. "Maybe just for a few hours . . ." He went back into Lucy's room quietly and came back out in less than a minute. "She wants me to go," he said, looking surprised and a little confused. "Maybe you can talk to her, Amanda. She's really really quiet, and I don't know what's going on in her head."

Amanda gave Will a tight hug and told him she would take care of Lucy and the baby tonight. Will looked like he was going to cry at that point so he left quickly.

Amanda knocked softly on Lucy's door and went inside.

Lucy was turned away from her, and Amanda was shocked at how small she looked. Lucy turned and her eyes were full of tears. "Oh, Lucy." She sat gingerly on the edge of Lucy's bed and hugged her gently while she cried and cried. Finally Lucy let out a deep sigh, and Amanda got up to get her some tissues. Lucy blew her nose and tried to pull herself together while Amanda got situated on her chair.

"I hate this," Lucy finally said. "I can't see my baby. He's still supposed to be with me. He's supposed to be inside of me!"

"Why can't you see him now? Could you go down there?"

"I went down there once, but now they want me to wait until I get done with this IV because they have so many babies in there right now.

But I won't be done until about 3: 00 a.m. They've been bringing me pic-tures, but it's not enough."

Amanda shook her head. One thing she had learned about doctors was that sometimes things were more flexible than they made them seem. "Let's get your nurse in here, and we'll tell her that you are going to see Javier tonight, and see if you need to finish your IV early, or if they will make room for you."

"Really?" she asked weakly.

* * *

THIRTY MINUTES LATER LUCY was in the NICU, and Amanda went back to the cafeteria and got all of Lucy's favorite foods. By the time she returned to Lucy's room, a nurse was wheeling her back into her room. The nurse needed to hold Lucy's arms and help her stand and transfer back to her bed. Amanda had done the same thing countless times with her mother.

Lucy settled back in her bed while Amanda unloaded her booty from the cafeteria. Lucy was worn out but seemed to feel better.

"He would almost fit in my hand," Lucy's chin quivered as she said it, but she also managed a tiny smile. "He has Will's nose."

Amanda nodded and unwrapped a Hershey bar, passing Lucy a square. She eyed it like she wasn't sure if she should, and then just took a nibble off one corner and laid her head back on her pillow with a deep sigh.

* * *

LUCY DOZED MOST OF THE EVENING while Amanda watched TV. The chair was more comfortable than most hospital chairs, likely because of the dads often spending the night. Sleep came between episodes of *Friends* and *Cheers*. She dreamed about Chandler and Monica, Lucy and Will, and Blaze and Justice, Judge Bach and Skip Husman. They were in a hospital, and then gathered around a campfire, discussing Amanda's life and whether she should go back to school. Even in her dream Amanda was embarrassed and ashamed of the mistake she had made, but no one was too upset about it in her dream. She finally turned off the television at mid-night and tried to settle in for some real sleep.

Amanda awoke every time the nurses came in to check on Lucy, which was about every two hours. Lucy had to pump her breastmilk be-cause Javier had to stay on the respirator, and Lucy needed to make sure her milk would come in for when he could finally take it. The nurses were coming in frequently to help her pump, and Lucy almost cried with frustration and exhaustion every time.

Will was back by 9:00 a.m. the next morning. Amanda was using her courtesy hotel toothbrush when Will came in. He sat on the bed and whispered to Lucy for a few minutes. Amanda was getting ready to leave for a while when Will asked to see her in the hallway. His eyes told her that he knew something. Amanda stood outside Lucy's door and waited.

"Dear God, Amanda," Will said, closing the door behind him. "Your apartment."

She shook her head. "I know, I know. It's fine. I'm getting it figured out."

"Jake said they think it's arson."

Jake. Amanda wasn't ready to think about him yet. And suspecting arson and hearing it from Will were two different things. She felt certain that Chuck Thomas and his family were responsible.

"Yeah, I thought it probably was arson," she finally said.

"Do you need anything? You know you can stay with us." Amanda wasn't used to thinking of Will and Lucy as "us."

"Thank you. I'm getting things figured out. You need to focus on your baby. I'm okay."

"I am focused on my family, but you're family too. He pulled his keys out and took one off his ring. "Here's our house key, so just come and go as you need to." She was incredibly touched by the gesture. Lucy and her sisters had come to feel like sisters, but for the first time she felt like she also had a brother.

* * *

THE REST OF THE DAY passed quickly. Amanda called her insurance agent and was able to get through to him on an emergency line. He already knew about her apartment and was waiting for her call. They discussed options, including getting a cash advance from the Red Cross. Amanda decided to call her credit card company to ask for her credit limit to be extended to give her enough money to buy clothes and necessities until her insurance money came through.

Amanda didn't have much of a credit limit in the first place, but she was able to get it extended enough to give her some breathing room. Her insurance agent said that they have an agreement with Super 8 Hotels to rent a room by the week, so she made a reservation at the Apple Falls Super 8 starting that night.

Shopping just for the essentials was probably more enjoyable than it should have been. It was fun to have a clean slate and start over with a brand new everything. Her cart was overflowing with clothes, pajamas, underwear, shoes, toiletries, and a few groceries.

Back at the hospital, Amanda was finally able to see Javier when Will pushed his glass crib to a viewing room. She choked back her shock and alarm at the sight of his purplish skin, his toothpick limbs, and his head that was barely larger than a plum. She blew him a kiss and waved goodbye at Will. Stopping in Lucy's room she gave her one more hug and headed back to Apple Falls. She had promised to check in when she got to the hotel.

The sky was streaked with a dozen shades of pink, purple, and gold, and the day's warmth had already melted several inches of Friday's blizzard. Streams of snowmelt ran down the highway, and Amanda guessed that the snow would be gone in a week, leaving little sign of the record-setting spring storm that coincided with one of the worst days of her life.

The next day was Monday, and Amanda would finally have to face reality, apologize for her mistakes, and hope that the only casualty of her lack of judgment, other than the victims who weren't ready for anyone's help right now, was herself.

* * *

THE HOTEL WAS OLDER BUT CLEAN, and as she checked in, Amanda wondered how long this hotel would be her home. Wishing she had bought a duffel bag, Amanda carried her shopping bags to her room. She brushed her teeth with a real toothbrush and took out a t-shirt and boxer shorts from her purchases and put them on.

Remembering her promise to Lucy, Amanda fished her phone out of her purse and turned it back on as she crawled into bed. Her phone beeped and showed that she had eight voicemail messages and even more text messages. She looked at the text messages screen and saw they were all from Jake.

"*Where are you?????*" Friday, 2:32 p.m.

"*I just heard about Lucy. Call me.*" Friday, 8:10 p.m.

"*I'm worried about you, Amanda. Please call me. I've been trying and I know your phone is off. I hope you check it soon because we need to talk.*" Friday, 11:12 p.m.

"I heard Lucy is okay. Thank God. Now please call because we really have to talk." Saturday, 7:56 a.m.

""Please call me, Amanda." Saturday 9:02 a.m.

"I don't know if you are upset with me or just have your phone off, but there are major things happening here right now and I HAVE to talk to you." Saturday, 7:44 p.m.

"Call me." Saturday 11:49 p.m.

""There are huge things going on here, and they affect you. Lots of people here need to talk to you, but I want to explain things to you first. You have to call me." Sunday, 4:17 p.m.

"There is a court hearing on Monday at 9:00 a.m.. You should be there, but PLEASE PLEASE talk to me first. Call me as soon as you get this." Sunday 7:09 p.m.

"I've talked to Will. I know you're at the hotel. I know you're avoiding me. You don't know how serious this is, and I don't want you to hear it from anyone else. Please call me before you go to the hearing." Sunday 7:58 p.m.

The last message came thirty minutes earlier. Amanda hesitated for a moment trying to decide what to do. It was hard to know what he meant by "serious things" but she assumed it was about the fire. Reality had to return tomorrow, and Amanda wanted to be ready for it. During her entire life she had shut down, avoided, and run away from difficult things, but to be fair to herself, she had done so because most things in her life had been so damn difficult.

Somehow this time was different. This time the avoidance was temporary, a need to get away and regroup. Thinking about her mistake still brought a wave of shame, but also a growing sense of indignation. Those girls had come to her looking for help, and she offered help the best way she could at the time. If they fired her, she could live with it, but it felt so unfair.

Amanda sent Lucy a quick text saying she was at the hotel and was fine. Then she turned her phone back off and set in on the nightstand. Tomorrow would come soon enough, and she would deal with all of this then. For now, Amanda was exhausted and needed sleep.

While she hadn't been exposed to church a lot in her life, Amanda prayed for strength to get through the next day.

chapter thirty-one

STALE POWDERED DONUTS, a pitcher of orange juice, and some paper cups comprised the continental breakfast. Amanda started to feel a little pathetic as she rifled through her plastic Target bags to find a box of granola bars among her new underwear and hair products. When she realized her only pair of shoes didn't really match her new Target dress pants, sudden and unexpected tears sprang up. *I cannot cry today,* she thought fiercely. This day was going to be hard enough.

Gathering her purse and phone, she remembered that she had loaned Lucy a pair of boots because her feet were too swollen to fit into any of her shoes. Grateful for the house key that William gave her, she drove across Apple Falls to Will and Lucy's house. The garage door had been left open and Will's car was already gone.

The mess inside was surprising, but the trail of blood made her knees weak. She could imagine the scene of Lucy suddenly hemorrhaging and Will frantically trying to get her to the car. Drops of blood had turned to dark, sticky pools by the garage door. She couldn't stand the thought of Lucy coming home to that, so she found the cleaning supplies and started scrubbing.

It was after 10: 00 a.m. when Amanda put away her rag and forced herself back to her car. She was halfway to Terrance before she realized that she forgot to pick up her boots.

The March sun was intense, and last week's snow was melting fast. Terrance was starting to feel like home, and she wondered if this was one of her last days there. Her heart pounded as she parked in front of her building and went inside.

"Amanda!" Maddie, the front desk receptionist startled her. "You are to go directly to court. Everyone is over there already. Jacob from the County Attorney's office has called about five times this morning already." The mention of Jake made her look at her phone and realize it still wasn't on. Since it had to be off in the courtroom anyway, she just left it off.

Amanda splashed her way across the street, cringing at her unmatched shoes. The parking lot was full. Inside there was a crowd gathered by the courtroom doors, and a bailiff standing watch. Despite being at court only a handful of times, the bailiff recognized her and told her to go inside. A prickle of uneasiness crept up her spine. Why would he specifically invite her inside when there were so many people left in the hall?

It was the largest courtroom available, and the bench seating was packed with nearly one-hundred spectators. There were no seats available, but the bailiff inside motioned for her to stand against the back wall. Even from the back, she recognized Chuck Thomas leaning back defiantly in his chair, Skip Huseman impeccably dressed by his side. She didn't recognize the female judge sitting at the bench. She did recognize the witness, who was seated below the judge in the witness stand—Judge Matthew Bach. Hard to know what to make of that.

Barb Cloud and Jacob were seated at the prosecuting attorney's table. Jake was questioning Judge Bach.

"How long have you been a judge?" Jake asked, still seated at the table.

"Three years." Judge Bach was wearing a dark jacket, white shirt and dark tie. He looked distinguished, somber . . . different than Amanda was used to seeing him in her dreams.

"And are you still on the bench?" Jake's voice waivered, and he cleared his throat. Jake's voice always cracked when he was nervous. It had to be intimidating to question a judge, more so with the crowd.

"No." There was shuffling as people reacted to this news. The former Judge Bach glanced down and clenched his jaw. As he looked back up, pain and anger seemed to have washed over his face, and Amanda was surprised how sad she felt for him.

"Could you explain how you know the defendant?" Amanda wanted an answer to why he was no longer a judge, but she sensed that would come soon enough.

"Mr. Thomas and I were teammates in high school. Hockey and base-ball. We were co-captains of the hockey team. After high school, he and I had little contact until a few days ago."

"What was the nature of the contact a few days ago, and to which day are you referring?"

Bach looked up briefly. "Actually, I ran into him about two weeks ago at the Y. He asked several questions about my personal life, and I was uncomfortable with that so I ended the conversation quickly."

Chuck Thomas shook his head and leaned over to his attorney at that. Almost imperceptibly, Skip Huseman put a hand up motioning him to stop.

"Why were you uncomfortable?" Jake asked.

"I would say that Mr. Thomas and I were not on the best terms in high school, and he and I had . . . we had words when we were in school about . . . uh . . . my personal life. I didn't know why he would ask, and I didn't want to have that conversation with him again."

"When you say 'you had words in high school,' would you say that you argued?"

"Objection. Relevance." Skip Huseman's voice echoed so loudly in the cavernous courtroom that Amanda jumped. "It's also leading on top of being irrelevant." Skip's voice dripped with condescension and disgust.

The judge turned toward Skip. Her voice was soft but held admon-ishment. "Mr. Huseman. I have already established for the purpose of this hearing that there will be latitude. I have also established that if you keep interrupting, I will set maximum bail of $500,000 and that will be that." Amanda was impressed with any judge who wasn't afraid of Skip Huse-man.

"I'll ask again," Jake said, his voice growing in confidence from that small victory. "Would you say that you argued in high school?"

"It was more than an argument. As co-captains of the hockey team we had to work together, but we tended to disagree frequently. Mr. Thomas wanted the team to be together on the ice and off. We were a very talented team, and we had a great chance of making it to state." So strange to hear a man in his forties talk about his high school team like they were still a team. Amanda's team won the state tournament, but she couldn't imagine referring to her team like they were still a unit. She wondered who was more typical, but in this small town knew that he was.

"So what was the argument about?" Jake asked.

"In essence, he didn't like my girlfriend." Judge Bach shook his head and shrugged. "Mr. Thomas wanted the guys on the team to . . . date only certain girls. He didn't think my girlfriend measured up. The first time he said something to me, I didn't think he could be serious. He told me that I shouldn't be with a girl 'like that.'" He crossed and uncrossed his hands in front of him. "My girlfriend was like me. We were both poor, and our families didn't have . . . status . . . for lack of a better word. Mr. Thomas thought I should be with someone with 'status.'"

"So was that the extent of the argument?" Jake asked, quickly glancing to his right in anticipation of an objection. None came.

Matthew Bach hesitated and appeared to be composing his words carefully. "He had a party at his house after a playoff game that we had won. Chuck, er, Mr. Thomas had a lot of parties. Mr. Thomas had a girl that he wanted me to spend time with at the party, and he was angry when he realized that I had brought my girlfriend. When my back was turned, he told my girlfriend to get out of his house, but he told me that she left because she was mad at me. I knew that wasn't true, and I knew that she didn't have a car and wouldn't just leave. I tried to follow her but she was long gone. I got in his face and told him I was going to be with my girlfriend no matter what. And he said . . ." Matthew paused, and the room grew still. "He said that I was not going to be with her, and that he was going to get rid of her."

The room reacted with shuffling and whispers. That Chuck Thomas would make a threat like that didn't surprise Amanda a bit. Chuck shook his head almost violently. Skip Huseman didn't move.

"How did you take that statement?" Jake almost braced for the objection that never came.

"It was a threat. At that time I thought he meant he would start a rumor or harass her in class."

"Did those things happen?" Jake spoke quickly, building toward something he knew was coming next. Amanda was holding her breath in anticipation.

"There was never any opportunity," Matthew said, his face growing dark and angry. "Her house burned to the ground that night." There was an audible gasp from someone in the room.

"Your honor!" Skip Huseman was on his feet, clearly surprised at this revelation. "This is highly prejudicial, not to mention libelous—"

"This historical information is a necessary part of the argument of why bail cannot be granted—" Jake also rose to his feet matching Skip's volume and tone.

The judge lifted her hands and glared at both attorneys hard enough that they both stopped mid-sentence. "I will allow it in this context." Her words were clipped, her anger apparent. Skip Huseman opened his mouth to argue again, but stopped when the judge put her hand on her gavel. Both attorneys sat back down with visible efforts to recompose. Amanda looked back at Judge Bach to see that his anger had morphed into visible sadness and regret.

"So Ju . . . Mr. Bach," Jake said, rearranging his papers and seeming momentarily lost. "What happened to your girlfriend?"

"No one was hurt, but she dropped out of school and left town. That was the last time I saw her." Matthew looked at Chuck when he said it.

"Your girlfriend's house burned to the ground, and you never saw her again." Amanda knew Jake repeated the words for effect. "Are you aware if there was ever any cause determined for the fire?"

Skip spoke quickly but with restraint. "Objection. Mr. Bach is not an expert on house fires and could only offer hearsay." Jake started to reply, but she lifted her hand.

"The objection is sustained." She offered no further explanation, and Jake looked slightly flustered but moved on.

"So now, Mr. Bach, please bring us back to the present. What did Mr. Thomas say to you a few days ago?" Jake turned around quickly to scan the room, and his eyes flickered when he saw Amanda. Now he clearly looked flustered, and Amanda wondered if she should leave.

Matthew held his hands together in front of his chin, and he also looked clearly uncomfortable. "Last Friday, Mr. Thomas was arrested for criminal sexual conduct. I signed the criminal complaint. A few hours later the County Attorney's office dropped the charges and Mr. Thomas was released." Amanda's face grew hot with shame at the news that the charges had been dropped. The feeling grew as she realized that everyone in the room might soon learn that it was her fault.

Jake nodded and seemed to want to move on quickly. "Then what happened?"

"Mr. Thomas met me at my car as I was leaving my office that evening. He told me that he held me responsible for the arrest, and he was going to sue the entire county. I kept walking." Matthew held his hands together and rested his chin on his hands. "He followed me."

Chuck Thomas was shifting in his seat. He tried again to talk to Skip Huseman, but he raised his hand and Chuck sat back again. Jake was sitting up straight in his chair. "Then what happened," Jake asked.

Matthew shifted in the witness stand. "He told me that the arrest ruined his reputation. He told me that I needed to make sure that everything 'went away' with the child protection case. I told him that I couldn't dismiss it and I wouldn't. Then he, uh, he just lost it."

Jacob looked pointedly at Chuck Thomas. "Please describe what you mean when you say, 'he lost it.'"

"Mr. Thomas got very close to me and started yelling and pointing. He said he would take care of the case by himself, but I wouldn't like that." Matthew was talking quickly now. He looked agitated and seemed to just want to get his words out and get this testimony over with. "Then he threatened me personally. He said that he knew about me, and why I shouldn't be on this case. He said that he would report me to the Board of Judicial Review because I didn't excuse myself. I told him that I hadn't done anything wrong, but actually he was right. I should have excused myself. I told him that he needed to stop talking to me about the case or it could be considered ex parte communication."

"Which means what exactly?" Jake asked.

"Communicating with a judge without the other parties present. But he just kept talking. He said that all of this needed to end today, and he had already taken care of a big part of the evidence." Matthew had been talking quickly, and he slowed down again. Chuck Thomas had been surprisingly quiet and was actually looking away from the judge, staring blankly at the back wall. "He just kept saying that he knew about me. Then he said, 'you know what I'm capable of. You need to take care of this.' I wasn't sure what he meant. I hadn't thought about that fire for a long time."

"The fire at your girlfriend's house?" Jake glanced back around at Amanda again. At that moment, something tickled in the back of Amanda's mind and her heart started to beat faster.

"Yes. She left town after the fire, and I graduated a few months later. I went to Alaska right after graduation to start working before I started at the university that fall. I never knew . . ." Matthew looked around the room and suddenly made eye contact with Amanda. He looked apologetic. "I never knew," he said more quietly this time.

"Knew what?" Jake's tone matched Matthew's.

"What Chuck knew. He figured it out. He told me that he took care of the evidence this time just like he took care of my girlfriend in high school. And he said it wouldn't stop there, and if I wanted to protect my family I needed to make everything go away." Matthew was clenching his jaw.

"Did he specifically say how he took care of the evidence?"

"Not exactly."

"But his exact words were, "If you want to protect your family you need to make everything go away." Jake's voice was louder as he made the point that Chuck Thomas had threatened the judge.

"Yes." The former Judge Bach looked straight at Jacob. "He was very clear."

"Then what happened?" Jake asked more quietly.

"He told me there were all kinds of ways he could get me. He knew I had a wife and young children." Matthew's voice grew steely. "He knew about my older daughter too." He paused. "And then he said, "Isn't it ironic that I got your daughter the same way I got her mom.""

Amanda's breathing quickened before her brain could comprehend.

"Could you explain what you think he meant by that?" Jake asked quietly, glancing over his shoulder again.

Daughter?

"He knew I have a twenty-three-year-old daughter." Matthew's voice got quiet as he looked at Amanda with apology. "And he figured out . . . that she is the social worker on this case."

The room swayed under Amanda's feet.

Jake's voice was faint. "Your daughter is Amanda Danscher?"

Matthew nodded and looked at Amanda, his eyes brimming with grief and pride. "Amanda Danscher is my daughter."

chapter thrity-two

SOMEHOW THE INTENSITY OF BLUE sky and golden warmth of the sun were soothing. Water almost poured down the boulevards the snow was melting so quickly, and the sounds of rushing mini rivers of snow melt combined with the optimistic chirp of robins. Spring brought universal relief.

All Amanda could do was drive and wipe away bewildered tears. Huge pieces of her life had suddenly dropped into place. The woman she had been remembering for months was her paternal grandmother, and she was flooded with memories of playing knee hockey in her house, "just like daddy plays." She had given Amanda blue-and-gold pompoms because those were daddy's colors, and Amanda could actually remember that pompom in her toybox before she and her mother moved to their trailer and got rid of all of her old toys. There had been arguments between her mom and her grandmother, and all memories of her grandmother seemed to stop by the time Amanda must have been about five.

I have a dad. She tried to reach for some type of emotion, but everything felt muffled and confused. Amanda felt desperate for some normalcy, something to grab on to and help her feel grounded and sane. But she was homeless and possibly jobless. Even if she didn't get fired, it would take more than she had in her right now to sort out her job. She just kept driving.

Amanda passed Dairy Queen and thought of her summer with Jake almost six years ago. Had it really been six years since her mom died? Jacob's house was one of the first places she had ever felt safe and sane. She knew that the Mann family had saved her that summer, but she also realized now that they inexplicably loved her too. Somehow they were family. But the feelings were too much at the time for Amanda, so she ran away and started college. After two years of partying and goofing off, Amanda met Lucy. That feeling of family returned, and she hadn't really felt lost since. It wasn't biological, but it was still unmistakable. Lucy was family.

But now things were different because her family wasn't just made anymore. Now it was born. She had biological, "next-of-kin" family. But this man, the former judge, her father, was also a stranger.

After driving for a long while, Amanda crossed the railroad tracks and found herself in front of her grandmother's house. She got out of her car and trudged through the sloppy wet snow to the backyard. Just the rim of the tractor tire sandbox was visible through the snow. The edge of the yard against the house had been protected from snow, so the gnomes were only buried to their little knees. Amanda crouched in front of those gnomes and knew that she had played there a lot. Their faces were amazingly familiar, and she smiled at the girl gnome that she knew had been her favorite.

Amanda didn't realize a car had parked by hers until she heard a car door slam. She looked over to see Matthew Bach getting out of a very expensive looking SUV and making his way through the slush to the yard. He was wearing a leather jacket instead of his suit coat. He held up a hand in a greeting and awkwardly dropped it by his side. His hands were wide, but his wrists were narrow, just like hers.

"Hello, Amanda."

"Hello." It came out as a whisper.

He clasped his hands in front of his face. After watching him testify today she learned that must be his nervous gesture. "I just want you to know . . . well, there are so many things that I want you to know. But I just wanted to say that Jacob Mann tried to contact you all weekend. Neither one of us wanted you to find out this way."

She nodded. "I know." She looked around the yard because it was just too intense to make eye contact with him. "But I just needed to get away from everything for a while. It's my fault for not calling him."

"No." He shook his head. "None of this is your fault. No one would begin to expect that this is why he was calling you."

"I suppose." They both grew uncomfortably quiet.

Matthew motioned around at the backyard. "So do you actually remember being here?"

"A little. I've had memories that I didn't understand." A thought suddenly dawned on her. "How did you know I was here?"

"Jacob talked to one of your coworkers. Zoe maybe? He asked her to watch for you when you came to court, and to, well, to follow you if you left."

Amanda glanced over at her car. "So Zoe followed me here?" Amanda had no clue someone had followed her.

He looked sheepish and concerned. "Jake said that you might leave. He obviously cares about you very much. I spent a good part of the weekend in his office, and it was clear that you were on his mind the entire time."

Jake's concern brought a lump to her throat.

Matthew cleared his throat. "Amanda. I need you to know some things. First, I am just so incredibly sorry. I didn't know about you until last fall. My mother had kept you a secret from me until just before she died. She had had a massive heart attack and needed to go to a nursing home. I was packing up her belongings and trying to get her house ready to sell when I found letters and newspaper clippings and photos. They were all about you. I went to her and asked who this person was, and she finally told me the whole story."

Letters, newspaper clippings, and photos. This woman, her grandmother, had been following her life.

"Your mom was pregnant at the time of her house fire, but she didn't tell me. It happened in March, and I was in Alaska by June. April went to my mother that summer because she needed money. April's family, your family too, I guess, scattered after the fire, and your mom was on her own. My mother helped her, and your mom actually lived here for a while, both before and after you were born." Amanda turned around and looked at the house that was actually her first home.

"I lived here." Being homeless, it felt good to know that she had belonged here at one time.

"I was at college and my mother never said a word to me about you. When I talked to my mother about you last fall, she admitted that she kept you a secret from me because she didn't want me to quit college, which I probably would have done. Apparently you were here for a few months until your mom got a job in Apple Falls and you two moved back there."

It was fascinating to hear about her life from his perspective. She had never thought about what it had to be like for her mom as a teen mom. She did know that April had never gotten along with her family and said they basically abandoned her. From Matthew's account, that was true.

"Amanda . . . I have something else to ask you." He looked even more nervous and kept rubbing his hands together. Amanda felt a strange little jolt every time she saw those familiar hands.

"Okay," was all she could think of to say.

"Would you like to stay here, in this house? It's pretty much empty, but I kept the heat on so the pipes didn't freeze. I know you need a place, and I would like to do this for you."

Amanda looked up at this stranger who had spent more time in her dreams than in her actual life. While she intended to say no, there was no way that she could accept his offer, somehow she found herself nodding. There was no desperate urge to run, only the desire to stay and try to absorb everything that had happened. And to maybe just let herself get to know this man who called himself her family.

"For a while . . . I'll stay."

* * *

WHILE THE FORMER JUDGE, Matthew, her father, ran around finding the basics for her to live in this house, Amanda sat in the living room that was barely, vaguely familiar and looked through the box of stuff that encapsulated her life. There were a few older photos of Amanda as a baby, sitting in the sandbox and by a foil Christmas tree—she actually had remembered the tree. There were a few pictures in the Apple Falls weekly newspaper that she had never ever seen—one from her third-grade school concert where she was front and center in a group shot of her class, and another of her fifth-grade softball team when they won a tournament. There were more photos as she got older—of softball and volleyball team photos and action shots. The paper actually printed the list of kids who made the honor roll, so there were at least a dozen of those articles. Eerily there were also a few actual photos from her games, including when she played in the state softball tournament that they eventually won. Her grandmother had been watching her for most of her life, and Amanda never knew her. Through all these years, how could she never have tried to make contact?

Amanda found her mother's brief death notice. Since she was the only family member, there had been no obituary because Amanda didn't know it was her job to write one. It hurt to think about her grandmother being the one of the only people in the world who read that notice and knew who April Danscher was.

As it grew dark that evening, Amanda found herself in a house with a new futon, bath towels, a few kitchen necessities, and a new flat screen TV and DVD player. Matthew was grinning sheepishly as he brought in the TV. "I'll call the satellite company this week. I thought you should be able to see the weather at least."

Amanda watched as he hooked up the TV and DVD player, and was able to locate a single channel that she could get without any cable. "At least this will help for tonight," he said, gathering up the boxes and putting them in the utility room by the kitchen.

"Thank you," Amanda said shyly. "I really do appreciate it. Everything is so up in the air, I don't know where I'm going to be yet. I may only be here a few days. You really didn't have to do all this."

"I know. If you decide not to stay here, that's fine. You can take these things with you, if you like them. We can settle it with your insurance company, or you could just have them. It's such a small gesture compared to how much I've missed . . ." He looked at her with such affection that Amanda had to look away. His kindness was overwhelming, but too much for one day. He sensed her discomfort. "If you're okay now, I'm going to head home. I've got two kids, you know. Two other kids I mean. Boys, eight and four. Maybe you could meet them . . . ?"

Amanda nodded briefly. "Maybe. Sure."

He headed toward the door, and then turned. Awkwardly, he lifted his arms like he was going to hug her, then put them down and just held out his arm to shake her hand. Amanda shook his hand, and he took her hand in both of his. "I'm very happy you're here." He fumbled in his pocket. "Here's a house key for you," he said as he took it off his key ring. I have another one at home, as long as you don't mind, of course. I would never just walk in . . ."

"That's fine. It's your house." Amanda smiled at him. "Thank you again." He turned around and left.

Amanda looked back at the bare living room with the futon and the television resting on the floor. She suspected that Matthew might be back the next day with more to fill up the house. And that would be just fine.

* * *

AMANDA HAD NO SOONER sat on the futon to watch her one channel when there was a knock at the door. She got up and answered it expecting to see Matthew with a recliner or a bedroom set, but instead it was Jacob holding a pizza and two blizzards. Stepping back to let him in. It felt foreign to invite someone into this home.

"Matt told me you were staying here." Jake stood in the doorway and looked around.

"He's 'Matt' now, huh?" Amanda smiled shyly.

"We spent a lot of time together this weekend," Jake said seriously. "He's a really good guy."

"He seems like it. Obviously I don't know him." Amanda said it without anger or sadness, just exhaustion.

They went to the kitchen and found that Matthew had purchased a box of dishes—four plates, cups, saucers, and bowls—in plain white. "He really thought of everything." Jake helped himself to pizza and Amanda went right for the ice cream, suddenly remembering that she hadn't eaten anything since the powdered donuts and was starving. She leaned against the kitchen counter while Jake stood by the sink not eating.

"Amanda." He put his food down and put his hands on his hips, a gesture she remembered from the summer she had lived at his house. "I'm so sorry I was so rude to you last Friday. I know you were doing the best you could in a crazy situation. I feel like a complete ass."

Amanda hardly knew how much she needed the apology until it came. Tears welled up and she wasn't sure she could keep them away any more. "You're right. I did do the best I could, but I still screwed up. That's what makes this job so scary."

"You're good at this. Max and Zoe both said so. Please don't let this situation scare you away." His voice was thick and pleading.

"I thought for sure I was going to be fired already. If they let me stay, then I'll stay. I like it here, and I like my job."

Jake looked visibly relieved and nodded. "They set bail for Chuck. Five hundred thousand dollars. It's the maximum for arson and aggravated criminal crime sex."

"I'm surprised he got that much after the initial charges were dropped." She couldn't meet his eyes.

"Your landlord saw his sons start the fire, and we have a tape of a phone call from the jail when Chuck told them to do it. We were able to get a search warrant for his house, and you cannot believe all the nasty stuff we found there. It's pretty much a slam dunk case at this point. The hearing today was to make sure that he sits in jail until his criminal trial." Jake looked exhausted and proud at the same time.

"I'm glad there's good evidence," Amanda said. "It would be terrible for him to get off on a technicality."

"This sex stuff goes way back, and there are tons of victims. Kemper and about five other investigators have been doing interviews for days. Once it got out that Chuck got arrested, a lot of girls came forward."

More than anything, Amanda felt relieved. Relieved that the victims would get some justice, and relieved that her mistake didn't ruin the entire case.

"So, Amanda. I want to tell you something. I've wanted to talk to you about it for a long time." He took a deep breath and couldn't meet her eyes. "I've been going back to Mayo Clinic."

Suddenly she thought back about the pills in his medicine cabinet and her eyes grew wide. He was sick again. The cancer was back. She felt her heart speed up and her tears fell before she could stop them.

Jake was looking down and trying to get his words out quickly. "I went back because I wanted to know if the cancer was back, or if it ever could come back. I had been on yearly checks and there's been nothing. But with leukemia, there's a bigger chance of recurrence. So they put me in this clinical trial where they are trying a new preventative drug." He paused, waiting for her reaction, and he saw her tears and shook his head. "It's okay. It's been six years, so they think I'm in pretty good shape . . . for it not to come back, I mean. They can't guarantee, but the odds are on my side." He tilted his head as he looked at her, and he had tears in his eyes too. "I needed to know . . . for you. I couldn't try to . . . be with you if I wasn't going to be around very long. I couldn't put you through that. I wouldn't."

Amanda almost dropped her ice cream.

"I know you stop talking when you're upset, so I'm just going to keep going." He rubbed his hands over his hair. "I've loved you since I met you that summer. And you left, and I never got over you." He took the ice cream out of her hands, and held her hands in his. "Would you ever think about being with me . . . or dating me . . . or whatever it's called?" Jake cringed. "God, I sound stupid. I'm just nervous. It took me a long time to work up to this because I was so afraid it would wreck our friendship if you said no."

Stunned, Amanda just stared at Jake.

"So, maybe this is too much right now." Jake dropped her hands and started to move toward the door. "That's okay, Amanda. I shouldn't have said anything . . ."

At that, she found her voice. "I love you too." She blurted it out, and Jake stopped and turned back to her. She shrugged and smiled at him shyly. Jake lunged at her and wrapped his arms around her and kissed her. The worry and fear of the past few days, and much of the loneliness that had been with her for her entire life, seemed to lift away, and Amanda was flooded with completeness and happiness and relief. Jake pulled back and pushed her hair back from her face, grinning at her.

As always, Amanda could barely find her words, so all she could do was grin back. And finally, she didn't feel the need to run away. In fact, she wanted nothing more than to stay.

Epilogue

JUNE IN MINNESOTA CAN USUALLY make its residents forget about winter. Low humidity, few bugs, and glorious sun make the state feel like an ideal place to live. The windows were open in Amanda's bedroom, and a light breeze came through, smelling of grass and sunshine.

As she awoke that day, the feeling in Amanda's belly was familiar and aching. Her initial instinct was to push it down, but this was supposed to hurt, so she tolerated it with a shuddery sigh. Jake rolled over and wrapped his arms around her, nuzzling his face into the back of her neck. She smiled through the tears that dripped off her nose, wetting her pillowcase.

"You don't have to do this today," he said pulling her close. They spent six nights out of seven together most weeks, usually at her place, and waking up next to him had never stopped being anything but wonderful.

Amanda had decided to stay in her grandmother's house, reluctantly at first, until they worked out a ridiculously low purchase price that Amanda couldn't refuse. Trix kept bringing over throw pillows, framed watercolors, and patterned curtains, so it was starting to feel like home.

"I know," she finally said, "but I want to."

"Okay." Jake reached down and squeezed her hand.

* * *

AMANDA AND LUCY HAD MADE FOOD the day before—sandwiches, salads, fruit, and bars. Amanda was only expecting seven people including herself and Jake, but she wanted to serve food because that was how these things were done.

267

Jake and Will had spent all of Saturday in the yard raking and landscaping. The four of them, with Javier in the portable crib, spent Saturday night playing Euchre and drinking margaritas—one small one for Lucy, many more for the other three—so by Sunday morning they were all hungover and weary. Luckily Trix arrived with enough energy for all of them, her arms loaded down with paper plates and plastic silverware, followed by Michael carrying a large, heavy box. With Trix clearly and happily in charge in the kitchen, Amanda made her way outside to prepare for the funeral.

* * *

THE YARD WAS SURPRISINGLY large and open, lined on one side by the railroad tracks. The grass was sparse, and Jake and Matt had spent one Saturday evening walking around the yard, pointing out different types of crabgrass and discussing products that may help. Matt was coming up with all kinds of excuses to come over. At first, it was hard to even make eye contact with him because his face was foreign yet eerily familiar at the same time. He and Amanda had the same hairline, the same shape to their chin, and the same eyebrows. He always seemed nervous around her, and she learned that he was pretty insecure, a surprising quality in someone of his stature. It seemed that he could never forget that once he was poor.

Amanda stood in the area they had designated for the burial, if there had been anything to bury. For the hundredth time, she regretted her hasty, semi-drunken scattering of her mom's ashes in the Mississippi River. She had been with a group of guys her freshman year in college, and they were bored and drinking. Wanting to impress them, she said that she had her dead mother's ashes and wanted to dump them in the river. No one believed her until she produced the cardboard urn, supplied for free by the funeral home. They piled into someone's car, drove to a bridge in St. Paul, and they all took turns reaching into the ashes and throwing out handfuls of her mother's remains. The mistake dawned on her then, but she was orphaned and angry so she didn't stop or care. The shame and disrespect came the following day and had stayed with her ever since. Today, she wanted to right her wrong.

Lucy, William, and Javier arrived, with Rosie and the girls right behind them. Amanda was surprised and honored that Rosie would come. They spread out blankets and the family gathered around Javier, cooing at the sleeping miracle baby.

Jake came out of the garage with the potted tree that they would be planting in her mother's honor. Jake had insisted on inviting Matt, who came in behind Jake and stood unobtrusively near the garage. Then surprisingly, Zoe, Max, and Leah came around the side of the house and stood near Matt quietly chatting. Jake must have invited them too.

The show of support was deeply touching. Jake carried the tree and stood next to Amanda, his hand warmly resting on her back. Amanda was struck with stage fright fueled by myriad emotions, but she forced herself to muster her courage and speak.

"Thank you, everyone for coming." She had thought about what to say, but didn't write anything down because she wanted to force herself to speak from the heart. "My mom died almost six years ago after fighting cancer for three and a half long years. It was just my mom and me, and sometimes that was really lonely. But even though it was the two of us, we were a family. Sometimes she didn't know what to do with me. She never took my picture on the first day of school, and she rarely came to my games and concerts. Sometimes I was so mad at her because there were so many things she didn't do right. But every mom makes mistakes, and most of them are doing the best that they can. My mom always did her best for me. And the one thing she always did right was that she loved me, unconditionally and completely. She made me feel important. Her love and support helped me believe in myself, and I wouldn't have that without her."

She took a deep breath and let out a shaky sigh. "I didn't appreciate her enough. In her last days, I wasn't there because I was more focused on myself and what I needed. But I was eighteen, and I did the best I could too." Trix was nodding and smiling through tears. "I never buried my mom. She was cremated, and I . . . well I scattered her ashes, but not in the way I should have. I can't bury her again, but I want to plant this tree in her memory. It's an apple tree, because she loved apple blossoms, and because I want to be able to pick apples and share them with people who are important to me. An apple isn't much, but it would be something from me and from her, to show my gratitude. I also chose a tree because it symbolizes family, something I never really thought I had."

A lump rose in her throat as she looked around at the faces of the people who were there with her today. Trix, openly crying now, and Michael—they had accepted her that summer and loved her beyond words, for reasons that she still didn't fully understand. Zoe, Leah, and Max—

more than just coworkers, they were part of her work family, there to support her and truly care about her. Her job had not only provided her income, but it gave her another place to belong. Rosie and her daughters, who had welcomed her into their home and their family. They had given her the gift of expecting her to come home to them every holiday. Her sweet best friend, Lucy, and Will, were endlessly supportive, and Lucy was truly the sister she never had. Matt, always full of pride and apology, whom someday she might actually call her dad. They shared biology, but he also knew that it was his job to earn her trust. That he loved her was apparent, and she thought she might be starting to love him back. And Jake, who had been there for her in every way possible, and had pledged to love her forever. These people were her family, in every sense of the word.

Jake started digging a hole for the tree. Matt came up and joined him, and together they dug a hole deep and wide enough. Jake lifted the tree into the hole, and Amanda pushed the dirt, soft and black, around it. Lucy, with Javier asleep in her arms, and William came forward with a large basket of perennial flowers that Lucy and Amanda planted around the base of the tree. Zoe brought forward a set of garden stepping stones that she said came from everyone at work. Amanda arranged them in a row by the tree. Rosie had a small statue of the Virgin Mary that she set at the base of the tree. Matt carried a small garden bench from the garage and set it near the tree. Carved in the side was a large cursive A, for April or Amanda, or both. Trix and Michael brought out a bird bath and feeder and set them near the tree.

Amanda stood back as her family continued to tend her Mother's Garden. The sky was brilliant blue, the sun was golden, and the air was fragrant with blooming flowers and fresh cut grass. Rosie sat on the bench and held baby Javier, Jake and Amanda's godson. Rosie's little girls ran after a butterfly. Michael and Matt were chatting about baseball. She thought about finding some closing words to honor her mom, but this day, this garden, and this family were a fitting tribute to any mother. Jake made his way over to Amanda and wrapped her in a hug.

"Looks great, doesn't it?" Jake asked.

Amanda nodded, so full of joy she couldn't find words.

"Come on, folks, let's eat," Trix hooked her arm in Will's and motioned everyone inside for lunch.

"She's just not happy unless she's feeding people," Jake said, his arm still around Amanda's shoulders. Marina pushed her little sisters, hard, so

Leah grabbed each girl by the shoulder and told them to quit. And miracle baby Javier let out a squeal and started to cry. That perfect moment gave way to real life—hunger, irritation, dirty diapers, and humor. But this was family, so perfection was never the goal. She followed them inside, where today it was her turn to serve her family a meal of ham sandwiches, gratitude, and love.

acknowledgements

First, I want to thank my sister, Lisa. She gave me a push to finish the book that I had barely talked about. Then she showed me how to turn a finished manuscript into a published book. Without her, this book would be nothing more than a very big document on my laptop.

It is also necessary to say that this is not an autobiography. The characters are most definitely fictional, and Amanda is certainly not me. More importantly, Amanda's mother is nothing like my mom, who is truly the most selfless, humble, and generous person I have ever known.

I also want to thank my wonderful friends, Michelle, Melissa, Bonnie, Ellie, Katie, and Julie who read and proofread my manuscripts and gave helpful suggestions and encouragement. And to countless other friends whose enthusiasm and support had made this project so much more meaningful, rewarding and fun.

I want to thank my husband, Gary, for photographing the cover art, and my daughter, Abby, for being the cover model. Somehow they knew just what I wanted the cover to be.

And finally, I want to dedicate this book to my family . . . my husband, Gary, and my kids, Abby, Sam, Gracie, and Lucy . . . you are my heart and my soul.

2